THEIR FIRST KISS WAS PRELUDE
TO AN OBSESSION
THAT NEITHER COULD ESCAPE

"Larissa, Larissa," Nathan soothed, stroking her back comfortingly. Desperately hoping to calm her before his wildly pulsing maleness overwhelmed his reason, he lifted her chin and gently kissed each of her eyes, sliding his cooling tongue over her swollen lids.

Limp and drained in his arms, Larissa suddenly realized how she craved the touch of another human being. The warm, heaving chest beneath her cheek seemed to give her strength and awoke a curious, unfamiliar tingling in her body. She lifted her head and whispered, "Nathan, kiss me. Please kiss me."

LARISSA

Lynn Lowery

LARISSA

A Bantam Book / November 1979

ISBN 0-553-12961-9

Published simultaneously in the United States and Canada

PRINTED IN THE UNITED STATES OF AMERICA

For Mona Alice Lowery

Prologue

�֍

The Indian Ocean
1838

Josiah Bennett sighed contentedly and stroked the long, shining, black hair of the woman snuggled against his chest. Six years ago when his wife Laura had died, he had lost himself in the China trade, certain his heart would remain numb for the rest of his life. But Ai-ling had taught him to love again, and now he was taking her home to Boston to become his wife.

He smiled as he imagined how his sister, Harriet, would greet the news. No doubt she would rant for hours about how he was lowering himself by marrying a yellow-skinned heathen. But he cared little about Harriet's opinion. It was Larissa he worried about. How would she accept a foreign stepmother who was scarcely older than she?

Time after time he had sat down in his office in Canton and tried to write to his daughter about Ai-ling. Somehow, he had never managed to finish those letters. Thinking of the thirteen-year-old girl he had left in Boston four years ago, still mourning her mother's death, he could not bring himself to write to her of another woman. Of course, Larissa would be seventeen now, old enough to understand a man's needs for a woman. Surely when she met Ai-ling, she would love her just as he did.

Ai-ling shifted against him, lifting her head to look into his eyes. "You are too pensive, Josiah," she murmured. "Does something displease you?"

"No." He smiled reassuringly and traced a finger across her cheek and down her silky throat. "With you beside me, nothing in the world could displease me."

Stretching gracefully, she twined her arms around his neck and slid on top of him, allowing her silk robe to fall open. She giggled, then nibbled at his throat. "Then show

2

me how pleased you are to have me here," she demanded.

"Ai-ling," Josiah groaned, "you'll be the death of me before this ship even reaches Boston. I'm too old for all this foolishness."

"Ah, no," she replied confidently, sliding a hand down to feel his hardness straining against his trousers. "Here is proof that you are not too old at all."

Giving a mock sigh of defeat, he lay back while she removed his trousers. Then her hands moved over him, stroking and caressing until he growled with pleasure. His own hands traveled down her body, lingering to cup her small, rounded breasts, then sliding lower to knead her firm buttocks. She lifted her mouth to meet his, whimpering as she flicked her tongue between his lips.

His sensations spiraled to a feverish pitch, until he could wait no longer. Holding her tightly to him, he rolled her to her back and pressed into her. Expelling a long sigh of ecstasy, he waited a moment before beginning to move within her. He opened his eyes to meet her gaze and seeing all the love and trust reflected in her dark eyes, he felt filled with tenderness. How blessed he was to have found her, just when he thought this part of his life was at an end! Closing his eyes again, he surrendered himself to the full rapture of the moment.

They moved in concert, soaring together toward the heights of fulfillment, oblivious to everything around them. Several moments passed before the pounding on the cabin door penetrated their consciousness.

"Mr. Bennett? Josiah? Are you there? The barometer's dropped something fierce. Looks like we're headed for a typhoon."

Josiah froze, confused by the sudden interruption of his ecstasy. "Typhoon?" he repeated numbly. "Typhoon?"

Raising his head, he focused on the walls of the small cabin. Was it possible the whole ship was shuddering? Suddenly he became aware of the wind shrieking outside his porthole. The realization descended over him with terrifying force. A typhoon could crush his beloved *Queen of Cathay,* the ship he had personally designed for his trading firm—crush it and send them all hurtling to their deaths without a chance of ever reaching Boston.

Instantly, he vaulted off the bunk and pulled on his trousers. Throwing a blanket over Ai-ling's shivering body, he wrenched open the cabin door to face Nathan Masters, his assistant agent in the trading firm of Bennett and Barnes. "Where is Captain Evans?" he demanded gruffly.

"Already on deck, directing the crew to shorten sail. I didn't want to disturb you, but it looks like it could be a bad one, and I thought you ought to know."

Nodding, Josiah stepped into the passageway, closed the cabin door, and started for the companionway ladder. "You did the right thing. Evans is the most competent master on the seas, but at times like this he can use every hand available. We'd better go up and see what we can do to help."

Nathan followed, his blood racing with exhilaration. At twenty-nine, he was pleased with his life. He enjoyed a relaxed, friendly relationship with his employer, and the voyages between China and the United States provided enough excitement to make up for the dull months spent in dreary Canton warehouses. Technically, he was a business agent, not a sailor, so he was not responsible for manning the ship. But he had acquired a working knowledge of sailing over the years and was only too glad to assist Josiah Bennett and his amiable captain, Charles Evans, in any emergency. Besides, even if he wasn't needed, he couldn't bear to sit idly in his cabin while the storm raged around them.

Both men braced themselves as they emerged on deck. The sails were trimmed, but the ship was scudding with the storm, rolling uncontrollably. Before their horrified eyes, the fore topmast studding sail booms, which controlled the auxiliary sails, rolled under, snapping off from the mast and dangling treacherously over the deck. The wind swirled and howled, tearing into the shortened sails and ripping them from the yards one by one, until only tattered bits of canvas waved above the deck.

Josiah and Nathan fought their way to the quarterdeck, where Captain Evans was battling unsuccessfully to control the wheel. As they reached him, a sailor rushed up from the foredeck.

"The jib boom's gone, sir," he said, panting. "Snapped right off the bow and plunged into the sea."

Captain Evans nodded in resignation and turned to Josiah. "I'll try to save her for you, Josiah," he shouted above the wind, "but Lord knows it won't be easy. If we're lucky, we'll get into the eye of the typhoon and have a chance to chop away some of the wreckage before we're hit again."

Two hours passed before the wind hurled the *Queen of Cathay* into the typhoon's center. By that time the tops of all three masts had snapped off, but the ship was still afloat, and miraculously, no one had been injured. In the brief lull, every man aboard set to work chopping away the wreckage. They were all soaked through from the sea's spray, but they worked at a frenzied pace, praying that they would be spared the storm's further fury. In his anxiety to preserve his ship, Josiah did not think of Ai-ling.

Scarcely had they cleared away all the broken bits of masts, sails, and booms, when a raging wind forced the *Queen of Cathay* back out of the relative calm of the typhoon's center and into its whirlwinds. Josiah watched in horror as a towering spindrift descended over the ship. The wall of spray seemed to be at least twenty-five feet high. It wavered slightly, then crashed into the ship's hull, sending it listing violently to the starboard.

"Josiah! Josiah!"

Suddenly, over the screeching winds, he heard Ai-ling's frightened shriek. Looking down from the quarterdeck, he saw her struggling to the main deck. "Ai-ling!" he screamed. "Go back below! It's not safe for you up here!"

She stopped, trying to get her bearings as his voice drifted to her. Lifting her gaze toward the quarterdeck, she caught sight of him coming toward her through the wall of spray. "Oh, Josiah!" she screamed. "I was so worried about you! I kept waiting for you to come back to the cabin when things got calm. But then, when the storm started all over again—"

"Get below!" he shouted urgently. "We'll talk later, when it's all over."

His words never reached her. The ship tipped precariously, and she began to slide sideways on the flooded deck. She fell to her knees, clawing wildly at the floorboards as she slid toward the rail. At that moment, the spindrift hit again, enveloping the crippled ship in a curtain of spray. Descending the ladder from the quarterdeck, Josiah lost sight of her for a moment. When the mist cleared, she was gone.

"Ai-ling!" The anguished cry tore from his throat as he

jumped to the tilted main deck. Hurling himself at the rail, he glimpsed a ragged bit of silk in the churning sea below. "Ai-ling!" he sobbed again.

He was halfway over the rail when Nathan grabbed him from behind and threw him back to the deck. "Ai-ling!" Josiah repeated, struggling back to his feet. "I've got to save her!"

Nathan shook his head and pinned him flat on the deck. "You won't save her by killing yourself!" He glanced back at the swirling sea, gritting his teeth as he saw she had already disappeared. Still, to calm Josiah, he called to a passing sailor, "Arnold, see if you can fish the girl out!"

The sailor glanced from the sea to Josiah, then back to Nathan before he nodded in understanding and moved cautiously toward the rail.

Struggling frantically, Josiah tried to break the younger man's hold. "Let me go! Ai-ling needs me! You've no right to hold me prisoner on my own ship!"

The ship lurched suddenly to the port side. As Nathan fought to maintain his balance, he lost his grip on Josiah. The older man wrenched away from him and staggered toward the rail. Around them, the wind intensified to a deafening howl, tearing one of the quarter boats from its davits. The boat flew through the air like a thin piece of kindling and crashed into Josiah, its hull cracking loudly against his skull, knocking him unconscious. Nathan lunged for him, dragging him away from the rail before he could be swept over.

On hands and knees, Nathan dragged Josiah's limp body back toward the companionway. Somehow, in between the ship's violent lurchings, he managed to maneuver Josiah down the ladder, through the passageway, and into his cabin. Panting from the exertion, he hauled him onto the bunk and examined his head.

There was a gash several inches long at the crown, and it was bleeding profusely. Already, his hair was matted with blood. Tearing off his own wet shirt, Nathan used it to wipe away the blood and attempted to staunch its flow. Then he tore the sheet from the bed, ripped it into strips, and bandaged Josiah's head.

Josiah regained consciousness an hour later. Blinking, he focused on Nathan. Then his eyes darted around the cabin. "Ai-ling" he asked weakly. "Did they save Ai-ling?"

Nathan frowned and hesitated, considering how Josiah

would react if he learned the girl had disappeared. Nodding curtly, he replied, "She's resting in my cabin now."

"Oh." Josiah struggled to raise himself on his elbows. "I'll go to her then."

"No. It would be better not to disturb her now. Later, when you've both rested." Inwardly, Nathan winced, dreading the moment when he would be forced to tell Josiah the truth.

Nodding dully, Josiah touched the bandage swathing his head. "Is it—bad?"

Forcing a smile, Nathan quipped, "The bandage? It's atrocious, but I'm no doctor, you know."

Josiah smiled weakly. "You know what I mean. The wound—how does it look?"

Nathan shrugged. "It can't be too bad if you're lying there talking to me. Next thing I suppose you'll be issuing orders."

Closing his eyes, Josiah smiled again. "No. No orders. Too tired to think right now. Just look after Ai-ling." Within moments, he had slipped back into unconsciousness.

Twenty hours passed before the *Queen of Cathay* limped away from the typhoon, battered but still afloat. Drained and exhausted, Captain Evans knocked at the cabin door. Nathan opened it.

"Well, it's over," the captain said, sighing heavily. "The *Queen* is a sorry sight, but it's over. We had to hack away most of the masts to get her upright and keep her from taking on too much water. Nothing to do now but build a jury-rig and take her back to Sumatra for repairs."

Glancing past Nathan, he cocked an eyebrow at Josiah's prone form. "How is he?"

Nathan shrugged. "It's hard to say. He was conscious for a bit soon after I brought him down here, but since then, he's been out." He paused and swallowed. "There wasn't any sign of the girl, was there?"

Captain Evans shook his head. "No. Two of our men were swept overboard as well." Sighing, he rubbed his red-rimmed eyes. "Well, if I don't get some rest, I'll never be any good again. Call me if there's any change in Josiah's condition."

Two hours later, Nathan awoke from a fitful sleep beside the bunk to hear Josiah's plaintive cry. "Larissa! Larissa! Oh, my poor Larissa! My poor little girl! Larissa!"

Josiah's breathing grew raspy. Nathan sat in the dark, listening. Then suddenly Josiah was silent. Gripped by apprehension, Nathan leaned forward to lay a hand on Josiah's chest. He could not feel even the slightest movement. He reached up to touch the bandage, recoiling as his fingers met sticky wetness. His fingers shaking, Nathan lit a candle, and in its dim light he saw that the bleeding had never really stopped. The bandage was saturated.

Josiah Bennett had completed his last voyage on his beloved *Queen of Cathay*.

Part One

✻

1839

Chapter One

"Andrew! Stop it!"

Larissa Bennett irritably brushed the young man's mouth away from her ear. Lifting the spyglass to her eye again, she aimed it at the white speck of sail on the horizon, hoping it might be the *Queen of Cathay*. The ship was nearly two months overdue, and she was beginning to think she couldn't bear to wait for it another day.

As she tried to focus, she felt a hand moving up from her waist to cup her breast. Sighing in exasperation, she slapped the hand away and turned to face Andrew Allerton. "Would you please try to behave? God only knows why Aunt Harriet let you come up here with me!"

Andrew smiled smugly, his blue-gray eyes sparkling with self-assurance. "God may not know, but I do! Your aunt adores me—just as every other woman in Boston does!"

"All but one!" Larissa responded tartly, setting the spyglass aside and strolling to the far end of the widow's walk, the railed balcony that topped her Aunt Harriet and Uncle Hiram's red brick house.

The tall, well-built young man followed her, casually brushing back his raven-black hair. "You might as well say so, Larissa. You want me just as much as any other woman. You're just too damned proud to admit it! And if you ask me, you've got little enough to be proud of. Who are you, anyway? The daughter of a struggling China trader who leaves you in Boston for years at a time while he luxuriates in the exotic Orient."

"That's not being fair to papa!" she protested. "He wouldn't spend so much time away if he wasn't so lonely since mama died. Besides, I intend to ask him to take me with him on the next voyage. I'm seventeen now, and my schooling is completed, so I don't see how he can object."

Andrew laughed derisively. "Don't be ridiculous, Larissa. You're not a sailor. You belong at home having babies —*my* babies! Why don't you admit you'd love to flaunt the Allerton name? Most girls would throw themselves at my feet for the chance of marrying the son of a senator."

"Then why don't you amuse yourself with one of those girls?" She stared out at the harbor, wishing he would go home and leave her to watch for her father's ship in peace.

He chuckled. "You may be sure I take advantage of every opportunity!" His arms reached around her, holding her captive as he placed his hands on the rail. He nibbled at the nape of her neck.

Disgusted, Larissa shook her head angrily. "Andrew! Have you no respect for me at all? What would someone think if they looked up here and saw you carrying on so?"

"I doubt anyone would think anything is amiss, since all of Boston knows you and I are to be married."

Larissa grimaced. For months, her aunt and the Allertons had been telling people she and Andrew would wed. Deaf to her protests, they had put off a formal engagement announcement only because she had insisted on discussing the matter with her father. When he knew her feelings, Larissa was sure her father would not consent to the marriage.

"Of course," Andrew mused, "if you are really so opposed to a public display, we could adjourn to your bedroom. Since your aunt is occupied serving tea to my mother, I doubt that anyone would disturb us."

"How dare you suggest such a thing!" Larissa whirled on him furiously, shoving him backward.

Stunned, Andrew lost his balance but recovered enough to grab Larissa's waist, pulling her down on top of him as he fell to the floor. "Well," he said, grinning and wrapping his arms tightly around her, "I had no idea you were so anxious to bed me!"

Before Larissa could recover her breath, he rolled on top of her, and his mouth came down hard against hers, his tongue forcing its way between her lips. Just then, his mother called to him from the stairway.

"Andrew? It's time you drove me home, dear."

Andrew and Larissa had just enough time to scramble to their feet before Mrs. Allerton and Larissa's aunt appeared on the widow's walk. Embarrassed and annoyed, Larissa hurried to pick up the spyglass.

"Any sight of Hiram's ship yet, dear?" asked Harriet, a thin, pale woman with gray-streaked hair drawn into a tight bun.

It always irritated Larissa when her aunt called the *Queen of Cathay*, "Hiram's ship." Her father and uncle owned equal shares in the firm of Bennett and Barnes. But she knew it was useless to argue the point.

"No," she replied wearily, setting the spyglass aside without even focusing it.

"Well then, come along and bid our guests goodbye."

Sullenly, Larissa followed the others to the street. She smiled stiffly as Andrew discreetly bent to kiss her hand.

"Ah, that Andrew is such a handsome young man," Harriet said as the Allerton carriage rolled away, up Pearl Street toward Beacon Hill. "And such a perfect gentleman. I wonder if you realize just how fortunate you are, Larissa."

Larissa looked away, thinking her aunt would not be quite so enthusiastic if she had witnessed the scene on the widow's walk. "If you don't mind, Aunt Harriet, I think I'll go back up and watch for papa."

Her aunt frowned. "I'll be glad when that ship finally arrives and you won't be wasting every afternoon up there. Remember, if you see the ship, you're not to go down there alone. The wharves are no place for a decent young lady."

Returning to the widow's walk, Larissa paced for several minutes, furious at Andrew and furious also at her aunt for allowing him to visit her unchaperoned. Sighing, she picked up the spyglass and focused again on the ship gliding toward the harbor. She drew in her breath sharply as she recognized the streamlined bow of the *Queen of Cathay*. While other China traders continued to sail full-bodied packet ships, her father had designed a more slender, swifter ship, along the lines of the Baltimore clipper. Its tapered shape made it easily recognizable. Suppressing a cry of joy, Larissa dropped the spyglass and hurried to her room to change into her best dress. Then, ignoring her aunt's admonition, she slipped outside and raced toward the wharves.

By the time Larissa reached India Wharf, the *Queen of Cathay* had docked and was unloading crates and baskets filled with tea, porcelain, silks, Oriental carpets, fragrant spices, and exotic Oriental artwares. Scanning the area, Larissa quickly concluded that her father must still be in his cabin. She elbowed her way through the crowd that always greeted the arrival of a China trader and ran up the gangplank to the main deck. Although she had not been on the ship in four years, she vividly remembered its layout, and brushing excitedly past the busy crew, she hurried to the stern of the ship and down the ladder leading to the officers' cabins.

By the time she reached the door of her father's cabin, she was breathless. As she paused to catch her breath, the door opened, and she threw her arms impulsively around a man's broad shoulders. Closing her eyes, she planted a resounding kiss on the man's lips. But she stiffened in shock as strong arms returned her embrace, and insistent lips answered hers with a searing kiss that forced open her mouth and left her gasping for breath.

Larissa pulled away as if burned, and her eyes flew open to stare into the dancing, amber-flecked eyes of a stranger. She swallowed hard and felt a flush painting her neck, then creeping higher to stain her cheeks.

"I—I beg your pardon," she stammered, stepping away abruptly from the tall, trim, chestnut-haired man in the passageway. "I'm afraid I thought you were someone else."

The corners of his eyes crinkled as he smiled. "I'm sure you did. But I can't say I regret the mistake. It's quite the nicest welcome to Boston I've ever had." His voice was a rich baritone and had an undertone of suppressed laughter.

He stepped to one side, pausing to study Larissa, his eyes moving appreciatively over her slender waist, full breasts, the sprinkling of freckles on her slightly upturned nose, and her jade-green eyes. "Yes," he chuckled, reaching out to brush a long, flowing strand of auburn hair away from her face, "quite the nicest welcome. I wish I might linger to continue our acquaintance. Unfortunately, I've work to do. Good day, miss." He nodded to her and strode toward the companionway.

Larissa stared after him, shivering at the memory of his lips pressed demandingly to hers. Realizing just how much his touch had excited her, she frowned and wondered why his kiss did not repulse her like Andrew's. For a moment, she forgot why she had even boarded the *Queen of Cathay*. Then she glanced into her father's cabin, the cabin the stranger had just left, and saw that no one was there.

Whirling back toward the companionway, she saw the

man about to disappear up the ladder. "Sir?" she called nervously, suddenly annoyed that this complete stranger could make her voice quiver so. He turned his head to her, cocking it in question.

"Would you know where I might find Josiah Bennett?"

He stared at her in perplexity. "I'm afraid Mr. Bennett is not aboard."

"Not aboard!" Larissa wailed. "But he must be! He promised me—"

The man froze on the ladder, a thunderstruck expression on his face. Slowly, he backed down the ladder and walked toward her. "Forgive my slow-wittedness. Since this had been his cabin, I should have surmised who you are. Don't tell me you're Larissa?"

She nodded, wondering numbly why he said it "had been" her father's cabin.

"Well, I'm Nathan Masters. I've been your father's assistant in Canton these last four years. He talked about you constantly, but from the way he spoke of 'little Larissa,' I assumed you were just a child. I never suspected he was hiding a beautiful, full-grown woman in Boston."

Larissa laughed self-consciously and lowered her eyes. "I suppose papa rather lost track of my growth in all his time away from home. But why didn't he come? What kept him in Canton?"

Nathan cleared his throat uneasily, and when Larissa lifted her eyes, she saw that his face was contorted. "I think perhaps Captain Evans should talk to you. If you'd like to sit down in the cabin, I'll go up and find him."

Feeling a lump of apprehension rising in her throat, Larissa leaned against the wall of the passageway to steady herself. "Mr. Masters," she whispered faintly, "as his assistant, you must know why my father is not aboard the *Queen of Cathay*."

Shifting uncomfortably, Nathan nodded.

"Then I beg you to tell me and spare me the pain of waiting for Captain Evans."

He swallowed, his eyes filling with compassion as he studied her, wondering how he could break the awful news. Her unwavering gaze met his, demanding the truth.

"Well, Miss Bennett, your father did leave Canton aboard the *Queen*. But, you see—" He stumbled, cleared his throat, and began again.

"I'm sure you're aware we're rather late in reaching

Boston. You see, we had to put in for repairs. Scarcely a week after we left Canton, there was a typhoon. A good part of the ship was wrecked. Masts and davits were snapping all around us and—" He swallowed the last phrase, unable to speak the horrible words.

"Mr. Masters," Larissa whispered in a trembling voice, hoping somehow she had misread the man's meaning, "you can't be telling me—did papa—perish in the typhoon?"

Nathan nodded miserably, feeling a lump rise in his own throat as her eyes filled with tears. Larissa turned and huddled against the wall, sobbing, overwhelmed by the terrible realization that she would never see her father again.

After watching helplessly for a moment, blinking back his own tears, Nathan stepped to her side, turned her gently by the shoulders, and enfolded her in his arms. Muffling her sobs against his chest, he held her tenderly, stroking her hair and murmuring words of comfort. Still holding her, he maneuvered her into the cabin, away from the curious glances of crewmen passing in the companionway. Gently, he sat down with her on the bunk.

Larissa clung to him, her sobs crescendoing as she recalled the day six years ago, when her mother had died of the grippe. Her grief-stricken father had lost himself in the shipping business, entrusting her to his stern sister Harriet and her husband, Hiram. He had not been home in four years. And now he would never come home again.

Nathan cringed as she pressed closer to him, bombarding his senses with her innocent femininity. Perhaps, he thought, the voyage had simply deprived him too long of the company of a woman. He had known countless other women, more mature and more beautiful, but, even as her eyes reddened and swelled from weeping, he found there was something irresistible about Larissa Bennett.

Why should she, who had been only a child when he began working for Josiah Bennett, affect him so strongly? As his groin began to throb insistently, Nathan pulled away from her abruptly.

Wailing, Larissa threw her arms around his neck, clinging to what seemed the one stable thing in her crumbling world. "Don't leave me!" she moaned imploringly. "Don't leave me alone. I can't bear it without papa. Tell me papa's coming home!"

"Larissa, Larissa," Nathan soothed, stroking her back

comfortingly. Desperately hoping to calm her before she became even more hysterical and before his wildly pulsing maleness overwhelmed his reason, he lifted her chin and gently kissed each of her eyes, sliding his cooling tongue over her swollen lids. He licked away the tears coursing down her cheeks, stifling his rising passions as her sobs seemed to subside. His fingertips gently massaged the tense muscles of her neck until she relaxed against him.

Limp and drained in his arms, Larissa suddenly realized how she craved the touch of another human being. With her father dead, and her stern aunt and uncle her only surviving relatives, she felt alone and unloved. The warm, heaving chest beneath her cheek seemed to give her strength and awakened a curious, unfamiliar tingling in her body. Unable to bear further thoughts of her father, she lifted her head and whispered, "Nathan, kiss me. Please kiss me." She raised her mouth to his, begging for his lips.

Nathan sensed that he should pull away then, before he completely lost control, but he feared she would start sobbing again. Sighing, he swallowed his doubts and lowered his mouth to cover hers. At first his lips were gentle, but as she responded instinctively, parting her lips and pulling him closer, the kiss increased in intensity.

For Larissa, the moment was a blessed gift, blotting out the horror of learning her father was dead. But for Nathan, it was the loss of the battle, the final blow that crumbled his resistance.

He eased her down gently on the bunk as his hands feverishly unfastened the hooks of her dress. She pulled away then, her eyes filled with fear, but he coaxed her to relax as he stroked her bare breasts. A tingling began in her breasts and gradually possessed her whole body. Now terrified, she squirmed away, trying to escape the sorcery of his touch. She beat her fists against his hard, immovable chest. Her breath came in short, uneven gasps as she cried, "No, Nathan! No!"

"Larissa, hush!" She heard his voice, hoarse and strained in her ear.

His mouth covered hers again, and Larissa felt herself weakening. She seemed to forget everything—who she was, what was happening, why she should protest. Then, suddenly, he was gone, and she was left floundering in a curious void.

Opening her eyes, she saw him swing his legs to the

floor and walk to the porthole. He stared out at the harbor for a long moment, breathing heavily, before he spoke. "I'm sorry, Larissa. I seem to have lost control for a few moments."

She frowned in confusion. All the magic of the moment dissolved as she stared incredulously at his back. Feeling a mixture of anger and despair, she realized that in another moment she might have surrendered her virginity to him. And she had met him only moments before.

Salvaging the remnants of her pride, she tossed her head and stilled the quivering within her. "Sorry!" she whispered bitterly. "You took advantage of my grief! You used me! All these years I've saved myself for love and marriage, and now you come along, practically rape me in my own father's cabin, and tell me you're sorry!"

He turned abruptly, staring at her with angry, flashing eyes. For the first time, she noticed that his long nose bulged in the center. Probably the result of a waterfront brawl, she thought bitterly.

A throbbing pulse at the edge of his jaw betrayed the tension building within him. "You needn't be so righteous," he said. "You were the one who begged me to kiss you."

"Only because I so desperately needed to be comforted. It never occurred to me you would be so callous as to take advantage of my grief." But she blushed as she admitted to herself she could have fought him harder. Could it be she had actually wanted him to take her?

He shrugged. "Well, angry words can't change what happened." Turning his back to her, he added, "Get dressed, and I'll take you home. It's getting dark, and I doubt that the waterfront is a safe place for a woman."

"It seems," Larissa replied tartly as she refastened her dress, "that this ship is not a safe place for a woman at any time!"

Harriet Barnes was pacing in the small, fenced yard in front of the house on Pearl Street when Nathan and Larissa arrived. Her head snapped up at the sound of their steps on the walk, and she rushed to Larissa.

"Where have you been?" she snapped, her eyes accusing. "Dinner is ready, and no one could find you. Didn't I tell you not to go to the wharves alone? Is the ship in? If it is, where is your father? Who is this man?"

Pushing Nathan's advances to the back of her mind,

Larissa had brooded about her father's death all the way
home. Now she threw up her hands and interrupted her
aunt. "Stop it!" she shrieked. "What does it matter where
I was or what you told me? I'll tell you what matters.
Papa is dead!"

Stunned, the older woman watched her niece brush past
her and rush into the house. Then she turned slowly back
to Nathan, her lips pursed in question. "Is this true? Is
Josiah really dead?"

He nodded. "I'm afraid so, ma'am. He was injured in a typhoon and succumbed soon afterward. Sorry
you had to get the news so bluntly. I'll be on my way now.
I don't imagine you feel much up to entertaining a
stranger at the moment."

As he turned toward the street, Harriet's voice stopped
him. "Young man?" Nathan turned, surprised by her un-
emotional, businesslike tone. "Just who are you that you
are privy to this information?"

"I'm Nathan Masters, ma'am. I was Mr. Bennett's assistant in Canton. I met Miss Bennett on the ship when she
came to greet her father."

"I see." Harriet nodded. "As Larissa may have told you,
I'm her aunt, Harriet Barnes. Josiah was my husband
Hiram's partner. I suppose that you'll be wanting to give
Hiram a full report?"

"Yes, ma'am. Captain Evans and I intend to call at his
office tomorrow."

Harriet shrugged. "No reason to put it off. I suggest you
stay for dinner this evening."

Nathan stared at her incredulously. "That's very kind of
you, ma'am. But under the circumstances—"

"What circumstances?" she interrupted tartly. "If you
are referring to Josiah's death, it's most regrettable, but we
can hardly benefit him now by postponing important business. You may come in and wait in the salon, Mr. Masters.
Dinner will be served in a few minutes."

He hesitated, thinking of the girl he had held in his
arms only an hour ago, then nodded curtly. "Very well,
madam. I accept your invitation."

Satisfied, Harriet led him into the salon, then went upstairs to find Larissa, who was lying across her canopied
bed, her face buried in a pillow. Closing the bedroom door
softly behind her, Harriet went to sit on the edge of the

bed. After a few moments, she spoke crisply. "You shouldn't have screamed at me that way—least of all in the presence of a stranger. One would think you never learned to show proper respect for your elders."

Slowly, Larissa rolled to her side, her tear-stained eyes wide with disbelief. "Is that all you can think about —some slight affront to your dignity? Papa is dead, and that's all you care about! He was your brother, you know! Doesn't it pain you at all to think he's gone?"

"Larissa!" Harriet said sharply, rising from the bed and turning her back to her. "I will not permit you to address me in such a manner!" She paused, cleared her throat, and made an effort to soften her voice. "Of course it saddens me to know Josiah is dead, but it will do no oné any good to mope about it now. The best thing we can do now is go on about our business."

"As if he never existed?" Larissa asked bitterly.

Turning back to her niece, Harriet raised her brows in warning. "Of course not." She sighed. "I suppose I cannot expect you to have the wisdom that comes with age, but you must try to be realistic about your situation. Now that your father is gone, it is more important than ever for you to think about your future—and think about making a good marriage for yourself. Not that Hiram and I begrudge you the hospitality of our home, but—"

"If you're trying to convince me to marry Andrew Allerton, Aunt Harriet, you can save your breath," Larissa interrupted sharply. "I've no intention of ever marrying that repulsive snob."

Suddenly Harriet grabbed Larissa's shoulders, squeezing them to emphasize her words. "You *will* marry him, Larissa! And in time you will thank me for seeing to your welfare when you would have been too stubborn to see to it yourself."

Harriet stared at Larissa for a moment, then released her and softened her tone. "Now, wash your face. Dinner is waiting."

"I don't believe I'm hungry," Larissa whispered.

"Nevertheless, you will eat. I won't permit you to waste away with grief. Now, don't keep me waiting any longer."

A few minutes later, Larissa reluctantly followed her aunt downstairs. At the foot of the stairs, they turned into

the salon, and Larissa froze, paling at the sight of Nathan
Masters. "You didn't tell me there would be a guest for
dinner," she whispered.

Harriet shrugged. "It seemed the least we could do after he was kind enough to escort you home." Hiram
Barnes, a robust, balding man in his mid-fifties, rose to
greet his wife, and the couple led the way to the dining
room.

Nathan offered Larissa his arm and whispered solicitously, "I hope you are feeling better."

Larissa stared at him, unsure whether he was alluding
to her grief or to what had happened between them.
Aware that her aunt was listening for her answer, she replied stiffly, "A bit, thank you. But it will take more than a
few hours to overcome my grief. I saw very little of my
father after mama died, but I dearly treasured our moments together."

"And he treasured that time as well," Nathan assured
her as he seated her at the long oak dining table. Harriet
indicated that Nathan should be seated across from Larissa,
and a maid brought in the first course.

As the meal progressed, Harriet and Hiram engaged
their guest in constant conversation. No mention was made
of Larissa's father, and the shipping trade was discussed
in only the most general terms. Larissa, totally ignored
by her aunt and uncle, picked at her food moodily, occasionally glancing across the table at Nathan. He seemed
bored by her aunt and uncle's conversation and impatient
to finish the meal.

Studying him discreetly through lowered eyes, Larissa
decided he was not really handsome in the flawless, elegant
way of Andrew Allerton. But he exuded a powerful magnetism, unlike any other man she had ever met. His cheekbones and jaw were ruggedly chiseled, indicating daring,
strength, and worldliness. Even the break in his nose
seemed somehow attractive, a badge of honor that promised resilience to whatever life had to offer. In their short
meeting, she had found him quite self-assured, but not
in the arrogant way of Andrew. Nathan had also proven
himself capable of incredible tenderness, which the young
aristocrat had never exhibited.

The clatter of the dishes as the maid brought dessert
shattered Larissa's thoughts, and she frowned guiltily to
herself. She knew it was wrong to idealize Nathan after

what had happened in his cabin. Still, his touch seemed somehow less sordid and infinitely more exciting than any of Andrew's stolen kisses and caresses.

At the end of the meal, as coffee was served, Hiram finally began to question Nathan about business. "It seems, my boy, that our profits have been slipping in the last few years. I hope you bring a better report this voyage."

Larissa watched as Nathan shifted apprehensively. "I'm afraid I'll have to disappoint you, sir. Even without the damage done by the typhoon, this year seems worse than the last."

Hiram's brow wrinkled as he studied the younger man. "And what do you suppose is the reason for that? My colleagues, Perkins, Hansen, Forbes, and any number of other traders, all seem to be making handsome profits."

"Yes, sir, but they deal in a commodity much more in demand than anything we have to offer."

"Which is?"

"Opium. The Chinese forbid its import, but the market is flourishing nonetheless."

"Aha!" Harriet interrupted. "Hiram and I thought as much. But my brother was too pigheaded to consider the opium trade."

Gasping in outrage, Larissa jumped to her father's defense. "Papa always said it was immoral to ship the drug. And surely if China has laws forbidding—"

"Morality has nothing to do with good business, young lady," her uncle cut her off irritably.

Turning to Nathan, he asked, "What is your opinion on the merits of the trade?"

Nathan's eyes moved from Larissa to her uncle. "As an employee, I feel I am not in a position to make a judgment. However, I do know that Captain Evans is strongly opposed to the opium trade and would never consent to carry the drug on his vessel."

"Captain Evans is also an employee," Harriet cut in. "And the *Queen of Cathay* is not his ship. It belongs to the firm of Bennett and Barnes."

Clearing his throat, Hiram pushed his chair away from the table and stood. "We can continue our discussion in my library, Masters," he announced. "I think you'll find I keep an uncommonly good stock of brandy."

"You may be excused to your room, Larissa," Harriet said firmly. "I know this has been a trying day for you.

No doubt you'll want to write a note to Andrew, to inform him about your father."

Grimacing at her aunt's suggestion, Larissa rose, nodded to Nathan and her uncle, and left the dining room. From the hallway, she heard her aunt explaining to Nathan, "We haven't made the official announcement yet, but everyone in Boston knows Larissa and Andrew Allerton are betrothed. They make such a lovely couple."

Larissa froze, annoyed by her aunt's statement. But she flushed with unexplainable pleasure as Nathan's reply drifted to her. "I cannot comment on Allerton, but your niece is, without a doubt, quite the loveliest young lady I have ever seen or met."

In her room, Larissa undressed, slipped into a white flannel nightgown, and flopped across her bed. She felt emotionally drained and terribly confused. She wanted to despise Nathan for the way he had fondled her, but she could not. She assured herself her conflicting emotions were not because she had actually wanted him to make love to her. After all, she thought, if her father had chosen Nathan as his assistant, he must be a basically decent man. Perhaps he had just succumbed to a moment of weakness. He did stop, when he could easily have overpowered her. And he did apologize.

She turned her thoughts again to her father, wondering if he had suffered much. Had he even had a decent burial or had his body simply been thrown into the sea? Had the poor man known even a moment of real happiness since her mother's death?

Throughout her musings, the image of Nathan Masters appeared over and over in her mind: Nathan working beside her father in his Canton office; Nathan aiding her father during the fury of the typhoon; Nathan's face twisting in agony as he told her of her father's death; Nathan's arms cradling her against his chest; Nathan's lips responding to her misplaced kiss of greeting and his later kisses, filled with what could only be described as passion.

Larissa extinguished her lamp and slid under the comforter. But she tossed for what seemed like hours, her mind a confusing jumble of thoughts and emotions. Finally, she got out of bed and slid into an embroidered silk wrapper her father had sent from the Orient the previous year. After pacing for a few minutes, she decided to go downstairs to borrow a book from her uncle's library.

Lighting a candle, she carried it to the stairway and descended. At the foot of the stairs, she saw light spilling from beneath the door of her uncle's library. She hesitated, considered returning to her room, then shrugged and continued toward the library door. If her uncle was alone, it might be a good time to discuss a memorial service for her father. Despite his ignoring her at dinner, he had always treated her much more kindly than her aunt, and she had always felt that he liked and respected her father.

A few steps from the door, she froze, surprised to hear voices coming from the room. Could Nathan have stayed so late? The very thought of seeing him again made her tremble, but curiosity prompted her to creep closer to the door. She frowned when she heard her aunt's voice.

"Well, Hiram, the business is finally ours! Didn't I always say that in good time we would own it all? Tomorrow, you can have the name Bennett stricken from the title. It will be Hiram Barnes, Limited!"

Hiram cleared his throat uneasily. "We mustn't be so hasty, Harriet. Have you forgotten the girl? She's a spunky one, and I wouldn't be at all surprised if she demands her father's share as her inheritance."

"Larissa will be no problem," Harriet laughed lightly. "In a few months, she'll be married to Andrew Allerton."

"Even if she marries him," Hiram said dubiously, "what assurance is there she won't still demand her inheritance?"

"Andrew will take care of that," the woman assured him. "Once Larissa marries him, her property becomes his, and he will gladly sign away any rights to the firm."

"How can you be so sure?"

Harriet sighed in exasperation. "Sometimes I swear you are almost as dimwitted as Larissa! The Allerton family is old aristocracy. They won't want to dirty their hands with the new money of the China trade. You can be sure that even if Andrew considered it, his parents would never permit it. They're a family of lawyers and public servants, not traders. Rest assured, Hiram dear, the business is as good as ours."

Stifling a gasp of dismay and outrage, Larissa backed away from the door. Blinded by tears, she stumbled back to

her room, replaying her aunt's spiteful words in her mind.
Now it was all too clear why her aunt had shown no
grief over her father's death and why she had seemed
more anxious than ever for Larissa to marry Andrew.

The grief and confusion that had overwhelmed her
only moments earlier were now drowned by anger and
determination. Pacing in her room, she vowed she would
not be used as a pawn in her aunt's plan for wealth and
power. Her father had given his life to building a prosperous, respectable business. That, and his memories, were all
she had left of him, and she was not about to let anyone
wrench that legacy from her.

But what could she do? Legally, her aunt and uncle
were her guardians and the trustees of her inheritance.
She was still too young to demand an active role in the
business partnership. She would, of course, refuse to marry Andrew, but what then? Surely they would devise some
other plan. In the meantime, it would be unbearable to
remain in the same house with her aunt and uncle. But
she had no money of her own and no other relatives to
whom she could turn.

To Larissa's surprise, the rough-hewn face of Nathan
Masters reappeared in her mind. She recalled how concerned he had been about her. And suddenly she began to
see a solution to her problems.

Chapter Two

Larissa huddled behind the sea chest in Nathan's cabin. She felt cramped and a bit afraid, and she was beginning to wonder if she had made the right decision in stowing aboard the *Queen of Cathay*. The ship lurched suddenly, telling her it was too late to reconsider. The *Queen of Cathay* was beginning to move, gliding out of Boston harbor on its way to the Orient.

Thinking back on the weeks just passed, she smiled to herself and decided her temporary discomfort was more than worthwhile, considering how Aunt Harriet and Uncle Hiram would suffer when they discovered she was gone. They had planned a lavish party for that evening, to announce her engagement to Andrew Allerton. How would they explain to the one hundred guests that the prospective bride had disappeared and that they had no idea where she was?

Of course, she thought, frowning, she might have an equally difficult time explaining her presence to Nathan. She had been lucky enough to slip aboard unnoticed in the predawn hours and had found his cabin unoccupied. But eventually he was bound to return, and she would have to face him.

She had seen him only twice since that first day. The first time was when he had attended the memorial service for her father. The second was when he had stopped at the house to discuss some business with her uncle. Both times he had been polite, though somewhat distant, never alluding to the incident in his cabin. But she had sensed an underlying tension in him, and she suspected he might be less than pleased to find her in his cabin.

After the way he had taken advantage of her at their first meeting, she supposed it made little sense to trust him.

Still, there was no one else to whom she could turn, and she had convinced herself he had an underlying sense of decency. After all, her father must have respected him, and at the memorial service Captain Evans himself had described to her how Nathan had struggled to save her father's life. If he had cared so much for her father, surely he would not harm her.

At the sound of footsteps in the passageway, Larissa tensed, overcome by a new wave of apprehension. The door opened abruptly, and she could hear someone moving around the cabin. From her hiding place, she could not see the person. What if it was not Nathan? The bunk creaked as someone sprawled across it. Then the cabin was silent.

Hoping to reassure herself that the sleeping person was indeed Nathan, Larissa crept forward on her hands and knees. She raised her head and sighed inwardly as she recognized the tall, lean form. But just as she began to sink back down behind the chest, the shoulder of her dress caught on the brass reinforcement riveted to its corner. Before she realized what was happening, the fabric ripped. In the small, still cabin, the sound seemed as loud as a thunderclap. Instantly, Nathan sat up. His eyes focused on the auburn head bobbing back down behind the chest. In three strides, he was standing over the chest, staring down at her.

"What the devil are *you* doing here?" he demanded, grabbing Larissa by the shoulders and dragging her to her feet.

Hoping to regain at least some of her dignity, Larissa stared at him defiantly. "I should think the answer is quite obvious. I'm sailing to China!"

"And you just thought to avail yourself of my cabin!" he said angrily.

"Well, you needn't get so huffy about it! The arrangement is only temporary."

"Damn right it's only temporary! It's going to last just about as long as it takes to turn this ship around and get you back to Boston!"

Larissa stiffened, suddenly afraid he would spoil her plan. "No! No, you mustn't do that," she pleaded. "Even if you do take me back to Boston, I'll absolutely refuse to get off this ship! Besides," she added, injecting a bit more bravado into her voice, "you can't order me off. I'm part owner of this shipping firm, you know. And if I want to take over my father's position in China, that is entirely up to me. In fact, if I wished, I could order you out of this cabin and take it over for myself!"

"Is that so?" Nathan's eyes narrowed, and he loosened his grip on her shoulders. "Then what puzzles me," he said sarcastically, "is why your uncle never mentioned these arrangements. And why weren't you a party to any of my meetings with your uncle?"

Larissa wrenched away from him and turned so he could not read the wavering determination in her eyes.

"Look," he said, his voice softening, "if you've had a misunderstanding with your fiancé, this is hardly the way to get even. I doubt that we'll be returning to Boston for more than a year, and by then I'm sure you'll regret your hasty decision."

"I have no fiancé, and I'm not likely to regret sailing on the *Queen of Cathay!*" Larissa snapped, whirling to face him again.

His eyebrows arched in question. "But your aunt led me to believe—"

"My aunt has led all of Boston—not least of all my supposed fiancé—to believe I am betrothed. But I have never had any intention of marrying Andrew Allerton."

"Still," he chided gently, "that hardly seems reason enough to stow away. I imagine your aunt and uncle will be frantic when they discover you're gone. Did you at least have the decency to leave a note explaining what you have done?"

Larissa sighed irritably. "No, I did not. And I can assure you that the only thing they will be frantic about is that I've ruined their plans."

Nathan shook his head. "I'm sure you're mistaken. They're your flesh and blood. Surely—"

"I think," Larissa interrupted calmly, "that I'd better explain the situation. Then you can decide for yourself if I've judged them too harshly."

Nodding, Nathan sat down on the edge of his bunk and listened to Larissa recount the conversation she had overheard in her uncle's library. By the time she finished, Nathan was frowning.

"From the first moment I met her, I didn't like that woman," he muttered. "And now it appears her husband has little more to recommend him. So," he concluded, raising his head to study Larissa's determined gaze, "you decided to turn to me."

She nodded. "I'm not asking much of you. Only that you let me hide in your cabin for a few days."

"But why didn't you approach me in Boston? Did you suppose you could not trust me to help you?"

"It was not a question of trust. I simply knew you would never agree to take me on the ship, and I refused to remain in Boston with my aunt and uncle. At least in Canton I can take over papa's work without interference from them."

Nathan frowned at her last statement, but did not debate it.

"You were right to assume I wouldn't bring you aboard," he said. "I think you'll find soon enough that life aboard a China trader is no lark. And I can't say I relish the idea of sharing my cabin—even with someone as desirable as you."

Blushing, Larissa sighed irritably. "I told you my presence is only temporary. As soon as we're a few days out to sea, when it would be imprudent to turn back, I'll reveal myself to Captain Evans, and we can make different arrangements. I would have gone to him directly—I've known him since I was a child—but I was sure that, sympathetic though he might be, he still would not have allowed me aboard."

Seeing that Nathan was about to speak, she grasped his hand and stared into his eyes imploringly. "Please, Nathan," she whispered, "try to bear my presence for just a few days. Please don't tell Captain Evans I'm aboard. In a few days, I promise you, I'll tell him myself. And then I'm sure he can find me a place in his cabin. After all, he's practically a second father to me."

Sighing, Nathan shook his head sadly. He reached up and stroked her cheek. "You're so innocent," he murmured. "You think the whole problem can be solved as easily as that. But I'm afraid your problems are just beginning. For one thing, Captain Evans is no longer master of the *Queen of Cathay*."

Larissa stared at him, aghast. "But he's sailed this ship for nearly seven years!"

"Nevertheless, the *Queen of Cathay* has a new master

this voyage. His name is Captain Clinton, and I seriously doubt that he will welcome your presence on his ship."

"But what's become of Captain Evans?"

Nathan shrugged. "I hardly thought it my place to ask." He paused, smiling cynically. "As part owner of this vessel, I should think you would be more likely than I to know the ship's business."

She frowned. "I'll thank you not to make light of my situation! It was only by the greatest stroke of luck that I even managed to find out when the ship was departing."

"Once you meet Captain Clinton, you may decide your luck was not so great. Of course"—Nathan cocked an eyebrow in question—"I could still go and inform him of your presence now. He'll be angry about having to turn the ship around. But I suspect not half as livid as if he discovers you later and has to bear your presence for the entire voyage."

Larissa defiantly shook her auburn curls. "And what can he do to me? Throw me into the ocean and bid me swim back to Boston?"

"He might," Nathan answered calmly.

"Ha! He wouldn't dare!" she proclaimed with more conviction than she felt. "You're just trying to frighten me, Nathan Masters, and you shan't succeed. I am staying aboard this ship until we reach China."

"And I suppose I have nothing to say about your decision? Despite the fact that you choose to occupy my cabin?" There was an undertone of amusement in Nathan's voice.

"Nothing whatsoever!"

"That is where you are wrong, Miss Bennett." He rose and towered over her. Larissa swallowed awkwardly as she watched the rise and fall of his bare, bronzed chest. "If you stay in my cabin, it will be at my consent and on my terms."

She opened her mouth to retort, but he raised his hand in a warning gesture. "I heard you out, Larissa, and you will do the same for me." She sat back, pressing her lips firmly together, and he continued in a cold voice. "I will grant you that your story about your aunt and uncle is no less than shocking. But I still think that you are an utter fool to embark on this voyage. Traveling to China is hardly the exotic adventure you might think. In a few days, we'll be out of fresh meat and vegetables. I can promise you that long before we reach Canton, you'll be sick to death of salt pork, dried bread, and beans. And you'll be even sicker of being cramped in this cabin. Besides all that, I am quite sure you'll be sadly disappointed by your reception in China. The Chinese people look down on all foreigners. They think themselves superior to the rest of the world, and they are especially cold to Western women."

"You needn't lecture me like some silly child," Larissa broke in. "I didn't come aboard because of some romantic dream of visiting faraway places. I came because it was the only way I could think of to protect what is mine. And nothing you say can dissuade me."

"Very well," Nathan nodded curtly. "Since you have made your position clear, perhaps we should discuss my terms. I will allow you to stay in my cabin, and I will say nothing of your presence to Captain Clinton. I might even be induced to protect you from his certain wrath. But, in return, I must expect some payment."

Remembering their first encounter, Larissa knew immediately what he was implying. Ignoring the sudden rush of warmth pulsing through her body, she replied coyly, "I'm afraid I have nothing you could want, sir. I brought only a small bundle of clothes, and I have no money other than a few coins. In time, of course, I shall collect my inheritance, and I will be glad to pay you handsomely—"

Her voice trailed away as his fingers slid beneath her chin, moving lower to caress her silky throat, then lower still to cup her breast. "My dear Larissa," he murmured, "you mustn't underestimate yourself. You have everything any man could want."

Her head snapped back and her hand lashed out to slap his cheek. Her green eyes blazing, she jumped to her feet. "Do you really think I am as low as that?" she whispered fiercely. "Just because I was desperate enough to choose your cabin, do you think I will willingly agree to become your whore?"

Nathan caught her by the arms, laughing at her anger as he pressed her to his chest. "What else am I to think when I find you hiding in my cabin, knowing full well what happened the last time you visited here? What did you really expect, Larissa? Can you honestly say you find my touch abhorrent? Do you mean to tell me you have not thought of me with even a touch of desire since that afternoon?"

"Oh!" She gritted her teeth in exasperation, hoping he could not feel how she quivered at his touch. "I despise you!"

"Indeed?" He raised his eyebrows in amusement. "How do you explain despising me so much that you seek my company for a four-month voyage? Strange, don't you think?"

She could feel his heart thumping against her cheek, and even through her skirt and petticoats, she was aware of his maleness growing hard as he pressed his groin against her. No, she told herself sternly, she did not want him! That strange magnetism she had felt at their first meeting had not influenced her to hide in his cabin. She would not believe that her heart was pounding as excitedly as his.

His mouth came down over hers, demanding that she give in. For a moment, she felt herself drifting helplessly, floundering in a rising tide of desire. She fought the weakness, determined not to respond. Somehow she sensed that if she succumbed to him now, he would feel he could bend her to his will whenever he wished. Without Captain Evans aboard, she had no one to protect or support her against him. She must never admit, even to herself, that he had any power over her.

With an effort, Larissa pulled her lips away from his, and her eyes sparked with determination as she met his amused gaze. Throwing back her head, she spit in his face, delighting as she saw his amusement turn first to shock, then anger.

Nathan flung her down on the bunk and strode to the door of the cabin. Without turning to look at her, he paused and spoke through gritted teeth. "Never let it be said that I forced myself on a woman against her will." He left, slamming the door behind him.

Larissa waited, fearful that he had gone to summon the captain. But the hours passed, and no one came to the cabin. She could not be certain, but it seemed the ship had not changed course. Pacing in the small cabin, she wished she could go on deck for some exercise and fresh air. But she knew she dared not show herself yet.

Sighing, she sat down on the bunk, rubbing the bruised spots where Nathan had clutched her arms. Perhaps, she admitted to herself, she had been foolish to stow aboard.

In two weeks of thought, while the *Queen of Cathay* lay at anchor in Boston harbor, it had seemed the only logical course of action. Once she reached Canton, she intended to take over the management of her father's office. She imagined she would be able to oversee all the purchases made in Canton, free from her aunt and uncle's meddling, and she would be able to insure that she received her just share of the profits. But perhaps she had not thought enough about the voyage itself. It seemed now that she had placed herself in a terribly vulnerable position. She had fought Nathan this morning, and he had stormed away. But he could easily overpower her whenever he wished, and no one aboard the *Queen of Cathay* could be expected to rescue her.

Somehow, she would have to appeal to the honorable part of his nature. He must never think her afraid of him, yet she would have to be careful never to push him too far. Above all, she must never let him know how his very presence made her tremble with desire.

It was dark when Nathan returned to the cabin, and Larissa, drained from the long day, had fallen asleep on the bunk. He shook her shoulder roughly and handed her a plate of fresh roast beef and succotash. "You'd better eat," he said gruffly. "We'll be out of fresh food soon enough. And I don't want you getting sick on me."

She sat up, rubbing her eyes as he lit a lamp. For a few moments she ate silently, mulling over his words. Then she looked up at him, her eyes filled with gratitude. "Then you didn't tell the captain? We're not going back to Boston?"

"No, I didn't tell the captain." He stared out the porthole into the night. "But I still think you're a fool." He paused, watching her hungrily attack her dinner. "And I know I'm an even greater fool for allowing you to stay here. Before this trip is over, we're both bound to regret it."

He was silent while she finished her meal. Then he went to his sea chest and took out a blanket and a heavy wool jacket. Larissa watched him, wondering at his apparent change in attitude. Throwing the blanket and jacket over one arm, he picked up her empty tin plate and started for the door.

"You can go back to sleep now," he said. "I won't bother you again tonight."

"Where will you sleep?"

"On the quarterdeck." He turned, grinning at her impishly. "As you said yourself, as part owner of this ship, you have first right to this cabin."

Before she could reply, he ducked out and closed the door. Larissa extinguished the lamp, undressed, and put on the only nightgown she had brought. Turning down the rough wool blanket, she slid into the bunk, frowning to herself. She knew she should be elated that she had won her first battle with Nathan so easily. But something within her warned that she had not won at all. Unknown to her, she had just begun a long succession of losses.

Chapter Three

For six days the tension between them built. Nathan brought Larissa her meals each day but spent most of the day on deck and slept on the quarterdeck each night. Larissa worried that he must be cold sleeping outdoors, but she could not invite him to share the cabin lest he read something more into her invitation. In truth, she was not at all sure she could resist him if he chose to press his advantage.

By the sixth evening out of Boston, Larissa was aching for some fresh air and exercise. Perhaps, she thought, the change could erase her incessant daydreams about Nathan's embrace. When he brought her dinner that night, she said wistfully, "I wish I could go for a stroll on deck. This cabin seems to get smaller every day."

He smiled. "Exactly what I had in mind. Eat your dinner quickly, and I'll accompany you myself. I heard the captain say he was retiring early, so I don't think we'll run into him."

"So what if we do?" she asked recklessly, though it was her fear of meeting Captain Clinton that had kept her in the cabin so long. "I'm not afraid of him! Anyway, he's bound to find out about me sooner or later."

"Certainly, but I guarantee you will prefer that he finds out later. The man has a mean streak in him. He's already had three seamen flogged for minor infractions of rules."

Larissa shivered. "Well, he wouldn't dare treat me that way! I'm not one of his crew. If I don't like the way he acts, I can have him dismissed."

"Whatever you say, madam." Nathan made a mocking bow. "Just see that he gets us to China first. My knowledge of sailing is far too limited for me to take over command."

34

A few minutes later, exhilarated by the prospect of fresh air and exercise, Larissa followed Nathan to the companionway and up the ladder. Nathan guided her to the stern rail, pointing toward the horizon.

"Look," he said, his voice tinged with a curious tenderness. "I think there's nothing more beautiful than a sunset at sea."

Larissa nodded, gazing at the red-orange glow spreading across the western sky and reflected in the blue-green expanse of sea. She stood mesmerized by the breathtaking sight. Then an upsetting thought crept into her mind. Either the sunset was in the wrong place, or else they were traveling in the wrong direction!

Since the sun always set in the west and the sunset was directly behind the ship, they had to be heading due east. But she knew the *Queen of Cathay* would not take an eastern route to China. Her father had told her it always sailed south and then west, around Cape Horn. Of course, she told herself, papa had mentioned stopping a few times at the Cape Verde Islands on the way to the Horn, which would require an initial southeasterly route. Still, if that were the case, the sunset should appear more to the port side of the stern. Puzzled, Larissa turned and strolled toward the binnacle, the case in which the ship's compass was mounted.

Nathan's voice cut in on her thoughts. "Larissa, what's bothering you? From the furrows in your brow, I'd say you're brooding about something."

"It's nothing," she said offhandedly. "I just thought I'd like to have a look at the compass. Captain Evans taught me to read one when I was only eleven years old."

Stepping to the binnacle, she pursed her lips as she saw they were, indeed, traveling due east. Perplexed by her discovery, she turned to the helmsman, a boy no older than she.

"Tell me," she asked innocently, "in what direction are we headed?"

"Due east, ma'am," the young man stammered, overwhelmed that there was a woman aboard and that she was talking to him.

"I see. And where will our first port of call be?"

"Smyrna, ma'am."

"Where is that? Is that a port in the Cape Verde Islands?"

The young sailor smiled indulgently. "No, ma'am. It's a port of—"

"Leave the sailor alone, Larissa," Nathan interrupted irritably. "He's got all he can do to keep us on course."

"Oh, no, sir," the sailor said quickly. "I enjoy a bit of conversation. Especially," he blushed, "with such a beautiful woman. Smyrna's in Turkey, ma'am."

"Turkey! But why would we be going to Turkey? I thought this ship was bound for—" She stopped abruptly, thinking back to a conversation at her uncle's dinner table. "Of course," she mumbled. "I should have known when I learned Captain Evans had been dismissed."

Whirling, she glared accusingly at Nathan. "It's for opium, isn't it? The Turks will give you opium to carry to China."

Nathan sighed. "Yes, we're going to Smyrna for opium. Now that you know, are you satisfied?"

"Of course not, and you know it! Papa would never have allowed it, and neither will I! The very idea is disgraceful—taking advantage of the Chinese weakness for some terrible drug. Why didn't you tell me sooner?"

He shrugged. "It would have made no difference. At least I was spared your righteous indignation for a few days. We're going to Smyrna, so you might as well relax and enjoy the trip, for there's nothing you can do about it."

"Oh, yes, I can!" She turned back to the helmsman. "Correct your course at once! We're to head southeast, toward the Cape Verde Islands."

"I can't do that, ma'am." Flustered, the young man looked away. "Captain's orders are to continue due east, and I dare not disobey orders."

"Do you know who I am?" Larissa snapped. "I'm Larissa Bennett. My father, Josiah Bennett, was half owner of this ship, and since his death, I have taken over his share. Now, I command you to correct your course to the southeast."

The sailor shook his head. "I can't, ma'am. Not without the captain's leave."

"For God's sake, Larissa, leave the lad alone," Nathan said, grasping her by the shoulders.

Larissa shook him off, and shoving aside the bewildered helmsman, she grabbed the wheel and strained to turn it hard to the right. Recovering his wits, the young sailor grasped the wheel, battling to regain control. Nathan grabbed Larissa and dragged her away from the wheel.

"My, my, what have we here? An attempted mutiny?" All three froze at the sound of a dry, commanding voice. Larissa looked up into the scowling face of a husky, dark-haired man she judged to be about forty years old.

"Is there some problem, Dillard?" the man barked.

"No sir, Captain Clinton," the sailor mumbled as he corrected the course.

"That's strange," the captain said, smiling grimly. "I could have sworn I just saw you wrestling with a woman over control of the wheel. That couldn't have been the case, could it, Dillard?"

"No, sir." The young man's whisper was barely audible.

While the captain addressed the helmsman, Nathan tried to maneuver Larissa away, but the older man quickly stepped to block their way. He peered at Nathan in the waning light of dusk.

"Mr. Masters, isn't it?"

"It is," Nathan replied stiffly.

The captain's eyes slid over Larissa. "Mr. Masters, you did not inform me you had brought your wife aboard my ship."

"You did not ask. In any case, I have no wife."

At that, the captain pursed his lips peevishly. "Well, I do not approve of carrying whores! This ship is not a floating brothel!"

"I'll thank you to reserve your judgment, sir!" Larissa lashed out. "If you're not careful, you'll find yourself without a job. I'm far from a whore! I am Larissa Bennett."

Captain Clinton's eyebrows raised in mock concern. "Forgive me, madam, but your name means nothing to me. And your threats even less."

Ignoring Nathan's warning squeeze of her arm, Larissa plunged ahead. "Then allow me to clarify matters. I am the daughter of the late Josiah Bennett, which means I am part owner of this ship."

"Really?" The captain eyed her skeptically. "Perhaps we had best continue this discussion in my cabin. My helmsman has been bothered enough for one evening."

He turned to Nathan. "Mr. Masters, if you will be so kind as to escort the young lady below?"

Nodding, Nathan took Larissa's elbow and guided her toward the companionway. "Try to get hold of yourself, Larissa," he whispered as they descended the ladder. "Don't push him too far."

Larissa tossed her head in answer and gave Nathan a withering look.

Inside his cabin, Captain Clinton slammed the door, waved Larissa and Nathan into two heavy oak chairs, and stood glowering over them. "Now then," he growled, "suppose you begin by explaining the meaning of that disturbance on deck. I refuse to stand for such actions on my ship."

"As I tried to explain to you, captain," Larissa said calmly, "this ship is more mine than yours. You are the captain, but I am half owner. And, as such, I must insist that you change our course. I will not allow this ship to go to Smyrna."

The captain shook his head incredulously. "In twenty-five years of sailing, I've never taken an order from a woman. And I'll be hanged if I'll do so now. In port, I listen to the owners, but on the high seas I am the sole master of this vessel. Besides"—his eyes narrowed as he studied Larissa—"what proof do I have that you're who you say? I was hired by Hiram Barnes, and he made no mention of a partner named Larissa Bennett."

"I'm quite sure he did not," Larissa said bitterly. "My uncle would like to forget I have any claim to the company, and no doubt he wishes I would do the same. But you needn't take my word for it. Mr. Masters can tell you I speak the truth."

"Well, what about it, Masters?" Captain Clinton growled.

Nathan hesitated, unwilling to be caught in the controversy. Then he shrugged in resignation. "The girl isn't lying, sir. Her father was Hiram Barnes's partner, and agent of the firm until his death a few months back."

Smiling coldly, the captain turned back to Larissa. "And so you intend to look after your late father's interests."

"Exactly," Larissa nodded curtly, ignoring the savage gleam in the captain's dark eyes. "And we must begin by changing course immediately. Papa did not approve of opium smuggling, and I won't disgrace his memory by engaging in such trade."

"My dear Miss Bennett," the captain broke in, "if we are not to carry opium, what do you suggest we offer the Chinese in trade?"

"Why, furs, wood, all the things papa has always—"

He dismissed her suggestion with a wave of his hand. "Do you really suppose we had time to take on a full stock of trading goods in only two weeks in Boston? I can assure you we did not. Furthermore, Mr. Barnes saw no reason to carry more than a minimum of other cargo— because we will not need it. My instructions are to sail to Smyrna, take on a full load of opium, then continue on to Canton. I intend to follow those instructions."

"No!" Larissa sprang from her chair. "I won't allow it!"

"You have no choice in the matter." The captain smirked, and his beady eyes seemed to bore into her. "Tell me, Miss Bennett, how do you explain your presence on my ship? How is it I was not aware of you earlier? Just where have you been staying?"

"In Nathan's—I mean Mr. Masters' cabin," she answered, realizing too late what the captain was implying. She swallowed, and a blush stained her cheeks.

"I see," Captain Clinton murmured, clasping his hands together. "Yes, I believe I am beginning to see everything quite clearly now."

"No, you don't understand—" Larissa protested weakly.

"Ah, but I do! How convenient that your lover should vouch for you! For all I know, you're nothing more than some dockside slut Masters picked up to amuse himself with on the voyage. Perhaps the two of you thought you could cheat Mr. Barnes of his business by fabricating some flimsy story of a partnership. Do you think me such a fool that I would believe a girl barely out of diapers when a respectable businessman like Hiram Barnes made no mention of a partner?"

"But you must believe me! The name of the firm is Bennett and Barnes. Where would such a name come from if Uncle Hiram had no partner?"

Captain Clinton raised his brows. "It came from your imagination, I'm sure. I am employed by Hiram Barnes Limited."

"That's what my aunt and uncle would like to call it, but surely you know better. Everyone in Boston knows—"

"I am not from Boston, as your lover no doubt informed you. I came recently from Charleston. But I won't be taken for a fool. I know who my employer is.

"As for you, Masters," he said, turning to the silent Nathan, "I am surprised at you. Mr. Barnes led me to believe you were a respectable agent. But I suppose you are not the first man to fall prey to the whims of a comely wench. I ought to have both of you thrown in chains for the rest of the voyage."

Nathan bristled, rising slowly to tower over the captain. "I'll grant you the girl is foolish and impulsive," he said slowly, "but she is who she says. I may be a fool for allowing her to stay in my cabin, but I'm not a liar, and I'm not a cheat. Nor am I one of your crew, to be bullied and slandered by a power-hungry captain. I'll thank you to remember that, Captain Clinton!"

Astounded that anyone should challenge him so boldly, and just a bit afraid of Nathan's obvious strength, the captain waved them toward the door. "Get her out of my sight," he snarled. He cleared his throat, trying to regain a spark of authority. "On the slim chance that she is, in fact, Barnes's niece, I'll let her remain in your care, Mr. Masters. But I refuse to take orders from her, no matter who she claims to be! She hardly looks old enough to be prancing around the world unescorted, let alone giving orders to experienced sea captains."

As Larissa opened her mouth to protest, Nathan took her arm and firmly pulled her into the passageway. He didn't speak until he had guided her into his cabin and closed the door behind them.

"I thought I made it clear Captain Clinton is not a man to tangle with," he said angrily. "You behaved like a damned fool! I'm not sure you'll ever convince me to take you out of this cabin again."

She turned on him, her green eyes snapping with fury. "You're a fine one to be judging the way I behaved! What did you do that was so noble? You sat there without saying a word most of the time!"

He smiled wryly. "I did vouch for your identity. What more could you want?"

"You might have supported my stand against opium smuggling. If you worked for papa for four years, you must have known his feelings on the matter."

"True enough. But no matter how much I might object to the trade, I'm practical enough to know this shipping firm can't survive without opium. The Chinese have enough furs and wood now. They want opium. If we don't provide it, someone else will—and we'll be run out of business."

Annoyed, Larissa turned her back to him. "Another

thing. You might have defended my virtue a bit. You never blinked an eye when Captain Clinton accused us of being lovers."

"Does it matter what he thinks?"

"Certainly!" She whirled on him indignantly. "Just because you nearly raped me at our first meeting, you can hardly call us lovers."

Nathan gritted his teeth. "I'm warning you, Miss Bennett, I've grown a bit weary of your self-righteousness. I've apologized for what happened that day and explained that it is not my usual way of becoming acquainted with a woman. But I will not have you throwing the incident in my face for the rest of this voyage. You must admit I've treated you with uncommon respect since then—especially considering the fact that you took it upon yourself to commandeer my quarters. But if I'm called a rapist once more, I might feel forced to justify that label."

Pressing her lips firmly together, Larissa turned away from him again and stared out the porthole. She flinched, but did not turn to watch him as he stormed out of the cabin. Her eyes stung with tears that she furiously blinked back.

As if to taunt her with the power he could so easily wield over her, Nathan did not sleep on the quarterdeck that night. He returned to the cabin, but made no attempt to share the bunk with her. Instead, he made an elaborate show of spreading a bedroll on the floor, then kept Larissa awake most of the night as he tossed on the hard surface.

The next night, Larissa was so exasperated that she told him to take the bunk, while she rolled herself in a blanket on the floor. In the bunk, Nathan sighed rapturously. "Ah, the exquisite luxury of a soft bed." He reached down to pat Larissa's shoulder. "Sure you wouldn't care to share it with me? There's plenty of room."

Roughly shaking off his hand, she rolled away from him on the floor and tried to ignore his chuckle. But she could not ignore the aching within her, nor the unexplainable desire she felt to have him take her into his arms again. She only hoped he could not sense her feelings.

Within a few minutes, she could hear his regular breathing. But she lay awake for hours, alternately despising and desiring him. She puzzled over how she could care at all for a man so brash and sarcastic. At times, he seemed too much like Andrew Allerton. Yet he was not at all like Andrew. He had been tender and caring in telling her about her father's death. Even in the face of his later boldness, she could never forget the sympathy and suffering she had read in his eyes at that moment.

But what had happened to all that tenderness? Was it possible it still lurked beneath his cynical, sarcastic shell? Larissa sighed. Perhaps it was better if the gentle side of Nathan's nature remained hidden. Then she could go on playing her own role, pretending she did not care for him at all. If he ever again approached her with a tender word or touch, she might be tempted to let her own feelings show, and that could lead to disaster. She must never forget she had undertaken this voyage for business purposes, to protect what her father had built, not as some foolish quest for romance.

Chapter Four

The *Queen of Cathay* docked at Smyrna in midmorning on a hot, sunny June day. Nathan, who had left the cabin early that morning, returned to collect some papers and announced that he would be gone for the rest of the day. "My business may keep me ashore till evening, so if you get hungry, you'll have to find your own way to the galley," he said.

Larissa turned from the porthole, where she had been studying the swirling blue and green Aegean Sea. "Couldn't you take me with you?" she asked, trying to control the plaintive note in her voice. "I would so love to feel firm ground beneath my feet again."

Nathan shook his head adamantly. "Out of the question. I've serious work to do, and I can't be bothered with attending to your whims. I'm sorry if that makes you unhappy, but—" he paused and shrugged, "I never invited you on this voyage, and I warned you it was no pleasure cruise."

He left without giving her time to retort, and Larissa turned moodily back to the porthole. She had long ago decided she would not beg him for anything. If he did do as she asked, she could well imagine what he might demand in return. More and more lately, she had sensed the building tension in him whenever they were near one another. She could not escape a feeling that he might attack her at any moment, despite his cool exterior and mocking attitude. And the most upsetting thing about the whole situation was that she almost wanted it to happen.

Nathan had been gone two hours when Larissa climbed to the deck. The ship seemed strangely quiet, and it occurred to her that she was probably one of the few people left on board. No doubt most of the crew had gone ashore to enjoy their short time in port, while she remained behind, a virtual prisoner on her own ship.

She stared at Mount Pagos, rising behind Smyrna, and thought about the grim irony of the situation. At the moment, she did not feel much like the part-owner of a shipping firm. She had no power over the ship and little control over her own destiny. Still, she was free for the day from the harassment of Nathan and Captain Clinton. Determined to enjoy the day, she tilted back her head and closed her eyes, basking in the warm sun and letting the playful Aegean breezes ruffle her hair.

At the sound of steps behind her, Larissa opened her eyes and whirled around to face the young sailor Captain Clinton had called Dillard. He smiled awkwardly. "I'm sorry, ma'am. I didn't mean to startle you."

She returned his smile sweetly as a plan began to form in her mind. "No harm done. I was only dreaming. This certainly is a beautiful day for dreaming, isn't it?"

"Yes, ma'am." Dillard stared bashfully at the deck.

Larissa gestured toward the shore, where the thin, white minarets and the dome of Yahli Cami mosque rose tantalizingly over Smyrna. "I was dreaming about how delightful it would be to go ashore and explore that intriguing city. Don't you agree, Mr. Dillard?"

The sailor flushed with pleasure, flattered that she remembered his name. They had not seen each other since that evening almost two months ago, when she had battled with him for control of the wheel. "Oh, yes, ma'am," he agreed.

Noting his reaction, Larissa smiled and moved closer to him. "Mr. Dillard?" she paused and stared at him imploringly. "Do you think you could take me ashore with you?"

He exhaled, obviously flustered, and his cheeks turned scarlet. "Oh, ma'am, I wish I could, but I'm assigned to watch, and I dare not leave the ship."

"Oh!" She pursed her lips in an appealing pout. "But I don't see any reason for you to be on watch now. The ship isn't going anywhere, and I very much doubt that anyone is going to steal it, especially in the middle of the day!"

He shrugged. "True enough. But I think the captain fears if he gave us all shore leave at once he'd end up without a sober man in the crew in the event of an emergency." He laughed nervously.

"But would anyone really miss you just for a couple of hours?" she wheedled. "I mean, as long as you don't come back drunk, who would even know you'd been ashore?"

The sailor squirmed uncomfortably. "I'd like to take you, ma'am, I really would. But this is my first voyage under Captain Clinton, and I don't think I ought to take any chances. Besides, I'm not sure it would be proper for me to be squiring around Mr. Masters' woman."

Larissa stamped her foot irritably. "I am not Nathan Masters' woman! Whatever gave you that idea?"

"Well, I—"

"Never mind." Larissa waved his explanation aside, anxious to press her advantage. "If you won't go ashore with me, perhaps we can settle on a compromise. Suppose you just row me to shore, and I'll continue into the city alone?"

He stared at her speechlessly.

"You could still keep an eye on the ship," she continued, "and you'd only be gone a few minutes. Surely no one could chastise you for that."

"You can't be serious," he whispered. "You won't be safe on those streets alone. The people here are heathens. I suspect they have little respect for decent Christian women."

"Mr. Dillard," Larissa said flatly, "I am my own woman, and I intend to go ashore whether you take me or not. I can assure you, I am well able to defend myself. Now, for the last time, will you row me ashore?"

He shook his head. "No ma'am. I'm afraid I couldn't live with myself if anything happened to you. One of the few things my father managed to pound into my thick skull was that women should be protected at all costs. You being about the prettiest woman I've ever seen, I'd be double-damned if I forgot his advice now." He paused and cleared his throat. "Pardon the profanity, ma'am. I hope I didn't offend you."

Larissa shook her head, then sighed. "Well, since it's clear that you will not help me, I suppose I shall have to find my own way to shore." Watching him from the corner of her eye, she turned slowly toward the rail and gazed appraisingly toward the shore. "Yes, I suppose the distance is not too great. Of course, I'm not the strongest swimmer, but—" Shrugging, she raised her dress above her ankles and swung one leg upward, toward the rail.

"No! Wait! You can't do that!" Dillard caught her by the waist, then instantly backed away, embarrassed by the contact.

"And why can't I?" Larissa asked indignantly.

"Well, you just can't! You might drown. And even if you don't drown, you can hardly walk into Smyrna dripping wet, with your clothes plastered to your skin." He blushed at the image evoked by his words.

"Then what would you suggest, Mr. Dillard?" Larissa raised her brows questioningly. "As I've already told you, I have every intention of going ashore. And, as you may recall from our first meeting, I am a very determined woman."

The young sailor stared at her for a moment, remembering how she had grappled with him at the wheel. Again Larissa turned back to the rail and began to raise her skirt. Watching her, Dillard sighed apprehensively. "All right, I'll row you ashore. Not because I like the idea. But I can't very well stand here and watch you throw yourself into the sea."

"You're very kind, Mr. Dillard." Larissa smiled sweetly and heaved an inward sigh of relief. She had not relished the thought of plunging into the sea, but she would have gone through with her threat, just to prove she was serious. Impulsively, she stood on tiptoe to kiss the young sailor's cheek. Sliding her arm through his, she suppressed a giggle at his embarrassment. "Shall we go, Mr. Dillard?"

As Larissa stood on the shoreline, watching Jonathan Dillard row back toward the *Queen of Cathay*, she felt a small quiver of apprehension. Perhaps she had been foolish to insist on coming ashore, but she was too proud to call to the young sailor to come back for her now. Turning away from the sea, she swallowed the lump in her throat and took a few hesitant steps toward the city. To her surprise, she noticed many men in western dress—traders, no doubt, from England, France, Holland, and America. But the majority of the men were swarthy Turks in billowing white robes and trousers. Holding her head high, Larissa tried to convince herself that their whispered comments in their strange language had nothing to do with her.

She followed what she assumed to be the main road into the city, passing red-roofed houses hidden behind mud-walled courtyards. The streets were parched and dusty. Smells of baking bread and roasting lamb wafted on the breezes from the courtyard cooking areas. Several blocks from the shore, she paused to stare in awe at a sprawling brick structure composed of countless archways and a high, vaulted ceiling.

After standing for a few moments observing the constant flow of people in and out of the structure, Larissa ventured toward the massive iron gates, which stood open at the main archway. Stepping inside, she found herself swallowed up in the mystifying world of a Turkish bazaar. She walked slowly down the main passageway, allowing her eyes to adjust to the dim light within. Looking up, she saw that the ceiling was a continuous row of small domes, each with a hole cut in its center to allow a few rays of sunlight in. She soon discovered the bazaar was a maze of streets and alleyways, a miniature city within the city, crammed with intriguing shops and vendors' stalls.

As she wandered in the maze, Larissa noticed several figures moving along, completely enveloped in long, black robes. Even their faces were veiled. Seeing a shopkeeper graciously bow and help one of the shrouded figures into his stall, Larissa realized that these must be Turkish women.

She smiled to herself. No wonder the men had observed her so curiously! Compared to these black shadows, she must look only half-dressed. With her auburn hair flowing freely, she must appear utterly shameless by Turkish standards. In fact, even now, it seemed that a hush fell over the crowded bazaar wherever she walked. For an instant, she shuddered, wondering again if it was safe for her to wander here alone. Then she pushed her misgivings to the back of her mind. The bazaar was so exotic that she simply would not let her imagination spoil the experience.

With a determined toss of her head, she stopped at a shoe stall, ignoring the proprietor's open-mouthed stare as she fingered a pair of soft red leather women's slippers, with turned-up toes and metal heels. At a jewelry stall, she stopped to stare at copper, bronze, and silver bracelets and caught a glimpse of sparkling gems being displayed to a black-veiled figure within the stall. Turning down another alleyway, she looked in on a carpet dealer displaying an enormous stack of Persian and Turkish rugs in rich shades of blue and red.

Wandering into another section of the bazaar, Larissa was overwhelmed by the pungent smell of tobacco leaves hanging from the ceilings of several stalls. As she paused to stare curiously at the strange assortment of pipes, their stems attached to large vessels by snakelike arms, she heard an anxious shout behind her. She managed to flatten herself against the side of an archway just in time to avoid being trampled by a camel.

Larissa blinked in amazement as an entire caravan passed through the bazaar. Many of the swaying camels were richly decorated with tufts of red, yellow, and green silk and brocade. The tinkling of camel bells was deafening as they passed.

Larissa continued to wander, gradually becoming immune to the stares and comments of the scowling Turks. She realized that, despite the many Western men in the city, she had not seen any European or American women. But she was too fascinated by the sights and sounds of the bazaar to feel alarmed. If the Turks stared at her and whispered about her a bit, it was only natural. After all, she was rather strange looking in comparison to the Turkish women.

Engrossed in her exploration of the bazaar, she did not at first notice that she was being followed by four burly Turks. When one of them reached out to tug at a wisp of her hair, she simply turned her head and smiled sweetly. They were only curious, she assured herself. In time, when they discovered she was no different from any other woman, they would leave her alone.

Fifteen minutes later, however, the men were still following her, and Larissa was beginning to feel less confident. She glanced about frantically, noting that all the European and American traders seemed to have disappeared. What if the men following her really did intend to harm her? Who among the sea of strange faces would help her?

Fighting a wave of panic, Larissa quickened her step and tried to reassure herself. Surely the men would not dare to accost her in a crowded bazaar. She could always scream, and a scream was understandable in any language. Certainly someone would come to her rescue.

Quickly she turned into another narrow alley, hoping to elude her pursuers. Then she noticed the passage was less crowded than the others. In fact, there seemed to be fewer occupied stalls in this area, and soon she and the four men were the only people in the passageway. Now truly panicked, Larissa broke into a run, desperate to reach the next, more traveled crossroad before the men overtook her.

Glancing frantically over her shoulder, she saw all four men running easily behind her, grinning broadly. They were just waiting for her to tire. If only she could outlast them, then dart among the crowd at the next intersection and lose them. She wished she were wearing a long black veil like the Turkish women. At least then she would not feel so vulnerable. Now she felt as if her auburn hair streamed behind her like a beacon.

As if in answer to her thoughts, a billowing black cloth suddenly descended over her. Stunned and blinded, Larissa tried to push it off and continued to run. She heard the men chuckling behind her. She stumbled and felt iron-hard arms enclosing her, dragging her back to her feet. Wildly, she kicked, but her captors eluded her feet, chuckling louder as her legs futilely slashed the air. Summoning her last ounce of strength, Larissa screamed, hoping the cloth would not completely muffle her cry. She screamed desperately, the one word that came to her lips. "Nathan!" The sound reverberated in her ears until a heavy fist clubbed the side of her head and she sank into unconsciousness.

Larissa awoke to the sounds of female voices giggling and chattering in a foreign language. She opened her eyes and focused slowly on a marble ceiling, inlaid with bits of gold and polished green malachite. Looking around, she saw that she was lying on a velvet divan in a great hall occupied by at least thirty women. Marble and malachite pillars, decorated with gold leaf, stretched from the floor to the ceiling, where sunlight filtered in through a many-paned skylight. Two towering, bare-chested men guarded the door. They were dressed in flowing silk trousers and stood with their feet spread and their arms crossed at their chests.

As she sat up, a young woman with dark brown eyes and blue-black hair approached her. Like the other women in the hall, she wore satin trousers, tightly fitted at the waist, then flowing full to the ankles, where they ended in gathered bands. A short, filmy silk blouse scarcely covered her full breasts, leaving several inches of olive flesh exposed between her waist and bosom. "Welcome to the harem of Ibrahim Pasha," the woman said, sneering as she gestured at their surroundings. "I am Roxana."

Larissa blinked. "You speak English?"

The woman shrugged. "Yes, I was taught as a child. It amuses the pasha to have women who speak various languages. Of course"—she scowled at Larissa—"he may find my English less enticing now that you are here."

"Oh, but I won't be staying," Larissa said quickly. "I'm sure my presence here is a mistake."

Roxana continued to scowl. She came closer and roughly grasped a lock of Larissa's hair. "No, I doubt that their bringing you here was a mistake. The pasha will be very pleased with this addition. This hair and your creamy skin will be quite a novelty. All of his friends will covet you."

"But you don't understand! I don't belong here! I didn't ask to come here. I must get back to my ship."

The woman laughed harshly. "Foolish woman! One does not ask to join the pasha's harem, one is chosen. And since you have been chosen, you must not question the wisdom of that choice. You will find that life here can be easy, if you are diligent in your duties and seek only to please the pasha. But, of course, there is always the chance he will sell you to the grand seraglio in Constantinople."

"The grand seraglio?" Larissa repeated weakly, still unable to believe the situation.

Roxana nodded. "The sultan's harem. That would indeed be an honor."

Larissa tossed her head defiantly. "I'm not a slave, and I won't be sold to anyone! Where is this pasha? I demand to speak with him immediately!"

"No one demands anything of Ibrahim Pasha," Roxana said, smirking, "except, of course, the sultan. In due time, of course, I suspect you will be accorded an audience with the pasha. For now, I suggest you relax and await your master's pleasure."

"No!" She jumped up from the divan and rushed at the door, hurling herself between the two turbaned guards. They caught her easily, their faces remaining expressionless as she flailed her arms and kicked. As they returned her to the center of the room, the other women continued chattering as if nothing unusual had happened. Only Roxana looked up at her with a taunting smile.

Nervous and agitated, Larissa paced in the great marble hall, wondering if she could ever manage to escape. Even if she did, would it be too late? Would the *Queen of Cathay* already have departed? Would Nathan even care when he returned to the ship and found her gone, or would he be pleased to be spared her company for the rest of the voyage?

She turned abruptly and almost collided with an old woman carrying a bundle of satin clothing. The woman spoke to her in a rapid, guttural tongue, and Larissa waved her away irritably. The woman persisted, shoving the clothes at her.

"She wants you to change into harem dress," Roxana explained.

Larissa shook her head adamantly. "That's out of the question. As I told you, I shan't be staying, so I refuse to change into such a disgusting outfit."

"Disgusting, is it?" Roxana raised her thick black brows in outrage. Turning to a group of harem women, she uttered an angry string of Turkish words.

Before Larissa knew what was happening, at least ten women descended on her and ripped her plain blue cotton frock from her body. Then her petticoats and even her most intimate lingerie were torn to shreds.

"Now will you accept our harem costume?" Roxana taunted.

"You seem to leave me little choice." Larissa snatched the clothing from the old woman and quickly slid into the apricot-colored trousers. The satin felt cold against her bare skin. The blue satin jacket was trimmed in gold and, like the other women's, left a considerable portion of her ribs exposed.

"Now you look more like one of us," Roxana nodded approvingly.

"But I'm not one of you, and I never will be!" Larissa glanced nervously toward the door. "How could you do that to me? It was embarrassing enough in front of all the women, but to have those men see me naked—"

"Men?" Roxana gave a bitter laugh. "They are hardly to be called men. They are eunuchs. You know—deprived of their male equipment."

Larissa stared at her, horrified.

"I assure you, the practice is quite common. The men who brought you here were also eunuchs. The pasha would be a fool to entrust his women to any normal men."

Larissa closed her eyes, trying to hold back the hot, acid vomit she felt rising in her throat. What sort of man was this pasha, she wondered, that he would mutilate his own men? What might he do to her if she displeased him? Would her carefree visit to Smyrna cost her her virginity or even her life?

For the first time since leaving Boston, she began to wish she had remained in the home of her aunt and uncle. Compared to the horrors that faced her now, her aunt and uncle seemed only a minor threat.

Chapter Five

In the receiving chamber of Ibrahim Pasha's palace, Nathan Masters rose slowly and offered his hand to the pasha. "Then our terms are agreed upon. I will return tomorrow morning with men to transport the cargo to my ship. At that time, I will bring the balance of the payment."

Grasping Nathan's outstretched hand, the pasha, a handsome man in his mid-thirties, nodded and smiled. His white teeth flashed, and his dark eyes sparkled with the exhilaration of a hard-driven bargain. His voice was smooth and lightly accented. "Very well, my American friend. Until tomorrow then."

As one of his men showed Nathan out of the palace, the pasha turned to another of his servants to inquire whether anyone else was waiting to see him. His carefully cultivated poppy fields gave a rich yield of opium, and he was the prime dealer for ships stopping in Smyrna on their way to China. His servant informed him that no other dealers were waiting, but a new candidate for his harem had arrived that afternoon.

Ibrahim Pasha leaned back in his chair and smiled. "Good. I could use a bit of relaxation. The American drives a hard bargain, and my mind has been well-exercised for one day. Bring in the girl, so I may see what delights she offers the body."

Two eunuchs, holding her firmly by the elbows, escorted Larissa into the chamber. The pasha relaxed in his satin-cushioned chair, stroking his chin absently as he eyed the girl. Before she had left the harem, the women had attached a gauzy apricot veil to her head. It flowed past her shoulders, almost to the floor, billowing out behind her as she walked. Now, feeling the pasha's gaze on her bare

53

skin, Larissa felt tempted to draw the veil around her for
the small cover it offered. Instead, she forced herself to
face him boldly, lifting her chin defiantly as she returned
his gaze.

When he did not speak, she took it upon herself to begin the conversation. "Will you kindly tell your men to
release me? I have tried to explain they have made a mistake in bringing me here, but it appears they do not understand English."

Her words echoed in the large, cool marble hall, seeming
to bounce back at her from the three marble steps leading to the pasha's chair. He continued to study her, then
smiled slowly and issued a command in Turkish. Instantly,
the two eunuchs let go of her arms and moved back a
step.

"Thank you," Larissa said coolly. "Now perhaps you
could arrange for me to have some decent clothing so I
may return to my ship."

Ibrahim Pasha's teeth flashed in another smile, and he
spoke gently. "You do not seem to understand, little one.
You are not going anywhere. You are mine, now, a
member of my harem. Is that so difficult to accept?"

She stamped her foot irritably. "I belong to no man! I
demand to be set free!"

He gestured amiably toward the carved copper doors at
the far end of the chamber. "The doors are there, child.
You have only to use them."

Whirling, Larissa raced toward the doors. She had almost
reached them when a heavy hand clamped over her shoulder and the pasha's laugh sounded behind her. As the
eunuch dragged her back to the foot of the stairs, she
raised snapping green eyes to Ibrahim Pasha.

"You tricked me!" she spat. "You never intended to let
me go!"

He shrugged. "You tricked yourself, my copper-haired
beauty. I said only that the doors are there for your use.
If you can devise a way of escape, you may go with my
blessings. But I must warn you that my men are watchful
and wary. They know it would displease me greatly to
lose one of my women, and they do not relish the thought
of incurring my wrath."

"But you can't keep me here against my will! I'm not
one of your Turkish women. I'm a citizen of the United
States!"

He cocked a bushy black brow. "But need I remind you we are not in the United States?"

Seeing that demands and threats had no effect on him, Larissa swallowed her pride and began to plead. "Please let me go. You have so many women already, what possible use would I be to you?"

He smiled. "A man's interests are many and varied. As to your use, we shall determine that tonight. I will send word to have my private bedchamber prepared in the harem, and you and I shall become much better acquainted."

She stiffened, staring at him icily. "We will not! I will refuse!"

"My dear, no one in this palace refuses me anything." His eyelids drooped over his dark eyes. "But for now I fear you have begun to bore me. A touch of spirit in a woman is commendable—in bed. But at other times she should conduct herself in a manner less shrewish."

He issued a series of commands to the eunuchs, then waved them away. They dragged Larissa back to the harem, numb to her kicks and deaf to her protests.

When evening came, Larissa still refused to go to the pasha's bedchamber, so a swarthy eunuch picked her up and carried her there. Muttering a curse, the servant threw open the door, dropped her unceremoniously on the huge, satin-covered bed, and turned to leave the chamber.

Hearing a chuckle, Larissa turned her head and saw Ibrahim reclining on a divan a few feet from the bed. He wore only white satin trousers, and she saw that his broad chest was covered with dark hair. Leaning on an elbow, he selected a treat from a tray of figs, dates, and raisins before him.

"Still the feisty one, eh?" he inquired, popping the fruit into his mouth. "Well, we shall see how long that spirit lasts." He patted a spot beside him on the divan. "Come, sit by me and feed me."

Larissa continued to stare at him from the bed.

"I said, come!"

His steely tone frightened her. Trembling, she sat up and walked slowly toward him. Perhaps, she thought, if she placated him, she could still secure her release.

He smiled as she sat down, and his hand idly stroked the naked flesh of her ribs. When he spoke again, his voice was gentle. "You are trembling, dearest. Do you fear me so?" When she bit her lip and did not answer, he continued, "You must not think I will treat you harshly. They have told me you are a virgin, and I can assure you I will be gentle."

Larissa's jaw dropped, and she turned to meet his gaze. *"They* told you?" she repeated weakly.

He nodded. "The eunuchs who brought you here. They examined you when you were unconscious. You mustn't be embarrassed. It is only natural for me to want to know the condition of my women. And of course they have no carnal interests in women."

She shuddered, wondering where and how they had examined her. She was glad she had not been conscious for the ordeal.

"You must relax now," the pasha continued, "and accept what happens. I realize you have not had the training of my other women, but I was so anxious to have you that I will train you myself. In time, I am sure, you will become one of the most pleasing women in my harem."

His hand slipped up beneath her thin silk jacket and caressed her breast. The other hand traced the crease where her thigh met her body, then plunged between her legs, gently pinching her. She felt her nipples straining and tightening, even while she tried to swallow her revulsion. An image of Andrew Allerton pawing her on the widow's walk flashed through her mind.

"Please! I can't!" She jumped to her feet, cringing as she heard the fastenings of her jacket rip loose.

He grabbed her by the waist, turning her to face him, and she shivered as she realized her breasts were now fully exposed to his gaze. "You will not be coy with me," he ordered in a tightly controlled voice. "I own you, woman, and you must learn to do my bidding!"

He bent toward her quickly, and his mouth covered her nipple, sucking noisily as he pulled her closer. Fighting the sensations evoked by his mouth, Larissa screamed and raked her fingernails across his bare back. His hand shot up and slapped her face, and she bit her lip, choking back a sob. Silent tears coursed down her cheeks, and she closed her eyes to blot out the image of the hungry beast clinging to her. His mouth moved away from her breast, nibbling and licking as it made its way to her waist. His hands kneaded her buttocks, rough in their urgency, all promises of gentleness forgotten. Then he loosened her trousers, letting them drop to the floor.

The sight of her nakedness seemed to ignite him even more. Standing, he picked her up and carried her to the satin-draped bed. In one frantic movement, he lay her on the bed and sprawled atop her, struggling to remove his trousers. Feeling his maleness, naked and hard against her thigh, Larissa bit back a whimper. His mouth took hers roughly, demandingly, and she willed herself into a protective oblivion as she felt him probing for an entrance.

Suddenly the door of the chamber flew open. Larissa gasped in shock as she saw Nathan, struggling in the arms of two towering eunuchs. Seeing her crushed beneath the pasha, his features froze in horror, and he groaned in agony. "My God, Larissa, what has he done to you?"

Rolling off of her, the pasha sat up and faced the door, his eyes snapping in fury. "What is the meaning of this intrusion?" he demanded.

The two eunuchs began an explanation in rapid Turkish, but Nathan cut them off with a shrill cry. "I'll kill you, Ibrahim! I swear I'll kill you with my bare hands if you've harmed her!" He attempted to lunge at the pasha, forgetting for a moment that the two eunuchs held him.

Ibrahim Pasha's voice was deadly calm as he stood and slid into his satin trousers. "You are, of course, aware that I could have you beheaded for daring to set foot in my harem?"

Nathan stared at him with raging eyes, refusing to answer or to show the slightest fear.

The pasha shrugged. "Why did you do it, my shrewd American friend? This afternoon you impressed me as quite wise. But now you show yourself to be a fool. Is the girl so precious to you?"

Hesitating, Nathan considered what story might win Larissa's release. "She is my wife," he said slowly.

Smiling, the pasha shook his head. "Either you lie, or you Americans are not very amorous creatures. I happen to know the girl is a virgin."

Nathan's eyes shot to Larissa, who had slid off the bed and was nervously stepping into her harem outfit. She nodded, blushing with embarrassment as she mouthed the word "still."

Clearing his throat, Nathan moved his eyes back to the

pasha. "All right, I admit she's not my wife. I'm her—guardian. I'm responsible for her."

"Indeed?" The pasha's eyebrows raised in amusement. "I might say you are rather a poor guardian since you somehow allowed her to be kidnapped. How did you know to come here?"

"I stopped in the bazaar after concluding our business. There was talk among the European traders of a woman being abducted this afternoon. Some even said they heard a scream sounding curiously like my name." He paused, cocking his head at Larissa, who nodded shyly. "When I returned to the ship and learned she was missing, I knew immediately. You are, I believe, the only one in Smyrna to keep an extensive harem."

Ibrahim Pasha nodded, obviously pleased by his reputation. "So. Now what do you expect me to do?"

"I expect you to do the honorable thing—release the girl and me."

"Honorable? Was it honorable for you to creep into my harem and disturb me in my carnal relations? What if the girl had not been here? What if I were engaged with another woman?"

Nathan shrugged. "Your questions need no answer, since she is, indeed, here."

The pasha stared at him a moment, a half-smile playing across his face. "I fear, my friend, that I cannot do as you ask. I might consider selling the girl to you, but I doubt that you could offer enough to match what the grand seraglio would pay for so rare a specimen. Still," he mused, "I admire your courage in coming here. Such spirit demands that I give you some chance to regain your prize."

Nathan's eyes narrowed. "Are you suggesting a duel?"

Larissa felt her heart lurch. Nathan could not win, she thought despairingly. Surely the eunuchs would intervene if they saw their master begin to falter.

"No!" she blurted. "Please, don't!" She turned pleading eyes to the pasha. "I'll—I'll stay here in your harem. Just let him go."

Chuckling, the pasha twined a hand possessively in her hair. "You needn't fear, little one. Your friend may disagree, but I have never felt a woman was worth staking my life for. How can the life of a mere woman be worth the life of a man? No, I was thinking of a game of skill. The winner will have the girl, and the loser must be content without her."

Nathan scowled. "I don't approve of gambling with human life."

"But you have little choice. Either accept my terms or"—he shrugged expansively—"I could still have you executed."

Glancing at the eunuchs, who still flanked him though they had relaxed their grip, Nathan sighed and nodded. "You are very persuasive, Ibrahim Pasha."

The pasha grinned. "You are familiar with backgammon?"

"I've played it once or twice."

"Good." The pasha's eyes sparkled, anticipating an easy victory. "We shall play one game only. If you win, the girl leaves with you tonight. If you lose, I may dispose of both of you as I see fit."

Larissa gasped, still fearful for Nathan's life. "No, Nathan," she cried, "don't agree to this foolish plan!" Again she pleaded with the pasha. "Let him go now, I beg you, and I will remain your most willing servant."

Nathan scowled, and the pasha cocked an eyebrow quizzically. "Have you so little faith in your countryman's skill?" He shook his head. "No, the bargain has been made, and now we must see it through."

Turning away from her, he issued a curt order to the eunuchs, who immediately left the room. Then he addressed Nathan. "Let us adjourn to my sitting room, where the backgammon board awaits. The girl will accompany us. Her presence will, I believe, add an extra measure of challenge to the game."

The sitting room was a small, cozy room with a Persian carpet and silk wall hangings. A servant had preceded them into the room, lighting a lantern and placing it near the gaming table. The low cedar table had thin legs and bits of malachite and ivory inlaid on the top in the pattern of a backgammon board. Leaving Larissa to stand uncertainly near the board, the pasha waved Nathan into a seat on one side of it and seated himself on the opposite side.

Larissa watched silently as each man positioned his fifteen stones, flat polished circles of ivory. Each man threw one of his dice. Seeing he had the higher number, the pasha smiled and took the first turn. She remembered that her father had owned a backgammon set, but she had never seen him play and knew nothing of the game. Uncle Hiram and Aunt Harriet, with their stern, businesslike attitude, had not approved of games, so there had been little chance of learning the skill in their house. Now she desperately wished someone had taught her. It was nerve-racking to watch, not knowing who had the advantage in the game.

Larissa closed her eyes, praying that, somehow, Nathan would win. Earlier, she had found the thought of her own fate unbearable. But the idea that her foolishness might also result in Nathan's death was even worse. Tensing, she listened to the click of stones against the table and the clatter of the rolling dice. The game seemed agonizingly slow as she stood in self-imposed darkness, afraid of what she might see if she opened her eyes.

Finally, she heard the pasha expel a long, decisive sigh. "So, the girl is yours, my friend. I suggest you disappear with her before I throw honor to the winds and renege on our agreement."

Still afraid to open her eyes, afraid to believe her ears, Larissa felt Nathan's firm grasp on her elbow. "Let's go, Larissa," he said in a cool, bored voice. He led her toward the door, and in another moment they were outside the palace.

She felt herself trembling with relief as she struggled to match his rapid, angry stride. His hard grip continued to bite into her arm as he steered her into the street. He paused to take off his blue broadcloth jacket and throw it over her shoulders, scowling as he buttoned it over her almost naked breasts. Then, before she even had time to catch her breath, he was hustling her through the nearly deserted streets again.

"Nathan," she panted, almost running to keep up with him, "how can I thank you? If you'd been a moment later—"

"Save your breath," he snapped, "we're not safe aboard the ship yet."

Afraid of irritating him more, she was silent. When they reached the shore, she saw Jonathan Dillard, looking small and frightened, waiting in a rowboat. Dumping her over the side, Nathan gave the boat a hearty shove off the beach before climbing in beside her.

Jonathan took up the oars, pulling in smooth, slow

strokes toward the *Queen of Cathay*. "You were so long," he said, "I'd begun to fear the worst."

In the moonlight, Larissa could see Nathan scowl. "Can't we go any faster?" He waved Jonathan away from the oars and took over, stroking in swift, angry, powerful motions.

Watching him, Larissa felt a great rush of warmth. Now that all the tension and fear were behind her, she was overwhelmed by one thought. He had saved her. He had come after her, damning the risks, and he had saved her! Closing her eyes, she saw again the anguish in his gaze when he first saw her sprawled on the pasha's bed. Was it possible he cared for her more than he would admit?

They did not speak again until they were aboard the *Queen of Cathay*. Leading her to the cabin, Nathan shoved her in ahead of him, then slammed the door and glared at her.

Exhausted from the ordeal of the last several hours, Larissa sank down on the bunk and looked up at him meekly. Ignoring the angry glint in his eyes, she asked, "How did you know you could beat him at that game?"

His voice was bored. "Backgammon was one of my main diversions for four long winters on Macao. Your father was an expert player, but I managed to beat him often." He strode toward her and grasped her shoulders roughly. "However, my skill at backgammon is hardly the main issue at the moment. Do you realize, Miss Bennett, that your foolishness and willfulness could have cost both of us our lives? I had a long talk with young Dillard when I first discovered you were missing, and he explained to me exactly how you came to be ashore."

"You mustn't blame him," Larissa interrupted anxiously.

Nathan frowned, annoyed that she was so quick to defend the young sailor. "I don't blame him at all. It's obvious you used your beauty and charms to manipulate the lad. I can hardly blame him for capitulating to your pleas when I myself am fool enough to allow you in my cabin. But, I repeat, Miss Bennett, your willfulness could have cost both of us our lives."

"I'm sorry," Larissa whispered. Then she added, with a touch of defiance, "If you'd taken a moment to warn me of the dangers, I would never have gone ashore."

He scowled, waving aside her defense. "I doubt that, since I warned you about Captain Clinton's nature, and you still saw fit to take him on at your first meeting. Now that I think of it, perhaps I should have left you to the pasha. At least then I wouldn't be plagued with you for the rest of the voyage."

Larissa bristled. "I said I'm sorry!"

"Sorry isn't enough!" Nathan thundered, releasing her and beginning to pace in the cabin. "You heard the pasha. His word is law in Smyrna. He could have had me executed, just for entering his harem. I'm damned lucky his eunuchs didn't break my neck when they first caught me. You don't seem to understand—I risked my life for you! I'm not in the habit of doing that for any woman!"

His tone was bitter, but his eyes betrayed wavering emotions. For a moment, Larissa wondered what angered him more, the fact that her actions had endangered his life or the fact that he had shown more concern for her than he normally showed for any woman. She smiled faintly, wondering again if it was possible he cared for her more than he would admit.

Nathan stopped pacing and stared at her irritably. "Do you find the situation so amusing?" he demanded.

"Oh, no!" She shook her head, but could not dispel the smile. "I suppose I'm just so relieved to be here, safe and whole, that I can't help smiling."

He shook his head. "No. I think it's more than that. I think you actually enjoy tempting the fates. It's all a game to you, isn't it? Why don't you admit it—you enjoyed tempting the pasha, and you enjoy tempting me. Let me tell you something, Miss Bennett. If I had been a moment later, you might have found the game less pleasing. The pasha would have extracted his price, without a second thought for your honor. Perhaps I should have done as much long ago."

He advanced toward her, his eyes blazing as his hands dug into her shoulders. "Tonight, I think you will pay for tempting me these many weeks. And for endangering my life. I hope to God you prove yourself worth the price."

"Nathan! Please!" She shivered under his fiery gaze, knowing it would be impossible to stop him. And in the secret recesses of her heart, she knew she did not want to.

In an instant, his mouth was upon hers, bruising in its harsh possessiveness. His hands forced her down on the bunk, and his body flattened hers. She could feel the pulsing hardness of his maleness growing against her thigh, and she fought to stifle the answering throb in her own loins. When she tried to pull her mouth away from his, his fiery tongue pushed inside. Her nails raked his back in protest, but he pressed even closer, as if she were encouraging him. She heard the fabric rip as he tore away her scanty harem costume, his movements frantic with desire.

His flesh felt hot, moist, and demanding against hers as his legs slid between hers and his fingers glided over her inner thighs, working ever higher to her private treasure. Gasping, she felt her powers of protest draining away. Strange, pleasurable sensations rippled through her body. Then a stab of pain penetrated her dream world, and she jerked away.

"Don't fight it, Larissa," he whispered. "It's too late to deny me now, and you'll only rob yourself of pleasure. Relax, Larissa, and enjoy."

His voice had a tenderness that caught her off guard. A part of her demanded that she remain limp, pretending he had no effect on her. But as the pain diminished and her body thrilled to his touch, passiveness became more and more impossible. As he moved within her, her passions mounted to an uncontrollable height. Unable to hold back, she found herself moving in rhythm with him, willing the moment to go on and on as her body tingled with almost unbearable ecstasy. She felt herself floating, mindless of all but the thrilling response his body was coaxing from hers.

She and Nathan became one as he carried her again and again to new peaks of sensation, until finally his passions culminated with hers and she lay shuddering in the aftermath. Tenderly kissing her forehead, he slid off of her and pulled a blanket over them.

Cradling her in his arms, he whispered, "I won't say I'm sorry—because I'm not. And neither are you."

For several moments, she lay silent, basking in the afterglow of ecstasy. But she could not dispel the question that lurked in her mind. "Nathan," she ventured shyly, "why did you tell the pasha I was your wife?"

He sighed. "It was the first explanation to come into my head. But don't get any foolish ideas. I've no intention of marrying anyone, ever."

Swallowing the lump in her throat, Larissa turned away from him. She blinked back her tears as all the magic of the moment dissolved, leaving her feeling soiled and discarded.

Chapter Six

Nathan was gone when Larissa awoke the next morning. Stretching slowly, she pondered the strange way the night had ended. She was sure Nathan had meant to take her brutally, to punish her for tormenting him and for endangering his life. But his harshness had turned to tenderness, and her own pain had turned to unbelievable sweetness. She had not been able to fight him, and she had not truly wanted to fight him. Guiltily, she admitted to herself that she had been waiting for that moment, longing for it since their first meeting. But his statement about marriage had brought her brutally back to reality. Last night had awakened her to what it was to want a man. But wanting was not enough.

Frowning thoughtfully, she wondered what would become of their relationship for the rest of the voyage. Having claimed her virginity, would he expect to take her whenever he wished? She knew her body would welcome him, but her conscience could not allow herself to give in to a man who bluntly denied any intention of marrying her. It was bad enough she had surrendered so easily last night.

Did he love her? she wondered. Despite what he had said about marriage, was the fact that he had risked his life for her proof enough? Or had he come after her only because of loyalty to her father—to save Josiah Bennett's daughter? And what about her? Did she love him? Did she even know what love was? She knew she was grateful to him. Perhaps she even cared for him more than any other man she had known. There was no denying she wanted him in a physical sense. But did she love him? Sighing, she decided it was useless to speculate about her feelings. Even if she concluded she did love Nathan, she would be a fool to tell him so unless he softened and made some commitment to her. All she could do was wait. And for the sake of her own pride and conscience, she must resist him.

In midafternoon, she climbed to the deck, where Jonathan Dillard informed her Nathan had gone ashore to complete the opium purchase. For an hour, she paced, worrying that the pasha might have felt less benevolent that day. But when she finally saw the opium boats approaching, she forced herself to stand calmly on the quarterdeck, watching nonchalantly as Nathan led a group of sailors to the main deck and directed them in unloading the boats. Midway through the operation, he glanced up and saw her. With a curt word to one of the crew, he ambled toward the quarterdeck.

"So, you decided to stay on board today. Have you lost your wanderlust so soon?" His voice had a new element of tenderness that made Larissa flush. She wondered if everyone around them could perceive the change in their relationship.

"Not at all," she replied quickly. "I simply thought I'd save you the trouble of coming after me today."

Nathan grinned. "Thoughtful of you." For a few awkward moments, they both stared at the baskets being raised to the ship. Then Nathan turned his gaze back to her. "You ought to go below. Your cheeks and nose are already turning pink from the sun. If you're not careful, you'll lose a layer or two of skin."

She shrugged, still staring at the baskets, unwilling to believe that her father's ship, her ship, would really be carrying opium. If only she could find a way to stop it. "Where will they store it all?" she asked casually.

"In the hold."

"That's a part of the ship papa and Captain Evans never showed me. I'd be interested in seeing it."

"You wouldn't find it very pleasant," Nathan said quickly. "It's dark and damp, and most holds have at least a family or two of rats. Anyway, there's nothing to see. It's just a storage area." He changed the subject, sensing that she was scheming something. "Will you go below now, before the sun takes its toll?"

"Why?" she replied shortly. "Would you object to shar-

ing your cabin with a flawed face? Or," she continued recklessly, "would you just object to seeing the ivory complexion you gambled for ruined?"

Nathan's features hardened. "I was thinking only of your
welfare. But do as you like. You may be sure I don't give
a damn!" He turned and strode back down to the main
deck.

Larissa stood on the quarterdeck several minutes more,
at least partly in defiance of Nathan's advice. She felt
touched by his concern, but was not about to let him
know that. As she stood, she studied the movements of the
crew, watching carefully as they passed the baskets of
opium to others standing in an open hatch. Assuming that
the hatch led to the hold, she decided she would explore
the area later, whether Nathan approved or not.

That night, when Nathan came to the cabin to retire,
Larissa was already huddled beneath her blankets on the
floor. Giving her a quizzical stare, Nathan said, "As we
proved last night, there's ample room in the bunk for two.
Or did you find my touch so repulsive?"

"No—I mean I—" she stumbled, flustered. "I'm really
much more comfortable on the floor."

"All right, have it your way."

Nathan chuckled as he blew out the lamp, but he wondered how long he could play her new game. Last night
had only confirmed how much he wanted her. One taste
of her sweetness would not be enough to satisfy him for
the whole voyage. And, unless he had misread her response, it could not satisfy her, either.

There was no denying he wanted her, but he wanted her
to admit she desired him, too. For tonight he would leave
her alone and hope that tomorrow she would weaken.
Smothering a groan, he rolled toward the wall.

Larissa lay still, listening for the steady breathing that
would signal Nathan was asleep. Even then, she waited a
while longer before she crept out the door to the passageway. At the head of the companionway ladder, she
froze, listening for the sound of the deck watch. Cautiously, she poked her head above the deck. Satisfied that no
one would see her, she scurried to the main deck and
rushed to the hatch where she had watched the opium
baskets disappear.

It took all her strength to pry open the hatch. Glancing around to be certain she was unobserved, she gingerly felt her way down the ladder to the dark hold. Aided only by the shaft of moonlight streaming in through the open hatch, Larissa found the first basket of opium and pulled it toward the ladder. It was heavier than she had imagined, and she suddenly despaired of getting it up to the main deck.

Grunting, she lifted the basket and struggled to stand upright. Somehow, she managed to get her foot on the first step of the ladder, then slowly began to inch her way up. Midway to the top, she almost lost her balance. She swayed, grabbing wildly for the ladder's side, while she held the basket wedged between her body and the ladder. By the time she managed to heave the basket to the deck, she was streaming with perspiration, plastering her dress to her body.

Fortunately, the night watch was still on the foredeck, engrossed in a game of cards with several other crew members. Pushing her perspiration-soaked hair away from her face, Larissa dragged the heavy basket toward the rail. She gritted her teeth and once again managed to lift the basket, balancing it against the rail for a second, before she gave it a determined push and watched in satisfaction as it fell toward the sea.

The basket hit the water with a loud splash, which alerted the card playing watch. "Hey, who goes there?" a sharp male voice shouted.

"Oh, don't be so jumpy," a second man's voice teased. "It's probably just a dolphin."

"I don't think so," said the first man. "It sounded too close to the ship. Clinton'll have my head if anything goes wrong while I'm on watch."

"All right," his companion said, "go ahead and take a look. But don't think you're gonna get out of this game now, when I've got you twenty dollars down."

"Don't worry," the watchman grumbled as he shuffled toward the main deck. "I ain't quittin' till you owe me!"

Larissa had frozen at the rail. Now, panicked by the thought of being discovered, she rushed back toward the hold and hurried to climb down the ladder. In her haste, her foot slipped on the third rung from the bottom, and she fell backwards into the baskets of opium below. A squeaking rat scurried from beneath her falling body, and Larissa forced herself to stifle a scream of terror. She might as well have screamed, for the thud as she hit the baskets had already given her presence away.

"Here! Who is it?" a man's voice cried. Then, seeing the open hatch, he called to his companion, "Quick, a lantern! Something's amiss in the hold!"

Paralyzed with fear, Larissa lay motionless as she listened to feet thudding above her. In a moment, light flooded the hold and revealed her lying among the baskets of opium. Some of the dry opium particles had been knocked from the baskets and flecked her dress.

Above her, four faces peered down in anger and consternation. Regaining her composure, Larissa jumped to her feet and brushed off her gown. She started up the ladder, acting as if they had just discovered her on a stroll and there was nothing unusual about her being in the hold. But the four sailors were older and more seasoned than Jonathan Dillard, so they were less easily dazzled by her beauty.

As she reached the top of the ladder and attempted to brush by them, one grabbed her roughly by the arm and demanded, "Now just a minute there, missy. What the devil were you doing down there?"

Larissa shrugged. "Just exploring."

He sniffed, eyeing the brownish flecks of opium clinging to her dress. "Is that so? You wouldn't maybe be an opium user, would you? Maybe just looking for something to ease the pain of a long voyage?"

"Certainly not!" She shook her head indignantly. "I find the trade thoroughly disgusting. Now, if you'll let me pass—"

He tightened his grip on her arm. "Not so fast. You still haven't given me a decent explanation of what you were doing down there." He peered at her closely, noting her disheveled hair and sweat-stained dress. "Whatever you were doing, you seem to have worked yourself into quite a state."

"Hey, look at this!" A cry from the rail interrupted them. As the sailor who held her looked up, Larissa thought she could take advantage of the situation and break away. She tried to run, but he held her fast, dragging her with him toward the rail. His mate pointed to a basket bobbing on the sea beside the ship.

"Remember the splash you heard a while back? It looks like we've found its cause."

The man looked from Larissa to the basket, slowly comprehending what had happened. "So, you don't approve of the opium trade, eh? That couldn't, by any chance, explain how that basket got in the water?"

Larissa tossed her head defiantly, refusing to respond.

"Of course not," the sailor continued sarcastically. "A frail little thing like you couldn't have dragged a big, heavy basket full of opium all the way up from the hold, could you?"

When she still refused to answer, he shook her roughly. "I said, could you?"

She stared at him, her eyes snapping, then answered coolly, "Why ask me when you seem to have answered the question yourself? As a lady, I am not accustomed to being treated so harshly, and I must demand that you release me immediately."

"Oh, no!" he replied. "You don't go free till the captain himself orders it. I ain't gonna be held responsible for no missing basket of opium.

"Atwell," he said to one of his mates, "go fetch Captain Clinton. No doubt he'll want to deal with this situation himself."

Larissa stood silently while they waited for the captain. She would not deny what she had done, neither would she give the men the satisfaction of admitting it. And, above all, she would not let them think she was afraid of their bullying captain.

Captain Clinton arrived several minutes later, grumbling about being disturbed in the middle of the night. He wore a hastily tied green satin dressing gown and a matching green-tasseled nightcap. When he saw Larissa, his eyes widened in fury, and he suddenly snapped wide awake.

"You!" he growled. "I should have known you would be at the bottom of any trouble! There hasn't been a single problem aboard this ship since the night I first discovered you—presumably because Masters has kept you in check. But now—" He shook his head angrily and turned his attention to the man holding her. "Well, what did the wench do?"

The sailor pointed to the empty, bobbing basket. "It appears she disposed of some of the opium shipment."

"What?" The captain's enraged roar seemed to shake the ship. Angrily clenching and unclenching his fists, he glared at Larissa. "Didn't I tell you, girl, that I would tolerate no interference on my ship?"

"And didn't I tell you, sir," Larissa replied quietly, "that this ship is more mine than yours?"

A shocked murmur rippled through the group of sailors, as each wondered how his captain would respond to such insolence. Sensing this, Captain Clinton knew he could not let her go unpunished. After all, she had not only attempted to destroy his shipment, but she had dared to question his authority. If he allowed a mere girl to get the best of him, the hardened image he had so carefully cultivated among his crew would be ruined.

"How much did you destroy?" he demanded.

Though she was beginning to quiver inside, Larissa stared at him contemptuously and answered coolly, "I had intended to destroy the whole shipment. Unfortunately, your lackeys discovered me after I had dumped only one basket."

"Only one basket, eh?" the captain muttered, stroking his chin thoughtfully. "You should count yourself fortunate the watch discovered you when they did, my dear. I doubt you could have survived the punishment I would feel forced to inflict had you destroyed more."

He turned to two of the waiting crew. "Lash her to the mizzenmast, and someone fetch my whip."

Larissa drew in her breath and tried not to shudder. She must not let them think she was afraid. Somehow she must keep herself from giving any of them that satisfaction. Knowing she could not possibly overpower them, she docilely let them drag her to the mast. As they tied her wrists to the post above her head, she heard the captain pacing behind her, cracking his whip in anticipation.

The cool evening breezes bit through her wet gown, and she began to shiver. She breathed deeply, trying to still her nerves before the first stinging blow. The murmurs of the crew around her faded, and in the silence she heard Captain Clinton draw back the whip. She forced herself to stare straight ahead, not daring to glance over her shoulder at the snarling whip, bracing herself for its inevitable bite. The moment seemed to hang as she tensed herself, waiting, willing the beating to be over quickly.

The first lash struck, tearing away her cotton dress and

biting into the tender flesh of her back. She sucked in her breath, determined not even to whimper, as she heard the whip's deadly whistle again.

After the sixth stroke, Larissa lost count of the lashes. Her back seemed to be on fire, and she slipped into hazy semi-consciousness as the lash bit into her back again and again. Finally, she heard the captain's voice, coming, it seemed, from a great distance.

"Cut her down, tie her hands and feet, and throw her into the hold. In the morning, after she's had time to think about her predicament, I'll dispose of her."

Someone stepped to the mast and unfastened the ropes that bound her wrists. As she crumpled to the deck, too weak to protest or struggle, two of the crew stepped forward to bind her ankles and wrists. Then another sailor threw her unceremoniously over his shoulder and carried her to the hold. He backed halfway down the ladder before dumping her to the floor. Ignoring her moans, he lumbered back up the ladder and closed the hatch, plunging the hold into darkness.

Larissa snapped back to full consciousness as she felt something furry scurrying along her back. Shrieking with terror, she struggled to sit upright. More furry creatures squealed around her as she shook herself to keep them away.

More than an hour passed as she sat shaking, trying to control her panic and keep the rats away. Her back burned with every movement, and her wrists and ankles chafed from the tightness of her bonds. With the hatch closed, the hold was pitch dark, and its musty odor was beginning to nauseate her.

She caught her breath at a sound above her as the hatch creaked open and dim moonlight streamed in. "Larissa? It's Jonathan Dillard. Are you all right?"

"Jonathan," she repeated, afraid to believe her ears. "Jonathan? Can you help me?"

"Yes. But we'll have to be quiet and fast, so we're not discovered. The captain would never approve of my meddling in his affairs." He descended the ladder and began to cut through her bonds. "Oh God, Larissa," he moaned, "I'd give anything to have saved you from this. I was asleep in the forecastle when some of the men came in, all excited about what had happened. At first I couldn't believe even Captain Clinton could be so cruel. Then they started talking about giving you time to recover and then coming down here to—violate you. That's when I knew I had to believe it. And I had to get down here to save you."

He finished sawing through the ropes and pulled her to her feet. "Can you make it up the ladder?" he asked anxiously.

Larissa swayed and winced as the blood rushed back to her chafed ankles. "Yes," she gasped, "I can make it."

In the moonlight, she saw Jonathan regard her dubiously before he nodded. "All right. I'll go first to be sure the coast is clear. You follow close behind so you can slip out of the hatch as soon as I say it's safe."

She nodded, reaching out to squeeze his hand before he started up the ladder. At her first step, pain shot through her ankles, and she wondered if she had been too optimistic. But she managed to cling to the sides of the ladder, hauling herself up, rung by rung, behind Jonathan. Reaching the hatch, she thankfully grasped Jonathan's helping hand, letting him drag her to the deck.

Collapsing on the deck, she panted, "Jonathan, I don't think I can walk too well. I'm sorry. I'm just so weak—"

He stared at her, noting for the first time how the whip had torn away one shoulder of her dress, leaving the bodice flopping awkwardly, exposing a breast. "Captain Clinton ought to be flogged within an inch of his life!" he muttered. "What a despicable creature he is!"

Raucous laughter coming from the foredeck companionway jolted him back to action. "I'd better get you out of here before we're outnumbered," he said, lifting her easily into his arms and holding her tightly against his chest. He strode aft and started down the companionway leading to the officers' cabins.

"Where are you taking me?" Larissa whispered, nestling her head securely against his chest.

"To Nathan Masters' cabin."

"No!" she sat upright, struggling in his arms. "We can't go there."

Jonathan frowned. "Why not? That's where you've been staying, isn't it?" His frown deepened. "Has Masters mistreated you in some way?"

"No—I—" she stuttered, "I'd just rather he didn't know about what happened tonight."

"Well, there's no way you can avoid him finding out. Besides, I can hardly take you up to my quarters in the forecastle—unless you want to take your chances with the rest of the crew."

"No, but I—"

"Hush, before you wake the captain or alert the other men."

Reaching Nathan's cabin, he shifted her to one arm while he opened the door and stepped inside.

On the bunk, Nathan shifted, disturbed by the noise. "Larissa?" he mumbled sleepily. "Something wrong? You change your mind about sharing my bunk?"

She felt Jonathan flinch at Nathan's last words, but when he spoke, his voice was steady. "Something *is* wrong, Mr. Masters. Larissa's hurt pretty bad."

At the sound of Jonathan's voice, Nathan sat upright and fumbled to light the lamp. As the light flared, he came to his feet, his eyes snapping at the sight of Larissa, her dress tattered, in Jonathan's arms.

"What in God's name did you do to her, Dillard?" he demanded harshly, rushing toward him, his fists clenched.

"All he did is save me!" Larissa cried defensively. "You can blame Captain Clinton for the lash wounds on my back."

"Clinton!" Nathan spat, enraged. "I'll kill him!"

"Perhaps first you'd better take care of Larissa's back," Jonathan said calmly, crossing to lay her on the bunk. "I'll go to the galley and get you some fresh water."

As Jonathan left, Nathan sat down on the bunk beside Larissa. Gently, he began tearing away the remnants of her gown. She drew in her breath sharply as he pulled away bits of fabric that clung to the partially dried wounds.

A few moments later, Jonathan returned with a pan of water. After setting it down beside the bunk, he stood staring at Larissa's ravaged back. Looking up at him irritably, Nathan demanded, "Is there something you wanted to tell me about all this?"

"No. I didn't actually witness it. Larissa can tell you more than I."

"Then I suggest you stop staring and get out of my cabin!"

Jonathan shrugged and was almost out the door when Nathan turned to him, his voice choked with emotion. "Jonathan—I—that is—Larissa and I appreciate your help."

Turning back to Larissa, he bathed her back gently.

Neither of them spoke until he was finished. Then he turned her to her side and said, "It'll hurt like the devil for a few days, and you may have some lasting scars, but I suspect you'll live. Now"—he grasped her chin and turned her face toward his—"suppose you tell me exactly what happened."

She looked away from him, shrugging. "It's obvious, isn't it? The fine Captain Clinton staged one of his famous floggings."

"That much is quite apparent," Nathan said, a note of irritation creeping into his voice. "What I would like to know is why?"

When she did not reply, he prodded, "I don't approve of what he did, but even a man of Clinton's character does not flog someone without some provocation. What were you doing out of the cabin, anyway? Did you go up to meet Dillard after I was asleep?"

"Why would I have done that?"

"The lad is obviously infatuated with you. And how am I to know how you feel about him?"

Larissa bristled. "What kind of a woman do you think I am? After what happened here last night, could you really think—"

Nathan cut her off. "All right, forget I even mentioned Dillard. Just tell me what you did to incense Captain Clinton."

"Well," she whispered, "you're bound to find out eventually, so I might as well tell you myself." Her eyes met his defiantly. "I was destroying the opium."

"What!" Nathan grabbed her shoulders, squeezing so hard she winced in pain. "No wonder the captain was so furious. I ought to take you over my knee myself! What a little fool!"

"Nathan, please! You're hurting me!"

Glowering, he released her. "What does it take to make you see that Bennett and Barnes needs that shipment? If we don't have the opium, we won't have anything to sell the Chinese. And we might as well return to Boston and let your uncle declare bankruptcy."

"I don't care! I don't want to live on money that comes from the opium trade!"

"Well, you've got to live on something, you know! And I don't imagine your aunt and uncle will welcome you back with open arms when they find out you've ruined them."

"I haven't ruined anyone!" Larissa shouted. "I only managed to dump one basket before the watch stopped me."

"Well, thank God for that! But one basket is still one too many. I had a hard job bargaining for every basket in that shipment—but you just toss one into the ocean without a second thought!"

"So turn me back over to Captain Clinton!" she cried. "Better yet, I'll go find him myself." Gritting her teeth against the pain, she struggled to her feet and stumbled toward the door.

Nathan's hand shot out to grip her wrist, whirling her back toward him. "You're not going anywhere," he said coldly. "Do you really think that I'm such a cad that I'd throw you back to the mercy of that fiend? No matter what you did, no one should degrade a woman that way. Besides"—he pulled her closer, wrapping his arms around her waist, his eyes glowing as he studied her torn dress and heaving, bared breasts—"if he saw you like this, he might be tempted to do more than flog you."

Bending his head, he kissed one nipple. His tongue teased it, until she felt it growing, hardening, sending a tingling through her whole body.

Larissa squirmed, pushing his head away from her. She frowned and tried to control the quiver in her voice. "Please, Nathan! Don't—I can't "

Pursing his lips, he shook his head. "No, I suppose in your current condition you'd be in too much pain to enjoy it. We might as well just try to go to sleep." He pulled her into his lap, then eased her down on the bunk. "But you're not sleeping on the floor any more tonight or on any other night. You're sleeping right here in my arms. It seems to be the only way I can keep you out of mischief."

Chapter Seven

Larissa was still locked in Nathan's arms the next morning when they were awakened by a pounding on the cabin door. "Masters? Let me in! I know you've got the girl in there, and I demand that you turn her back over to me!"

Sighing irritably, Nathan swung out of bed, pulled the blanket up to cover Larissa, and slid into his trousers. He stood in the middle of the cabin, feet braced, arms crossed on his bare chest, and said coolly, "The door's not locked, Clinton. Let yourself in."

Cursing, the captain threw open the door and started into the cabin. Blocking his way, Nathan demanded, "Did you come to examine your handiwork? I can tell you, it's the most disgusting thing I've ever seen. Any man who would treat a woman that way—"

"She deserved what she got—and worse," the captain growled. "I warned both of you that I would not tolerate any further interference on my ship."

"I think you made yourself quite clear last night," Nathan said crisply. "Now, I suggest you let her nurse her wounds in peace."

"Oh, no! I'm not taking the chance that the little slut will cause any more problems. When this ship sails today, she's staying behind in Smyrna."

"I think not," Nathan replied, his tone cold and unyielding.

"See here, Masters, you have nothing to say about this. What I choose to do with the girl is my business, and you've no say in it." He paused and cocked an eyebrow. "How did she get back to your cabin, anyway?"

Nathan shrugged. "I found her when I went to check the shipment early this morning."

76

"Liar! Some of my men have already told me she disappeared last night."

"Indeed?" Nathan's voice had a hard edge. "And why were any of your men looking for the lady last night?" When the captain remained silent, he continued, "It makes no difference how Larissa came to be in my cabin. The fact is she's here, and she'll remain here."

"No, she won't!" Captain Clinton pushed past Nathan and lunged at Larissa, who was cowering wide-eyed under the blanket.

"Take your hands off her, Clinton," Nathan said in a tightly controlled voice.

The captain's hands tightened on Larissa's quivering form. "Give me one reason why I should?"

"I'll give you two. Number one, if you hurt her again, I swear I'll thrash you within an inch of your life."

Smirking, the captain tightened his grasp. "I doubt you'd wish to be accused of mutiny."

"Number two," Nathan continued, "as we've told you before, she is Hiram Barnes's niece. Mr. Barnes is an influential man, and I've no doubt he could see that you never command another ship for the rest of your life."

The captain released Larissa and stepped away from the bunk. "I'm still not sure I believe your story of who she is."

Nathan shrugged. "Can you really afford not to believe it?" He stood before the captain, towering over him by more than a head, clenching and unclenching his fists meaningfully.

"You don't frighten me, Masters," the older man growled. "If you want a fight so badly, I've a whole crew to back me up. But," he spat disdainfully, "that little harlot is hardly worth the trouble. For the moment, I'll let you keep your plaything. But, I'm warning you—if there's any more trouble of any kind, I'll have you both thrown into the hold in chains!" Without waiting for a reply, he stomped out of the cabin and slammed the door behind him.

On the bunk, Larissa turned toward the wall, trying to hide the tears that sprang to her eyes. Sitting down beside her, Nathan turned her gently toward him, a half-smile playing across his face. "Does the thought of sharing my cabin for the rest of the voyage make you so sad?"

"No—I—" She paused and forced a smile. "I can't help it. After last night, that man terrifies me."

Nathan frowned. "And you didn't think I could handle him? Or didn't you trust me to protect you?"

"No—I don't know—I just—"

He gathered her into his arms, planting soft kisses in her hair, making her tremble as always with his nearness. "Ah, Larissa," he murmured, "you really are an incorrigible little fool. But at least this time you had the good sense to keep quiet and let me do the talking." He was silent for a moment before adding, "For both of our sakes, I'd appreciate it if you would try to behave, at least until we reach China. You can only push Clinton so far, and last night was only a taste of his fury."

"All right," Larissa sighed. "I'll do whatever you say."

Nathan's white teeth flashed against his tanned face. "Anything? Is that a promise?"

She blushed. "You know what I mean."

"Yes," he murmured, tilting her chin back to kiss the throbbing hollow of her throat. "I know. Perhaps I know even better than you."

During the next week, as they sailed out of the Mediterranean and down the west coast of Africa, Larissa reveled in Nathan's protectiveness and tenderness. At night she slept securely wrapped in his arms, her whole body tingling at his embrace. She told herself she was glad he did not try to make love to her again, glad she did not have to fight him off. But as the first week moved into the second, she found it more and more difficult to deny the yearning for more than kisses and caresses.

She was almost asleep one night when she felt him nudge her legs apart and slide on top of her. She moaned as his mouth covered hers, her hips rising to meet him as his pulsating maleness slid deep within her. Then, remembering her resolutions after the first time, she forced herself to go limp and concentrated on fighting her rising desires. As if to break down her resistance, Nathan drew out the experience until she had to bite back her sobs of ecstasy. Finally, when she had begun to fear she could control herself no longer, his passions were satisfied and he rolled away from her.

Only after she heard him breathing peacefully in sleep did she allow her tears to course silently down her cheeks.

Every particle of her being wanted him, but she was so afraid to let him know. He was good to her—caring for her and protecting her—but her pride and her conscience demanded more than that. She craved for him to say that he loved her, that he wanted to marry her. But she feared he was too independent ever to give himself completely to a woman. He wanted her now, in a physical sense, and he was willing to care for her to get what he wanted. But how could she know he would not stop wanting her? Hadn't he said he would never marry?

Neither Nathan nor Larissa spoke of the incident the next morning. Several nights passed before he made love to her again, and again she fought to hide her own desires.

In the next weeks, Nathan, preferring a more willing partner, denied himself night after night, until he could no longer resist the enticing form beside him. Larissa ached to pull him close and revel in the full ecstasy of their love-making, but she stubbornly battled her own passions, refusing to surrender her pride for what she was sure could be no more than a passing affair. Only once did her control desert her, letting her respond to him fully. But her afterglow was dulled by shame, and she renewed her resolve not to give in again.

But no matter how she reacted, Nathan treated her the same. By night, as they shared his narrow bunk, he was tender and solicitous. By day, his mood varied from kind, to gently teasing, to gruff. He never expressed disappointment with her coldness. He never spoke of love. And he certainly never mentioned marriage.

By the time the *Queen of Cathay* maneuvered through the Spice Islands and into the China Sea, Larissa had still not resolved the conflicts within her. In her heart, she knew she treasured every moment with Nathan. But she guarded her emotions closely, afraid even to hint at how she felt. So long as he made no commitments to her, she would not reveal her true feelings. For the moment, they seemed to share a relaxed, affectionate comradeship, and she was reluctant to upset that balance with any discussion of love.

Early in September, Larissa and Nathan stood on the quarterdeck, watching a magnificent sunset. In the distance, they could see the Portuguese-leased port of Macao, an island near the entrance of the Pearl River, which led to Canton.

"Well," Nathan said, gazing toward the island forts, "in another few days your journey to China will be at an end. Tomorrow we'll draw closer to Macao, and Captain Clinton will send a mate ashore to get a pilot. After we receive *chop*—Chinese government permission to enter their waters—the pilot will guide us into the Pearl River. Then we've only about a day and a half journey up the river to Whampoa."

"I thought our destination was Canton."

He smiled indulgently. "The ship has to stay at Whampoa, about twelve miles downriver from Canton—a silly Chinese rule."

"Oh, I see. But the actual trading is conducted in Canton, isn't it?"

"Yes," he answered shortly.

Not noticing his thinly veiled uneasiness, Larissa stared back at the western horizon and whispered mischievously, "So the voyage is almost over. I must say it hasn't been terribly exciting."

Nathan swatted her rump playfully. "Not since you made your own excitement at Smyrna, eh? I suppose you'd like more kidnappings and floggings and having me risk my life."

She smiled impishly. "No, I suppose not—but those things did add a little life to the trip."

"As one who knows, I can tell you you wouldn't have welcomed some of the excitement we might have encountered. For instance, from the time we neared Java, we've been in some of the world's most pirate-infested waters."

Larissa turned doubtful eyes to him. "Pirates? Here?"

He nodded. "And believe me, Chinese pirates are ruthless. We've been most fortunate not to sight any. Now that we're so near Macao, I don't imagine there is any more reason to fear them. They wouldn't risk coming near the Portuguese harbor cannon."

Larissa turned back to the rail to watch the final fading glow of the sunset. As she watched, three Chinese junks slid out of a cove of the nearby Ladrone Islands, their angular sails etched black against the red-orange horizon. "Look," she said, pointing at the ships, which seemed to grow larger as she watched. "Aren't they beautiful?"

As Nathan squinted at the junks, noting the rhythmic moving of the oars, bringing them quickly closer to the

Queen of Cathay, he muttered, "Beautiful, my eye! They look to me like pirate craft, and they're headed straight for us! You'd better get down to the cabin immediately!"

When Larissa continued staring at the ships, Nathan grasped her shoulders, turned her away from the rail, and shoved her firmly toward the companionway. "Get below, *now*! I don't want you on deck if they draw abreast."

Hearing the authority in his voice, Larissa sighed and started down the ladder. Nathan's voice carried to her as she descended.

"You, Martens, run and get Captain Clinton. Tell him it's an emergency. Adams, tell the crew to get those sails unfurled. Lawson, see that the anchor's weighed. We're going into Macao tonight. Well, don't just stand there, all of you, get a move on! I guarantee Captain Clinton will second my orders. Right now, there's no time to waste!"

Larissa stood motionless on the ladder, listening to the thud of feet overhead and swelling with pride at the competent way Nathan was taking charge. Just then, Martens galloped down the ladder to find Captain Clinton and almost knocked Larissa over. Larissa, instead of returning to the cabin, scurried back up the ladder to the deck.

Nathan was nowhere in sight. On the quarterdeck she saw Jonathan Dillard struggling with the crossjack brace. Rushing to his aid, she strained to help him, ignoring the pain as the running ropes burned her hands. Glancing over her shoulder, she saw Nathan explaining the situation to Captain Clinton. The three junks were no more than four lengths away now.

A moment later, the *Queen of Cathay* rocked as the nearest junk released a volley of shots. Around her, the crew rushed to wheel the portable cannon into place and return the fire. Still, the pirate junks drew closer. Larissa stared in open-mouthed horror as she saw the crew aboard the nearest junk begin to swing huge grappling hooks toward the rail of the *Queen of Cathay*. They meant to draw alongside and board her ship!

"I thought I told you to go below!"

Larissa whirled to see Nathan scowling beside her. "I had to see what was happening," she whispered. "I had to try to help."

"Well, now you've seen. And you've done all you can. Unless you're adept at handling a pistol or a sword, you'll just be in the way here." Even as he spoke, a passing sailor slapped a pistol into Nathan's hand, and Nathan turned his attention to seeing that it was properly loaded.

A bloodthirsty roar tore the air as the first hook found its mark. On board the junk, the exuberant pirates hurried to toss another. Stripped to the waist, their yellow skin glistening in the waning light, they looked horrifying. Their long queues swayed in rhythm with their movements.

Larissa paled, suddenly fearful that this would be her last moment with Nathan. "Nathan, I—" She stopped, groping for words, wondering if she dared admit all she felt. Indeed, was there even time to say it?

The pirates roared again as their ship lurched closer. "For God's sake, Larissa, get below!"

She shook her head helplessly. "I have to say—"

"There's no time to say anything!" He swept her into his arms and carried her to the companionway. His lips pressed her forehead before he dropped her to the floor below.

"Nathan—" She stopped helplessly, realizing he was already gone and that her voice was drowned out by the roars and cries overhead.

She retreated to the cabin, where she paced fretfully, listening to the clomping feet and frantic cries above. Fearing what might happen to her if a pirate found her there, she locked the door and continued to pace. She wondered how many of the pirates had boarded the ship and if the other two junks had drawn abreast yet. New cannon fire rocked the Queen of Cathay, and Larissa had a horrible vision of drowning right there in sight of the Chinese coast.

Why didn't the ship move, she wondered frantically. Then she remembered that there had been no wind when she stood on deck, watching the sunset with Nathan. The ship had lain becalmed, and at the time she had thought it beautiful to view the sun reflected in a mirror-smooth sea. Now she desperately wished for a wind to help them escape the pirates. The junks were powered by oars, so they could move without wind, but the Queen of Cathay depended on wind. If they did not move, all three shiploads of brigands would surely board the Queen of Cathay and murder or enslave everyone on board.

Larissa shuddered, thinking what enslavement would mean for her and resolved she would kill herself rather than let anyone enter the cabin and take her. Glancing frantically around the room, she looked for some weapon.

She went to Nathan's sea chest and rummaged through the contents until she located a small knife. Weighing it in her hand, she decided it was probably too small to pierce her heart. She might be forced to slash her wrists. Cringing at the thought, she tucked the sheathed knife into her bodice, convincing herself it would be better to die at her own hands than to suffer cruelties, indignities, and slow death at the hands of the pirates.

The cries from the deck above became louder and more exuberant. Going to the porthole, she strained her ears and realized the happiest cries were coming from the Americans. A glance at the water told her at least part of the reason for their excitement. The *Queen of Cathay* was moving! A wind was blowing, and they were drifting toward Macao.

Elated, she stared at the sea. Still, the noises overhead continued, and she worried that the pirates who had come aboard might kill all of the crew before they reached the security of Macao's harbor. She wrung her hands. What was happening to Nathan? Would he be one of the survivors, or was his blood, even now, staining the deck?

The ship began to move faster, and the noise overhead subsided a bit. New cannon shots thundered for several minutes, and cries of terror blended with the roar. Then the ship was gripped by a ghostly silence. They had ceased moving, and the waves lapped loudly against the side of the ship.

Terrified, Larissa sank down on the bunk, clutching the knife to her bosom and wondering if she would be forced to use it. Unable to bear the suspense any longer, she jumped to her feet and unlocked the door. Taking a deep breath, she decided to go on deck and find out for herself what was happening. If necessary, she would defend herself with the small knife.

Brandishing the knife, she threw open the door and rushed blindly into the passageway. She had gone only a few steps when strong hands grabbed her wrists. She shrieked.

"For God's sake, Larissa, what do you intend to do with that knife?"

"Oh, Nathan," she blurted, "I'm so glad you're—" She stopped suddenly as her eyes focused on his pale face and the red splotch spreading through his white shirt. "You're hurt!" Clutching his hand, she led him back into the cabin.

"It's not as serious as it looks," he said, wincing as he lay back on the bunk. "Just a flesh wound, really."

Taking a deep breath, Larissa forced herself to tear away his shirt and expose the gash, which was just below his ribs.

"Lucky for me the fellow didn't jab it in any further," Nathan joked feebly, "or he would have seen what I had for supper."

"Nathan," she chided, "don't jest. You might have been killed!"

His eyes softened, and his fingers caught her hands. "Would you have cared that much?"

"You know I would," she replied softly. Then, afraid she had admitted too much, she snatched her hands away and added lightly, "What would I do if I was left at the mercy of Captain Clinton or, worse yet, the pirates?"

"Is that your roundabout way of telling me you need me?" Nathan smiled faintly.

"It's not my way of telling you anything." Quickly she turned away, concentrating on ripping one of her two precious petticoats into bandage strips. "If we don't get you bandaged, you may bleed to death on me anyway."

Nathan chuckled, watching her tenderly as she worked. She pressed her lips firmly together, trying to maintain an air of businesslike severity, though she quivered inside as she touched him. While she wound the bandages tightly around his middle, she asked about the outcome of the battle.

"Everything stopped so suddenly, for a few moments I thought we had been defeated," she said.

He smiled grimly. "No doubt we would have been if the wind hadn't picked up. We started to drift just as the other two junks pulled abreast. They were too busy rowing to keep up and couldn't board us—a good thing, since we had our hands full with the first crew of pirates. Anyway, we eventually drifted right into the range of Macao's harbor cannon. The pirates were foolhardy enough to continue their pursuit, and the big artillery blew them right out of the water."

"What about the ones who boarded the *Queen of Cathay*?"

"When they saw they were defeated, a good many of them plunged into the sea without waiting for the final outcome. Whether they will be able to swim to safety before providing some shark's supper is no concern of mine. The crew is dumping the rest of them—those who can no longer make their own choice—right now."

Larissa shivered. "Were many of our own hurt?"

"There were a few casualties. No more than two or three killed, and another handful wounded." He paused, then added in a teasing tone, "You'll be glad to know Captain Clinton came through without a scratch. Of course, your young friend Dillard was not so fortunate."

She gasped, thinking of the boyish young sailor. "Was he badly hurt?"

Nathan pursed his lips. "Not *too* badly."

"Nathan, don't tease! Tell me!"

He raised his brows. "Is the lad that important to you?"

"He's a nice, pleasant boy," she answered, "and I hate to think of him being in pain."

"Well, you can put your mind at ease. His pride is injured more seriously than his body. It seems he nicked himself with his own cutlass. In fact, I hear he was so clumsy when he swung the thing that all the pirates thought he was a madman and wouldn't come within two feet of him."

Larissa could not suppress a smile, but she quickly hid it behind her hand and frowned at Nathan reprovingly. "You shouldn't make fun of Jonathan. He tries very hard. Besides," she added as she finished tying his bandage and patted his ribs, "you must have had a touch of clumsiness yourself to end up with this."

He chuckled. "At least my wound wasn't self-inflicted." Grimacing, he sat up and gingerly twisted his torso. "I suppose I'll turn out as good as new, but this damned bandage is bound to restrict my activity for a few days." Frowning, he stared at Larissa peevishly. "Are you sure you didn't purposely bind me up too tight?"

Raising her eyebrows, she smiled and shrugged. "Why in the world would I want to do that?"

"Exactly the question I would ask, since I know you enjoy our little romps just as much as I—no matter how you try to hide that fact."

Larissa's face reddened, and she turned away. "I don't know what you're talking about, Nathan Masters."

"Don't you, now?" In an instant, he was behind her, turning her quickly by the shoulders and enfolding her in his arms. His golden-flecked eyes smoldered as he lifted her chin and brought his face close to hers. "Will you force me to demonstrate?"

His lips were burning, insistent. Overwhelmed by the events of the evening and finally giving way to a flood of relief, Larissa melted in his embrace. As their interlocked bodies inched slowly toward the bunk, it became obvious that his wound would not impair his skills. In the heat of the moment, Larissa admitted to herself she was glad. But she did not admit that fact to Nathan.

Chapter Eight

The next day, as the *Queen of Cathay* glided up the Pearl River toward Canton, Larissa stood beside Nathan at the rail, not wanting to miss a single sight. They passed Macao's crescent-shaped bay, leaving behind the Portuguese forts as they traveled up the straits known as the Macao Roads and on through the swirling yellow-brown waters of the Pearl River.

Soon after passing Macao, Larissa sighted a desolate, rocky island poking out of the river. Its gray and brown expanse of soil and rock, almost unbroken by trees, shrubs, or grass, was a far cry from the exotic Oriental gardens she had expected to see. Anchored in the coves around the island were several dilapidated ships, from all appearances abandoned there to rot. With a start, she realized the *Queen of Cathay* was altering her course and sailing straight toward the island.

Turning puzzled eyes to Nathan, she asked, "Surely that Godforsaken bit of rock is not Whampoa?"

He looked amused. "No, it's Lintin Island."

"Then why do we seem to be going in?"

"Perhaps I failed to mention this to you earlier, but we do have to make a brief stop at Lintin to unload the opium. It would never do for the customs inspector in Whampoa to discover it on board—though he will, no doubt, realize we have carried it."

Larissa sighed. "Well, I'll be glad to have it off my ship, anyway." She glanced toward the island. "I must say this looks like an appropriate place for such shady dealings. Who would expect any real trading to take place among all these abandoned ships?"

"Those ships are hardly abandoned," Nathan said. "They are storage ships. If any officials should start poking

87

around, it appears that the ships store all sorts of trading goods. But in reality their main purpose is to hold the opium until small Chinese smuggling boats—fast crabs, they're called—can transfer it to Canton." He pointed to the nearest storage ship. "Look closely among the flowerpots along the railing and tell me what you see."

She squinted into the sunlight and caught a glint of steel. "Cannon?"

He nodded. "To keep the pirates away—and any Chinese official that gets too nosy. But the officials don't pose much of a threat. Most of them know what's going on here, and they gladly look the other way in return for a sizable bribe."

"You see!" Larissa exclaimed. "That's exactly why I don't want my ship involved in the opium trade. Everything about it is abhorrent—the things papa told me the drug does to people who use it, the deceit, the corruption—"

Nathan turned away. "We've been through all this before, Larissa, and nothing you say is going to change the fact that for this trip this ship is carrying opium." His eyes settled on a small boat rowing quickly out to the *Queen of Cathay*. "Now, if you'll excuse me, I believe I have some business to attend to."

She ignored him as he left her, turning to watch him only as he reached the main deck and the boat pulled alongside the ship.

Nathan leaned over the rail and waved as a tall American stood up in the boat to call a greeting. "Nathan Masters, what a surprise! I never thought I'd see the *Queen of Cathay* stopping at Lintin Station."

Nathan shrugged. "Well, situations change."

"Aye, they do." The man looked troubled about something. "I think I'd best come aboard and discuss matters with you."

While the man climbed to the deck, Larissa, unable to contain her curiosity, strolled nonchalantly down from the quarterdeck and stopped at the main rail, within earshot of Nathan and the man. She stood staring at the water while she listened.

After their initial greetings, the man, whom Nathan called Alex, said, "Things have changed around here since you left, Nathan. The old emperor is getting tougher on the opium business."

Nathan frowned. "He's always making idle threats. What makes you think this time is any different?"

"For one thing, he's appointed a new imperial commissioner."

"So there's a new official to bribe, so what?"

"You don't understand," Alex shook his head. "Lin Tse-hsu is different from the others. In May and June he destroyed the entire British opium shipment—twelve million dollars worth!"

Nathan whistled softly. "The man must be insane!"

"Not insane, just dedicated to eliminating the opium trade. The British have all withdrawn their ships to Macao, but they're mad as hell, and I've even heard rumors of war."

"And the Americans?"

Alex shrugged helplessly. "What can I say? The fact that we're still here must speak for itself."

"So, the Lintin Station is still accepting shipments?"

He nodded. "We are. But we don't make any promises about the safety of the operation."

A voice at Larissa's elbow interrupted her concentration. "Enjoying the view, little troublemaker?" She looked up to see the cynical smile of Captain Clinton. "I don't suppose you had anything to do with that pirate attack yesterday?"

She opened her mouth to protest, but he continued before she had a chance. "But of course not! Even *you* couldn't be that adept at troublemaking! Besides, it seems to me that Masters has kept you far too busy lately. I've noticed how satisfied he always looks."

His jeering voice was so loud it distracted Nathan, who looked up and scowled. Noting his reaction, the captain continued, "I am sure Mr. Masters will confirm my conclusions. Tell me, Masters, have you bedded the slut yet? If not, I daresay I question your manhood."

Alex's questioning gaze shifted between Larissa and Nathan, and Larissa felt her cheeks turning scarlet. Nathan was furious. "I believe, Captain Clinton, that I warned you once before—I will not be treated like one of your crew. The lady, likewise, is not under your command, and I must demand that you treat her with more respect. Now, if you will excuse me, I must resolve the question of disposing of this ship's precious cargo." Giving a curt nod, he turned back to Alex.

Captain Clinton frowned at Nathan's back for a moment, then strolled away to bully a hapless member of his crew. Larissa stood a moment longer, trying to hear the rest of Nathan's low-toned conversation. But Alex's constant sidelong glances in her direction embarrassed her, and she went below to the cabin.

Nathan entered a quarter of an hour later, looking tired and worried.

"Did Alex advise against selling the opium?" Larissa asked hopefully.

He looked at her sharply. "You'd like that, wouldn't you? You'd love to see the whole shipment destroyed. If you had been here a few months ago, I suppose you would have volunteered to help the imperial commissioner dump the British stock into the river and pour lime over it."

"I only asked a simple question," she retorted. "I merely heard the man describing the problems, and I wondered if the venture is safe."

Nathan sighed. "Safe? I suppose not. But we can't scrap the shipment now. We're going to wait until dark, then draw closer to the island to make the transfer. If all goes well, we'll be on our way to Whampoa before morning. If not—the penalty for opium smuggling is death."

Larissa blanched, and Nathan smiled feebly. "You needn't worry. If you stay below, out of sight, I doubt that you'll be implicated, even if we are caught. In fact, just to make sure you keep out of the way, I think I'll lock you in."

Her eyes became stormy, and she tossed her head indignantly. "You needn't go to the trouble. I don't approve of opium smuggling, but I'm not enough of a fanatic to meddle when every lost second might endanger your life."

His brows raised quizzically. "You've changed, Larissa. In Smyrna, you didn't give a second thought to endangering my life."

Ignoring his sarcasm, she persisted. "Nathan, I don't care what you say. I'm coming with you tonight."

"It would be better for you to stay here. Then if something goes wrong and we're caught, you can always claim you didn't know what we were doing."

Studying him carefully, Larissa whispered, "Does it really matter to you whether or not I have an alibi?"

Shrugging, he kept his voice noncommittal. "I'd simply

hate to see a woman hurt for something for which she was not responsible."

He turned abruptly and started out the cabin. "I think I'd best go and inform the crew of the plans for tonight."

As the door closed behind him, Larissa smiled wistfully and blinked back her tears. He must care for me, she told herself. Surely the concern he had shown today, coupled with his tenderness last night, was proof enough. But why did he still refuse to admit his feelings?

Soon after sunset, the *Queen of Cathay* began moving closer to Lintin Island. Returning to the cabin for a heavy jacket, Nathan found Larissa wrapped in a woolen shawl, waiting to accompany him. He glanced at her, his eyes filling with tenderness for just an instant, then shook his head in resignation.

"All right," he said, then sighed, "I haven't time to argue with you, so you might as well come along. But for God's sake, try not to get in the way."

On deck, the crew had already assembled a large number of the opium baskets. More baskets were being passed up from the hold. The quarterboat had been lowered and bobbed beside the ship, a Jacob's ladder dangling over it. Silently, Nathan guided Larissa to the rail and helped her over to the ladder. They descended to the boat, and the crew began passing down baskets of opium.

They all worked wordlessly, acutely conscious of the dangers of discovery. Without being directed, Larissa found herself arranging the baskets, stifling her grunts of exertion as she moved them to fit as many as possible into the boat. When the boat was full, Nathan gave a signal and a sailor began rowing in quick, strong strokes toward the nearest of the storage ships. The moment they reached the storage ship's side, they began handing up the opium baskets, still working silently and efficiently.

The first two trips between the *Queen of Cathay* and the storage ship went smoothly. They were unloading the third group of baskets when Larissa caught sight of a small, flat-bottomed boat slipping noiselessly toward them.

"Nathan," she whispered urgently, catching his sleeve.

He paused with a basket of opium in his arms as his eyes moved to the approaching sampan. "Damn," he muttered, "just when we've almost finished."

Keeping one eye trained on the sampan, he hefted the basket to waiting hands overhead and whispered to Larissa, "How many more have we got?"

"Twelve," she replied quickly, struggling to lift a basket herself.

"All right. I think we can get them all off."

He took the basket from her and called to a man in the storage ship overhead, "Carlin, there's a sampan coming in. Can you see that we're covered until we finish unloading?"

"No problem," a muffled voice replied.

They worked twice as fast as before. In her panic, Larissa found herself lifting baskets, hardly noticing their weight. She was just passing Nathan the last basket when a shot rent the air. Dropping the basket, Nathan dove for her and flattened her in the bottom of the boat. Another shot whistled over their heads, and he muttered, "Damn, they've got a carronade on board!"

"Don't they even ask questions before shooting?" Larissa breathed.

"What for? There's only one reason a ship would stop at Lintin Island."

Above them, the storage ship began to return the fire. But its cannon were aimed too high, and the balls whistled harmlessly over the sampan. Someone on deck fired a rifle, but in the dim light it was difficult to aim at the shadowy figures aboard the sampan. The sampan's carronade sent an answering shot.

On the floor of the boat, Nathan crawled to the oars and began rowing toward the *Queen of Cathay,* raising his head to check the course, then ducking to avoid the shots exploding around them. "Hopefully," he grunted, "the storage ship can keep them diverted until we make it back to the *Queen* and get out of here."

Behind them, a piercing shriek announced the rifleman had found one of his targets. Larissa lifted her head to see a form hurtle over the sampan's edge into the water. She realized suddenly that the Chinese boat was moving after them and that someone was leaning over the carronade. There was a flare of light as the shadowy form lit the weapon, and she screamed, "Nathan, they're still after us!"

A moment later, the boat exploded into splinters, and Larissa was floundering in frigid water, sputtering as she fought to stay afloat. A hand grasped her shoulder, and

Nathan pulled her to him. "Easy," he whispered. "We're going to make it. Just relax and trust me."

He began swimming, his arm tight around her chest, towing her toward the ship. The water erupted around them as more shots exploded from the carronade. When they reached the hull, he pushed her before him, clamping her hands tightly around the sides of the Jacob's ladder. As they paused for breath, both Nathan and Larissa looked back at the advancing sampan. A cannonball shot from the deck of the storage ship and crashed into the center of the sampan. The boat lurched, then tipped precariously to one side as water streamed in through its hull. The crew abandoned the carronade to fight for their own survival.

Giving a hoot of victory, Nathan pushed Larissa up the Jacob's ladder to the helping hands waiting above. Scarcely had they climbed over the rail when the ship began moving up the Pearl River, away from Lintin Island and toward Canton.

In the cabin, they stripped away their wet clothing. Shivering, Larissa knelt to find her flannel nightgown. Behind her, Nathan watched a moment before gently grasping her shoulders and drawing her to her feet. Turning her in his arms, he pulled the nightgown from her hands and tossed it across the cabin.

"I know a better way to warm you," he whispered as he tipped back her head to find her lips.

A weak protest flickered through her mind. But by the time he eased her down on the bunk and covered her body with his, it was forgotten.

Now that the hated opium cargo had been disposed of, Larissa found the remainder of the trip upriver wonderfully exotic. They passed countless huge Chinese junks on their way downriver to the open sea. From the quarterdeck, she watched enchanted as sailors on the passing junks burned bits of red and silver paper and scattered them over the water. Once she jumped in alarm, fearing another attack, as fireworks exploded nearby. Laughing, Nathan explained that the fireworks, the paper, and the gongs that often sounded on the junks were offerings to the Chinese ocean gods.

As they passed particularly close to one junk, Larissa sniffed the deliciously pungent odor of burning sandalwood.

"Another offering to the gods," Nathan explained, "to accompany the prayers for fair winds. Sometimes, if the wind dies, they throw little gilt paper boats into the river as a way of asking the gods to break the calm."

Larissa nodded, her eyes glued to the passing ships. "Papa always told me China was a land of great mystery and beauty, but he could never have told me enough. I think I shall find my stay in China quite intriguing."

"Perhaps," Nathan said softly, brushing a lock of hair away from her face. "I just hope you're not disappointed."

She glanced at him quizzically, wondering at his meaning. But the sights, sounds, and smells around her were too enticing for her to spend time brooding about his words. Within a few moments, she had completely forgotten them.

By midafternoon, they were sailing through a narrow, rock-lined channel called the Boca Tigris. Nathan told her it was named for a tiger's mouth, with the rocks representing the animal's teeth. The channel was lined on both sides by the Bogue forts, guardians of the mouth of the vast Canton harbor. Just beyond the Bogue forts lay Whampoa. More than twenty vessels from European and American ports lay at anchor there, and the harbor had room for at least twenty more.

Looking through the clusters of masts, sails, and foreign flags, Larissa could see the city of Whampoa, with its colorful nine-story pagoda. "Oh, Nathan," she exclaimed, "can we go ashore immediately?"

He frowned. "I'm afraid not. Perhaps in time, but no one and nothing is permitted off this ship until the hoppo— the customs inspector—has levied his fees." He hesitated, considering saying more, then changed his mind and turned away. Anxious to change the subject, he pointed to a small Chinese boat sailing near the *Queen of Cathay*. "Look—see the eyes painted on the bow, looking down?"

Larissa nodded.

"That means it's a fishing boat. The eyes are supposed to help it locate fish. Seagoing boats sometimes have painted eyes looking heavenward, to follow the stars."

She smiled in amusement before her eyes moved to some of the other boats crowding the harbor. Small, flat-bottomed sampans floated among the foreign ships, exchanging outgoing Chinese cargo for the incoming foreign cargo, which they would then carry the twelve miles up-river to Canton. There were boats with stately bamboo cabins and shuttered windows, and there were houseboats, carrying entire families. Some boats were powered by oars, some by small sails, and some by a combination.

Once Larissa watched in horror as a child tumbled over the side of his family's boat and into the river. But a wooden buoy, tied to his back, kept him afloat until someone could fish him out. From the way everyone aboard the houseboat laughed, Larissa assumed the accident was not unusual. Indeed, she soon noticed that children on other boats also had buoys tied to their backs. She found the harbor traffic so fascinating that the afternoon seemed to pass quickly.

Toward sunset, an ornate sampan approached the *Queen of Cathay*. A plump Chinese man emerged from the silk-draped cabin and stared thoughtfully at the ship. He wore flowing black silk trousers and a long coat of deep blue silk, embroidered with yellow and orange fire-breathing dragons. A long, thin, black queue dangled from the nape of his neck, but the rest of his head was covered by a dome-shaped hat with a wide, upturned brim and with a peacock feather protruding from its center.

Nathan leaned over the rail and waved to the man, whispering to Larissa, "That's the hoppo. He'll board now and assess the size of the ship and the cargo so he can levy customs fees. But first we'll have to go through another little ritual of the Canton trade—offering him cumshaw."

"Cumshaw?"

"Gifts for himself, his wife, his mother, and anyone else he wishes. Bribes, if you will. We carried a small stock of watches, clocks, musical snuffboxes, and perfumes for that purpose."

Larissa pursed her lips dubiously. "It's all because of the opium trade, isn't it? I mean, if we hadn't carried that hideous drug, we wouldn't have to bribe the officials."

"No." Nathan shook his head. "Cumshaw was an established tradition long before the first load of opium was imported here. Perhaps the drug trade has made the bribes a little larger, but it is not totally responsible for them." He paused, seeing she was still unconvinced, then added, "Even your father participated in the ritual."

"Oh. Then I suppose it can't be all that bad." Larissa watched the hoppo lumber up the ladder to the main deck, where Captain Clinton hurried to greet him.

"I suppose I'd better join them," Nathan said. "You

might prefer to stay here, away from the captain's brutal tongue."

She waited while Nathan went down to join the captain and hoppo, then followed, stopping several feet from the group. A few crewmen carried some chests of gifts onto the deck, and the bargaining began. One by one, Nathan and Captain Clinton lifted the objects out of the chests for the hoppo's inspection.

Ordinarily, Larissa would have been fascinated by the collection of delicate gold, silver, and crystal gifts. But she was so mystified by the hoppo that she scarcely saw the objects. Occasionally during the bargaining, he smiled or laughed, but not in a happy, friendly way. There was something sinister about his laugh, and Larissa instinctively felt the man could be quite cruel.

After examining all the objects, the hoppo chose three gold pocket watches in elaborately engraved cases, a gold pendant watch embellished with rubies and sapphires, a chiming clock of silver and painted porcelain, and a delicate music box, decorated with tiny dancing figurines that revolved in time to the music it played. Still, he stood stroking his beard and twisting the ends of his mustache, as if he were not quite satisfied. His eyes shifted from side to side, and then he slowly lifted his gaze to stare at Larissa. He drummed his fingertips thoughtfully against his mouth as a wicked smile slowly spread across his face.

Unnerved by his stare, Larissa scowled at him defiantly, hoping he would shift his attention back to the array of cumshaw. But he simply smiled more broadly and took a few steps toward her. Nathan and Captain Clinton watched in confusion as he approached her.

"What is your name?" he inquired in a soft, whistling tone.

Larissa took a deep breath and drew herself up straighter, determined not to appear nervous or afraid. After all, why should she be afraid of him on her own ship? "My name," she said in a firm, cool voice, "is Larissa Bennett."

"La-ris-sa," the hoppo repeated as he came closer to her. Larissa thought that he made her name sound lewd. Stopping less than one step away from her, he eyed her green cotton dress disdainfully. "Very pretty dress. But not Chinese."

"No," she replied coolly, "not Chinese."

"You would look much better in Chinese fabric, Chinese

fashions." He reached out to finger a lock of her hair, casually brushing a breast as he did so.

Angrily, Larissa slapped his hand away. "I'm not a piece of your cumshaw to be scrutinized and handled," she snapped.

The hoppo raised his thin black eyebrows and smiled. "Ah, La-ris-sa has spirit. Not like Chinese woman." He turned quickly to Captain Clinton and raised his voice authoritatively. "You give me La-ris-sa, and this ship pays no tax."

Dumbstruck, Larissa stared open-mouthed. Captain Clinton smiled slowly. "That's an interesting proposition, inspector, but surely the girl is worth far more than the paltry tax you would levy on this vessel." His eyes glowed as he continued. "Take another look at that auburn hair and those green cat's eyes. You won't find the likes of them anywhere in China—"

"Wait a minute!" Nathan broke in sharply. "This is insane! You're talking as if she's a commodity, something for sale. You can't do that!"

"Why not?" the captain demanded. "The girl has been nothing but trouble. It would be a relief to be rid of her."

The hoppo cleared his throat, and they turned to face him. "Gentlemen," he said briskly, "you are wasting my time. I will have the girl." He grabbed Larissa's wrist and pulled her toward him.

"No!" she screamed, kicking furiously at his shins. Stunned by her vicious kicks, the hoppo dropped her wrist.

In the same moment, Nathan stepped between them, shielding Larissa behind him. He glared at the hoppo. "I believe the lady asked you not to touch her," he said crisply.

Captain Clinton quickly intervened. "You'll have to make allowances for the young man. These past months the girl has been his whore, and—"

He never finished the explanation as Nathan whirled on him, crashing his fist into Clinton's jaw. Before the captain even hit the deck, unconscious, Nathan was turning back to Larissa. "Go below to the cabin. Lock the door behind you and don't unlock it for anyone but me."

She nodded, glad to have him take control of the situation and fled toward the companionway without another look at the hoppo. As she left, she heard Nathan address the hoppo. "If you will kindly inform me of your government's fees, I will see that you are paid so you can leave this ship."

"You are a very foolish young man," the hoppo replied. "I promise you, this shall not be the end of the matter."

Almost an hour later, Nathan knocked at the cabin door.

"Is that evil man gone?" Larissa asked as she let him in.

He nodded. "Paid and gone. Though I do think his fees were rather exorbitant this time."

"I'm sorry," she said. "I heard him threaten you as I was leaving. Do you think he'll cause us any more trouble?"

"I doubt it. His pride was injured, so he felt forced to threaten me. But there is really nothing else he can do."

She shuddered, thinking again of the hoppo's sinister smile. "I hope not. Is the captain all right?"

"Yes. He came to, just before I came below. Madder than hell at me. But he'll get over it. He'll have to. It's not within his power to fire me and hire a new agent."

He sat down on the bunk to remove his boots, and Larissa sat beside him. She trembled at his nearness, breathing in his heady, male scent. "At first I thought you'd killed him," she said softly.

He nodded. "At the time, I was so furious I wished I had." Softly, he added, "This time he just went too far. No man wants to hear the woman he cares about slandered."

Larissa sucked in her breath, then felt his hand gently turn her face toward his. He smiled, but his amber-flecked eyes held a strange combination of amusement and hurt. "Does my statement surprise you so much?"

"I—that is—" she stumbled, aware that she was trembling and that he knew it. "It's just that you've never given me any indication."

"Indeed? I've cared for you, rescued you, made love to you. Even though I've desired you more than any other woman, I've never taken you harshly. I've held myself in check rather than bruise your delicate sensibilities. I've endured your taunts, your foolish female habits, your coyness. And you say I've given you no indication! Are you blind and deaf, or just totally naive? What more would you have me do or say?"

"You could say—" She stopped herself, on the verge of declaring he could say he wanted to marry her. It was better, she thought, not to press matters tonight. It was enough for him to admit he cared. The rest would surely come in time.

"I could say what?" he prodded gently. "That I love you? Would that hollow word mean more to you than all that has passed between us?" Without waiting for an answer, he continued, "Well, I can do better than speak the word with my tongue. I can speak it with my whole body. And you can too, if you will only let yourself. I've sensed it in you time after time." His mouth met hers, while his fingers found the fastenings of her dress.

Wrapping her arms around his neck, Larissa pulled herself closer to him, releasing all the yearning she had kept bottled within her all through the voyage. This time she would not lie indifferent. She would give and take as a woman, confident that she and Nathan shared love.

She was surprised to find her own fingers loosening his clothing as he gently laid her back against the pillows. When they were both naked, he guided her hand to his growing member. Feeling its size, she gasped, and she began to imagine how it would feel within her. But he made her wait, teasing her as his tongue flicked over her body, tempting her nipples, leaving a searing trail along her flat, white abdomen, burning her inner thighs.

She was straining with desire as never before, and when at last he plunged into her wet readiness, she cried out in ecstasy. She rose to meet him, unashamed of her passion as one thought reverberated in her mind: He loves me! He loves me! In that moment, she forgot the purpose of her trip, forgot how she had scoffed at the idea of romance. She floated in relieved pleasure as she admitted the fact she had stifled for so long: she wanted his love because she loved him, too.

Afterwards, she lay with an arm flung across his chest, feeling the strong beat of his heart as she nestled against his side. "Nathan," she whispered, "I do love you."

He did not respond, and his steady breathing told her he had already drifted into contented sleep. She sighed but told herself it did not matter. Surely he knew. And surely, in time, he would ask her to become his wife.

Chapter Nine

Larissa was still nestled against Nathan when a knock at the cabin door awoke them the next morning.

"Mr. Masters," the first mate called, "the captain's commissioned a boat into Canton. Says you should be ready to leave in half an hour."

Nathan groaned, smiling sleepily as he patted Larissa. "All right, Mr. Stephens, I'll be up immediately," he responded.

He sat up, squinting at the dim light streaming in the porthole. "Damn, it can't be much past six. I swear the captain's punishing me for knocking him out last night." He gazed down at Larissa, then leaned over to kiss the tip of her upturned nose. "I would much prefer to linger here and sample your sweetness again."

Smiling back at him, she stretched lazily. "You'll just have to hold your passions in check, sir, until we can contrive to find some privacy in Canton."

Nathan straightened and looked away from her. "I'm afraid that won't be possible."

"Now who's being the coy one? What do you mean it won't be possible? Surely we will have private sleeping quarters in Canton."

"I mean," he said, getting out of bed and reaching for his trousers, "that you won't be going to Canton with me. You'll have to remain behind on the *Queen of Cathay*."

"That's ridiculous," Larissa cried, sitting up, then jumping out of bed. She planted herself in front of him, feet braced, hands poised on her hips, oblivious to her nakedness. "After what happened between us last night, how can you go off to Canton and leave me behind?"

He sighed wearily. "It has nothing to do with my feelings, Larissa. The Chinese simply forbid any foreign women in Canton. They think that if the traders bring their women, they'll want to establish permanent homes there, and they're totally opposed to that idea. As it is, they confine us to one small area of the city and force us to leave during the winter."

She frowned at him. "Why is it you can break their laws about opium smuggling, but you can't take me with you? I think you just don't want me with you, Nathan Masters! You don't love me at all! You just used me last night and all through the voyage. You probably have a pretty little Chinese girl waiting for you in Canton right now!"

"For God's sake, Larissa," he broke in sharply, "don't get hysterical! Everyone breaks the law about opium smuggling, but no one brings their women into Canton. You can only push the Chinese so far. I wish the rules were different, but it's just not possible for you to come with me, and that's final."

"But I have to come," she pouted. "I have to attend to my business. That's the only reason I came on this voyage anyway, to take over papa's position. You knew what I intended, so you might have told me earlier about this silly Chinese rule."

He sighed. "What good would that have done? Must I remind you that you didn't seek my advice before stowing away in my cabin?"

Ignoring his sarcasm, she waved him to silence, and her eyes narrowed as she thought of a scheme. "Suppose I disguise myself as a man?"

Nathan cocked an eyebrow and stared at her full, round breasts. "That, my dear, would be extremely difficult. Anyway, there's no time for that now. As for the business, you needn't worry. I'll give you a full accounting and be sure your uncle doesn't cheat you out of your share."

She continued to stare at him accusingly as he sat down on the bunk and pulled on his boots. "How long will you be gone?"

"Perhaps two months, perhaps less. As I said, no foreigners are permitted to stay in Canton over the winter. We'll have to retreat to Macao by December at the latest."

"And what am I to do all that time?" she asked petulantly.

"Stay here with the crew and keep out of trouble. I've already asked young Dillard to look after you. After the

way he rescued you from the hold, he seems to be someone I can trust."

Crossing the cabin, he took her by the shoulders, gazing
down tenderly at her. "Look, Larissa, I'm sorry it has to be
this way, but you've got to admit your presence on this
voyage was all your idea. If you had consulted me in Boston, I never would have permitted you to come. Now,
won't you get dressed and come up on deck to see me off?"

She shook her head. "I'd rather not."

He sighed heavily. "All right, whatever you say. You'll
be all right here. You'll probably find you're glad to be
rid of me for awhile." He bent to kiss her, but she turned
her head away, determined to remain cool and distant.
Sighing again, he released her and left the cabin.

Larissa stared sullenly at the houseboats gliding around
the harbor. Nathan had been gone more than two weeks,
and she still had not reconciled herself to being left behind.
Waving absently at one of the children on a passing boat,
she wondered if it would be possible to bribe one of the
families to take her into Canton. Surely she could take
some clothes from Nathan's sea chest, alter them to fit her
well enough, and disguise herself as a boy. She could
imagine Nathan's face when she stepped into his office in
Canton, proving he had been wrong to leave her behind.

"Larissa?" Jonathan Dillard's shy voice broke in on her
thoughts. "Perhaps you'd like to go ashore today. I know
Whampoa is not as magnificent as Canton, but I understand it has some interesting curio shops."

Larissa shook her head. "I'm not really interested."
Hearing him sigh disappointedly, she turned to him and
added, "You go, Jonathan. I know it's been a bore staying here with me every day, and it's really not fair for me
to keep you tied to the ship. You ought to enjoy your
time in port, like the rest of the crew."

"No, I promised Mr. Masters I'd look after you, and I
won't leave you alone. You know, you needn't worry that
he'll return while we're gone. I'm sure he won't be back
for at least another two weeks."

Larissa stiffened. "Why should I care at all when Nathan
Masters returns?" she asked bitterly.

"Because," Jonathan replied softly, "it's quite obvious
you care about him."

"You're wrong, Jonathan!" she snapped. "I've told you before, Nathan Masters means nothing to me."

"Would you change your mind if I told you you mean a great deal to him? He was very concerned about my looking after you while he was gone."

She shrugged. "He's an old friend of my father's. No doubt he feels responsible for me."

"I see." Jonathan sounded unconvinced.

For several moments they were silent while Larissa mulled over Jonathan's words. It occurred to her that it was quite logical for him to assume she was pining for Nathan. Why else would she insist on brooding on the ship when she could be exploring the town? Forcing a bright smile, she reached out and squeezed his hand impulsively. "You're right, I'm being silly. Let's go into Whampoa."

The afternoon in Whampoa was a pleasant change of pace. In the crowded marketplace, which catered to the sailors from the many surrounding ships, Larissa and Jonathan strolled hand-in-hand, examining a variety of delicate Oriental curios. Jonathan made it obvious that he was proud to be Larissa's escort. He insisted on buying her a pair of tiny, carved ivory earrings and would have bought her any number of silk scarves, exquisite paintings on silk, and carved jade figurines if she had not insisted he save his money.

Munching on lichee nuts purchased from a strolling vendor, they did not notice the thin Chinese figure who shadowed them as they made their way back to their boat. Jonathan rowed their boat back to the ship, and laughing and talking, neither Jonathan nor Larissa noticed an elegant sampan following them at a distance.

By the time they climbed aboard the *Queen of Cathay*, the sun was setting. They lingered on deck to watch, then went below to the galley for a leisurely late supper.

Afterward, Jonathan escorted Larissa to the door of her cabin. She smiled at him, squeezing his hand affectionately. "It was a lovely day, Jonathan. I'm so glad you convinced me to go ashore. There was so much to see. Perhaps we can go again soon."

He nodded enthusiastically, his dusty blond hair falling boyishly across his forehead. "Tomorrow, if you like."

"We'll see." Impulsively, she stood on tiptoe to brush her lips across his cheek. To her surprise, he caught her by

the waist and pressed his lips to hers. She swallowed awkwardly, sensing that this was the first time he had kissed a
woman.

Blushing, he released her. "I'm sorry, Larissa," he stammered. "I don't know what came over me."

"Don't be sorry, Jonathan," she replied softly. "It was
very nice." She opened the cabin door and stepped inside.
"Good night, Jonathan."

Closing the door behind her, she listened to Jonathan's
retreating footsteps and thought about his innocent kiss.
Whenever Nathan kissed her, indeed if he even touched
her, she quivered with anticipation and desire. But Jonathan Dillard's kiss had had no such effect. It was pleasant
enough, but not at all exciting.

Flopping across the bunk, she wondered why fate had to
be so cruel. She had not come on this voyage in search of
romance, but if she had to fall in love, why couldn't it
have been with someone like Jonathan, instead of Nathan?
Jonathan was so innocent and sincere that she felt sure he
would never take advantage of her as Nathan had. He
would not profess his love, then cast her aside the very
next morning.

She had hoped that her afternoon with Jonathan would
help her forget about Nathan. Instead, it had made her
ache for him more than she had in all the days since he
had left. No matter how much more innocent and noble
Jonathan might seem, he could not fill the void within her.
She might successfully deny her feelings to anyone who
asked, but in the end she could not deny what was in her
heart.

Groaning, Larissa got to her feet, certain that she
would not be able to sleep for hours. The ache within her
was too strong, and Nathan's image was too vivid in her
mind. Without even closing her eyes, she could see his
chestnut hair and amber-flecked gray eyes. She could almost feel the hard, rigid muscles of his shoulders and back
and the surprisingly soft caress of his leathery hands. She
could hear his gentle laugh and the sometimes sarcastic
tone of his voice. She cringed, wondering whom he was
entertaining that night. Or who was entertaining him? An
uncontrollable throbbing began in her groin, and no one
was there to assuage it.

She reached for her shawl, deciding she would go up and

pace on deck until she was exhausted. She knew no one would bother her, since most of the crew were still ashore, probably enjoying the delights of some Whampoa beauties. With Captain Clinton gone, the mates, themselves eager to be ashore, had relaxed discipline and seldom posted regular watches. Larissa smiled to herself as it occurred to her that innocent Jonathan Dillard might well be the only sailor on board, alone in his own bed.

The crisp night air helped clear her head and made her feel better. As she paced, her feelings toward Nathan began to mellow. Perhaps, she thought, she had judged him too harshly in deciding he did not love her. Since the Chinese really did forbid foreign women in Canton, he might have feared her life would be endangered if she accompanied him. And she could hardly expect him to remain behind when he was responsible for conducting the firm's business. After all, he would be looking out for her interests.

All things considered, she realized she had acted like a foolish child, screaming at him, making accusations, and refusing to see him off. They would have the rest of their lives to nurture their love, but business matters could not wait. If she wanted to keep Nathan's love, she would have to start acting more like a mature woman.

Worried that her shrewish behavior the morning he departed might have turned him away permanently, she felt more impatient than ever to see him—to tell him she loved him and reassure herself he still loved her. Her thoughts flew back to the morning when she had considered disguising herself as a boy; now the plan became even more tempting. If she took pains with her disguise, she was certain it would be convincing, and it would be easy to find a friendly family to transport her to Canton. After her reunion with Nathan, if he still thought it better for her to return to the *Queen of Cathay*, she would return immediately, without question.

Elated by the thought of seeing Nathan again, Larissa turned back toward the companionway, intending to return to the cabin and begin work on her disguise. Immersed in her thoughts, at first she did not hear the rustle of silk behind her. As the sound penetrated her consciousness, she turned her head to glance over her shoulder. Briefly she caught sight of a long, narrow, Oriental face. Then a hand clapped tightly over her mouth, and another hand grasped one of her arms, twisting it brutally behind her back, until she was sure it would be torn from her shoulder.

Despite the white-hot pain shooting through her body, she kicked wildly, trying to turn to face her assailant, flailing with her free arm. It was no use. She felt her strength ebbing away.

A heavily accented voice hissed in her ear. "Will be much easier if you do not fight. You will come with us, regardless, but I should hate to bruise so lovely a body. Will you come peacefully, now?"

Larissa shook her head violently.

"Ah, well," the Chinese man said softly, "then I shall be forced to take certain measures. No doubt the master will understand."

He removed his hand from her mouth, but before Larissa could scream, she saw a long, curved blade glittering in the moonlight. The blade whistled through the air, stopping only a hair's breadth from her throat. Involuntarily, she shrank back against the man behind her as the blade slowly followed her. She felt the cold steel against her throat, and then she felt a thin trickle of blood warming the edge of the blade.

Oh, God, she thought, is this to be the end? Here? Now? Before I can even tell Nathan that I understand? Before I can apologize and show him how much I really do love him?

Aware now that she was bargaining for her life, she whispered, "What do you want with me?"

"Only that you come with me," the voice hissed. "If you agree, I promise you that you will meet no further harm."

She hesitated, battling her fears. The man's promise meant nothing to her; she had no reason to believe him. But what was her alternative? She might try screaming, but the sword at her throat would quickly end that.

As if reading her thoughts, the man counseled, "There is no one on board to aid you, so please do not do anything foolish. We have watched all evening. All the crew is gone, except for your young friend, and I fear he can do nothing."

Larissa gasped. "Did you kill him?"

"No, no," the man chuckled. "We are not so cruel. He will awake tomorrow with a large lump on his head. Now then, will you come?"

Feeling the cold blade against her throat, Larissa allowed herself to be pushed ahead of the man to the rail of the ship. There seemed nothing else to do. If she pretended to give in to him now, perhaps she would later find a way to escape. Her other alternative was instant death. Inexplicably, she thought again of the pirate attack, remembering how she had resolved to kill herself if necessary. Now she knew she would not have been able to do so. She loved life too much.

At the rail, the man lifted her roughly into his arms and climbed nimbly over the side to a waiting sampan. As he dropped her to the floor of the boat, she glanced at the river, gauging her chances of swimming to safety. Thinking him engrossed in conversation with the sampan's crew, she crept slowly to the side of the boat and dangled an arm in the water. Flattening herself against the boat's side, she glanced quickly back toward her captor, then pushed herself over the edge and into the water.

"Ho!" the man's cry sounded louder than her splash. Her skirt and petticoat tangled between her legs, and before she had time to take even one stroke away from the boat, he grabbed her by the hair and dragged her back aboard.

"A pity you cannot be trusted," he said, an evil smile twisting his face. He hauled her to the sampan's mast and called out a command in Chinese. Instantly, two young men appeared and lashed her to the mast. While they worked, her captor stuffed a gag into her mouth and tied it securely at the back of her neck. Then he produced another silk kerchief and waved it before her eyes, shaking his head sympathetically.

"Too bad you will not be able to enjoy the lovely scenery. It is difficult to see at night, but I would not want you planning an escape route for yourself." He tied the scarf around her eyes.

They left her alone for the rest of the trip, while they talked among themselves in Chinese. Larissa could only guess that they were gliding north, towards Canton. For a while she struggled with her bonds, but they were firmly tied and eventually she gave up. In her wet dress, lashed to the mast where every night breeze could assail her, Larissa shivered and felt utterly miserable. When the boat finally stopped and they untied her to carry her away, the warm rays of the sun were striking her face, telling her dawn had come and she had survived the first night of captivity.

Chapter Ten

"So, I see you were at last successful in your mission."

Still blindfolded, Larissa felt her captors set her in a hard, broad wooden chair. She frowned, trying to recall why the soft, whistling voice seemed so familiar. But the pungent odor of burning incense assailed her senses, making it difficult to think.

Several moments passed, and then she felt someone untying her blindfold and loosening her gag. As both scarves fell away from her face, the man spoke. "Welcome La-ris-sa."

Uttering a moan of despair, Larissa looked into the eyes of the hoppo. Glancing around, she saw they were seated in a small, dimly lit entry hall.

Noting her distress, the hoppo gave a short laugh, then frowned pensively. "You are not happy to be my guest?"

She glared at him. "Guest, you say? Do you always kidnap your guests?"

His eyes narrowed. "Not always. Only when they refuse to come willingly. In fact, you are the first to be brought to me by this means. But then, you are most extraordinary. I have tried to remove you from my thoughts, but I fear I was unsuccessful."

"I won't stay, you know," Larissa said, forcing her voice to remain calm. "I've no desire to be your guest, and I won't accept your so-called hospitality."

"Ah, but you shall," the hoppo assured her. "I have gone to great expense to acquire this house for you. I feel quite sure that in time you will come to love it. In time you will learn to act like a Chinese woman, and you will greet me with proper warmth and serenity when I visit this house."

Larissa regarded him carefully. "You mean you will not be living here, too?"

"Alas, no," the hoppo sighed. "I have two wives, several concubines, and children, too—six, I believe it was at the last count. All of my women are dutiful, adequate, but I fear they would not welcome you to my house. You, my little auburn-haired beauty, shall be the joy of my life! This house is my humble gift to you, in return for your charms and favors. It shall be your home—and my haven."

Larissa stared at him, absorbing his words, and her eyes brightened with a spark of hope. If this was to be her home, perhaps she would be allowed some freedom. Perhaps, in time, she would be able to devise a means of escape. She smiled sweetly. "If this is to be my home, I should very much like a tour of it."

The hoppo returned her smile. "Your request is easy to grant. I will conduct the tour myself, and I know you will be quite pleased." Standing, he offered her his arm and led her out of the dimly lit entry foyer into the main part of the house.

Under different circumstances, Larissa would have been charmed by the house. The rooms were small and cozy but elegant. The floors were of marble, with lavish velvet and silk carpeting in various shades of purple and lavender. The polished cedar furnishings featured elaborate latticework, and the chairs in the parlor and dining room all had patterned seats of woven bamboo. An exquisitely painted set of delicate porcelain was displayed on a low sideboard in the dining room. In the parlor, there were several hanging scrolls, on which were painted delicate landscapes.

Avoiding the kitchen, the hoppo explained that the cook was a testy creature who refused to have her domain invaded. He also avoided the servants' quarters and led Larissa to the master bedroom, the room he obviously considered most important. A large, low, carved bed dominated most of the space. It was covered with a lavender satin spread decorated with intricate embroidery, featuring a crescent moon, a peacock, and a pair of doves seated on a flowering plum branch. Embroidered silk tapestries on the walls repeated the birds and flowers motif.

An adjoining room held a sunken marble bathtub, surrounded by an array of bath oils and perfumes. One glance told Larissa the tub was more than large enough for two. The hoppo chuckled at her horrified expression.

Sliding doors at one side of the bedroom opened onto

the elegantly landscaped gardens that surrounded the house. Taking her hand, the hoppo pulled Larissa through the doorway to stroll along the pebbled paths bordered by bellflowers, lilies, cockscomb, and chrysanthemums. They paused to watch and listen to a crystal-clear waterfall splashing into a reflecting pool, then crossed an arched bamboo bridge under which several swans gracefully swam.

"Look," the hoppo said, pointing to a peacock strutting proudly, its tail feathers elegantly fanned. But a glance at Larissa told him she was looking beyond the peacock, to the high stone walls that closed in the grounds. His voice hardened, and he squeezed her hand in warning. "I hope you are not thinking of leaving me, La-ris-sa, for you shall not succeed. The grounds are well guarded, day and night. I have invested too much in you to lose you. If you stay here and behave yourself, your reward will be great. Try to escape, and you shall be very sorry."

Turning abruptly, he pulled her back toward the house. "Soon I will be forced to leave you for the day. You may rest and become acquainted with your new home for the rest of the day. Tomorrow, your servants will begin teaching you the ways of a Chinese woman. I have found an old woman who speaks English. She will see that you are properly clothed and cared for, and will teach you how to please me. I will not visit you again until I am satisfied you have learned all your lessons."

They reentered the house through the bedroom door, and Larissa followed the hoppo to the main entrance, where a sedan chair awaited him. Touching her cheek, he whispered, "Goodbye, La-ris-sa. Remember, do not try to escape!"

His threatening tone made her shiver. But even as she watched his chair being carried toward the massive iron gates, she knew she would seize the first opportunity.

Larissa awakened the next morning to the sounds of water filling the great tub in the adjoining room. Opening her eyes, she reached for her dress and discovered it was gone. A petite woman entered from the bathroom. She was smiling and bowing. Her black hair was streaked with gray and was drawn into a tight bun that reminded Larissa of her Aunt Harriet.

"Your bath is all prepared," the woman said in almost perfect English.

Larissa nodded. "But where is my dress?"

The woman smiled serenely. "You will not be needing that any longer. It would only remind you of your former life. Today you become a Chinese woman and will learn to wear Chinese clothes. I will go now and get your new clothes. After your bath, you will dress in Chinese fashion."

The woman shuffled toward the door with small, mincing steps, and Larissa noticed that her feet had been tightly bound and were crammed into slippers half the size of her own. She shuddered, wondering if she would be required to adopt even that oddity of Oriental dress. If so, the likelihood of escape would be severely limited, for it was obvious every step pained the woman.

As the door closed behind the woman, Larissa slid out of bed and went into the bathroom. After her months aboard ship, where a sponge bath had had to suffice, it seemed an unbelievable luxury to step into a full-sized freshwater bath. Sinking neck-deep into the delicately jasmine-scented water, Larissa felt grateful for this one luxury and for the quiet moments it gave her to consider her plight.

After the hoppo had left, she had been too exhausted to do anything but sleep, but today her mind was alert, and she began thinking seriously about escape. Instinctively, she knew it would be foolish to try to flee at once. It would be better to take a few days to become acquainted with the house and the grounds and to discover the servants' habits and weaknesses. After she had convinced them all that she was resigned to her new position, it would be a simple matter to escape.

The woman, who identified herself as Soong Ching, returned with fresh clothing, a flowing white silk robe embroidered with pink, green, and lavender hibiscus blossoms. As she helped Larissa dress, Soong Ching explained that she was the widow of a Chinese merchant who had traded extensively with the English and Americans. She had learned to speak English because her husband had often entertained foreigners in his home.

"And now, I suppose you will be teaching me to speak Chinese," Larissa said.

The woman shook her head briskly, as if the very idea horrified her. "Oh, no! The emperor forbids teaching the language to any foreigners."

"I should think," Larissa said bitterly, "that your emperor would also forbid kidnapping."

Soong Ching regarded her strangely. "Do you forget that you are the honored guest of the hoppo? Already he has showered you with gifts and luxuries. You must learn to show your gratitude by learning to please him. There is much that I must teach you."

Biting back an angry retort, Larissa reminded herself that she must appear docile and willing if she hoped to win Soong Ching's trust and eventually devise a plan of escape.

Soong Ching spent most of the first day instructing Larissa in the Chinese tea ritual. Quoting from *The Classic of Tea,* a code devised more than a thousand years ago, she explained that there were seven stages in making perfect tea. The water went through three stages just in the boiling process, and the tea leaves might take any of nine basic shapes while brewing. Stressing the importance of serving tea in exactly the right way, she assembled twenty-four implements before Larissa and explained when and how each should be used. Then she drilled Larissa on the proper usage, making her begin the whole ritual again whenever she missed a step.

Nodding gravely, she said, "If one of the twenty-four implements is missing or if one of the steps is omitted, it is better not to serve the tea."

Larissa grimaced at all the seemingly meaningless hocus-pocus, but she gritted her teeth and began the ritual again and again, until her teacher was satisfied with her progress. By the end of the second day, she had finally mastered the procedure.

In the next days, Soong Ching introduced her to various Chinese foods, including sharks' fins, plovers' eggs, and octopus, and explained the proper methods of eating them. She began teaching Larissa the fine art of silk embroidery, a pastime Larissa found nerve-racking. Gradually, her instructions also turned to the bedroom, explaining what would be expected of Larissa and what she in turn could expect from the hoppo.

"When the master takes you to bed," Soong Ching said sagely, "you must be subservient and must do all in your power to bring him pleasure. But in the end, you may find you enjoy even greater pleasure than he."

Larissa wrinkled her brow distastefully. "I sincerely doubt that."

"Ah, but you will learn." The older woman smiled

knowingly. "He has many ways of bringing you pleasure and will delight in seeing you writhe in ecstasy. But he will never allow his own pleasure to climax."

"What do you mean?"

"Are you really so naive?" Soong Ching regarded her incredulously. "I mean, of course, that he must always cease making love to you before he releases his seed. This is the accepted practice for relations with a concubine. A man must save his seed for his wives so they can bear him strong sons and heirs."

"Then you mean I will never bear the hoppo's children?"

Soong Ching nodded. "Yes, but do not concern yourself. Being spared the rigors of childbirth, you will remain as thin and firm as a young girl. As the years pass and all his heirs have been conceived, your master will find his wives less and less desirable, while you shall remain his joy and reap the rewards of his affections."

Larissa smiled obligingly, but not with pleasure at Soong Ching's words. She was thinking instead that she would not be available to receive the hoppo's so-called rewards. She was determined to escape long before that.

The days developed a definite pattern of studying in the mornings and afternoons, then strolling in the gardens in the early evening. A week passed, and the hoppo did not return. With each passing day, Larissa became more and more hopeful she would find a way of escaping before he ever reappeared at the house. Soong Ching was her constant, watchful companion, but surely some day the woman would relax her guard.

The answer to Larissa's hopes came on the evening of the tenth day. As they finished dinner, Soong Ching patted her stomach ruefully and complained that she felt a bit of indigestion. "Perhaps, if you do not mind, I will not accompany you on your stroll tonight," she said. "I think I would prefer to retire immediately."

Suppressing her excitement, Larissa nodded. "Are you quite sure you will be all right?" she asked, hoping she sounded suitably concerned. "I would enjoy a walk, but perhaps you would like me to remain here with you."

"No, no," Soong Ching said, waving her away. "If I need anything, I'll call one of the servants. You have been most diligent in your studies, and I believe you need some time of respite."

Stepping into the garden, Larissa could hardly keep herself from dashing for the wall. But knowing some of the house servants might be watching her, she strolled demurely along a path, gradually working her way toward the edge of the property. In her walks with Soong Ching, she had taken special notice of an old peach tree that stretched its boughs over the wall. She had also noted that the nearest guards were located some distance from the tree. If she was quick and wary, she might be able to slip over the wall unnoticed.

Looking around to make sure no one was observing her, she walked to the tree, then removed her woven bamboo slippers. For a brief instant, she hesitated, remembering how, at the age of nine, she had climbed into her parents' apple tree and, unable to get down, had been forced to hang there uncertainly until her father had come in the yard. Well, she thought resolutely, she was bigger now, and she would have to manage on her own. Reaching up, she grabbed a low-hanging bough and hoisted herself upward.

She pulled herself from the first branch to the second. On the third branch, she paused to catch her breath. Glancing back toward the house, she saw movement near her bedroom door. She frowned to herself, thinking Soong Ching had recovered from her indigestion a bit too rapidly. Hurriedly, she crept along the branch, anxious to slip over the wall before the old woman discovered what she was doing.

"La-ris-sa! La-ris-sa!" Soong Ching's cry drifted to her.

Glancing back again, Larissa saw the woman heading directly toward the tree. Fighting her fear of discovery, she continued to move along the branch. Another foot and she would be past the wall. She prayed that the guards would be out of sight and that she would be able to drop to the ground unnoticed. Lifting her eyes, she surveyed the surrounding countryside. The estate was located some distance from a city, in an area with little vegetation other than cypress and willow trees. Larissa estimated she would have to run at least two miles before she reached any real shelter. But it was worth the try. Ten more days might pass before she had another chance for escape.

Still eyeing the landscape, she crept forward on the branch. The red roofs of the distant city beckoned to her, and she wondered if the city might be Canton. To her left, not more than five hundred yards from the grounds, flowed a river. Catching sight of a small boat bobbing near the shore, Larissa decided to board it and float downriver toward the city. Perhaps the river could even take her to Whampoa! Excited by the prospect, she continued to watch the boat when she should have been watching the branch in front of her.

Too late, she felt the branch begin to give way. While she was planning her escape route, she had crawled too far, to a point where the branch was too thin and weak to support her. Cautiously, she tried to inch backward, but the damage had already been done. With a thundering crack, the branch tore loose from the peach tree, dumping Larissa on the dusty, dirt roadway on the outside of the wall.

The fall knocked the breath out of her, and it was a moment before she realized she had made it to the other side. As she struggled to her feet, a searing pain shot through her ankle. Gritting her teeth, she tried to push the pain to the back of her mind and began a wild rush toward the river.

She had taken only five steps when she heard the babble of Oriental voices coming at her from all directions. She tried to continue her flight, but it was useless. Before she could take even two more painful steps, six guards were upon her. They seized her savagely and dragged her back to the house.

Trying to soothe her aching body, Larissa soaked in the tub until the water grew cold. She felt battered and defeated, but she knew she would continue to watch for another chance to escape. Soong Ching had greeted her with a stern expression, saying little as she helped her undress and guided her into the bath. Now, as she rose from the tub, she realized the woman had taken her robe when she had left her soaking in the tub.

"Soong Ching," she called as she padded into the bedroom, looking for some clothing. The chest that had held her silk and satin robes was empty.

Soong Ching entered, shaking her head and frowning. "You are a very foolish girl, and now you must be punished. The master left word that if you were caught trying to leave us, I must remove all your clothes from this room. You must remain in this room, naked, until you learn to submit."

Larissa gasped. "But that's inhuman, degrading. I won't stand for it!" Determinedly, she marched toward the door.

"For the sake of your modesty, I would not open the door," Soong Ching counseled. "There are two guards stationed there, and two more at the doors leading to the garden. You shall have no further chances to escape."

Thinking the woman might be bluffing, Larissa opened the door a crack. Two smiling guards bowed mockingly. Quickly she closed the door and faced Soong Ching. "It won't work, you know," she said defiantly. "I will never be pleased to be here, and I will never call the hoppo master."

Soong Ching gave her a knowing smile. "We shall see, in time. Now, it is time to sleep. Tomorrow we shall continue your instructions." Indicating that Larissa should get into bed, she extinguished the lamp and lay down on a pallet near the sliding doors.

Sighing, Larissa slid into bed, sure that the night would offer no more chances for escape. It would be best to rest and build her strength for the next time.

Early the next morning, Soong Ching roused Larissa and informed her it was time she learned the *k'o-t'ou*, since the hoppo would no doubt require this ritual greeting to show respect and submission. Instructing Larissa to watch carefully, she demonstrated the ritual, which involved kneeling three times and lying prostrate on the floor nine times as one approached the honored person. Each of the times she lay prostrate, Soong Ching banged her head against the floor.

When she rose at the end and commanded Larissa to follow her example, Larissa shook her head adamantly. "The whole ritual is utterly demeaning, and I refuse to participate in it."

Soong Ching shrugged. "I cannot force you, of course, but I think you shall grow very tired of being without clothing."

Larissa remained steadfast in her refusal that day, but by the end of the second day, she agreed to learn the hated ritual, reasoning that she would never find a way out of her prison if she had no clothes and was kept in a constantly guarded room. The next day, as part of her plan to regain the trust of the staff, she submitted to an even stranger practice.

"This is a ritual usually confined to the bedchamber of the emperor," Soong Ching confided. "But the hoppo fancies it and has expressly asked that it be taught to you. When the hoppo wishes to engage in sexual relations, he will retire first. Then you must enter the bedchamber, remove your clothing, and stand naked at the foot of the bed. When he invites you to join him, you will raise the coverlet, press it to your lips, and bow before your master. That done, you will enter the bed at the foot and crawl up under the coverlet until your head has reached the pillows. Then the hoppo will take you as he sees fit."

Larissa scowled distastefully, angered by the continual talk and symbolic gestures of submission. But with the sole aim of regaining her clothing, she learned the ritual. Somehow, she still felt confident she would escape before the hoppo returned to demand a demonstration of all she had learned.

That night, as she tried to sleep, Soong Ching's voice drifted to her from the pallet. "You have done well, La-ris-sa, and tomorrow your clothing shall be returned to you."

Larissa's hopes soared, only to crash with the old woman's next statement. "It is well you have finally learned all your lessons, for tomorrow evening the hoppo comes to dinner."

Chapter Eleven

Larissa sat apprehensively in the parlor, dreading the coming hours. All day she had searched for some means of escape, but the servants had been especially watchful, never allowing her out of their sight. Now it seemed there was no avoiding the meeting with the hoppo.

Moments before, she had stood before the looking glass in her bedroom, unable to believe the face staring back at her was Larissa Bennett's. She wore a plum-colored silk robe, embroidered with lotus blossoms and butterflies. Her hair was swept into a loose chignon. Rice powder lightened her complexion, while charcoal emphasized her brows and eyes. Her lips had been painted with a deep red lip rouge. She felt prepared for some masquerade, and it occurred to her that perhaps she was. Whatever the hoppo might eventually force her to do, she would not be acting as Larissa Bennett.

For a fleeting instant, she wondered what Nathan would think if he could see her now. But she pushed the thought of him out of her mind, just as she had done all through the two weeks of her captivity. It was foolish to think of him and long for him. She could expect no rescue such as in Smyrna. In all likelihood, he was still in Canton, completely unaware that she had disappeared.

The front door of the house opened, and she heard the hoppo exchanging low-toned greetings with the servants. Then she heard him shuffle down the hall and enter the parlor. She kept her eyes averted as he entered.

"What, have you no greeting for me?" The hoppo's tone was lightly mocking. "Soong Ching tells me you are most adept at the k'o-t'ou."

She remained frozen, refusing to look at him, and he laughed. "Ah, but perhaps you would prefer to perform it

naked. I understand you are at your best without clothing
—a fact which surprises me not in the least. But you
were foolish to try to forsake my hospitality. I warned
you there would be consequences."

Revulsion boiled up within Larissa, and she struggled to
remain impassive as he walked to her and grasped her
chin, pinching it as he turned her face toward him. "Look
at me," he commanded harshly.

She swallowed and lifted her eyes to meet his, her
green gaze flashing defiantly.

The hoppo chuckled. "Still the spirited one, I see. But
I suppose that is part of your charm. In time you will
learn to bend to my will." He nodded sagely, still grasping
her chin as he brought his face close to hers. "Yes, I have
no doubt that in time you will become the most satisfying
of all my concubines."

Releasing her chin, he clutched her hand and pulled her
to her feet. "Now, let us go in to dinner. I have ordered
a special feast to forever imprint this day on our memories."

Dinner was a long affair, stretching on for hours. They
began with *samshu*, a fiery Cantonese wine that Larissa
almost choked on. Smiling, the hoppo explained that the
wine's name meant "thrice-fired." Next they sampled
bird's nest soup, lichee nuts, delicately fried bits of octopus, and sharks' fins. The cook served nearly twenty
courses, each of which the hoppo attacked with relish.
Larissa picked at her food moodily, glad that the long meal
put off the inevitable. Watching the hoppo from beneath
discreetly lowered lids, she began to hope that the huge
quantities of food and wine would make him too tired
and full to attack her.

They ended the meal with the tea ritual, which the
hoppo insisted that Larissa perform herself. Leaning back
in his chair to observe her, he pulled a small, painted
porcelain figurine from his robes. The figurine was a perfect tiny likeness of a mandarin, and as he opened one
end of it, Larissa realized it was a snuffbox. Taking a
pinch of tobacco and inhaling it, first in one nostril, then
in the other, he smiled euphorically, then put away the
snuffbox.

"One of my very few vices," he explained. "At least I
have not allowed myself to become enslaved by opium, as
so many of my countrymen have." His eyes narrowed as he

stared at Larissa. "I know for a fact that the ship you arrived on carried opium. But the foolishness of others is not my concern. Your young man paid well for the privilege of trading in Canton." Gazing meaningfully at Larissa, he added, "I wonder if he realizes yet just how well he paid?"

Biting her lower lip, Larissa refused to be baited. She completed the seventh stage in making the tea and handed a cup to the hoppo. He sipped it slowly, savoring the flavor, then flashed a broad smile. "You have learned this lesson well, La-ris-sa. The tea is excellent."

Bowing her head, she did not acknowledge the compliment, but silently sipped her own tea. Servants entered quietly to clear the table, emphasizing to her that there were no further courses. There could be no further stalling. Soon he would rise, retire to the bedroom, and expect her to follow. She could fight and refuse and try to flee, but in the end there would be no escaping him. If the hoppo himself could not restrain her, he had an ample number of servants and guards who could.

She heard him push his chair away from the table, and she tensed as she sensed him approaching her. His hands rested heavily on her shoulders, and he squeezed them a bit too hard to be affectionate. He chuckled as she winced.

"It is unfortunate I am unable to linger and see how well you have learned your other lessons. But business dealings demand that I leave you now. Perhaps tomorrow—" He left the sentence dangling, allowing her to imagine the worst.

Larissa did not look up as he called a servant to see him to the door. As she heard the door close behind him, she sighed with relief and collapsed in her chair. Another day had passed, and the worst had still not happened. Perhaps tomorrow would bring her a new chance to escape.

The week wore on, but there were no new chances. Each day Soong Ching and the other servants seemed to watch her more closely than the last. And each evening, the hoppo came to dine with her. Each evening, Larissa nervously shared his table, sighing in relief when he finally pushed back his chair and left at the end of the meal.

The situation puzzled Larissa, and the constant anticipation made her nervous. Nevertheless, she was grateful for each reprieve and prayed fervently that the hoppo would not return the next day. She refused to argue with him or even to speak with him when he visited. Remembering how he had called her spirit part of her charm, she deliberately remained passive, hoping he would become bored with her and set her free.

The dinner visits continued unchanged for seven days. But as the eighth dinner with the hoppo began, Larissa knew immediately that this evening would end differently. Instead of the usual first course of soup, the servants brought only a simple meal of rice with stir-fried chicken and vegetables. As they placed the plates on the table, the hoppo spoke to them curtly in Chinese. They nodded, bowing as they left the dining room. A moment later, Larissa heard the front door open and close.

Frowning in puzzlement, she lifted her eyes to observe her dinner partner. His dark eyes met her gaze, as he idly twirled the ends of his long, drooping mustache. A half-smile played across his face. "Tonight," he murmured, "we shall see just how well you have learned all of your lessons." He raised his silver wine cup and his smile broadened. "A toast, La-ris-sa, to our first union."

She raised her own cup, smiling beguilingly, then drew back her arm and hurled the cup at him. The cup hit the astonished hoppo squarely in the jaw, and its contents splattered over his mustache and beard, dripping down to stain his white silk jacket.

"So!" he roared, overturning his chair in his haste to jump from the table, "that is how you think to repay my hospitality! Well, I will not accept such actions. I have been excruciatingly patient, but tonight I will have you. Nothing will prevent it!"

As he strode toward her, Larissa pushed herself away from the table and screamed. The hoppo's lips curled in a cruel smile. "You may scream until your throat is raw, but it will do you no good. Some of my serving girls are softhearted and might have responded to your screams, which is precisely why I sent them all away for the evening. You and I are the only ones in the house, my beauty. Need I explain that you are too weak to elude me for long?"

He laughed at her as she struggled to her feet, but Larissa nimbly dodged his hands. Feeling on the sideboard behind her, she located a large, heavy porcelain vase. As he reached for her again, she swept the vase around and smashed it over his head. Bits of rose and white china crashed to the floor around them, and a dark red gash opened on his forehead.

While the hoppo stood stunned, Larissa fled to the parlor, grabbing a plate from the porcelain display as she ran. Giving an enraged bellow, the hoppo lumbered after her. She turned, hurling the plate at him. Desperation had dulled her aim, and the plate missed him completely, sailing harmlessly into the wall, where it shattered into hundreds of pieces.

Glancing around frantically, her eyes fell on a bronze statue. She sidled toward it, hoping she could reach it in time. The hoppo's hands clutched at her, and his fingers locked in a fold of her flowing silk robe, but her body eluded him. Knowing that he could capture her in only one more step, she leaped at the statue, ignoring the loud ripping sound as her robe came away in his hands. Her fingers closed around the foot-tall bronze statue, and she whirled to face him as he advanced, staring hungrily at her exposed flesh.

Summoning all her strength, she raised the heavy statue over her head and slammed it down at him. He ducked, raising an arm to protect himself. The statue grazed the side of his head and hit his neck with crashing force. The hoppo's eyes widened, and he moaned, clutching desperately for her as he sank to the floor. Larissa felt her knees weaken as blood began to spurt from the side of his neck, pulsing out to stain his white silk robe and the lavender carpeting. For a moment, her fingers tightened around the statue. Then she dropped it on the floor beside him and fled to her bedroom.

As she knelt to take a fresh robe from her chest, she heard a movement behind her. Turning toward the garden door, she screamed at the sight of a figure outlined by moonlight, dressed in Oriental silk trousers and jacket and brandishing a huge sword.

The figure stepped toward her and spoke. "Larissa, are you all right?"

She almost swooned with a combination of relief and disbelief as the smooth, baritone voice caressed her. "Nathan?" she whispered incredulously.

"Yes!" He dropped the sword and rushed to enfold her in his arms. She clung to him, feeling suddenly weak and drained, drawing strength from his heaving chest.

"But how—why are you dressed this way—how did you know—"

"Later," he crooned, "we'll discuss it all later. Right now we've got to get away from here. Where is the hoppo?"

She shuddered as the full realization of the scene in the parlor swept over her. "I think—I think I may have killed him. I left him in the parlor, bleeding all over the carpet."

Nodding, Nathan picked up the sword. "I'll go and take a look. If necessary, I'll finish the job."

"No!" She clutched his arm. "Stay here!"

He regarded her quizzically. "Don't tell me you're feeling compassion for him now?"

"No—it's not that." She shook her head. "But I don't want you to leave me, even for a moment. And I couldn't bear to go back out there myself."

He sighed. "All right. I'd feel better knowing for sure the scoundrel's dead, but I'll do as you ask." He paused, noticing for the first time that she was naked. He asked sharply, "He didn't—"

"No." She cut him off before he could complete the sentence. "He intended to, but I was not as compliant as he wished."

Nathan nodded. "We'll talk about it later. Hurry and get dressed now. The place seems to be unguarded for the moment. I saw a number of servants and guards leave about half an hour ago, and I personally took care of the guard at the gate."

"You didn't kill him?" she asked as she quickly slipped into a green silk robe and fastened the ornate white satin frogs.

He shook his head. "Just knocked him out. We'd better hurry before he comes around."

She fastened the last frog and slid her hand into his. "I'm ready, and God knows I'm anxious to get away!"

Moments later, she was seated in a sampan, gazing lovingly at Nathan as he shoved it away from shore and climbed in opposite her. He hoisted its small sail, and a brisk wind began to carry them downriver. As they floated past the Canton harbor, Nathan pointed to a grim line of buildings crowded between the shoreline and the city walls.

"That's where I spent the weeks since I left you in

Whampoa. The hong warehouses. Not very exotic looking, are they?"

Larissa shook her head. She was silent for a few moments, then asked, "Did you really have to spend all your
time in those awful-looking hongs? Didn't you go into
the city from time to time?"

Nathan snorted. "Those walls are twenty-five feet thick,
and they aren't about to let any foreigners in to contaminate their city. In the old days, some of the hong
merchants entertained foreign traders in their homes, but
that's all changed since the eruption of the opium hostilities." He paused to gaze at her searchingly. "You had
the rare treat of enjoying Chinese hospitality."

She shuddered. "It wasn't such a treat."

"I know. You're sure you're all right?"

"I am now," she nodded. "It was horrible, but I guess
he didn't really harm me. I won't bear any scars for life."
She paused, remembering the hoppo lying on the parlor
floor, and she knew she would always be haunted by the
thought she had killed a man. Smiling bravely, she whispered, "Do you know what the worst part was?"

"What?"

"Thinking I would never see you again—that I'd never
be able to tell you I love you."

He smiled tenderly. "When I left you in Whampoa, I
doubted that I'd ever hear you say it. You were more than
a little angry that morning, as I recall."

"I know. I behaved like a child, a spoiled, irrational
child. I hope you can forgive me."

Nathan reached across and pulled her onto the seat beside him, wrapping his arm comfortingly around her.
"Hush now. You've had quite an ordeal, and you must be
exhausted. Try to sleep a bit if you can. By morning we'll
be at Whampoa, safe aboard the *Queen of Cathay.*"

Larissa huddled gratefully under his arm, feeling secure as she surrendered her future to his care.

Larissa awakened at sunrise, as Nathan gently lifted her
and carried her aboard the waiting ship. In his cabin, he
lay her gently on the bunk and brushed his lips across her
temple. She smiled drowsily as she focused on his Chinese
clothing.

"Even in silk, you don't look very Chinese by daylight,"

she teased, reaching up to brush a lock of chestnut hair off his forehead.

"I suppose not. But these clothes served me well for the last five nights. I would never have gotten out of the foreign sector of Canton in American dress."

"Five nights?" she repeated.

He nodded, rising and beginning to unbutton the blue silk jacket. "After young Dillard discovered you were gone, he spent a number of days searching the Whampoa area. I suppose he was embarrassed to admit anything could have happened to you while you were in his care, but he finally sent word to me in Canton. It took me another week to track down the hoppo's estate, and then I wasn't even sure you were there. The place was so well guarded, it would have been impossible for me to just break in, so I waited and watched for five nights, trying to figure out a way to get to you.

"I'll have to admit I'd just about decided you weren't there, for I saw the hoppo leave every night. I mean, I couldn't understand why he went to the trouble of kidnapping you if he wasn't going to spend the night with you. Then last night I saw all the servants leaving, and I knew something strange was happening. A couple of minutes later, I heard you scream, and that's when I knocked out the guard and headed for the house. I wasn't sure what might be waiting at the front door, which is why I went to the bedroom entrance."

He finished removing his silk trousers and jacket and tossed them casually out the porthole. "You can toss this, too," Larissa said, quickly slipping out of her green silk robe. "I don't want anything to remind me of that terrible man."

"As you wish." He bowed mockingly and took the robe, striding to the porthole and hurling it out. Larissa lay on the bunk, watching his magnificent muscular body. She was completely unembarrassed by his nakedness or her own.

He turned from the port, smiling as his eyes slid over her, and sniffed the air, heavy with the smells of breakfast drifting from the galley. "Hungry?" he asked softly.

"No. I—" She stopped, embarrassed, wondering how she could explain the special hunger she felt at that moment.

His eyes were burning as he came toward her. Instinctively her eyes lowered to his erect manhood, and she knew he shared her feelings.

"God, how I've missed you, Larissa!" he whispered huskily. "If you could imagine the torment I've suffered these last days—" He stopped abruptly. "But perhaps it's too soon after what you've been through. I can wait, if I must. Not patiently, I'm afraid, buy I *can* wait."

She smiled, touched by his tenderness and consideration, and spread her arms wide in welcome. "I *can't* wait, Nathan. I need to be touched and caressed and loved by someone who cares. You're the only one who can erase the horror of these last weeks. I need you. Love me, Nathan, please love me!"

Before she finished speaking, he was beside her, pressing his body full length to hers. He fondled her, caressed her, stroked her, every touch filled with infinite care. All her sensations seemed to spiral skyward as she opened herself to him, moaning at the almost unbearable pleasure as she felt him press in and fill her. She arched against him as he drove deeper, clutching at his back and wondering if she could possibly be bringing him even one tenth of the pleasure she felt.

They were one, and in that instant, she was sure they were meant to be one forever. As they finally drifted down from their heights, suspended in euphoria, Larissa whispered, "Please, Nathan, say we'll be together always."

He sighed, softly stroking her spine. "Tomorrow we'll be on Macao. We'll have the whole winter together, love. The whole winter, I promise you that."

"But I mean—" She stopped herself, aware that he had drifted into exhausted sleep. Cuddling close to him, she felt contented for the moment. For the moment, the whole winter seemed as promising as a lifetime.

Part Two

�

1840

Chapter Twelve

"No! No! Don't touch me!" Larissa screamed, sitting straight up in bed.

Nathan's arms encircled her, pulling her firmly down against him. "Hush, love," he crooned. "I'm the only one here. No one's going to hurt you."

She trembled in his arms, fighting back the tears. "It was him again," she whimpered. "He rose from the carpet, with the blood spurting from his neck, and he came after me! He grabbed me, and then he staggered and crushed me beneath him."

"He's not here," Nathan said firmly. "Try and convince yourself, Larissa. We're in Macao. The hoppo's in Canton, if he's even alive. It was only a nightmare again." He sighed. "I wish you would have let me make sure he was dead. Then maybe you'd stop imagining him alive. Should I ring for the maid to make you some tea?"

Huddled against him, she drew in large breaths of air and shook her head. "No, I'll be all right now. I'm sorry I woke you again. You must be getting weary of living with such a hysterical woman."

He brushed his lips tenderly across her temple. "Only when you wake me at three in the morning. The rest of the time I find you most delightful. Now, go to sleep, love. You'll feel better in the morning."

He was asleep again in moments, but Larissa lay tensely beside him, trying to drive away the leering image of the hoppo. They had been on Macao more than two months now, and she had had the same nightmare several times. Nathan was extremely patient with her, but even his constant understanding and reassurance could not quell her fears.

At first she had thought she simply felt guilty over

having killed a man. In time, she supposed, she would adjust to the fact that she had acted in self-defense, and the hoppo's image would no longer haunt her. But time had not solved the problem. Now she was gripped with an inexplicable certainty that the hoppo was not dead at all. He was alive. And somehow, he would manage to seek her out and punish her for what she had done to him.

When sunlight began to seep into the room, Larissa was still awake. Careful not to wake Nathan, she slid out of bed, slipped on a royal-blue velvet dressing gown, and stepped out onto the veranda adjoining the bedroom. As she stood looking down over the terraced hills of Macao, topped by the spires and towers of its twelve churches and monasteries, the specters of the night began to fade, and she felt enveloped in a wave of contentment.

Since arriving in the Portuguese port for the winter, she and Nathan had enjoyed a leisurely life. Like the other traders, Nathan had rented a spacious house, complete with a large staff of servants. It nestled among the island's hills, and the veranda looked out over the straits of the Pearl River, with its constant traffic of junks and sampans.

During the day, they attended horse races, cricket matches, and tea parties, while their evenings were often filled by balls, soirees, and theater productions. Under pressure from Commissioner Lin, the English had temporarily been ousted from the community. But the American, French, Dutch, and Portuguese traders continued to carry on a lively social whirl. Nathan appeared to be liked and respected by all who knew him, and so he and Larissa never lacked invitations.

Thinking of Nathan, Larissa sighed contentedly. Since the night he had rescued her from the hoppo's estate, he had never ceased to amaze her with his tenderness and concern for her. Their life together had become a romantic idyll, unmarred by even an occasional quarrel. When they were out in society, she could see other women watching her enviously, and she was proud to be seen with Nathan. She felt supremely secure and happy, except for one thing: he still had not even hinted at a desire to marry her.

Most of the bachelors in Macao, as well as the married men who had left their wives in their homelands, kept Chinese mistresses, so Larissa was not the only woman in the community living with a man without the benefit of marriage. But she was the only foreign woman to do so, and though she was never excluded from social functions, she sensed that the other traders' wives looked down on her and gossiped among themselves about her unmarried status.

What the other women said did not bother her, but she could not deny a yearning deep within herself to be Nathan's wife. She was prepared to devote her life to him, if only he would give her the same commitment. But he seemed perfectly content to live for the moment, and despite her underlying feelings of guilt, she was reluctant to upset what happiness they shared by broaching the subject of marriage.

Engrossed in her thoughts, she did not hear his footsteps behind her. His arms slid affectionately around her waist, and he lifted her hair to nuzzle the nape of her neck. Sighing, she leaned back against his warmth.

"You're up early," he observed. "I hope you're feeling better."

"Yes." She pulled his arms more tightly around her. "I love this time of day. It's so peaceful and beautiful, and Macao has to be one of the most enchanting places on earth."

"Better than your aunt and uncle's house in Boston?" he teased.

"To tell you the truth, I've hardly thought of them since we've arrived here. I suppose I don't make a very good businesswoman, do I?"

"As part owner, you don't have to worry about details. All you have to do is sit back and collect the profits, providing, of course, that you've hired a reliable agent—one who wouldn't cheat you."

She turned and lazily put her arms around his neck, her green eyes sparkling as she gazed up at him. "Would you?"

Nathan smiled rakishly, sliding a hand into the opening of her dressing gown. "Not as long as you keep me satisfied."

"Do I?"

His eyes glowed appreciatively as his hand stroked her flesh. "More than any man deserves to be."

She parted her lips as his mouth covered hers, and she felt his fingers loosening the sash of her gown. Her own fingers quickly untied his dressing gown, and they pressed their naked bodies together. Just as she felt him growing against her belly, he pulled away, laughing low in his throat and giving her rump a playful swat.

"Enough, vixen! If I followed my male instincts, we'd spend all our days in bed. Have you forgotten we're supposed to go to the races with the Jamiesons today?"

Larissa wrinkled her nose. Lawrence Jamieson, another American agent, was amiable enough, but Larissa was less than fond of his wife, Estelle. Haughty and aloof, Estelle Jamieson was probably the least friendly woman in the community. Larissa suspected she was also the most vicious gossip. "Couldn't we send word we're ill?" she asked, pouting.

"We could. But we won't. Look, I know Estelle isn't your favorite person, but once the races start, you'll hardly have to talk to her. I'll have the servants set breakfast on the veranda, and afterwards we can get ready to go."

"All right," she nodded, going into the bedroom to readjust her dressing gown and brush her hair.

At breakfast, she toyed with her food, barely conscious of Nathan across the table from her. Their morning conversation had reminded her of the unpleasant reason for her trip, and now she found herself wondering, for the first time in months, how Aunt Harriet, Uncle Hiram, and even Andrew Allerton had reacted to her disappearance.

She looked up as Nathan nudged her foot with his. "You're not still moping about going out with the Jamiesons, are you?"

Larissa smiled faintly. "No. As a matter of fact, my thoughts were back in Boston. I was wondering if Andrew Allerton—my supposed betrothed—has found himself another wife yet. I don't suppose I ever told you, but our engagement was to have been announced the day I stowed away on the *Queen of Cathay*."

Nathan's brows raised quizzically. "Are you sorry now that you didn't stay to marry him?"

"Of course not! I despised Andrew!"

His eyes narrowed to gray-gold slits. "But you are sorry you're not married."

She flushed, embarrassed that he could read her feelings so easily. "I've never said anything of the sort."

"You didn't have to. It's quite obvious." He sighed, and his eyes clouded as he reached across the table to take her hand. "Isn't it enough that I love you? I've never wanted to hurt you, but I've never deceived you, either. I told you at the beginning that I'm not a marrying man, and I have good reasons, though I don't wish to discuss them. Can you honestly say that I've made you unhappy?"

Blinking back her tears, she shook her head. "No. You've been wonderful. No woman could ask for more—"

"But—?" he waited expectantly.

"Well—what would you say if I said I was pregnant?"

Nathan frowned. "You're not, are you?"

"No."

"Then it seems pointless to speculate. If that's all that's bothering you, put your mind at ease. Since we've been living together this long—making love day and night—and you haven't conceived yet, I would guess that we might never have to face that problem. Some couples never have children, you know. Look at the Jamiesons, married eight years and they haven't any."

Larissa laughed nervously, anxious to change the subject. "But do they actually make love?" she asked lightly.

"A good question," Nathan said, grinning mischievously. "Estelle certainly is forbidding. I, for one, would be terrified to touch her."

"I doubt that any woman could terrify you that much."

He shrugged, then got up and kissed her forehead. "Well, there's no time now to debate the point. We've got to get dressed before the Jamiesons' carriage arrives."

Smiling, she let him pull her to her feet and lead her to the bedroom. But she was sighing inside, wondering why he was so strongly opposed to marriage. Whatever his reasons, she knew she loved him, and she believed with all her heart that he loved her, too. Perhaps, in time, when he saw how much they depended on each other's love, he would change his mind about marrying her. Until then, she would wait, stifling her conscience and trying to win him over with her constant show of love.

The stands at the racetrack were already crowded when they arrived, so they had to push their way to their seats. As they sat down, Larissa adjusted her green- and black-striped damask dress and smiled winningly at Estelle, determined to be friendly. The other woman patted her silver blonde curls and nodded curtly before turning her attention to the field. Miffed, Larissa pressed her lips together and looked away, ignoring Nathan and Lawrence chatting beside her.

"Well, Larissa," Lawrence broke in on her thoughts, "who do you favor, Dragon Prince or Black Mandarin?"

She shrugged, reaching for her opera glasses to examine the field. "I don't know," she said, feigning interest for Nathan's benefit. "I rather like that sleek chestnut over there."

Nathan squinted at the horse she had pointed at, then laughed lightly. "Larissa always was one to pick an underdog. That's Gallant Lad, and from what I hear, he hasn't a chance. What about you, Estelle, which horse do you favor?"

Estelle shot him a bored, reproachful look. "I hardly care, dear Nathan. It's a silly sport, and I come more to be seen than to see."

Embarrassed by his wife's attitude, Lawrence cleared his throat. "Well, we'll know soon enough. The first race is about to begin."

The crowd quieted as the jockeys lined up their mounts at the starter's gate. Then the starter's gun cracked, and the crowd began to roar again, everyone cheering for his favorite. By the first turn, Gallant Lad was far behind, struggling to keep up with the other horses. Although she was too tactful to admit it, Larissa was inclined to agree with Estelle's assessment of horse racing. Assuming that her horse had no chance of winning, she glanced away from the track, noting the fashions of the women seated around her. It was then that she saw him.

At first she did not believe it. She blinked, sure that her eyes were deceiving her, that her too-frequent nightmares were causing her to hallucinate. But the form was too familiar, too frighteningly real. Oblivious to the cheering crowd around her, she stared at the Chinese man. He was thinner than she remembered, but the small pointed black beard and the thin drooping mustache were the same. And his lips had the same cruel, sinister curve.

No, she told herself, fighting her rising panic, it couldn't be him. Plenty of Chinese men had small beards and drooping mustaches. Her mind was just playing tricks on her after her almost sleepless night. Besides, even if it was the hoppo, he couldn't harm her here in Macao, with Nathan on hand to protect her. Then the man lifted his head, and his gaze locked on her. She felt all her fears multiply. He stared hypnotically for what seemed an eternity, then smiled slowly and bowed to her. Larissa shuddered, immediately reading a threat in that smile.

Then she heard Nathan's voice, coming, it seemed, from a great distance. "Well, aren't you even a little excited, Larissa? We all thought you'd picked a loser, but Gallant Lad won!"

She turned to him, her face ashen, and whispered, "Nathan, he's here!"

"Who's here? What are you talking about?"

From the corner of her eye, Larissa saw Estelle leaning toward them, obviously expecting to glean some juicy gossip.

"Please, Nathan," she whispered, "I want to go home. Now!"

"What's come over you, Larissa? We've only seen one race. I was counting on you to pick me a winner in the next one. Perhaps we'd even place a wager."

"Please—"

"I say," Lawrence cut in, "she does look awfully pale. Perhaps it would be wise to take her home. You can take my carriage. Just tell the driver to bring it back after he's dropped you off."

"You're very kind." Larissa smiled gratefully. "I hope I haven't spoiled your afternoon."

"Don't give it another thought. Now, off with you."

Sighing, Nathan helped her to her feet and guided her out of the stands. During their conversation, the hoppo had disappeared. As they walked toward the Jamiesons' carriage, she kept glancing around frantically, expecting to see him following them.

"What are you looking for?" Nathan asked, in a tone that betrayed his irritation at having to leave the races early.

"The hoppo."

"Who?"

"The hoppo. He's here. That's what I was trying to tell you up in the stands."

"Good God, Larissa! It's enough you have constant nightmares about the man. Do you have to start imagining him during the day now, too?"

"I did not imagine him! I tell you, I saw him! And he saw me, too. He smiled and bowed to me, only it wasn't really a smile. It was his way of telling me he's going to get me. But this time there won't be any escaping. He'll make sure of that."

Nathan stopped and studied her terror-filled eyes. "You're really sure about all this, aren't you?"

Larissa nodded, tears running down her cheeks.

Wrapping a comforting arm around her, Nathan whispered, "All right, I'm sorry I acted so irritated at first. We'll get you home, and I'll see what I can find out about this man—where he's staying, what he's doing on Macao. But you've got to stop worrying. Do you really think I'd let him take you again?"

"I—I guess not," she sobbed. "But what about you? He must have seen you, too. What if he tries to kill you?"

"If he does, he won't succeed," Nathan replied coldly. "I promise you that. And he'll never so much as touch you again."

In the next six weeks, Nathan conducted a thorough search for the hoppo, exhausting all of his contacts in the Macao area, but he could find no sign of the man. Finally, he bribed a number of his Chinese acquaintances to investigate the hoppo's existence in Canton. They reported back that he had died at one of his estates, apparently the victim of a robber, nearly four months ago.

"So I couldn't have seen him at the racetrack that day," Larissa concluded when Nathan told her.

"It appears not. So, I hope now you can put your mind to rest. You were through quite a lot at his hands, so I suppose it was natural for you to imagine more horrors. I guess I should have sought information about his death long ago. Then perhaps you would not have been haunted for so long. But I had hoped that our life on Macao would make you forget that whole period."

"It's all right, Nathan." She smiled faintly. "You did what you thought was best for me. I'm only sorry I put you to so much trouble."

He smiled, gently kissing her forehead. "If it puts your mind at ease, my time was not wasted. By the way, I saw Larry Jamieson on my way back from town today. He invited me to a small card party at his home this afternoon. Said you should come along to have tea with Estelle."

Larissa wrinkled her nose at the prospect of an afternoon with Estelle. "You go, Nathan. You've had so little time to do anything you enjoy lately. I'd rather stay home and soak in a hot tub."

"You're sure you won't mind?"

She shook her head.

"All right, then. I'll see you at supper." After kissing her lingeringly, he called for a horse and went on his way.

Larissa had just climbed out of her bath and was wrapping herself in her dressing gown when her maid, Mei Ling, scurried in. "There's a man here, mistress. He asked to see the master, and when I told him he was not in, he asked to see you."

Larissa tensed, her thoughts flying back to that day at the races. No, she told herself firmly, the hoppo is dead. "What sort of man?" she asked.

"A young man, one who has not been here before. A Mr. Dil-lard."

"Jonathan!" Larissa exclaimed joyfully, quickly tying the sash of her gown and rushing to the sitting room to greet him.

He turned from the window where he stood, smiling broadly at the sight of her. At first glance, Larissa saw that the winter on Macao had made him older, wiser. She took his hand. "Jonathan, we haven't seen you since we docked. How good to have you visit."

He shrugged. "Well, I never wanted to intrude."

"Intrude? After the things we've been through together, you're practically family! Of course"—she smiled mischievously—"perhaps you've been too busy for old friends. What brings you here today?"

Jonathan shifted uneasily. "Captain Clinton sent me, Larissa. I was really supposed to see your husb—uh, Nathan Masters." He paused, blushing at his error.

"Well," she said, hardly noticing his slip, "even if Nathan were home, I would never have forgiven you if you'd left without seeing me as well. It happens that Nathan's out for the afternoon. If you'd like to stay to supper, he'll be back then. Otherwise, I'll be glad to deliver your message."

He smiled and gazed at her ruefully. "I appreciate your invitation, but I am a bit pressed for time. Perhaps you can just give him the message."

"I will, if you promise to come for a real visit very soon."

"I'm afraid that's not possible," Jonathan said regretfully. "You see, the message is that the *Queen of Cathay* sails for Whampoa at eight tomorrow morning."

"Oh. Then we'll have plenty of time to reminisce aboard ship, won't we?"

He stared at her silently a moment, before nodding and murmuring, "I suppose so." Backing uneasily toward the door, he added, "You'll have to excuse me now, Larissa. I really do have some important business to attend to."

She smiled teasingly as she followed him to the foyer. "Exotic, Oriental business, no doubt. I suppose it's just as well you can't stay, since I'd better begin packing."

She lay a hand on his arm and stood on tiptoe to kiss his cheek. "It really is wonderful to see you, Jonathan. We'll talk more tomorrow."

He hesitated, as if he was about to say something, then swallowed, nodded, and backed out the door.

Turning back toward her bedroom, Larissa wondered why he had acted so strangely. She smiled to herself, thinking he was probably slightly embarrassed by his new-found maturity. After all, she had known him when he was no more than an innocent, stammering boy, apologizing for kissing her. Of course, she thought as she took out a valise, they had both changed a great deal in the months since they had sailed from Boston.

Nathan arrived home about an hour later. He lounged unnoticed for a moment in the bedroom doorway, watching Larissa fold a dress into her valise. "Don't tell me you've found someone else and now you intend to leave me," he quipped.

Startled, she looked up, then laughed. "Yes," she replied lightly, "in your absence, another man was here and swept me off my feet."

"Did he, indeed?" He strode toward her, picked her up by the waist, and spun her around. Holding her off the floor at arm's length, he demanded, "And where is this rogue now?"

Giggling, she kicked her feet and squealed, "Put me down, Nathan." He complied, dropping her abruptly, and she fell against his chest, panting. Recovering her breath, she said, "Actually, Jonathan Dillard was here to say Captain Clinton intends to sail tomorrow morning at eight."

Nathan frowned. "I'm not surprised, though I can't say I'm particularly pleased. I've grown fond of this life of leisure. But you still haven't explained why you're packing."

Larissa stared at him strangely. "Obviously, so we'll be ready to go."

"You aren't going," he said without emotion.

She sighed. "I know I can't go into Canton with you, but I can at least accompany you as far as Whampoa. I understand the Chinese regulations now, and you needn't worry that I'll throw some kind of temper tantrum in Whampoa. I'll be very meek about waiting for you there."

"After what happened with the hoppo, how can you even think of going back to Whampoa?" Nathan asked incredulously.

"He has nothing to do with this decision. He was just one evil man, and you told me yourself that he's dead."

Nathan shook his head adamantly. "You're still not going. Even if Captain Clinton didn't absolutely refuse to carry you again—a position he made clear to me before we landed last November—I wouldn't take you. Try to understand, I'm only thinking of your welfare, Larissa. Here on Macao we've been rather insulated, but hostilities between the British and Chinese are intensifying every day. A small-scale war is likely to erupt at any moment, and Whampoa would be in the middle of it. It's true that Portugal only leases Macao from China, but as a Portuguese colony, it's not likely to be the scene of much fighting."

"I don't care about the danger!" she interrupted. "If you go to Canton and fighting erupts, you're sure to be in the line of fire. I want to be near you."

"Be sensible, Larissa. The fact is, I'm not even sure Captain Clinton and I will be allowed upriver to Canton. I've heard rumors the Chinese are stopping all foreign shipping. But, from a business standpoint, the best thing to do is go to Whampoa and find out—wait it out if necessary. Naturally, if things get too hot, we'll come back here immediately. Likewise, if anything goes wrong here, you can send me word, and I promise to return and take care of it. But I think you'll be perfectly safe here while I'm gone."

"I'm not staying here, Nathan! You can't tell me what to do!"

He pulled her into his arms. "You know, we're wasting valuable time arguing."

"Nathan, I'm serious!"

"So am I." His eyes smoldered, flashing golden fire as

he tilted back her head and pressed his lips to the throbbing hollow in her throat.

"Nathan, don't!" She tried to squirm away as his hands flattened against her spine, pressing her body to his. Her protests became weaker as she felt herself beginning to respond. She knew she could not fight him, and she also knew she could not win the argument. She would have to take this moment and treasure it through the long, lonely months while he was away.

Whimpering, she bent her head to catch his lips. They felt warm, moist, firm, demanding. Her lips opened, and her mouth accepted his tongue. She strained against him, almost unable to bear the delicious anticipation. Her hands loosened his trousers, then plunged inside to massage the firm flesh of his buttocks. Gradually, one hand slid forward to encircle his growing shaft of manhood.

Growling with delight, he squirmed out of his trousers and began to tear off her dressing gown. When they were both naked, he lifted her off the floor. Her legs wound around him as he carried her to the bed, and she felt him inside her even before they fell together to the satin counterpane. As he drove into her, he seemed possessed by a fury greater than anything she had ever known. Driven by a wild, surging passion, she matched his movements, wanting more.

At the height of the experience, he froze, forcing her to wait for the final, glorious sensation. She panted beneath him, writhing, aching with her need. As she opened her mouth to moan and beg, his lips covered hers, and he began to move again. The final burst of ecstasy was too exquisite to be real.

Long afterwards, she clung to him, trying to quell an unexplainable, gnawing fear that this act was his final goodbye.

Chapter Thirteen

Larissa woke slowly, possessed by delicious memories of the night just passed. After the first time, they had shared love again, slowly, savoring each delightful sensation. Then he had carried her to the veranda, where they had consecrated their love yet again, in the caressing light of the moon and stars. After that, she recalled being carried back to the bed, where they sampled even more of each other's sweetness, until they both drifted into sleep, exhausted but content. At some point in the evening, a maid had knocked at the door, summoning them to supper, but they had both ignored the knock, consumed by a greater, more demanding hunger.

Sighing dreamily, she reached out for Nathan. She could feel the indentation, still warm, where he had lain. But he was gone. Then she remembered the discussion that had preceded their lovemaking.

Opening her eyes, she guessed from the bright light streaming into the room that it was at least ten o'clock in the morning. The *Queen of Cathay* had left two hours ago, taking her beloved away from her. Suddenly, she felt more alone than ever before in her life, and she remembered her curious premonition of the night before. Frowning, she shook her head and pushed her fears to the back of her mind. He would come back for her, she assured herself. Perhaps after the agony of separation, he would even ask her to marry him.

Sitting up, she saw the note folded on his pillow. With trembling fingers, she picked it up and read:

Dearest Larissa,
  I did not want to wake you, since we had so little sleep last night, and I prefer to carry with me the memories of

last night rather than the tearful parting I know we would have this morning. I know that eventually you will see that this is the best course. I will rest easier, knowing you are safe here on Macao, and our reunion will be all the sweeter after our time of separation. Please understand that I would not be so concerned for your safety if I did not love you so completely.

I've left you money—more than enough to cover the household expenses while I'm gone, plus a bit more, in case of emergency. If fighting should erupt and Macao is threatened, I beg you to take the first available ship back to America. In the event of any other problem, remember that I am only a short journey away. If you need me, send word, and I'll do all in my power to return to you.

I hope you will find ways to amuse yourself while I am gone. My major amusement will be thinking of you, my love.

With love, forever,
Nathan

Refolding the letter, Larissa sighed wistfully and tucked it beneath her pillow. He had been right to leave her on Macao, she knew, but she wondered how she would survive the long months of the trading season without him.

To Larissa's surprise, the other traders' wives, who had also been left behind on Macao, continued to invite her for tea and to other small afternoon parties. She found their company pleasant enough and was glad for at least some way to fill her empty days.

Returning from tea one afternoon about a week after Nathan's departure, she realized she had dropped one of her gloves before entering the house. As she turned back toward the door, she heard someone knock. Thinking the carriage driver must have seen the glove on the walk and was bringing it to her, she opened the door immediately.

Her eyes widened, and she froze, unwilling to believe whom she saw. "No," she whispered hoarsely. "No! It can't be! You're dead! The men Nathan sent to check assured us you were dead!"

Smiling cruelly, the hoppo nonchalantly stroked his short, pointed beard. "A convenient ruse, girl. All of Canton, even my wives, believes me dead. But as you can see, I am quite alive. Are you not pleased to learn you are not a murderer after all?" He took a step toward her, placing one foot inside the foyer.

"No!" Larissa screamed. "I won't allow you in my house!" She started to swing the door closed, but his arm lashed out, knocking it out of her grasp so that it flew back on its hinges, crashing against the wall.

"I have things to say, and you will listen!" he thundered.

"What do you want?" she whispered coldly, trying to control the quivering inside her.

He smiled slowly, sinisterly. "You, of course."

"Well, you won't have me! Nathan won't let you take me!"

"It appears he will have little say in the matter, since he sailed last week. I would have called on you sooner, you see, but I thought it best to wait for his departure."

Larissa stiffened, fighting to keep command of herself. "I have servants who will protect me."

He shrugged. "Servants can be bought off more easily than you think."

"No. They are loyal."

"You may find in the end that they are more loyal to one of their own countrymen than to a foreign devil."

"I think you had better go," she said icily, "before I'm forced to call someone to throw you off the premises."

The hoppo bowed, unruffled by her threats. "I did not intend to take you today, La-ris-sa. I want you to have time to think about our future together—time to antici- pate the life that awaits you, just as I have anticipated it all winter. When I decide the time is right, you may be sure that I will not fail in my efforts to take you. In the meantime, I wish to leave you with something to think about."

He grasped the high collar of his red silk jacket, pulling it roughly toward his shoulder. Larissa could not suppress a gasp at the sight of the jagged white scar along his neck. She closed her eyes, sickened by the sight of it.

"What? Are you not pleased with your handiwork?" The hoppo chuckled. "Of course, the last time you saw it, it was red with my blood. Perhaps you preferred it that way. I was fortunate that my guard—the one your Nathan knocked out—was able to reach me in time. But we will have plenty of time to discuss that night. I'll leave you now, and while you wait for my return, you may dream of the ways I will repay you for what you have done to me!"

Laughing cruelly, he turned and strode away from the

door. He swung onto a sleek black stallion waiting at the street and waved gaily as he galloped away.

Larissa collapsed against the door, finally succumbing to the horror and fear that gripped her. He was alive! He was alive, and he intended to take her again. He intended to punish her for almost killing him. She closed her eyes, and the horrible white scar loomed in her vision, seeming to grow until it covered the hoppo's face and became a terrifying threat. She blinked rapidly, fighting back her tears. She had to think. She had to find the way to escape the evil, menacing hoppo.

Nathan, she thought desperately. She would send word to Nathan and beg him to return. He had promised to come back if she needed him. She would send a message to the *Queen of Cathay,* convincing him that he must return immediately. She wanted to go herself, but she was certain the hoppo would follow her and capture her before she ever reached Nathan. It would be better to send a Chinese servant, who could move unobtrusively among his countrymen. In the meantime, she would instruct the other servants to admit no one to the house, no matter who might call.

Her decision made, she went to Nathan's study and found pen and ink. Anxious to send the message on its way, she penned only a short note:

> Nathan darling,
> The hoppo is alive! He was here to see me this morning and said his supposed death was simply a ruse. He has threatened to kidnap me again and make me pay for scarring his neck. I am terrified. Please come home and protect me.
>
> > All my love,
> > Larissa

Folding the note, she called to Lin Po, one of the house servants, and instructed him to go upriver, in search of the *Queen of Cathay* and Nathan.

"It's extremely important that you find Mr. Masters as quickly as possible," she said. "The message must be given to no one else. Do you understand?"

The servant nodded. "Yes, mistress, you need not worry. Lin Po will take care of all."

Larissa smiled grimly. "Yes, I certainly hope so. Now, off with you, and remember, speed is most important."

Shooing him out the door, she called to Mei Ling and instructed her to assemble the other servants in the parlor.

When they had all gathered there, Larissa stared at the group of friendly, inquisitive faces, wondering how much she should tell them. Sighing, she began. "This morning I had a most unpleasant experience. A man—a Chinese man—threatened to kidnap me, possibly even to kill me!" She paused as shocked murmurs rippled through her audience. "He is gone for the moment, but he assures me he will be back, and I am quite certain it was no idle threat. I've sent Lin Po after Mr. Masters, and I am sure that when he returns, he will be able to handle the situation. In the meantime, no one is to be admitted to this house. I don't care who they say they are, what reason they give, or how well they say they know me, I do not wish to see anyone, and I do not want you to let anyone in. Is that clear?"

The servants all nodded gravely, shaking their heads over the seriousness of the problem. Gazing at them, Larissa felt a rush of warmth and reassurance. No matter what the hoppo might have said, she felt certain they were all loyal to her. She had always treated them well, and she knew they felt a great deal of affection for her and would repay her for her consideration.

As she left the room, Larissa heard nervous Chinese chattering breaking out behind her. She smiled grimly, imagining the wild speculations her words had begun. Well, she sighed to herself, let them think what they wished. As long as they kept the hoppo away until Nathan arrived, it didn't matter.

Lin Po did not return for a full seven days. Each day, Larissa paced nervously, expecting the hoppo to break into the house at any time. At night, she tossed for hour after hour, imagining his face at the veranda doors, his leering smile, his scar, stark and horrible in the moonlight. Several times, she got out of bed and looked out onto the veranda, sure the vision was too real to be imagined. But he was never there, and she returned to bed to be haunted again.

By the seventh day, she was frantic, imagining something had happened to Nathan, something had happened to Lin Po on his way to Whampoa, something was sure to happen to her before anyone arrived to save her. She questioned the servants a dozen times a day. Always their answers were the same. No one had come calling, and there had been no sign of nor word from Lin Po.

Finally, late in the evening of the seventh day, when Larissa was just about to send out another servant in search of both Lin Po and Nathan, Lin Po staggered into the house.

Hearing his voice in the foyer, Larissa hurried from the parlor to confront him. She stopped abruptly as her nostrils were assailed by the strong, cloying odor of jasmine. Lin Po smiled sheepishly, ducking his head and staring at his feet. She knew immediately that he had just come from one of the floating, flower-lined brothels located on boats in the Pearl River, south of Whampoa. After her days of helpless waiting and frustration, bitterness and anger seethed through her.

"Lin Po!" she snapped, "how could you disappoint me so? I told you speed was most important, and yet you found the time to dally in a brothel! I suppose you didn't even go to Whampoa and deliver my message."

The servant lifted hurt eyes to her and whined, "I did go, mistress. And I delivered the message to Mr. Masters, just as you instructed."

"Then where is he?" she demanded. "Don't tell me you left him in the brothel!"

Lin Po moistened his lips, shifting uncomfortably. "No, mistress. He did not come with me."

Larissa paled, unable to believe her ears. "What do you mean? He had to come!"

"No." Lin Po shook his head, then added sheepishly, "He did send a message, though."

"Then, for heaven's sakes, give it to me!" She extended her hand, waiting expectantly.

"Not a written message, mistress. A spoken one." At Larissa's surprised look, Lin Po hurried to explain. "He said he had no time to write an answer to your petty problems. He said you are just being crazy, hysterical—that you are imagining things again. He said the hoppo you wrote about is dead and he cannot be rushing back here because of your foolish fears."

Larissa listened dumbstruck, shaking her head dazedly. "No," she whispered, "I don't believe you. Nathan wouldn't do that. He wouldn't say those things. Even when I woke him with my nightmares time after time, he was always gentle and comforting. You're lying, Lin Po, I know you are! You never delivered my message, and now you're lying to cover up your laziness!"

The servant shrugged. "I am telling the truth, whether or not you choose to believe me."

"I can't believe you! I suppose you will even deny that you stopped in a brothel, even though my nose has given me all the evidence I need."

"No, I won't deny that fact. But it seemed pointless to hurry back here, considering the news I carried."

Larissa frowned. "I'm not interested in your excuses. Get out of my sight now, before I'm tempted to slap you for your disgusting, deceitful behavior."

Bowing quickly, Lin Po scurried off to the servants' quarters. Larissa paced in the study, replaying the conversation in her mind. No matter how she considered it, she could not believe Lin Po's story. After their months together on Macao, she knew Nathan too well to believe he could be so callous and uncaring. She could not believe he would dismiss her fears so easily, not when she told him the hoppo had actually visited her. Lin Po was lying to cover his own laziness and unreliability. That was the only plausible explanation. And his deviousness had cost her a full week of precious time.

Again Larissa considered going to Whampoa herself. But again she rejected the idea. No doubt the hoppo was just waiting for her to leave the house. On the street, it would be easy for him and his henchmen to snatch her. She felt safer inside. Besides, even if she did manage to reach Whampoa unharmed, there was still the possibility that Nathan might have continued upriver to Canton. Then she would be forced to wait for an answer in Whampoa. And if the hoppo had managed to kidnap her off the *Queen of Cathay* before, he could surely manage it again.

The only sensible course, then, seemed to be to send another messenger upriver and hope the servants could stave off the hoppo, should he arrive in the meantime. She searched her mind for a servant who would be more reliable than Lin Po and finally settled on Sun Yuan. He was still too young to be tempted by the brothels, and he had always seemed exceptionally ready to please her. In addition, his mother, to whom he was devoted, was also a member of the household staff, and it was unlikely that he would do anything to embarrass her.

She penned a quick note and summoned Sun Yuan, giving him instructions almost identical to those she had given Lin Po. As she watched him leave the house, she prayed that he would prove more reliable than the first messenger.

Larissa had to wait only three days for Sun Yuan's return. Three days of worrying about the hoppo, but neither hearing from nor seeing him. When Mei Ling came to her bedroom to tell her Sun Yuan had just arrived, she rushed to the parlor, stopping in stunned confusion when she saw the youth was alone.

"Were you unable to find Mr. Masters?" she asked. "Or has something happened to him?"

Sun Yuan shook his head. "I had no trouble finding him, and he appeared to be well enough."

"Then I don't understand. Why did he not return with you? You did give him my message, didn't you?"

The youth nodded emphatically. "I gave it to him immediately, mistress. But—" he hesitated, reluctant to continue.

"But what?"

"He said there was no reason to return, that he already told Lin Po as much—and that you should stop disturbing him."

Larissa stared at him, unable to speak, unwilling to believe the message. She moistened her lips and forced out a whisper. "You're sure that's all he said? Nothing more?"

Sun Yuan wrung his hands. "Nothing more."

"He gave you no written message for me?"

"No, mistress. He said that he hadn't the time."

She swallowed, blinking rapidly, lest her tears betray her before the servant. "I see. All right, Sun Yuan. Thank you for your trouble. You may go now. I'm sure your mother is anxious to see you."

Nodding obediently, Sun Yuan left the parlor. As she heard the doors close behind him, Larissa succumbed to the tears welling up within her. How could Nathan desert her so heartlessly, she wondered, when he had promised to return if she needed him? She still could not believe he had betrayed her so. But could she really doubt it when both servants returned with identical stories? Lin Po might have lied to mask his own irresponsibility, but what motive did Sun Yuan have for lying? Then she remembered the hoppo's words: "Servants can be bought off more easily than you think." But not Sun Yuan. Surely he would not betray her. Still, it was easier to think Sun Yuan had fallen prey to the hoppo than to believe Nathan could treat her so cruelly.

"Mei Ling!" she called sharply as she sank down on the settee, "please ask Sun Yuan to return here immediately. There's something I wish to ask him."

Sun Yuan entered a few moments later, his eyes downcast. "Yes, mistress?" he whispered.

Larissa stared at him for a moment, then pointed to a chair. "Sit down, Sun Yuan." She paused, wetting her lips nervously while he seated himself. "Sun Yuan, I want to ask you something, and I want you to give me an honest answer."

The servant looked surprised. "But of course, mistress. I am always quite honest with you."

She nodded distractedly. "What I mean is, you must not fear that I will punish you, no matter what your answer. I promise you, I will not be angry with you, so long as you tell me the truth."

Sun Yuan looked puzzled. "I don't understand, mistress. I have always been honest, and you have always been quite fair to me."

"Sun Yuan," she cut in urgently, "are you sure no one kept you from delivering my message to Mr. Masters?"

Blinking back tears, Sun Yuan repeatedly shook his head. "Why do you even ask?"

Standing, Larissa began to pace. "Because I can't believe Nathan would abandon me! You were here the day I told the staff about the man who has threatened to kidnap me. I'm certain that man would do anything to keep my messages from reaching Nathan. If he approached you and somehow frightened you, I can understand that. Just tell me the message you brought me was false."

"You must believe me!" Sun Yuan sobbed. "I know nothing of this man. Can you really believe I, who have been so loyal, would allow myself to be drawn into league with a man who has threatened you?"

"Not in league with him, Sun Yuan. But perhaps—" She broke off, overwrought, as the servant buried his head in his hands and sobbed wretchedly. "Oh, Sun Yuan," she cried consolingly, "you mustn't think it's *you* I doubt!"

"Then prove you don't doubt me," he begged, his words muffled by sobs. "Believe me! I carried your message to Mr. Masters, and I returned his reply exactly as he spoke it. I'm sorry for what he said, I wish I could have brought some other message, but I swear to you, I would not lie."

"No," she said quietly, "I suppose you would not. You may go now, Sun Yuan." Watching him stumble from the room, Larissa wondered how she could doubt the young man. Seeing how upset he had become, she found it difficult to question his sincerity. Even if the hoppo had approached him, she felt certain now the servant would have refused to deceive her, even if his refusal cost him his life.

But if she accepted Sun Yuan's words, she must also accept the fact that Nathan had, indeed, deceived and deserted her. Bitterly, she thought she should have realized he did not truly love her when he first refused to consider marrying her. He had simply wanted her to think he loved her so that he could use her for his pleasure during the winter on Macao. Even when he had rescued her from the hoppo's estate, he had only acted to satisfy his own lusts. No doubt he had grown tired of her in the past months and had already chosen a pretty Chinese woman for the next winter. And so he had abandoned her to the mercy of the hoppo.

Pacing despondently in the parlor, Larissa was gripped by a frantic desire to leave the Orient and all the heartbreak it had brought her. She could book passage on the first ship out of Macao, wherever it was bound. Somehow, she could make a new life, far from Nathan and from evil men like the hoppo.

Gradually, her despondency was swallowed by her rage against Nathan, a rage that far outweighed her fear of the hoppo. And that rage began to build a new resolve within her. She would not leave Macao yet. She would not run away. That would be doing exactly as Nathan wished, disappearing from his life without causing any problems or regrets.

For too long she had allowed herself to forget her original reason for coming to China. She had come to protect her business, not to find romance. Chinese regulations might prohibit her presence in Canton, but they could not keep her from directing the firm from Macao. She would not return to Boston, where her aunt and uncle still held legal sway over her, and she would not simply disappear, leaving her father's share of Bennett and Barnes to be swallowed by their greed.

If Nathan no longer wanted her as a lover, he would still have to contend with her as an employer. She would not leave Macao without collecting her share of the year's profits, and she might well remain permanently to oversee the trading business. As for the hoppo, tomorrow she would report him to the Portuguese authorities, something she should have thought to do immediately after his visit.

Chapter Fourteen

Larissa stood on the veranda, staring peevishly down at the harbor. It was late April, almost two months since Nathan's departure, and still there was no further sign of the hoppo. She suspected that he planned to torture her with anxiety until the last possible moment before the return of the *Queen of Cathay*. Perhaps he even knew that Nathan had refused to help her, so he was simply biding his time, making her suffer.

The Portuguese authorities had been only slightly helpful. The morning after Sun Yuan's return, she had summoned an aide of the Portuguese governor to the house. A sober, ingratiating little man, he had regretfully informed her there was little his government could do. Portugal leased Macao from China, so the Portuguese had only minimal control over any Chinese citizens in the area. Since the man in question had not actually harmed her, it seemed pointless to pursue the matter. However, he added, the governor could arrange to have a guard placed around the house to keep away any intruders.

Sighing, Larissa had agreed to the guard, but so far the only intruders had been a mother duck and her brood, who had set up a nest near the veranda. Since she refused to go out, she had not received any invitations in weeks, and none of her acquaintances from the foreign community even called on her anymore. Now, as she watched the Portuguese guard patrolling the perimeters of the house, she felt like a prisoner in her own home.

Turning abruptly from the veranda, Larissa entered her bedroom and called briskly to Mei Ling. "Have the carriage brought around. I'm going for a drive."

The maid looked at her fearfully. "Do you really think it wise, mistress?"

Larissa sighed. "I don't know, but I'm tired of being wise. I've been cooped up in here so long I can't stand it. I'll have Sun Yuan accompany me. He's young and strong. Besides, if I stay in a busy area, I doubt that anyone would dare to accost me."

Raising her eyebrows apprehensively, Mei Ling went to call for the carriage and summon Sun Yuan. A few moments later, Larissa was seated in the carriage, directing the driver to the Praya Grande, Macao's fashionable seaside promenade.

It was a balmy day, and as Larissa had expected, the promenade was crowded with strollers. Most of them were fashionably dressed European and American women, whose husbands were away in Whampoa. Sure she would be quite safe among the crowd, Larissa asked Sun Yuan to wait in the carriage while she strolled alone.

Walking past the white baroque houses lining the promenade, Larissa breathed in the fresh sea air. Since the hoppo's visit, she had missed the freedom to move around the city. But she knew there was something she missed even more. No matter how she tried to deny it to herself, she missed Nathan desperately. She had tried to harden herself against him, but not a day or a night passed without the memories flooding over her—memories of his tender touch, his rich baritone laugh, the flash of his eyes. The memories were always there, clawing at her heart, making her want him even when she knew she should despise him.

She kicked a pebble and stared at the stone promenade, absently removing her bonnet to let the light sea breezes ruffle her hair. Immersed in her thoughts, she hardly noticed the heat of the sun. Suddenly, she realized that she was becoming queasy. She lifted her eyes, and the landscape seemed to be swimming. Then, amid the wavering lines, she saw the gloating face of the hoppo, but she was not sure if it was really him or just another haunting vision of him. Her knees began to buckle, and she felt someone grab her from behind. Panic-stricken and powerless, she threw back her head and screamed.

"Easy, young lady. No one's going to hurt you, though I dare say you might have hurt yourself if I hadn't caught you. The way you were swaying, you surely would have gone down in another second."

The man's voice was soft and reassuring. Larissa turned slowly, allowing him to continue supporting her. Hearing running footsteps, she looked up and saw Sun Yuan approaching, ready to do battle with the man. She smiled weakly. "It's all right, Sun Yuan. The man is just helping me. I just panicked for a moment when I thought I saw the hoppo."

"The hoppo?" the man asked in a clipped British accent. "I believe all the hoppos are in Whampoa. That's where they check the shipments, you know."

For the first time, Larissa turned her attention to the man. He was tall and lanky, with sandy hair and watery blue eyes that seemed to be filled with compassion. She guessed that he might be in his mid-thirties, though he looked a good deal younger. She smiled. "The man I'm referring to is a former hoppo, but I don't know him by any other name or title. We met in Whampoa, but now he is on Macao."

The man frowned. "Has this former hoppo tried to harm you in some way?"

Larissa sighed. "Yes. But it's a long story, and I wouldn't wish to bore you, Mr.—"

"Farrell. Edmund Farrell. And I assure you the company of so beautiful a lady could never bore me. Perhaps you'd like to come into my home for a bit of refreshment."

"I really couldn't impose upon you, Mr. Farrell. I do appreciate your kindness and concern, but my carriage is nearby, so I'll just be going on home."

"It would do you good to sit down and have a cool drink, first," he cajoled. "After all, I'm not your insidious hoppo, and I give you my word I won't harm you. In fact, if it makes you feel more relaxed, you can bring your servant boy with you. I live right across the way on the Praya Grande, so you can hardly give the excuse that it's out of your way."

Larissa paused, considering the long drive back to her house and the visions of the hoppo that were sure to haunt tation."
her. Perhaps it would be good, after all, to have the company of another Westerner, at least for a little while. Smiling, she relented. "All right, Mr. Farrell, I accept your invi-

"Please," he said, taking her elbow and steering her across the promenade to one of the baroque mansions, "do me the honor of calling me Edmund."

She nodded. "Very well. My name is Larissa Bennett."

A short time later, Larissa was comfortably seated on Edmund Farrell's seaside veranda, drinking a cool julep and breathing in the refreshing aromas of its herbs. She studied her host carefully, feeling entirely at ease with him. Finally, she asked, "You're British, aren't you?"

Smiling, he nodded. "I guess that's rather obvious."

She hesitated, not wishing to appear too ill-informed or to pry into his business. "Then how do you happen to be on Macao? I mean—I thought the Chinese had banned all the British from the area."

He smiled indulgently. "Most people think that, though it's not strictly true. As a matter of fact, all the British citizens left on their own accord last August, when the Chinese were only threatening to throw us out. I just decided that eight months living on board a ship anchored off Hong Kong was too bloody much, so I decided to come ashore."

Larissa stared at him incredulously. "But will you be safe?"

He shrugged. "Before long, no one in the vicinity of China will be safe. If the reports from Parliament are true, we'll have a British war fleet here by June. And once that happens, there'll be no turning back. There'll be war for sure."

Involuntarily, Larissa thought of Nathan and paled. "You really think war is so certain?"

"No doubt about it."

She shook her head dazedly. "And all because of that horrible drug."

"Not entirely. The whole question of free trade is at issue. The Chinese have limited us to one small area of Canton for long enough."

He paused, and his eyes clouded as he considered his next words. "And, I might add, that drug is hardly as horrible as you might think."

Something about his last statement made Larissa shiver. Her gaze met his as she tried to read the hidden meaning in his words. Clearing his throat, he shifted his eyes uneasily away from hers.

"Well," he said briskly, "I really shouldn't be discussing

any of this with you right now. Political worries are for the men. Besides, you seem to have your own problems. What was it you were saying about a hoppo?"

"Oh," she flushed, "it's rather difficult to explain. Briefly, I was aboard my father's ship at Whampoa last fall, and this hoppo had me abducted. I was held prisoner on his estate, and he tried to attack me. We fought, and I—managed to escape." Her voice broke as she remembered Nathan helping her to flee. In a whisper, she added, "At the time, I thought I'd killed him."

"Oh, my God!" There was agony in Edmund's voice. "How horrible for you! But you say you've seen him on Macao now?"

"Yes. Two months ago he came to my home and threatened to kidnap me again. Since that time, I've seen nothing of him."

"Until today?"

She nodded. "I'm not even sure if I saw him today or if I was just hallucinating because of the heat."

Edmund pursed his lips and stroked his chin thoughtfully. "What has your father said about all this?"

"My father died over a year ago."

"I'm sorry. Then who is looking after you?"

Larissa sighed. "At the moment, no one. It's a long story, Mr. Farrell, one I'd rather not go into just now." Setting aside her empty glass, she stood and turned to stare at the sea. "I think it really would be best if I returned home now."

"I'm sorry if I seemed to be prying," he said softly. "It's just that you're so young, so vulnerable."

She turned back toward him. "I understand. Perhaps you'll feel better knowing Governor da Silveira Pinto has stationed a Portuguese guard around my home."

He smiled. "That is a relief. But the guard did you little good this afternoon. You really should not go out alone."

She shrugged. "I wasn't alone. I had Sun Yuan and my driver. Besides, I can't stay cooped up in the house all day."

"No—but now that you've met me, you could agree to let me be the one to accompany you."

"I really couldn't trouble you, Mr. Farrell."

"Please, I asked you to call me Edmund. When you address me so formally, you make me feel old enough to be your father—and I don't want to feel that way." Impulsively, he grasped her hand. "Really, Larissa, I'd be very pleased if you'd allow me to call on you and take you out from time to time."

"I don't think—" She left the sentence unfinished, suddenly wondering why she should refuse him. Why should she deny herself some innocent companionship? She doubted that their relationship would ever be more than that, but even if something else did develop, what did it matter? No one else had any hold on her. She need not even feel guilty about using Nathan's house to entertain another man. After all, it was really her house, paid for with her money from her shipping firm.

Defiantly tossing her head, she smiled at him. "I'd feel very honored to be seen with you, Edmund."

"Good." He returned her smile. "I'll begin by accompanying your carriage home now."

He rode a bay stallion beside her carriage, keeping a firm rein on the spirited animal so he could watch her and converse with her all the way to her house. At her door, he quickly dismounted and handed her down from the carriage, asking permission to call on her the next day. Larissa nodded, then entered the house to face a worried Mei Ling.

One glance at her servant's face made Larissa forget the relaxation of the last two hours. "Mei Ling, what's wrong?" she demanded. "Was he here? Did he threaten you?"

Mei Ling shook her head. "Nothing is wrong here. But you were gone so long I could not help worrying about you. I was sure that evil man had snatched you."

Larissa nodded grimly. "He might have, if Mr. Farrell, the gentleman who accompanied me home, hadn't saved me. As a matter of fact, anyone might have kidnapped me without much problem. I almost fainted right in the middle of the Praya Grande."

Her maid studied her, nodding thoughtfully. "That does not surprise me."

Larissa sighed. "I know. I shouldn't have taken my bonnet off, especially when I'm not accustomed to the hot sun. Edmund said the same thing, and you can be sure I won't be so foolish again. Edmund's going to call for me tomorrow afternoon, so be sure that he's admitted." She stopped suddenly, aware that Mei Ling was staring at her. "Mei Ling, whatever is the matter?" she asked.

Mei Ling chewed nervously on her lip before asking, "Are you quite sure it was only the sun that made you feel faint?"

"I don't see what else it could have been. What are you driving at, Mei Ling?"

"Have you felt any stomach sickness in these last months?"

"Of course. But that's only natural. I've been extremely nervous with all this worry about—"

Mei Ling interrupted. "Your woman's time has not come on schedule, has it?"

"No, not since before the hoppo—" She cut herself off abruptly as Mei Ling's meaning became clear. "Mei Ling, you can't believe I'm . . . no, that's just not possible."

"It is possible," the older woman nodded gravely. "Whenever a woman lies with a man, it is possible."

"But couldn't I just have missed my time because I've been so upset? I've heard that happens sometimes. That a woman thinks she's carrying a child when something else has just thrown her body off its normal course."

"It happens," Mei Ling agreed. "But I think you are really carrying a child. I have noticed when I help you at your bath that your tummy is not so flat as it once was."

"I haven't been getting enough exercise," Larissa insisted. "My body has gone lax because I've done nothing but sit around this house for two months, worrying about that dreadful man. But now that Edmund's going to be calling on me, I'll be getting out more. The fresh air will do me good, and perhaps we'll even go riding a few times a week. I'll be back to normal in no time at all."

Mei Ling shook her head slowly. "I think not. I only hope you won't do anything to harm yourself—or the baby."

"Nothing I do can harm anyone," Larissa said firmly, "because there is no baby. I'm sure of it."

Chapter Fifteen

By the middle of May, Larissa was sure she was carrying a child. She was also sure that Edmund Farrell had fallen hopelessly in love with her. Since their first meeting, he had called on her every day. Some days they went for a drive in his carriage, other days they went horseback riding together over Macao's terraced hills or simply sat at home, quietly conversing. Feeling totally at ease with him, she explained why she had come to the Orient, but she did not mention Nathan.

He always treated her with complete respect. In the three weeks they had been seeing one another, he had never even tried to kiss her on the lips, limiting their intimacy to an occasional circumspect kiss on the hand. But she could see in his eyes that he wanted much more, though he was too much of a gentleman to declare his desires.

For her part, Larissa enjoyed her time with him. She felt completely at ease with him, and she deeply appreciated his concern for her safety. She was also grateful that the hours with Edmund kept her from worrying about the hoppo, about the child growing within her, or about Nathan, who still plagued her mind all too often. She loved Edmund like an older brother, but she knew she could never feel anything more for him. Still, she doubted that it would do any harm to continue seeing him. After all, he would soon be leaving Macao, and he would forget about her in a short time. So sure was she of her assessment, that his proposal caught her completely off guard.

They had gone for a carriage ride and were stopped at the peak of one of Macao's highest hills, when Edmund turned to her gravely. "I'll be leaving Macao within the next fortnight, Larissa. I understand the British fleet will be arriving soon, and I've no desire to be caught in the midst of battle."

She nodded. "Where will you go?"

"To my estate in India, near Patna. If all goes well, our navy will soon convince the Chinese of our superiority, and I'll be able to return to resume trade."

"I see." She smiled and squeezed his hand. "I must say, I'll miss you, Edmund. I've enjoyed our time together, and I wish you nothing but the best in the future. I hope I'll be able to see you again before your departure."

He cleared his throat nervously and gazed earnestly into her eyes. "I hope I'll be able to see you for the rest of my life. I want you to come with me, Larissa." Seeing her frown and fearing she had misinterpreted him, he hastily added, "As my wife, of course."

She looked away, staring at the peach blossoms dotting the terraced landscape. "I—I'm very touched," she stammered, "but—"

"Please"—he lay a finger gently across her lips—"don't refuse me so hastily. At least say you'll think about it. I'll do anything in my power to make you happy, Larissa. I know that I'm thirty-four and you're eighteen, but sixteen years isn't really so great a difference. I could name you any number of good marriages with an even greater age span. I'd take good care of you, Larissa. For a start, I'd take you away from here so you'd never have to worry about the hoppo again. You could forget about your horrible, scheming aunt and uncle. I'd—"

"Oh, Edmund!" she cut him off tearfully. "It's not you I doubt, it's myself! There's so much you don't know about me. I'm afraid if you knew it all, you would never even have considered asking me to become your wife."

He shook his head. "I know all that's necessary, darling. I know I want to share my life with you. You're so young and innocent, I suppose my proposal came as somewhat of a shock to you. You need time to think about it. I'll drive you home now and leave you to your thoughts. Just remember that I love you and I want you, no matter what faults you may imagine yourself to have. Will you at least promise me that?"

Looking into his pleading eyes, she hadn't the heart to say no.

Larissa slept less than an hour that night as she worried about how she could avoid hurting Edmund. He was so much older than she, but it seemed that in some ways he was so much more naive. She knew she could not marry him. It would be unquestionably wrong when she did not love him and she was carrying Nathan's child. But if she rejected his proposal without giving him any reasons, he would be crushed, assuming she found him lacking in some way. For his sake, she would have to tell him the truth, even though it would surely damn her forever in his eyes.

Thinking of Edmund's kindness and consideration, she cursed Nathan for the ruthless way he had played with her emotions. If only he truly loved her! In a way, it would be so easy to accept Edmund's proposal and go away with him—so much easier than remaining on Macao to face Nathan's ridicule and scorn when he and his new mistress returned to find her big with child. She could never be truly happy with Edmund, but she supposed she could find a kind of contentment with him. No, she pushed the thought resolutely from her mind. Edmund was too decent for her to use and deceive. She would tell him the truth, and when he knew, he would no longer even want to marry her.

That course settled in her mind, she wondered what she would do after Edmund left. With the hoppo undoubtedly still at large and no one there to protect her, it would not be safe for her to go out any more. She would be confined to the house again, spending day after boring day inside, while her Portuguese guard patrolled outside. Eventually, assuming the hoppo did not get to her first, she would bear the child who, being a bastard, would be even more of a social outcast than she.

For an instant she considered sending one final message to Whampoa, telling Nathan about her pregnancy and appealing to whatever sense of honor and decency he still possessed. Even if he did not care about her, he might still marry her to give his son or daughter a name. No, she told herself stubbornly. If she could not have him for love, she did not want him at all. The child would be better off fatherless than living with a mother and father who despised one another. Besides, she had no reason to believe he would marry her, even for the child's sake. Remembering their breakfast conversation months before, when Nathan had so neatly evaded her questions about pregnancy, she became even more opposed to sending him another message. She was too proud to let him reject her again.

Somehow, she would find a way to make a life of her own. She didn't need the approval of society, and she didn't need Nathan, no matter how much she still wanted him. She still had her half share in Bennett and Barnes, despite what her aunt and uncle might be thinking back in Boston. Surely that would be enough to support her and the child. And in the end, she assured herself as she drifted into exhausted sleep, the child might be better off being raised on the fringes of society. It would make him or her tougher, more able to withstand the scheming and deceitfulness he or she would surely encounter later in life.

Her decision of the night made it no easier for Larissa to face Edmund Farrell the next afternoon. As she dressed slowly in a prim, pink damask dress with long, fitted sleeves and a high, close neckline, she realized that she wanted him, somehow, to continue to view her as chaste, even when she told him about the child she was carrying.

Larissa clasped a simple strand of pearls around her neck and was just putting on single pearl earrings when she heard Mei Ling admit Edmund to the house. Glancing fretfully at her pale reflection, she rose, squared her shoulders, and went to the parlor to greet him.

Dismissing Mei Ling, Larissa closed the parlor doors behind her as she entered. Edmund turned from where he stood by the fireplace, frowning when he noted her pale, haggard look. He held out his hand to her, and she accepted it, allowing him to lead her to the settee.

Still staring at her gravely, he asked, "Are you feeling all right? You look lovely, as always, but not quite well."

She smiled wanly. "I'm well enough, thank you. It's just that I did not sleep too soundly last night."

"Oh?" He raised his brows apprehensively. "Were you so worried about the decision I asked you to make?"

Nodding, she blurted, "I can't marry you, Edmund." Seeing him about to protest, she quickly raised her hand. "Please, hear me out, and then you'll understand, though I fear you'll hate me as well. I'm not good enough for you, Edmund. You see, I'm carrying a child."

His mouth dropped open as he stared at her, thunder-struck. "Surely you are mistaken," he whispered.

Miserably, she shook her head. Then, for the first time since they met, she saw anger flare in his soft blue eyes. His fist smacked into his knee as he exclaimed, "All these weeks I've smothered my desires for you, thinking you the naive innocent! And now it turns out you've been lying with another man! Who is the scoundrel?"

Getting up, Larissa went to stare out the window, un-able to bear the agony and accusation on his face. With her back to him, she whispered, "I don't see that his iden-tity is any concern of yours."

"Isn't it?" he asked bitterly. "Or is it just that you don't know his identity?"

Angrily, she whirled on him. "I know who he is! It could only be one person. Do you take me for some mindless harlot, sleeping with any man who happens my way?"

Edmund paled, and he cleared his throat uneasily. "I'm sorry, Larissa. I had no right to say anything so cruel. It was just the shock of your revelation. I would never have dreamed—" His voice trailed off, and he cleared his throat once more. When he spoke again, he seemed to have his emotions under control. "Where is the rogue now?"

"In Whampoa, I believe."

"Does he know you're carrying his child?"

"No. And I will never tell him."

"You don't—" He hesitated, then began again, "You don't love him after what he's done to you?"

Her voice was low and hollow. "I despise him."

"Ah. Then can it be—I don't mean to pry—but is it possible he took you against your will?"

"I—he—" she stumbled, not wanting to lie, and finally concluded, "he deceived me." Unable to look at Edmund, Larissa turned back to the window. Hearing his footsteps behind her, she tensed.

She felt his hands rest lightly on her shoulders, and he propped his chin on the top of her head. For a long mo-ment, he was silent, and she trembled, wondering what he was thinking. Finally, he asked, "When will the child be born?"

"November, I think."

"Then I suggest we get married and be on our way to India as soon as possible, before travel becomes too dif-ficult for you."

She froze, certain she could not have heard him correctly, then turned slowly to face him. "I don't understand. Knowing what you do, would you still marry me?"

He shrugged. "You'll need someone to care for you more than ever now. I was stunned and angry at first, but I think I am most angry at the man who did this to you. Nothing can change the fact that I love you. Besides, you still need to get away from that hoppo."

"But the child. How can you accept it when it's not yours?"

He ran a finger gently along her face. "You and I are the only ones who need to know that. It will be born in India, far from the snobbish Macao matrons counting off the months. Knowing it is your child is enough for me. I promise you I will love it like my own. And later we will have other children to share."

Larissa shook her head hopelessly. "There's still something else I have to say. And I don't know how to make you understand. You're the finest man I've ever known, and I wish I could make myself feel differently, but—"

Frowning, he cut her off. "You're going to tell me you don't love me, aren't you?"

She hesitated. "Not exactly. I mean, I do love you, Edmund. But not in the way a wife is supposed to love a husband."

"But you do feel some affection for me, and you—you're sure you don't love the man who fathered your child?"

She nodded mutely.

"Then I ask no more. Sometimes love can grow between two people after marriage. At any rate, I am sure my love for you can only increase over the years to come. I'll make very few demands on you, and even if you don't love me, I think you'll find life with me far easier than life alone with a child." Gently he tilted her head up so her gaze met his. "Now that I've eliminated all your reasons for not marrying me, won't you reconsider, Larissa?"

Gazing into his clear, blue eyes, so filled with compassion and concern, Larissa found herself forgetting all the resolutions she had made before falling asleep the night before. Suddenly, all she could think of was how wonderful it would be to get away from Macao, where she had begun to feel like a prisoner. Perhaps, she thought, it *would* be unfair to force the child to grow up without a father, never to know the kind of closeness she had felt with her own father. She would not be deceiving Edmund if she accepted his proposal now. He knew everything, and he still wanted to marry her. If this good, kind man was so willing to take her as she was, how could she possibly refuse him? She might not love him, but she would surely be much happier going away with him than if she remained on Macao. And he seemed convinced she could make him happy.

Still gazing at him, she took his hands. They felt cold and tense, but with an underlying strength she had not noticed before. It would be so good to surrender herself to someone else's strength and support.

Smiling slowly, she whispered, "If you are so certain, dear Edmund, how can I question your wisdom? You *are* certain you don't wish to reconsider? I mean, you are not willing to marry me now, simply out of pity?"

He shook his head. "I want to marry you for the same reasons I wanted to marry you yesterday. I love you. I want you beside me. Are you telling me you accept my proposal?"

She nodded, ignoring the dim warning bell in the back of her mind that told her she was making a mistake. Smiling broadly, Edmund bent to plant an exuberant kiss on her lips.

Larissa smiled faintly, reaching up to brush a stray lock of hair from his forehead. "I'll try to be the kind of wife you want," she whispered. Then, as a wave of relief washed over her, she collapsed, sobbing, against his chest.

For a long time, he held her quietly. Then he gently unwound her arms from his body and backed away from her. "I would love to hold you for the rest of the day," he murmured, "but we both have a great deal to do and little time in which to do it. We'll be married tomorrow morning at the Episcopal chapel, if you've no objections."

Larissa nodded numbly, still stunned by her decision and the enormous change it would bring to her life.

"Good. I'll go immediately and consult with the priest. By tomorrow evening, we'll be on our way to India aboard the *Sovereign of the Seas*. Upon learning she was departing so soon, I took the liberty of booking passage for both of us, hoping you would accept my proposal.

"Under the circumstances, I think a simple marriage ceremony would be best. If you wish, you may bring a few of your servants to act as attendants and witnesses, but I think it would be preferable not to invite other guests. Later, if you so desire, we can have a more formal celebration in India."

She shook her head. "That isn't necessary."

"Well," he shrugged, "we can discuss that more in the future. For now, I'm off to see the priest. I suppose you'll want to use the rest of the afternoon to pack. But don't worry if you haven't time to pack all your clothes. We can have more made in India. Indeed, we'll have to, as your stomach begins to grow."

There was no time to reconsider. Larissa spent the afternoon and evening packing and preparing for her wedding. When she told Mei Ling of her plans, the servant shook her head disapprovingly. "Mister Farrell seems to be a good man, but I think he is not the man to make you happy. He is not your Nathan."

"Of course he's not Nathan!" Larissa snapped irritably. "Thank heavens for that! Edmund is decent enough to want to marry me, which is more than Nathan would ever do. Nathan deserted me here to bear his child without a second thought."

"Do you not think," Mei Ling said slowly, "that you should at least send a message to him to tell him of the child?"

"Absolutely not! I've already sent him two messages telling him my life was in danger. He didn't care then, and he won't care now. I certainly don't intend to give him the satisfaction of rejecting me again."

Mei Ling sighed and shrugged in resignation. "I think you are wrong. But I also know you are very stubborn. I will not argue with you more, but if you are determined to go to India, I will, of course, come with you."

Larissa stopped folding a dress into her trunk and blinked back tears. "No, Mei Ling. I can't ask you to leave your homeland."

"You did not ask. It is my decision. I cannot allow some strange Indian woman to assist you in the child's birth. You will need someone you know, someone you can depend on."

Dropping the dress, Larissa rushed to embrace her maid. "Oh, Mei Ling," she sobbed, "you are too good!"

"Perhaps," the servant replied matter-of-factly, "but someone must look after you."

Larissa sniffled and pulled away from Mei Ling, regarding her in a new light. During her first months on Macao, she had been too involved with Nathan to think much about her relationship with the older woman. Later, her worries about the hoppo had pushed everything else from her mind. But now she realized she had come to rely on Mei Ling more as a beloved family member than a servant. It would be a great relief to have her beside her as she began her new life.

Forcing a smile, she asked, "Can you tell the others about my decision? I'm afraid I just haven't the strength to face them today. Tell them I will leave enough money for them to get by on until Nathan returns, but, in the meantime, they are free to seek employment elsewhere if they wish."

Nodding, Mei Ling went to make the announcement.

Edmund arrived promptly at nine the next morning to take Larissa to the chapel. She had chosen a pale yellow satin gown with a fitted bodice and fitted sleeves to serve as her wedding gown. Mei Ling had spent more than an hour arranging her hair into an auburn crown, into which she had woven a half dozen yellow lotus blossoms. As he took her arm and led her to the carriage, Edmund smiled fondly. "You look like a love goddess this morning, Larissa."

She blushed. "But you know I'm far too fallible to be any kind of goddess."

Mei Ling and the priest's wife were the only witnesses at the wedding, which lasted less than fifteen minutes. By ten o'clock, they were back in the carriage, and Larissa was staring thoughtfully at the wide, engraved band that proclaimed her Edmund Farrell's wife.

"It was my grandmother's," he explained. "She gave it to me years ago, hoping, I suppose, it would be an incentive to settle down and get married. I've carried it with me on all my travels, waiting for just the right girl to wear it. Now I'm convinced that I've found her, Mrs. Farrell." He kissed her tenderly, then leaned forward to give the driver directions.

Settling back beside her in the carriage, he said, "I hope you won't mind stopping at my house for a moment before we go up to your place. I sent all my trunks ahead to the ship this morning, but I had a little gift for you, and I stupidly left it lying on my bureau. It will only take a moment to fetch it."

"I don't mind," she said, smiling.

As the carriage stopped before his mansion, Edmund turned to her. "Would you like to come in with me?"

"Not unless you really want me to. It seems rather silly for me to just follow you in and out."

He hesitated. "Yes, I suppose you're right. You should be safe for a moment with Mei Ling and the driver. I'll hurry."

Watching him open the door and enter his house, Larissa smiled, thinking how sweet he was to be so concerned about her. As the door closed behind him, she shifted her gaze to the other side of the promenade and recoiled in horror.

Standing not two feet from the open carriage was the hoppo. Bowing stiffly, his hands hidden in his wide, brocade sleeves, he leered at her. "Did you think because I have not visited you in so long I had forgotten about you?"

She stared at him open-mouthed, and her voice caught in her throat.

Smiling evilly, he continued, "You needn't fear, Larissa. I did not forget you. I know all about you. I know, for instance, that today you married the Englishman and you plan to go with him to India. Did you really think you could escape me so easily?"

Larissa glanced back toward the door of the house, wondering what was keeping Edmund. Beside her, Mei Ling was frozen in horror.

"How do you know all this?" Larissa asked hoarsely.

"Did I not warn you that the loyalty of servants can be purchased?"

"What do you mean? Who told you my plans?"

The hoppo shrugged. "In good time, you will know everything. But now we must not delay any longer."

In three steps, he was beside the carriage. He reached out and grasped her wrist, squeezing and twisting as he pulled her roughly toward him.

Determined not to be kidnapped again, Larissa gritted her teeth and hung back, digging the nails of her free hand into the underside of the carriage seat as she tried to resist him. Shaking off her daze, Mei Ling screamed. At the same moment, Larissa heard Edmund's crisp, commanding voice.

"Take your hands off my wife, you filthy Chinaman!"

The hoppo's grasp tightened, and he smiled in amusement as he pulled harder and Larissa's hold on the seat gave way. She felt herself lurching helplessly toward him. Then there was a sharp crack. His green and gold brocade jacket exploded into brilliant red. For an instant, his grasp became even tighter. Then his hand went limp, and he staggered backward, sprawling on the hard rock promenade.

Larissa turned her gaze away from the horrible scene and saw Edmund climbing calmly into the carriage, holding the still-smoking dueling pistol. She closed her eyes and leaned back in the carriage as the world seemed to reel around her. Vaguely, she heard Edmund give directions to the driver and felt the carriage begin to move.

For several minutes, she sat with her eyes tightly closed, breathing deeply. She felt Edmund's arm slide around her shoulders as he whispered softly, "Are you all right, Larissa?"

She nodded, forcing herself to open her eyes and look at him. He seemed totally calm, almost as if the scene in front of his house had never happened. "You—killed him," she whispered, as the full realization finally gripped her.

His arm tightened comfortingly around her shoulder. "I had to, darling. I couldn't let him hurt you any more, and I couldn't bear the thought of him taking you away from me."

"But—shouldn't we do something—report it to somebody? I mean, we just left him lying there."

Edmund's face clouded. "There was nothing we could do for him now. And I doubt that the government would give us a sympathetic hearing, no matter how justified I was. Think, Larissa," he implored. "Under current circumstances, do you really think the Chinese would favor any Englishman over a Chinaman? They demand a life for a life. That means they could demand *my* life. Is that what you want?"

She paled. "Of course not. But this is Portuguese territory. Surely the Portuguese authorities could help you."

"Like they helped you? Make no mistake about it, the Portuguese are little more than puppets of the Chinese. But I must say I don't quite understand your attitude. I fancied myself the knight who slew your dragon, but you're acting as if I'm a common murderer."

"I'm sorry." She smiled faintly and patted his hand. "It was just such a shock to me to see his violent death. Of course I don't blame you for it. After all, at one time I thought I had killed him myself."

"You should not waste another thought on him," Mei Ling broke in. "He was too low even to be considered a man. I know I would not claim him as one of my people. Let him lie in the street and feed his brothers, the rats."

Edmund nodded. "My sentiments exactly. Still, it's probably just as well we're leaving today. I don't think anyone was around the Praya Grande to report what happened, but I wouldn't want to take any chances. As soon as we get to your house, we'll load your belongings and go on to the ship. Once we're aboard, no one can touch us. The British captain won't surrender one of his countrymen to the Chinese."

Larissa sighed. "All right. All I want now is to get away from this dreadful place."

"Oh! In all the excitement, I forgot," he said, then shoved a flat leather box into her hands. "This is what I stopped to pick up. Open it, darling."

With shaking hands, Larissa opened the box to reveal a sapphire pendant in a rose-gold setting. It was one of the most exquisite pieces of jewelry she had ever seen, but she felt too numb to fully appreciate it.

"It's a family heirloom," Edmund said. "Now that you're my wife, I wanted you to have it."

Forcing a smile, she whispered, "It's lovely, darling. I'll be very proud to wear it."

When they opened the door of Larissa's house, they found the servants in an uproar. All of them seemed to be crowded into the dining room and parlor, chattering distractedly in Chinese. A number of the women were gathered around Sun Yuan's mother, who was huddled in a corner of the parlor, wailing inconsolably. Hardly anyone noticed when Larissa, Edmund, and Mei Ling entered.

Turning to Mei Ling, Larissa saw her maid pale with horror as she picked up some of the words drifting around her. "What's the matter? What are they talking about?" she demanded.

Mei Ling swallowed uneasily. "I'm not sure. I will find

out." She pushed her way to the group surrounding Sun Yuan's mother and began questioning them in Chinese, her face growing graver by the second.

Beside her, Edmund gently squeezed Larissa's elbow and whispered solicitously, "All this excitement can't be good for you, darling, or for the baby. Why don't you show me where your trunks are, and I'll start loading them. In the meantime, perhaps it would be good for you to rest in the quiet of your room."

Nodding numbly, she led him to her bedroom and indicated two trunks, a portmanteau, and a valise. As he hefted one of the trunks to his shoulder, she threw herself across her bed, worried about the disturbance among the servants. It occurred to her that Sun Yuan had not been in the group surrounding his mother, which was strange since he was so devoted to her. Could it be that the problem involved Sun Yuan? Edmund had already taken the second trunk and was leaving the room with the portmanteau and valise when Mei Ling entered.

The servant waited until she heard Edmund's footsteps receding down the hall, then whispered, "The news is most unpleasant, mistress. I doubt whether I should tell you in your condition."

"If you don't tell me, I shall simply imagine the worst," Larissa said wearily. "So, I think it would be best for me to know the truth. Does it concern Sun Yuan?"

Mei Ling nodded.

"Well, out with it! Is he injured? Is he in some sort of trouble or danger? How can I help him?"

"You cannot help him," Mei Ling hesitated, shuffling nervously. "Sun Yuan is dead."

"Dead?" Larissa fell back against her pillows, feeling the color drain from her face. "It can't be! He was young, strong—"

"They found him less than an hour ago, hanging from the door frame of the kitchen. It seems he took his own life."

"But why would he do that?"

"Because he felt responsible for the unhappiness he saw in you. Because he felt he had betrayed you."

"Betrayed me?" Larissa thought of the young man who had always seemed so ready to please her. "How could he have betrayed me? That makes absolutely no sense."

Mei Ling perched on the edge of the bed and gazed at Larissa unhappily. "This morning before he took his life, he told his mother everything. It seems that evil man had a hold on him."

"You mean—the hoppo?" Larissa whispered incredulously.

"Yes," Mei Ling nodded. "He knew the boy was devoted to his mother, and he threatened to kill her if Sun Yuan did not cooperate with him. Only last night, fearing for his mother's welfare, he told that man about your marriage and your plans to leave Macao."

"So that's how the hoppo knew," Larissa mused. Suddenly, she recalled that day in the parlor when Sun Yuan had convinced her the hoppo had not intercepted her messages to Nathan. "How long had the hoppo had Sun Yuan under his power?" she asked urgently.

Mei Ling shrugged. "At least since March, it appears. The boy always thought that in the end the authorities would catch the hoppo, or that Mr. Masters would return to save you. But after last night, he began to fear—"

Larissa was only half listening as her mind fastened on the details of her two attempted messages to Nathan. Remembering how Sun Yuan had begged her to believe him, she understood suddenly why he had seemed so wretched. It was not, as she had assumed then, because she had questioned his loyalty. It was because he felt uncomfortable lying to her, but he was convinced he had to lie to protect his mother!

"But of course," she murmured. "Why was I so blind? It was easy to buy off Lin Po with drink and prostitutes. With Sun Yuan the hoppo had to use a different tactic, so he played on the boy's loyalty to his mother. For the hoppo, the results were the same, but how poor Sun Yuan must have agonized!"

Then the full impact of her discovery overwhelmed her: Nathan had never received her messages! Nathan had never rejected her—he had never had the opportunity. And now she was carrying his child, married to another man, and about to leave for another country.

"Oh, Mei Ling!" she wailed, "I'm afraid I've made a terrible mistake! Perhaps the worst mistake of my life." She rolled on her stomach, burying her face in her pillows, wanting Nathan, needing him.

"Larissa?" Edmund's gentle voice penetrated her fog of grief and despair. "Your bags are all taken care of, so I think it would be best for us to go."

"Go?" she repeated dumbly. No, she thought wildly, she couldn't go. She wouldn't. This was her home. Hers and Nathan's. She had to remain. She had to be there when he returned.

Grasping at straws, she rolled to her side and looked at Mei Ling. "What about Sun Yuan? He must be buried properly. I'll have to be present. What would all the servants think of me if I left without taking care of him? After all, the poor, misguided boy died because of me."

Edmund stared at her strangely, and Mei Ling shook her head. "They will understand if you go. The family will want to have private ceremonies, things you could not participate in. I think you should go with your husband. After what happened on the Praya Grande, it is important that you do not tarry."

"No, I can't leave—" She cut herself off as her gaze swept across the room to Edmund. Standing in the doorway, his face creased in confusion, his sandy hair falling boyishly across his forehead, he looked so vulnerable.

For a long, silent moment, she stared at him, forcing herself to digest the facts. He was her husband now. He cared for her. He loved her so much that he had not hesitated to kill a man for her. Now, every moment that she delayed might be putting his life in danger.

His eyes met hers, and she knew what she had to do. She sat up and smoothed her dress. "All right, Edmund," she whispered in a thin, hollow voice. "We'll leave immediately."

Part Three

�֍

1840-1842

Chapter Sixteen

Standing at the rail of the *Sovereign of the Seas,* watching Macao shrink into the distance, Larissa tried to convince herself that she was doing the right thing. After all, she told herself, no matter how much Nathan said he loved her, no matter how much he truly did love her, he had made his views on marriage quite clear. And despite her thoughts a few nights earlier, she supposed it really would not do to saddle a child with illegitimacy, which could mark him or her for life. She might be able to resign herself to living with Nathan without being married, but it really would be unfair to the child.

She had no doubts that Edmund loved her. He had brushed aside her past and married her anyway, when most men of breeding would have dropped her without a second thought. Within minutes after their marriage, he had killed a man in her defense. He had not even questioned her about her strange behavior at the house. The best thing she could do would be to forget Nathan and devote herself wholly to the man who had made her his wife. Perhaps being far away in India would help her to forget. She need not worry about Nathan. He would find someone else. No doubt he had had a score of mistresses before her.

As the sky began to darken to twilight, she felt Edmund beside her. He slid an arm protectively around her shoulders as he bent to whisper in her ear. "It's been a long and difficult day, darling. Don't you think you should come below now and rest?"

"Yes, I suppose so." Despite her answer, her grip tightened on the rail, and she continued to stare at the reflection of the rising moon in the China Sea. After all her nights with Nathan, it seemed silly to feel reticent about her wedding night. But she realized suddenly that she did. She was not afraid of disappointing her new husband by knowing too little. Rather, she was afraid she might shock him because she knew too much, and she wondered just how she should react to his advances. She had placed her future in his hands, and she did not want to displease him. She wondered just what he expected of her.

His voice broke into her thoughts. "You're trembling! Are you so afraid of me, Larissa? Remember, I love you, and I most assuredly will not hurt you."

"I know that, Edmund, and I'm not afraid of you. It's just that my life is changing so rapidly—I had scarcely become accustomed to China, and now I'm off to another strange land. I suppose I can't help being a bit fearful."

"I understand. But you must always remember that I will always be beside you to protect you and care for you. No doubt you will find some aspects of your new life difficult to adjust to, but you are my wife now, and I am confident that together we can handle whatever adversity comes our way."

Forcing a smile, she turned and put her arms around his neck. She stood on tiptoe to plant a quick kiss on his cheek. "Let's go below," she said evenly. "I'm very fortunate to be married to someone so wise." Perhaps, she thought fleetingly, if she said that often enough, she could blot out any further thoughts of Nathan.

In their cabin, she quickly discovered that her fears had been ill-founded. After watching her hesitantly begin to unfasten her dress, Edmund suddenly announced he had forgotten to finish some business with the captain. He left, saying he would be back in a few moments. By the time he returned, she had finished undressing, donned her white lawn nightgown, and slid beneath the covers. He stood by the cabin door for a moment, gazing at her and smiling wistfully. Sighing, he extinguished the cabin's solitary lamp.

She lay tensely, listening to him undress in the darkness. The mattress sagged as he sat down beside her on the bunk, then swung his legs up and lay back. His hands felt warm and damp with perspiration as they explored her body and pulled her close to him.

"Oh, Larissa," he murmured, "I've wanted this moment from the first time I saw you on the Praya Grande.

I've wanted to know you in the most intimate way a man can know a woman, and now, at last, I shall have my wish. We shall be one, my darling, for the rest of our lives."

She squirmed slightly, wishing he would go ahead with the act, that he would get it over with. She had never wanted him in this way. She had told him that, and she could not bring herself to lie now in response to his words. Still, it made her uncomfortable to listen to his sentiments and say nothing.

He sighed, a long sigh, full of frustrated desires. "There is nothing I would like more than to bring my love for you to realization tonight. But I would hate myself for the rest of my life if I did anything to hurt you or the child growing inside you. So I must be content to wait a few months more, knowing you are mine and dreaming of the sweet reward at the end of my wait. For now, just let me hold you, my darling. Let me hold you and dream."

She relaxed against him, letting him draw her closer. With the threat removed, or at least postponed far in the future, she could enjoy the warm security of his arms encircling her. She nestled her cheek against the softly matted hair of his chest and breathed in the comforting odor of his body. Within moments, he was sleeping contentedly, his chest rising and falling rhythmically beneath her ear. She felt a tear slide down her cheek as she thought that she was, indeed, fortunate to have Edmund for a husband, and she would be a fool ever to doubt that fact.

They sailed southwest through the China Sea, then turned north through the straits between Malaya and Sumatra and on into the Indian Ocean. Within less than a month, they had entered the Bay of Bengal and were gliding up the treacherous Hooghly River to Calcutta.

Mei Ling, whose stomach had been less than enchanted with its first ocean voyage, was delighted to learn they would soon be disembarking. Larissa was inclined to agree with her maid's sentiments, since the monsoon season had already begun, and the last several days of the voyage had been particularly rough. Edmund pointed out to both of them that they had been extremely fortunate not to encounter any typhoons, at which Mei Ling rolled her eyes and suggested it might have been easier to perish early in the voyage, rather than endure the whole trip.

Throughout the voyage, Edmund had been extremely attentive and solicitous, but as they neared the end of the eighty-six-mile journey upriver to Calcutta, Larissa noted that he seemed to become more and more agitated. She supposed that he must be anxious to get back to his estate and learn how productive it had been in his absence.

It occurred to her that she knew very little about her husband's business. In all their time together, he had volunteered almost no information about his work. She knew he was a trader, indeed a very prosperous one to afford a home on Macao's Praya Grande, but she had no idea what products he dealt in or what his estate produced.

As they packed their bags in preparation for disembarking, Larissa remarked casually, "Don't you think you should give me some briefing about your work, Edmund? As your wife, it seems I should know a bit more than I do now. I mean, it could be embarrassing if I became involved in a conversation with one of your colleagues and displayed my total ignorance."

He shrugged. "That hardly seems likely to happen. We'll be in Calcutta only a day or two before continuing on to Patna, so you won't have time for more than trivial conversation with most people you meet. Besides, a woman's not expected to be well versed on business matters. I'm an agent of the British East India Company, and I manage the estate under their direction. Beyond that, there's little you need to know."

Larissa was annoyed by his evasiveness, but she did not press him further. In time, she supposed, he would learn to be more open with her. At any rate, no matter how little he told her, she would eventually learn about his business just by living on the estate. A moment later, the ship slowed, and she quickly accepted Edmund's suggestion that they go up on deck for her first view of Calcutta.

The air was stiflingly humid, but she was fortunate enough to view the city unhampered by any of the seasonal downpours. Like Macao, the city combined European with Eastern architecture. One of the first sights to catch her eye was the soaring spire of the Neo-Gothic St. Paul's Cathedral. The cathedral shared the skyline with the minarets of a mosque and, further in the distance, a Hindu temple.

Edmund shepherded Larissa and Mei Ling off the
Sovereign of the Seas and hailed two rickshaws waiting
near the docks. He installed Mei Ling in one of them,
along with Larissa's valise, and gave the Indian pulling the
conveyance instructions. Then he helped Larissa into the
other and climbed in beside her. She watched in amazement as their Indian coolie, dressed in a simple white
robe tied up above his knees, grasped the poles extending
from the rickshaw and trotted forward, pulling them behind.

"Isn't this terribly difficult for him?" she whispered to
Edmund.

He shrugged, "He seems not to think so. Besides, he
makes his living this way."

Within moments they were traveling past a large, well-
groomed park, dotted with palms, teak, and tamarind
trees, heavy with red-streaked yellow flowers and brown
seed pods. Gardens of roses, heliotrope, jasmine, and scarlet hibiscus also decorated the area.

"It's called the Maidan," Edmund explained as she exclaimed at the grandeur of the park. "Oddly enough, all
this beauty came about as the result of military calcula-
tions. At one time the whole area was jungle. Sixty years
ago, when our government rebuilt Fort William, General
Clive decided our cannon needed a clear field of fire, so
he had the area cleared."

Looking beyond the gardens, Larissa shivered at the
sight of Fort William's protruding bronze cannon. "You
needn't worry," Edmund chuckled. "They've never been
used, except for ceremonial occasions. And the Maidan
has become the pride of Calcutta. It's the favorite rec-
reational area for British and Indians alike. We've even
built a racecourse at the far end."

Larissa settled back and enjoyed the view of the Maidan
on her right and the sprawling white government buildings
on the left. Edmund explained that the domed government house was modeled after an English hall built in the
last century. Two blocks beyond, on Dalhousie Square,
stood Writer's Building, headquarters for the clerks of
the East India Company.

The rickshaw turned right at Chowringhee Road, at the
southern edge of the Maidan. As they passed elegant
shops, restaurants, and theaters, Larissa began to imagine
she was in one of the fashionable districts of London. But

a glance at the street traffic, where cows wandered freely among women clad in bright silk saris and men in *dhotis,* the white cotton garment of the rickshaw coolie, reminded her that she was, indeed, in India.

"Doesn't anyone tend those animals?" she whispered to Edmund as she watched a cow lie down in the street, forcing traffic to go around it.

"Cows are sacred to the Hindus," he replied, "so they are free to do whatever they please. You'll soon become accustomed to it."

They stopped before a tall stucco building, where Edmund helped her out of the rickshaw and turned to help Mei Ling out of hers. Explaining that this was one of Calcutta's finest hotels, he led them into an impressive lobby and reserved a suite. The rooms were spacious and spotless, furnished with English furniture of the Queen Anne style and lavish velvet draperies.

"After all those days aboard ship, it's exquisite!" Larissa exclaimed, spinning around happily. "I must admit it's not at all what I expected Calcutta to be like."

"And what was that?" Edmund asked, looking amused.

"Oh, rather dirty, dingy, crawling with all sorts of vermin." She laughed self-consciously. "At home in Boston they say you can always tell when a ship from Calcutta's arrived—because all the dogs in town are seen fleeing from the wharves, pursued by an army of the largest, meanest cockroaches in existence."

He smiled indulgently. "I can assure you some parts of the city might meet your expectations. But we'll confine ourselves to the British section." He paused, then added pensively, "Enjoy your stay here. I'm afraid you'll find some of the villages between here and Patna less satisfactory. But I promise you, you will find the estate well worth the trouble of the trip."

Larissa nodded thoughtfully, hoping the trip would not prove too harrowing, then asked, "Do you think it would be possible for me to have a bath? I feel so gritty from this humid weather."

"Of course, darling. I'll order one for you on the way out."

"You're going out so soon?"

Edmund nodded apologetically. "I really must go over and check in at the office. You'll be perfectly safe as long as you remain in the room, and the rest will do you good.

I made arrangements for the ship to send over our trunks, so you can expect them within the hour. I suspect I'll be detained at Writer's Building for a number of hours, so I'll ask the hotel staff to send up some supper for you and Mei Ling."

"I'd rather wait and eat with you, whenever you return."

"No," he shook his head, "that would never do. It's important for a woman in your condition to eat at regular hours, and I'm afraid I might be dreadfully late."

She frowned, and he went to put his arms around her. "Come now, darling, give me a smile before I leave. I'm sorry it has to be this way your first evening in India, but you'll have Mei Ling, so you won't be alone. Besides, the sooner I get everything taken care of, the sooner we can finish our trip and get settled at the estate."

Forcing a smile, Larissa said, "All right, but promise you'll get back as soon as possible. After my past experiences, I can't help feeling edgy in a strange place, no matter how English it is."

"I give you my word." Lightly kissing the tip of her upturned nose, he left.

Edmund did not return until almost midnight. Mei Ling had long ago retired to her own small, adjoining room for a good night's sleep, but Larissa continued to pace uneasily, plagued by a feeling that something was wrong. She had eaten very little of her dinner, a rice and chicken combination, heavily spiced with curry and cardamon, and now her stomach was beginning to growl in protest. She was standing by the window, hoping to catch some bay breeze that would alleviate the stifling atmosphere, when the door finally opened and Edmund entered.

He smiled jovially, apparently oblivious to her agitation. "Did you have a pleasant evening?" he inquired lightly.

"Not particularly," she replied somewhat tartly, "but it appears you did. You seem quite pleased with yourself."

She flinched and frowned as he giggled, sounding almost like a giddy schoolgirl. "Yes, well, I did have a rather pleasant reunion with some of the old chaps."

He paused, as her displeasure finally registered. "Oh, now, darling, surely you can't be angry with me? I warned you I would be late, and I can assure you you wouldn't have enjoyed the evening at all. It was strictly a man's sort of gathering."

"I'm sure it was," she said, turning away in annoyance as she quickly concluded that he and his cronies had passed the last several hours drinking heavily, while she fretted in the hotel room.

He crossed the room to her, sliding his arms around her middle and pulling her back against him. "Tell me," he whispered, "what's bothering you? Was it so terrible to be without me these hours?"

"Of course not. I was just worried, afraid something had happened to you."

"Impossible!" he exclaimed. "India may look strange to you, but it's British territory. I'm as safe here as I would be on the streets of London!"

Larissa tensed, wondering how he could minimize the dangers so casually when only hours earlier he had spoken of India's less savory aspects. She supposed drinking had made him euphoric, but it suddenly occurred to her that she could not smell any alcohol on his breath. Turning in his arms, she gazed into his eyes, recoiling slightly when she noted their glassy appearance and how tiny, almost like pinpoints, his pupils were. Absently, she reached up to brush a lock of hair from his face, expecting to feel his forehead hot with fever. When it felt quite normal, she frowned in confusion.

"Edmund," she asked gently, "are you feeling quite all right?"

"I feel splendid!" he replied, lifting her off her feet and twirling her around. "Why do you ask?"

"Your eyes—"

"What about my eyes?" He laughed nervously. "Have they suddenly changed color? Have they fallen out of my head? Strange, I can still see!"

"Oh, never mind." Larissa sighed wearily, convinced she could not get him to be serious. "Let's just go to bed."

"Now, that sounds to me like a sterling suggestion!" Swinging her into his arms, he carried her to the bed.

The next morning, Larissa felt certain her anxieties and agitation had made her imagine the whole incident. Perhaps Edmund had only seemed so euphoric and insensible in contrast to her own agitation. Perhaps she had imagined the strange appearance of his eyes. At any rate,

he seemed quite in control of himself that morning. He
was up and dressed before she even awoke, and he entered the room carrying a tray of warm muffins and tea
just as she sat up to stretch.

Setting the tray across her legs, he leaned down to
kiss her forehead and said, "Eat quickly, darling, we've a
lot to do today."

She stared at his eyes as he stood up, noting that they
looked completely normal. "Is something wrong, Larissa?"
he asked.

"No." She shook her head and quickly bit into a muffin.
"Just what have you planned for today?"

"The start of our journey to Patna."

She blinked in surprise. "So soon? I thought you intended to stay in Calcutta a few days."

"I did, originally, but the fellows at Writer's Building
convinced me we ought to take advantage of the fair
weather and start for the estate as quickly as possible. The
monsoons appear to be a bit late here, so we may be lucky
enough to be able to sail up the Ganges before it floods.
Once the rains really start, it could become unnavigable.
We can see more of Calcutta another time, but in your
present condition, I think it really would be best to get
you settled on the estate as soon as possible."

"Of course. Whatever you think best. I'm anxious to
see the end of all this traveling, too."

While Larissa ate and dressed, Edmund removed their
baggage. By the time Mei Ling had finished combing Larissa's hair, Edmund had returned to take them to the river.
A carriage was waiting for them outside the hotel and
quickly transported them past the Maidan and Fort William to the muddy Hooghly River.

On the banks of the Hooghly, flights of irregular stone
steps, some of them wide enough to be terraces, led to the
water's edge. There, a long, low wooden boat lay moored,
their belongings already stowed aboard.

Edmund smiled apologetically. "It's not the *Sovereign
of the Seas,* I'm afraid, but it shouldn't be too uncomfortable." He pointed to a snug cabin at the bow of the
boat. "You can rest there, darling, during most of the trip.
At least it should provide a smoother journey than if we
went overland by elephant."

At that, Mei Ling rolled her eyes and scrambled aboard,
anxious to show how pleased she was with the accommo-

dations. Laughing, Larissa followed. A young Indian dressed in a dhoti, his head swathed in an immaculate white turban, also climbed aboard. Edmund introduced him as Banerjee, their Bengali pilot. Together, the two men hoisted the boat's single sail, and they set off northwest up the Hooghly.

Before the day was over, they had reached the main arm of the Ganges River and continued their journey up that sacred river of the Hindus. Along the way, Larissa noticed many flights of stone steps and terraces lining the water's edge, similar to the steps in Calcutta. Often she saw people standing or squatting on the steps, bathing.

Banerjee, who spoke perfect English, having been educated at the Hindu College built by the British in Calcutta, explained that the stone landings were called *ghats*. The people had built them, he said, expressly for bathing, since Hindus were required to bathe before saying their daily prayers. Since the Ganges was the sacred river, it had also become the most sacred bathing place. Many Hindus believed that bathing in the Ganges brought purity, wealth, and fertility.

For ten days they traveled upriver, past small villages of mud huts, and except for an occasional light shower, they encountered no rain. Every day and every night, Edmund expressed thankfulness for that fact, until Larissa began to wonder what could be so terrible about a little rainstorm. On the eleventh day, her wondering came to an abrupt end.

When they began sailing that morning, the sky was clear and blue, and it remained that way for several hours. Then early in the afternoon, white fleecy clouds began to dot the sky. Within moments, the clouds thickened, changing from white to gray, until the whole sky was covered with a gloomy, black mass. A flash of yellow-orange cracked the sky above the flat plain, and the heavens roared. Before Banerjee could begin to guide the boat to the shore, the skies opened, and they were pelted with torrents of rain. Edmund quickly helped Larissa and Mei Ling into the small cabin, where they huddled together, listening as pebble-sized raindrops drummed insistently on the roof.

Within moments, the boat was filling with water, and the cabin was flooding. Around them, the Ganges was rising, swirling furiously with mud and sand. Struggling together, Edmund and Banerjee were unable to control the boat. It scudded helplessly in the power of the wind and rain, while thunder and lightning continued to crackle around them. Standing ankle-deep in water, Banerjee fought his way to the mast to try to haul down the tattered sail. As he raised his arms to grasp it, his face froze convulsively, and he uttered a strangled moan. His body went limp, and he collapsed in the rising water. Afterwards, Larissa swore she had seen a bolt of yellow light reach from the heavens to claim him.

She saw Edmund kneel beside the Bengali, then shake his head and rise beside the mast. Watching him lift his arms toward the sail, she hurled herself from the cabin and screamed, "No!" With a sudden burst of strength, she grabbed his arms and wrestled them back to his side.

Eyes wide, he stared at her as if she had gone mad. "Larissa," he shouted above the storm, "the sail's got to come down! Otherwise, we'll never escape the wind. Go back to the cabin."

"No!" she sobbed. "I won't let you kill yourself! I saw what happened to Banerjee."

"We could all be killed if I don't get this boat under control! What happened to Banerjee was an unfortunate fluke. Now, let go of me. You've got to let me do this!"

Even as he tried to shake her off, the thunder boomed again, and there was an intense burst of light around them. With a resounding crack, the mast split down the middle. Edmund's arm swept her out of the path of the falling timber, and she clung to him, sobbing like a frightened baby. In the same instant, a scream rent the air, and they whirled to see that the other half of the mast had smashed the cabin roof.

"Mei Ling!" Larissa shrieked, rushing toward the crumbled structure. She tripped over a broken scrap of wood and felt Edmund catch her from behind. As she paused to regain her balance, the rubble of the cabin began to move, and Mei Ling emerged, shaken, but unhurt, smiling bravely.

Her smile faded in the next moment as a violent gust of wind caught the crippled craft, sending it spinning dizzily until it smashed into the bank. The boat shuddered, and for one agonizing instant, Larissa thought they would remain afloat. Then the wind slammed it against the bank again, and she found herself floundering in a whirl-ing mass of water, wood, and rock.

Edmund pulled Larissa to him. Holding her close, he lifted her out of the angry, muddy waters of the Ganges. As she felt him climbing stairs, she realized they had crashed into one of the river's innumerable ghats. He seemed to climb forever, until finally he collapsed with her on the muddy bank.

Larissa lay still, panting and miserable as the rain con-tinued to pelt her. Her mind struggled to make some or-der of the last several minutes. She felt Edmund move over her, attempting to shield her body with his own, and suddenly she remembered her poor maid.

"Mei Ling?" she asked weakly.

Edmund sighed and replied slowly, "I don't know, dar-ling. All I could think of was getting you to safety."

"Mei Ling!" she repeated frantically, struggling to sit up. "We've got to find her!"

Edmund caught her, holding her back as she tried to stand. "I won't let you go back down there, darling."

"I have to, I have to find her! She gave up her home for me! I won't desert her, no matter what!"

Firmly, he pushed her back down. Leaning over her, he said, "I'll go and look for her. But only if you promise not to move. I can't risk losing you down there."

"But—"

"No arguments." He lay a finger across her lips and leaned closer to brush his mouth across her forehead. "I'll be back as soon as I can."

Larissa sat up and watched until he was lost from view, hidden behind a murky curtain of raindrops. She watched and waited, feeling cold, weak, helpless, and sorry she had ever come to India. She wondered if the child inside her— Nathan's child—could survive the ordeal. Indeed, could any of them survive? Shielding her eyes with her hand, she tilted back her head and glanced toward the heavens. The sky was still a savage black, and the rain showed no sign of letting up. Perhaps they would all drown before they even found sanctuary. Perhaps that would be best.

The minutes passed with agonizing slowness as she waited for Edmund and Mei Ling. The rain intensified and the sky grew blacker, until it was impossible to see more than a few feet ahead. Larissa shivered in cold and fear, wondering how Edmund would find her again. After what seemed an interminable wait, she heard the sound of running feet. As she peered into the darkness, Edmund collapsed beside her, dropping Mei Ling to the ground between them.

Larissa threw herself on her servant, overwhelmed with joy to find her still alive. "Oh, Mei Ling!" she cried, "are you all right?"

"Yes, yes," Mei Ling assured her softly. "Only a few scratches and bruises. In a few days I will be fully mended."

A deep, wracking cough drew Larissa's attention to her husband, sprawled on the muddy bank. "And you, Edmund," she asked, gently stroking his cheek, "are you all right?"

He grasped her hand and drew a deep, heaving breath. "I will be, darling. Just give me a moment or two, and I will be."

Since the boat had crashed on a bathing ghat, they knew they must be near a village. But they soon found that little of the settlement remained. Near the shoreline, only mud and scattered rubble marked where crude shacks had stood. A few people wandered among the ruins, lamenting their lost homes, but most had fled to higher grounds at the first threat of flooding. The natives were accustomed to the monsoon's habit of washing away entire villages, and they had learned to value their lives and the lives of their animals above property.

Edmund guided Larissa and Mei Ling away from the river until they stumbled upon a partial shack, which would provide at least some shelter for the night. The abandoned shack was completely unfurnished, so they were forced to sleep huddled together on the cold, damp earthen floor, without even a blanket to warm their aching bodies. In the morning, when the rains had subsided, he scavenged the town for food. After an unsatisfying breakfast of rain-soaked bread and soured goat's milk, they set off on foot toward Patna. At first, Edmund tried to carry Larissa in his arms, but after only a few minutes, she insisted on walking.

"You'll tire yourself too quickly," she said reasonably, "and the trip will take longer than ever. I'd rather walk beside you and reach Patna as soon as we can."

"But your condition is too delicate," he protested, "the baby—"

Flinching, she cut him off sharply. "If the baby survived last night, I'm sure a bit of walking won't harm it. At any rate, only time will tell."

Seeing the hurt look in his eyes, Larissa was immediately sorry for her harshness. She knew he had suffered more than she in the last day, castigating himself for bringing her on so treacherous a journey.

Last night, after her initial relief that they had all survived, she had had to bite back bitter words of accusation. He should have warned her what to expect before they ever left Macao. She felt deceived and cheated, thinking she could still be in her secure house on Macao, waiting for Nathan to return. But, then, if she hadn't married Edmund, the hoppo would still be alive to threaten her, and she would still be facing the prospect of bringing an illegitimate child into the world. She owed Edmund a great deal, and it would be cruel and ungrateful to add to his suffering. She could not love him with the passion due from a wife, but she could at least be careful to spare him her contempt.

As he set her on her feet, she patted his arm affectionately. "I'm sorry, Edmund. I guess I'm still a bit overwrought from yesterday's events. But it's unforgivable to take it out on you."

He smiled sadly. "Never mind. Once we get to the estate, everything will be all right."

"Of course." She forced herself to return his smile, but she knew in her heart that she was only trying to deceive herself. She could work hard to make Edmund happy, but nothing in their marriage could really be right until she managed to forget Nathan. And how could she do that while she carried his child? Perhaps it would be best for all concerned if the child did not survive. No, she told herself firmly, she must never even think that. She had committed herself to Edmund, so she could never have Nathan, but she could have his child, and she would treasure that child, even while she struggled to honor her marriage vows.

For three days they plodded west on the banks of the Ganges, past village after village that had been washed away by the monsoons. The surviving villagers generously shared their meager food and shelter with the weary travelers. But they had no horses or mules to offer to speed their journey, and Edmund said it would be madness to build a boat and take to the treacherous, swollen river again.

Rain fell for a portion of each day, though never with the fury of that first storm. If they were near a village, they stopped to find shelter. Otherwise, they continued, learning to ignore the rain as they pressed toward their goal.

On the third day, Edmund, Larissa, and Mei Ling were plodding along, eyes downcast as the rain pelted their backs. Wearily, Larissa raised her head to squint into the distance. She stopped, focusing on a weird structure on the horizon. It swept skyward in tiers, shaped like a giant beehive. So mystified was she by the structure, that she failed even to notice the five-domed mosque rising beyond it.

Hurrying to catch up with Edmund, she touched his arm and pointed at the beehive structure. "What is it?" she asked.

His eyes followed her pointing finger, and he squinted for a moment. Then a joyful grin spread across his face. "It's the Golghar!" he exclaimed. "The granary Hastings had built after the last great famine. And beyond that is the Sher Shahi Mosque. They're landmarks of Patna, darling! We've almost made it!"

Chapter Seventeen

It was nearly dark when they stumbled into the city. They went directly to the Governor's Palace, a spacious, imposing neoclassical building. For the first time since the accident, Larissa felt embarrassed by her tattered dress. She felt even the lowliest servant must look more worthy than she of the gracious palace. But the governor's wife, a pert little British woman named Margaret, immediately put her at ease.

While Governor Pinckney received Edmund, Margaret ushered Larissa and Mei Ling up the sweeping marble staircase to a spacious suite. She ordered a hot bath for both women and set about finding some fresh clothing for them. Larissa found the pale green silk gown Margaret gave her a bit tight and a trifle short, but she was grateful for the feeling of clean, fresh clothing against her skin. Since their hostess had no Chinese clothes, Mei Ling accepted a blue cotton dress. Larissa suppressed a smile at her first view of her servant in Western garb.

Explaining that the men would, no doubt, be occupied with business for some time, Margaret had a late supper brought up to the suite. Bidding them good night, she left Larissa and Mei Ling to eat and retire.

Luxuriating in the feeling of a real bed with crisp, clean sheets, Larissa fell asleep long before Edmund stumbled into the room. She awoke to hear him moving about in the dark, bumping into the furniture as he undressed.

"You can light a lamp if you wish, Edmund," she whispered drowsily.

"Huh? Oh, sorry darling, I was hoping I wouldn't wake you." His speech was slightly slurred, as if he had downed too much of the governor's brandy.

"Well, I'm quite awake now, so I wish you'd light a lamp before you stumble and break something."

"All right." She heard him fumbling with the flint, and then the lamp on the bedside table flared up.

"What time is it?" Larissa asked, shielding her eyes behind a pillow.

"About two thirty."

"In the morning?" She threw the pillow aside and peered at him in surprise. "I should think the governor would have taken pity on you and let you retire a bit earlier after our grueling journey."

Edmund shrugged sheepishly. "Oh, the governor retired at eleven, but I had some business to attend to at the company office."

"So late? Couldn't it have waited until the morning?"

"No," he replied shortly as he climbed into bed beside her.

Concerned, Larissa watched him, noting the unusual appearance of his eyes. They looked like they had that night in Calcutta when he had acted so giddy. Deliberately, she leaned toward him and kissed him full on the mouth, but she found neither the smell nor taste of liquor on his breath. She looked puzzled.

"Whatever is the matter?" he asked.

"Nothing—I—are you feeling all right, Edmund?"

"Of course." He pulled away from her abruptly and snuffed out the lamp. "I'm just a bit tired. I need a good night's rest."

"Then go to sleep," she said gently, reaching out to pat him in the dark. She tried to settle back down to sleep, but her mind was gripped by a strange certainty that her husband was suffering from more than exhaustion. As he tossed beside her, she thought again of that night in Calcutta. Whenever he spent an evening with other men from the company, something strange happened to him. If only she knew what it was.

The next morning, just as in Calcutta, Edmund seemed perfectly normal. Instructing Larissa to rest through the morning, he went out and purchased a huge selection of fabrics so she could have a new wardrobe made at the estate. In the afternoon, he brought a doctor back to the palace, who examined Larissa and pronounced her remarkably strong and sound. To both Edmund's and Larissa's relief, he predicted that the baby would be just as healthy as its mother.

They stayed a second night at the palace and departed the next morning for the estate. As the carriage the governor had loaned them rolled toward the estate, Edmund explained a bit about the area and its inhabitants. "We're out of Bengal now, and into the province of Bihar. You'll find the region has a great number of Moslems, though Hindus are common too, and we've imported a good deal of Bengali labor. Most of the land here is managed by native *zamindars*, landlords who collect the rent and keep the farmers under control. Until recently, my estate was no exception, but the local zamindar became a bit swellheaded and hard to control, and so the company removed him and asked me to oversee operations for a bit."

Suppressing a sigh of relief, Larissa asked, "Then your position here is only temporary?"

He shrugged. "One might say so. I've lived here off and on for the last three years, and I've no doubt the company would gladly allow me to manage it in perpetuity. But, charming as I find the pastoral life, I inevitably begin to pine for the excitement of trade. Of course, if you fall in love with the area—"

"You needn't worry," Larissa said, smiling. "So far I've found India less than enchanting."

Her first glimpse of the estate almost made her retract her words. The main building, which could only be described as a palace, was set back several hundred yards from the Ganges so it would never be threatened by floods. It was an octagonal building of creamy white marble, topped in the center by a pointed dome. Four smaller gilt domes surrounded the main dome, and the building was fronted by a pillared pavilion of pointed arches, each edged in gilt. As the carriage drew nearer, she could see that the walls of the pavilion were decorated with intricately painted tiles.

Edmund smiled as she drew in her breath in awe. "I told you it would be worth the trip."

"Well, it's certainly no ordinary house!" she exclaimed, staring transfixed at the marble domes.

"No. The original owner was obviously one of the chief nawabs of the Mogul Empire. But this is nothing. Wait until you see the sculptured gardens. Perhaps now you can understand why I was never truly able to describe the place to—"

"Edmund!" His words were cut short by a shrill cry of joy. A slim, dark young woman, dressed in an apricot silk sari, her arms and ankles glistening with golden bracelets, a dark red spot of rouge accenting the center of her forehead, rushed out of the pavilion. She had almost reached the carriage when she caught sight of Larissa and stopped abruptly.

Flushing, Edmund climbed out of the carriage and helped Larissa and Mei Ling to alight. "Darling," he said smoothly, "I'd like you to meet Indrani, my housekeeper. Indrani, this is my wife, Larissa, and her maid, Mei Ling."

Ignoring Larissa's outstretched hand, Indrani stared at her contemptuously. Instinctively, Larissa knew that the young woman had been much more to her husband than a housekeeper. She wondered why that surprised her. After all, he was a normal, healthy man, and she could hardly have expected him to have been celibate for the entire thirty-four years of his life. Since her current condition precluded marital relations, she wondered if he would resume the liaison now.

For a long, strained moment, Indrani's gaze traveled over Larissa and Mei Ling. Then she turned to Edmund and asked caustically, "Does your wife think Indians so unworthy that she felt compelled to bring a Chinese maid? Would we, perhaps, contaminate her smooth, white skin?"

"Indrani!" Edmund said in a sharp, warning tone. "Mei Ling is devoted to Larissa and begged to travel with her. I felt it was wise for her to accompany us in case my wife required special assistance. It so happens Larissa is with child."

Indrani's eyebrows raised appraisingly as her eyes darted back to Larissa's abdomen. She smiled cynically. "Ah, so she carries your heir so soon! Some women, it seems, are unaccountably fertile. While others of us—" She let the sentence hang as she continued to smile knowingly.

Edmund cleared his throat irritably. "Enough, Indrani! We had a difficult journey, and my wife is tired. Please show her to her rooms. And remember, I shall expect you to accord her the courtesy due the mistress of this estate."

Indrani batted her eyelashes innocently and bowed mockingly. "But of course, master. But which suite did you intend me to show her?"

He frowned. "The blue one adjoining mine and overlooking the gardens, of course."

"Of course." She paused to stare at him slyly before adding, "Might I suggest that she enjoy a bit of tea in the salon while I have the room prepared? We did not know you would be bringing a wife, and I suspect she might find some aspects of the rooms are not to her liking."

Nodding curtly, Edmund took Larissa's elbow and steered her through the pavilion and into the house. "I'm sorry things aren't prepared, darling," he whispered. "I'm afraid I should have thought to send word ahead from Patna. You mustn't let Indrani upset you. She just needs time to get accustomed to you. She's run this household so long that I'm afraid she's developed rather a proprietary attitude."

"Please don't trouble yourself about it, Edmund," Larissa replied gently. "I'm sure that in time we will learn to get along quite well." To herself, she thought that Indrani had developed a proprietary attitude about a good deal more than the house.

As they walked through the cool, marble hall toward the salon, Larissa mused, "I am a bit concerned about Mei Ling, though. I hope all the servants will not treat her as harshly as Indrani."

Edmund sighed. "No. I think they will show more understanding. But you needn't worry too much. Mei Ling will not be quartered with the house staff. There is a room for her adjoining your suite."

"And what of Indrani?" Larissa could not resist asking. "Where is she quartered?"

"She—" he stumbled, "as housekeeper, she has her own suite."

Seeing how agitated Edmund was, Larissa instantly felt sorry she had asked. It was unfair of her to pry into his past affairs. After all, he had demanded to know very little about her past. Slipping her arm through his, she said sweetly, "I really don't feel much like having tea at the moment. Won't you show me the gardens you were telling me about?"

Edmund smiled and nodded enthusiastically. "I'd be delighted, darling." He led her through another hall and out an arched exit to a spacious, walled area with thin, graceful towers at the corners of the walls. Some distance from the house stood an open, vaulted pavilion, topped by a dome encrusted with bits of jade and mother-of-pearl. They stepped through the pavilion, and Larissa laughed in delight at the profusion of thin canals and geometric flower beds. Marigolds, roses, jasmine, fern, and other flowers were planted in elaborate arabesques, lotus patterns, and other intricate designs.

"It's like a dream palace," she breathed. "No wonder the last zamindar became swellheaded. Living here, one could easily imagine oneself the lord of the universe."

"Yes," Edmund agreed. "It is lovely. No doubt these gardens and this pavilion will provide you with a pleasant way to pass the hours during your confinement. But I'd rather you didn't come out here unguarded. An occasional jackal wanders through these parts, and they've been known to maul unsuspecting persons."

"I can't believe any animal could act so savage in so beautiful a setting."

"Can't you?" he murmured, drawing her close. "Not even a love-starved husband? I've often thought these gardens would be perfect for love." His mouth closed over hers, and Larissa tried to return his kiss. She stifled a sigh of relief as footsteps on the pavilion's marble floor startled them, and they moved apart.

Indrani stopped a few feet from them, again smiling cynically. "Madam's suite is ready now, if she would like to examine it."

Edmund smiled down at his wife. "Why don't you go up and rest a bit, darling? I really ought to ride out and examine the grounds. I'll call for you for dinner later."

"All right." Larissa reached out and squeezed his hand, then followed Indrani back to the house.

As they ascended the curved marble staircase, Larissa stared up in enchantment at the inside of the great dome. Semiprecious stones and metals, outlined in gilt, were arranged in patterns within the dome. Two marble-railed balconies ringed the bottom edge of the structure.

"The house is so huge," Larissa said conversationally, "that I wonder if I shall ever learn to feel at home here."

"Yes, it is huge," Indrani replied tonelessly. "The second floor has your suite, the master's, and the nursery. Guest suites are located on the third floor. Servants' quarters and workrooms are in another wing, and the ballroom and rooms for entertaining guests are in still other wings."

Reaching the second floor, she turned sharply to her right and walked toward an arched doorway.

Determined to be friendly, Larissa asked, "How long have you been the housekeeper here, Indrani?"

"Three years." She stopped at a door, stepping to one side so Larissa could enter before her. As Larissa passed, she murmured meaningfully, "Edmund brought me with him from Calcutta."

Without answering, Larissa continued into the room. It was a cozy sitting room with light blue walls and furniture upholstered in indigo silk. A small, blue- and white-tiled fireplace was built into one wall. An arched doorway led to the bedroom, where the same blue color scheme was repeated. The huge canopy bed was curtained in indigo silk and covered with an indigo and white satin counterpane. Two more doors opened off of the bedroom. One led to a bathing room, which featured an elaborate, sunken marble tub. The other opened into a small dressing room with another door at the opposite end.

"That connects to *his* suite," Indrani said.

The touch of bitterness in the Indian woman's voice made Larissa stiffen. She turned slowly, surprised to feel a sudden wave of sympathy for the housekeeper.

"Indrani," she said quietly, "I don't know quite how to say this but—I'm sorry. When Edmund asked me to marry him, I didn't know—how could I? What I mean to say is, I didn't mean to come and displace you in your own home."

Indrani shot her a dark, reproachful glare, then shrugged. "It was to be expected. A proper British gentleman would not marry a Hindu woman, and sooner or later he was bound to want an heir." She paused, pursing her lips as she chose her next words. "You have his name, and perhaps you even have his heart. But I fear there is much you do not know about Edmund Farrell. He is your husband, but there is a part of him I think you will never own."

Larissa looked puzzled, but Indrani merely smiled enigmatically. Backing toward the door, she said, "I have work to attend to. Have a pleasant rest, madam."

Troubled by Indrani's statement, Larissa wandered back into the sitting room, where she discovered another door. She opened it quietly to find it was a small bedchamber where Mei Ling, exhausted from the journey, was already deep in sleep. Closing the door carefully, she went to the sitting room window and gazed out over the grounds.

In the distance, beyond the walled gardens, she could see Edmund riding through the fields, fields of tall red, pink, white, and purple flowers. He stopped, dismounted, and examined some of the blooms, then remounted, and rode on. She strained her eyes, looking for evidence of some crops. Everywhere, she saw flowers, three to four feet tall, waving in the breeze. Puzzled, Larissa decided she would have to ask Edmund again just what the estate produced.

Turning her thoughts back to Indrani, she wondered exactly what the housekeeper meant about never really owning Edmund. Was Indrani so convinced that Edmund would return to her bed, even though he now had a wife? Or was she just playing the role of the jilted lover, striking back at Larissa by trying to make her jealous?

Whatever the Indian woman's implications, she had succeeded in making one fact clear to Larissa—there was a great deal she did not know about her husband. And perhaps she should not want to know everything.

Chapter Eighteen

The next morning at breakfast, Larissa learned from Edmund that the flowers were indeed the estate's main crop. The fields also produced small quantities of jute and enough food for the estate, but their fortune lay in poppies, the source of Patna opium.

"I never suspected *you* would be involved with that hateful drug," Larissa said angrily, after Edmund had reluctantly told her of the opium. "You might at least have warned me!"

"Well," he said apologetically, "I assumed you would know. After all, why else would the East India Company be interested in maintaining estates here? Really, darling, you must learn to be more objective about opium. Among other things, it provides us with laudanum and morphine, both highly respected drugs in Europe and America."

"But the bulk of it is shipped to China, is it not? To poison those poor, unsuspecting souls."

"We hardly propose to poison anyone. The drug simply provides a pleasant escape for the Chinese people, who are overtaxed and misused by their emperor. Naturally, a few individuals are not judicious in their use of opium, but if they did not have the drug, they would certainly find some other, less respectable way to escape their problems."

"Oh," she fumed, "I can see it would be impossible to make you see how wrong you are! You're just as stubborn as—" She swallowed the last word, having vowed never to mention Nathan to her husband.

He cocked his head. "I'm just as stubborn as whom?"

"As—as all the other opium dealers!" She pushed her chair irritably away from the table and stood. "I find

I've lost my appetite! If you'll excuse me, I think I need some exercise."

Forgetting his warning that she should not go to the garden unescorted, she fled through the halls and out to the marble pavilion. Her mind was in turmoil. Was all Asia obsessed with opium? Was there no escaping the drug?

Gradually, as she strolled among the roses and the fragrant, reddish-purple heliotrope, Larissa began to feel that she had reacted too harshly. After all, she had managed to overlook Nathan's involvement with opium. Could she not do the same for Edmund, who had committed his whole life to her?

She turned at the sound of footsteps to see Edmund approaching her. "Darling, I thought I explained that I'd rather not have you wander here alone. It's for your own safety. The jackals—"

"I know," she cut him off, smiling awkwardly. "I guess I was just overwrought and not thinking. Edmund," she paused, groping for the right words, "I hope you'll forgive my behavior at breakfast. I'm afraid I was a bit irrational. I've no right to meddle in your business affairs, particularly when my own ship carried opium on its last voyage."

Heaving a relieved sigh, he smiled and took her arm. "There's no need for apologies. I understand that when a woman is with child she sometimes becomes quite emotional. Now, will you come and finish your breakfast?"

She nodded meekly and allowed him to escort her back to the breakfast room, telling herself that somehow she would reconcile herself to the presence of opium in their lives. But she still could not erase the nagging, uncertain fear at the back of her mind.

Larissa spent the first weeks at the estate becoming acquainted with the magnificent house and the servants and having a selection of gowns made from the fabrics Edmund had purchased in Patna. Beyond that, there was little else for her to do. Indrani resented her interference in any of the household affairs, and her condition precluded planning a ball or other social gatherings, so the elegant, domed ballroom with its fourteen golden chandeliers remained unused.

Edmund was occupied with business for most of each day, so Larissa was left to wander from room to room, becoming more and more bored with each passing day. Occasionally, she walked or sat in the gardens, but she felt silly asking one of the Bengali footmen to accompany her each time. Never did she so much as glimpse a jackal or even one of the cobras the servants held in such awe. By the end of the summer monsoon season, she had read every novel and book of poetry in Edmund's small library and had even begun to tackle some of the more difficult geographical and agricultural treatises on India.

As the months dragged by, Larissa could not help but think of Nathan from time to time. Each time his child moved inside her, his flashing, amber-flecked eyes reappeared in her mind. She found herself wondering if he had returned to Macao yet. Were the British-Chinese hostilities endangering him in any way? She had heard that a large fleet of British ships had begun to blockade Canton in June, but there had been no further news. Calcutta may have received more recent reports, but news was slow in traveling up the Ganges. Inevitably, she thought of the happy months she had shared with Nathan on Macao—months that could never be recaptured.

In an attempt to find something else to occupy her mind, Larissa tried to talk with Edmund about her position with Bennett and Barnes, but he waved away her concern, telling her a woman should content herself with domestic matters and let her husband build their fortune by his own means. When it became obvious he would do nothing to help her secure her inheritance, Larissa secretly sent a messenger to Calcutta to make inquiries of incoming ships. The messenger returned two months later with no news of Bennett and Barnes.

She did not feel particularly unhappy in India, but neither did she feel happy. If she did not have the birth of the child to look forward to, her life would have seemed quite meaningless. Edmund treated her with infinite kindness, and she made every effort to return his affection. But with each passing day, it became more and more apparent to her that they could never even approximate the relationship she had shared with Nathan.

Despite his kindness, there were times when Edmund seemed distant. Larissa supposed that he was working too hard and wished he would let her help lighten his workload. Some days he disappeared for hours at a time, only to return with a faraway look in his eyes and an inability to concentrate on anything she said. His moods fluctuated wildly, from careless giddiness to dark concentration on some secret problem, but whenever Larissa asked him what was troubling him, he regarded her strangely, as if she were imagining things.

Larissa could not help wondering if Edmund had resumed his liaison with Indrani. Perhaps, she thought, his strange moods were the result of guilt over the affair. The housekeeper's haughty, aloof manner only strengthened her suspicions. Whenever Indrani looked at her, Larissa felt sure the Indian woman was gloating about something. But she felt too embarrassed to confront either Edmund or Indrani with her suspicions.

Still, as the months passed and she watched her husband growing further and further away from her, Larissa knew she could no longer ignore the situation. Meeting Indrani one day in the second-floor corridor, she demanded, "You told me once that I would never really own my husband. What is it you know about him that I do not?"

The housekeeper smirked. "A great deal, it appears, since he does not even share your bed."

Larissa flushed. "He sleeps alone in consideration of my condition. At any rate, our sleeping arrangements are no concern of yours—unless—unless he shares *your* bed."

Shrugging, Indrani replied tartly, "And my sleeping arrangements are no concern of yours."

"They are," Larissa said coldly, "if they involve my husband."

Sighing in disgust, Indrani pushed by her. "Do not trouble me with your accusations. If you are so concerned, speak to Edmund. This much I will tell you—no matter what your condition, you are a fool not to share his bed. It is written in the *Mahabharata* that a woman derives eight times as much enjoyment from carnal relations as a man does. I assure you, Edmund is quite capable of proving that."

Watching Indrani glide away, Larissa could not help imagining her husband in bed with the woman. As the days passed and her own relationship with Edmund did not improve, she felt more and more certain he was slipping away regularly to the Indian woman's bed. But she still hesitated to speak to him about the problem, desperately hoping all would be resolved as soon as her child was born.

By late November, Larissa had begun to feel so uncomfortably huge that she thought she could not bear to carry the child another day. At least the monsoon season had ended in September, and more temperate weather had replaced the heat and humidity. Larissa was sitting up in bed, picking moodily at her *macher jhol*, a soupy curry of rice, vegetables, and fish, when she felt the first strong pain. Her face contorted, and Edmund, who was eating at a small bedside table, almost overturned the table as he jumped up to grab her hand.

"What is it, darling?" he asked excitedly. "Is it the child?"

She nodded, taking a deep breath. "Yes. I think so."

"Oh, my God," he gulped. "And it's twenty miles to Patna and back! Do you suppose the doctor can get here in time?"

Larissa smiled weakly, touched and amused by her husband's concern and lack of knowledge. "I imagine there will be plenty of time. No doubt the child will not be born for several hours. I've heard that first births take an especially long time."

Edmund paled. "You mean you're to be in pain all that time?"

"Not all the time," she said, squeezing his hand reassuringly. "It will come and go."

"Well, I'll send Bhabani to Patna for the doctor at once."

"All right. And you might tell Mei Ling the pains have begun."

Edmund was gone for only a moment. When he returned, he refused to leave her again, even when Mei Ling insisted there was nothing he could do. When the pains gripped her, he stood beside the bed, allowing her to cling to his hand. Between pains, he paced fretfully, his sandy hair dripping with perspiration and his rumpled white shirt clinging to his back. He was there through the long night, and when the light of dawn filtered into the room, he insisted on remaining beside her, ignoring the hunger and weariness gnawing at him. The doctor, occupied with other patients, never arrived, so Mei Ling, assisted by the frantic Edmund, had to deliver the baby. Late in the afternoon, Larissa finally heard the child's first lusty cry.

She collapsed against her pillows in contented exhaustion, and through the haze of drowsiness that quickly descended over her, she heard Edmund murmur happily, "We have a son, darling. A healthy, handsome boy with hair that looks to be just the color of mine! Thank you, darling, for giving me a son!"

She squeezed his hand, grateful to him for caring for her all through the night and for calling the child his. Blinking back tears of joy and gratitude, she vowed to do all in her power to be a perfect wife to this good man, whatever his failings might be.

She smiled at him and murmured, "I'm so glad you're happy. Now rest, dearest, you've had as difficult a time as I."

They named him Sean, and he seemed to give Edmund a new zest for living. He was away from the house only as long as his business demanded, always hurrying back to watch the sleeping child, to rock him tenderly or to sit beside Larissa as she nursed him.

Within the first few weeks after his birth, the baby's hair darkened, becoming more auburn like his mother's and losing the light, sandy quality of Edmund's. But Edmund seemed not to notice as Sean lost the one trait they had shared. He continued to talk exuberantly about his son and began making plans for a grand ball to celebrate Sean's birth.

Larissa watched her husband happily, relieved to note his dark and distant moods seemed to have vanished. Since he spent almost all his time with her and Sean, she felt convinced his affair with Indrani had finally ended, and she was confident they could begin their marriage anew.

With a charming, healthy child and a devoted husband, she knew she should have felt supremely content. But every time she looked into Sean's gray, amber-flecked eyes, she saw the eyes of his real father, and she found herself pining for Nathan.

The ball was held early in February, as soon as Larissa had had ample time to recover from Sean's birth. Edmund invited more than one hundred people, every Briton employed by the East Indian Company in Patna, plus a number of dignitaries visiting Patna from Calcutta.

The guests began arriving early on the morning of the ball, in every sort of carriage and coach. Governor Pinckney, who loved ostentation, had commissioned a dozen elephants to carry him and his entourage. Larissa watched in awe as the huge beasts, bedecked with velvet, silk, and jewel-encrusted hangings, lumbered up to the front pavilion. At a signal from the turbaned Indian sitting on its head, the first elephant knelt before the pavilion and the governor and his wife emerged from the silk-canopied *howdah* atop the animal's back. Margaret, who looked a bit shaken by the ride, confided to Larissa that she would never again consent to one of her husband's showy schemes.

Edmund and Larissa greeted each of the guests at the pavilion, and Indrani and the other servants showed them to their rooms, where they rested until the ball began in the early evening.

For the ball, Larissa wore a new gown with an overskirt of luminous green silk, falling over underskirts of deeper green satin. The fitted bodice was just low enough to reveal a tantalizing hint of creamy breasts; short sleeves of luminous silk fell loosely over her shoulders. Around her neck she wore a heavy gold chain from which hung an emerald pendant. Matching pendant earrings, a gift from Edmund after Sean's birth, adorned her ears. When Edmund, dressed in an elegant black silk suit and emerald green brocade waistcoat, stepped into her room, he sighed appreciatively.

"Darling, you look exquisite. I wish I could give a ball every night, just to show you off."

She smiled coyly. "I fear you flatter me, kind sir. It is I who should be pleased to be seen with someone as handsome as you."

Edmund smiled, pleased by her rare compliment. "But not half so handsome as the little fellow in the nursery. I stopped to check on him before coming for you. He's sleeping soundly, with Mei Ling stationed nearby, so I think we can safely go down and open the ball." Bowing grandly, he took her arm and led her down the sweeping marble staircase.

Entering the grand ballroom, Larissa felt as if she were stepping into fairyland. She smiled wryly, thinking for a fleeting instant of how shocked Uncle Hiram, Aunt Harriet, and Andrew Allerton would be if they could see her. All fourteen of the golden chandeliers were ablaze with tiny white candles, casting flickering shadows on the multi-

colored tiled dome overhead. While they greeted their
guests, a group of native musicians played sitars and sang
in tones that seemed strained and harsh to Western ears.
Their melodies were haunting, sad, and mystifying, but
quite unsuited for dancing a waltz or a quadrille.

The guests talked quietly among themselves until all
had been announced and Edmund gave the signal for the
British musicians to begin. Then he took Larissa into his
arms and began the first dance of the evening. He
danced with a grace born of his euphoria. Looking into his
sparkling blue eyes, Larissa realized for the first time what
a handsome, sought-after young man he must have been.
She gave herself up to the music and his contagious joy,
letting herself float through the evening with an abandon
she had not felt since long before the day she had become
his wife.

After that first dance, Larissa was passed to the arms of
one man after another. She smiled at each of them, acting the perfect hostess as she responded to their compliments and small talk. Ralph Palmer, an imposing, white-
haired gentleman who had just arrived from Calcutta,
provided more serious conversation than the others. He
informed her that British troops, having captured the island of Chou-shan the previous July, had only last month
defeated the garrisons at the first of the Bogue forts guard-
ing the entrance to Canton harbor.

Larissa stiffened at this information but tried to keep
her tone conversational. "Do you suppose that presents a
threat to any of the foreign ships at Whampoa? I mean,
suppose the Chinese wished to retaliate?"

"My dear young woman," Palmer smiled indulgently,
"there are no ships at Whampoa—haven't been since the
blockade began last June."

"Oh, of course. How foolish of me even to ask. But
then, where did all the ships go?"

He shrugged. "Macao. Or back to their home ports. And
of course our own British merchant ships have remained
anchored offshore. Aside from the battles, there have been
a few other nasty incidents. But I suppose you already
know about the young man kidnapped on Macao."

Larissa paled, and she felt her heart pounding in fear.
Had one of the hoppo's cronies gone after Nathan? "No
—no, I hadn't heard anything about the incident. You
mean the Chinese kidnapped a civilian?"

Her partner nodded. "Some of them have just gotten to be fanatical in their hatred of the British. This poor fellow was quite harmless. In fact, he's a divinity student."

She almost laughed in her relief but forced herself to maintain a serious expression. "How horrible for him. Have they released him yet?"

"No. But I understand he's enjoying quite a comfortable captivity."

"And that's the only incident of its type?"

"The only one I've heard of. Of course, the usual prisoners of war have been taken on both sides, and I understand the Chinese are holding the survivors of a British brig that ran aground near Ningpo." He paused to study her searchingly. "You seem quite interested in the Chinese situation—more than I would think likely for a woman. Is there someone there about whom you are concerned?"

"I—" she stumbled, wondering why she felt as if he knew all about Nathan, "I have American friends involved in the China trade, people I grew up with in Boston."

"Ah, I see. Well, I can assure you I've heard no reports of Americans being involved in any of the hostilities. I think it's safe to say you can put your mind at ease. A charming, beautiful woman like you should not have to concern herself with matters of state."

Grimacing inside, she flashed him a smile. "That's precisely what my husband says. But, of course, my interests are more personal than political, and I thank you for your comforting words." They talked more about India until the music stopped, and Ralph Palmer surrendered her to another partner.

As the evening progressed and Larissa concentrated on her duties as hostess, she found she had very little time to reflect on Mr. Palmer's news. At any rate, she told herself, it hardly mattered, since he had assured her that no Americans had been involved in the British-Chinese problems. She could assume then that Nathan was safe, wherever he might be, and it would do her little good to learn more about his whereabouts. As a married woman, she was in no position to go to him or even to write to him. In time, she intended to make further inquiries about the status of Bennett and Barnes, and she supposed she might learn more about Nathan then. For the moment, she thought, it seemed it would do no harm to put off her interest in the firm, since Mr. Palmer had made it clear no business was being conducted in Canton or Whampoa.

The music, the constant stream of admiring men and chattering women, and the champagne made it easy for Larissa to forget, at least for the moment, that she had any interest in the business world. As the last of their guests finally drifted off to their guest rooms, she smiled at Edmund in blissful weariness, sinking gratefully against him as he slid an arm around her waist.

"I was so proud of you tonight, darling," he whispered. "Not another woman here could match your beauty, your grace, or your charm."

"And none of the men could match you," she assured him.

"Tired?" he inquired as he brushed his lips against her temple.

"Exhausted! I'm sure I've never danced so much or with so many men."

"Yes, I know. I'm exhausted, too. But I'm still rather keyed up over the success of the evening. I wonder if you'd mind taking a short stroll in the gardens with me?"

She shrugged. "I suppose not. A short stroll might be pleasant. No doubt it would help clear my head. I'm afraid I drank a bit too much champagne."

Smiling, he guided her out the back exit and into the gardens. The spicy scents of jasmine and bougainvillea wafted to her on the chill, evening breeze. Vaguely, she wondered why there was a torch burning in the pavilion, then assumed it had been put there to light the way of any guest who might have become overheated from dancing.

As they stepped between the columns of the pavilion, the flickering flames bathed the white marble in warm, yellow-orange flames.

"Lovely, isn't it?" Edmund whispered. Before she had time to respond, his mouth closed over hers. Lips that had always kissed her gently were now hot and demanding. She felt his body pressing against hers, and instantly she knew what he intended.

"Edmund," she gasped, as his lips moved to her throat, "not here!"

"Why not, darling?" His voice was muffled against the top of her breast, and she could feel his fingers fumbling

with the hooks at the back of her gown. "Don't you agree
this is a perfect setting for love?"

"But the guests—the servants—"

"The guests are all tumbling into their own beds.
And I can promise you that none of the servants will disturb us."

The certainty with which he gave that promise made Larissa realize that Edmund had planned the moment very
carefully. And why shouldn't he, she thought helplessly.
He was her husband, the lord of this estate. The fact that
he did not inspire the least bit of desire in her made no
difference. She had willingly pledged herself to him as his
wife, and it was her duty not to deny him.

Gently, as if he were peeling a delicate, easily bruised
fruit, he pulled her gown down off her shoulders and
loosened her chemise. Her breasts shimmered in the torch-
light, and he sighed rapturously as he bent to kiss each
one gently. "Ah, Larissa. I've waited so many months for
this moment, dreaming of the time when our marriage
would finally be fully consummated. You won't deny me
now, will you?"

She winced, thinking of all the months when she was
carrying another man's child and he had scarcely touched
her. And of the months since Sean's birth, when he had
kept his distance in awe of the suffering she had endured
to bring that child into the world. He had been more patient than she had any right to expect.

"No, dearest Edmund," she whispered, sliding her arms
around his neck, "I'll not deny you now—or ever."

Slowly he undressed her, savoring every moment, his
hands infinitely gentle on her body. She gazed at him affectionately, seeing a virile, handsome man, a man who
would do anything for her and the child he so generously
claimed as his own. Desperately, she wished she could
feel some stirring of passion, something to remove her
dread of the coming moments. She wanted to desire him
as she knew he desired her, and she knew she was a fool
not to. But she could not.

He undressed himself much more quickly than he had
undressed her. Swiftly, his desire mounting, he knelt and
spread his clothes on the marble floor of the pavilion, fash-
ioning a pallet to cushion her. On his knees, he turned to
face her, groaning in an agony of anticipation as he

gazed up at her. Impulsively, he threw his arms around her legs and buried his face in the soft, dark delta between her thighs.

Larissa's breath quickened as she felt his kisses covering her moist, private area. She did not really want him, and yet it had been so long since she had known any man. Whimpering, she ran her fingers through his thick hair. She felt her knees give way as he pulled her down beside him, cradling her against his firm, demanding body. He pulled the pins from her hair, and his fingers combed through her silky auburn tresses. Then his hands seemed to be everywhere, caressing her, kneading her flesh, burning her with his need.

Without protest, she let him roll her to her back and accepted his body upon hers. She felt his hard, throbbing manhood, and she moaned softly as it slid deep within her. To her relieved surprise, she felt a joyous tingling in her loins, and for a moment she imagined she might be able to love him as a wife should. Wrapping her arms tightly around his back, she murmured, "Love me, dearest. Love me and make me love you!"

He groaned hoarsely and moved spasmodically. Then it was over. They both froze as the realization washed over them. He groaned again, miserable at the thought that all his dreams had ended so quickly.

Turning her head away, Larissa tried to blink back the tears silently running down her face—tears of disappointment for herself, tears of pity for her husband. Her romantic imaginings of a moment earlier crumbled, and she cursed herself for her own past experience in love.

If only she did not know the full ecstasy that perfect love could bring, perhaps she could have convinced herself that that passing tingling sensation was all any woman ever experienced. Perhaps she could have been content with that, never expecting more. Now she wondered how she could endure the next twenty, thirty, forty, or however many more years they might share. Now she knew she had been deceiving herself, thinking she might be happy with only affection. She needed the fullness of love, in all its emotional and physical aspects. But she could never have that, because she was married to Edmund, and she must honor the vows she had made.

He shifted his body off hers and choked out the only

words he could think of. "I'm sorry, darling. I don't understand—"

"Hush." She reached out to pat his side, swallowing her own disappointment in her attempt to comfort him. He might be a miserable lover, but he was still a devoted husband and a blameless father to a son who was not even his. Indrani's jeering face loomed suddenly in her mind, and she could hear her voice telling her again how much ecstasy Edmund was capable of giving.

Biting back accusations, Larissa soothed, "It's not your fault, Edmund. You've had to wait far too long for this moment, and perhaps tonight was not the best time for it. We're both too exhausted. There will be other times. We've a whole lifetime still to share."

"But I wanted this night to be so perfect," he moaned. "This never happened bef—" He cut himself off abruptly and muttered, "This isn't the way it happened with Sean's —with that other man, is it? I could tell it wasn't. I could sense you were expecting something—"

"Edmund!" she cut him off sharply, trying to control the quiver in her voice. "I've put that man out of my mind, and I had hoped that you had, too. He means nothing to me! You are my husband. That is all that matters." She wondered if she sounded as unconvincing as she felt.

Slowly, he sat up and kissed her forehead. "You're right, darling. We're both overtired, and we ought to go to bed." Turning away from her, he began to dress.

Larissa sat up and was reaching for her chemise when she noticed a glittering movement within the trailing trumpet vines. She froze, focusing carefully, and she felt her heart begin to thump fearfully as she realized two eyes were staring back at her.

"Edmund," she whispered, reaching out to touch his thigh, "there's something out there watching us!"

He followed her gaze, and she could feel him tense as he saw the eyes. Slowly, he expelled his breath and confirmed what she had already guessed. "A jackal."

They watched, paralyzed, as the vines rustled and the beast moved nearer. "Damn!" Edmund muttered. "I meant to stop in the library for a rifle on the way out here, but I was in such a bloody hurry I forgot."

Swallowing awkwardly, Larissa said, "Do you think it will attack us?"

"Probably not," he replied uncertainly. "A lone animal is unlikely to attack when he can see that he's outnumbered. But they usually travel in packs. If his comrades are nearby—"

"What are we going to do?" she interrupted nervously.

"We'll take the torch and go back to the house. I've heard they're afraid of flame, so I think he'll keep his distance if we carry the torch and move very slowly and deliberately."

She nodded, staying close beside him as he moved toward the torch. The eyes continued to glow menacingly, making her shiver with fear. Edmund removed the torch from its bracket and held it before them as they moved toward the house. He wrapped his free arm comfortingly around Larissa's shoulders, whispering to her that she must not be afraid.

They stepped out of the pavilion, and Larissa flinched as she saw the yellowish-gray outline of the jackal following a few yards behind them. As they continued on the path, she could hear it padding through the vines. Her heart beat erratically as she imagined its glistening teeth tearing into her throat.

They were only a few yards from the darkened house when its piercing yelp sent shivers racing down her spine. Suddenly, glistening eyes seemed to be closing in on them from all sides.

Waving the torch wildly before them, Edmund clutched Larissa to him and plunged toward the house. The night air was punctuated by an excited chorus of yelps as he threw open the door and pushed her inside. She turned to see him hurriedly bar the door as a pack of at least ten jackals circled closer.

Larissa collapsed against the wall, sobbing with relief. Suddenly she sensed that she and Edmund were not alone. Raising her head, she saw Indrani step out of the shadows. Ignoring Larissa, the servant rushed to Edmund's side.

"I heard a disturbance and thought I should investigate," Indrani said. "I hope nothing is wrong?"

"Everything is under control," Edmund replied tersely. "We were strolling in the gardens when we encountered a pack of jackals, but no harm has been done."

"Ah, yes." Indrani's gaze shifted to Larissa, who had not had time to finish dressing and now clutched her gown awkwardly before her body. "But I have always believed," she continued sarcastically, "that the jackal gives little reason for fear. After all, it feasts mainly on the scraps left by the lion, and on this estate, the lion leaves little for the cheeky jackal." Smiling sweetly, she turned and walked away, carrying herself as proudly and regally as if she fancied herself a lion.

Larissa closed her eyes tightly, trying to ignore a sinking feeling that Indrani and Edmund had not ended their liaison after all.

Chapter Nineteen

A week passed before Edmund approached Larissa again. During that time, he retained his same doting good humor with Sean but seemed politely distant with her. Neither of them mentioned the incident in the gardens, but Larissa felt constantly plagued by Indrani's words. Did Indrani really think of her as the jackal, the cheeky intruder who was tossed the leftovers of Edmund's love? Was that why her husband could not perform with her—because he was too exhausted after his encounters with their housekeeper?

In all honesty, Larissa had to admit she was perfectly content not to share her bed with Edmund. She felt certain now that she could find no satisfaction in his embrace, and she did not wish to be reminded of that fact night after night. Still, her pride was wounded, and she felt cheated to think he was bestowing his favors on another. She also felt strangely guilty, knowing how much she owed him and feeling unable to repay him as a wife should. Worst of all, she feared Edmund's own guilt might drive him back to the moody, withdrawn state that had possessed him before Sean's birth.

She was almost asleep one night when she heard him open the door of the dressing room connecting their suites. Turning her head, she could see him standing in the doorway, outlined by moonlight. His maroon silk dressing gown swished as he moved toward her bed.

"Larissa? I'm sorry if I woke you, darling."

"You didn't," she replied sleepily. "Is something wrong, Edmund?"

"No, I—I just couldn't sleep. I thought perhaps we could talk. Would you care for a bit of brandy with me?"

She shook her head, frowning to herself as he went

into her sitting room and poured a snifter of brandy. Edmund seldom drank unless he was entertaining guests. Something must be troubling him if he felt he needed liquor to fortify himself. Perhaps now, at last, the whole question of Indrani would be resolved and put to rest.

When he returned to the bedroom, she patted the edge of the bed in invitation, stroking his thigh as he sat down beside her. "What is it, Edmund? What do you want to talk about?"

Staring into his brandy snifter, he shook his head slowly. "It's—I can't tell you right now. Oh, I never should have brought you here! I never should have married you!"

Pursing her lips, she asked, "Have I done something to make you regret marrying me? Is it because of Sean?"

"No! No! You and Sean are everything to me! But I've cheated you. There are things you don't know about me—terrible things!"

"And there are things you do not know about me," she countered. "Not to mention the terrible things you did know when you decided to marry me anyway. Edmund, dearest, marriage is a time for learning about one another. It will take us years to begin to learn it all."

"You don't understand," he moaned, downing his brandy in one gulp. "If you had known this, I feel certain you would not have married me. I'm not the man you think."

"What are you talking about? You're kind, loving, strong—the kind of man any woman would be proud to call her husband."

She paused. Then, deciding it was best to bring everything into the open, she plunged ahead. "If you're trying to tell me about your relationship with Indrani—"

"Indrani?" He cut her off with a sharp, nervous laugh. "If only it were that simple! I have no relationship with Indrani! I'll admit at one time she was much more to me than a housekeeper, but that changed long before my last trip to China. Now I suppose she is jealous and she would like you to believe there is something more, but I swear to you there is not."

His words were so impassioned that she could not doubt him. She felt sure then that Indrani had only pretended Edmund still shared her bed to salvage what she could of her hurt pride. If his liaison with Indrani really had ended long ago, what *did* cause his dark and distant moods? What terrible secret was he hiding?

Taking his hand, she rubbed it gently against her cheek. "Edmund," she whispered, "what would you have me say? What can I do to help you?"

He sighed and moved closer to her, sliding his arms around her. "Just promise me you'll never leave me. Promise me you'll stand by me, no matter what."

"Of course I'll never leave you. Don't you remember I pledged that on our wedding day? And I won't forget my pledge, dearest husband."

With shock, she realized there were tears glistening on his cheeks, and she felt him shivering in her arms. "You're cold," she murmured, lifting the edge of her blankets. "Here, get under the covers with me."

They lay side by side for several minutes, while she stroked his back consolingly. He snuggled against her, seeming to draw warmth and strength from her body. Gradually, he relaxed and began to return her caresses. With a wave of guilt, she tensed as she felt his manhood stiffen, knowing what would happen next.

"Oh, darling," he murmured, as he rolled her to her back and hovered over her, "I want you so much."

It was as dismal a failure as that first time in the gardens. Afterward, he slid away, stifling a sob, and they huddled on opposite sides of the bed.

In the next months, Larissa did everything she could think of to put him at ease, to show him she cared, to build his confidence, and to hide her own disappointment. But it was no use. Whenever he visited her bed, they both came away unhappy, until finally he stopped coming to her room at all.

Larissa tried to maintain an attitude that there was nothing wrong between them. She treated him the same as always, except for an added measure of compassion. But he seemed to become more and more withdrawn, sinking into deeper depression with each passing day. Even Sean, who was beginning to crawl and get into all sorts of mischief, no longer seemed to delight him. Edmund retreated into a private world, spending as little time as possible with Larissa and Sean.

She suffered through another sultry monsoon season, worrying about her husband and finding solace only in the hours she spent with Sean. But even the innocent child could not bring her untarnished happiness, for every time she looked at him she saw Nathan mirrored in his eyes, and she regretted the life she had left behind on Macao.

At times, she wished they could return to Macao. There, Edmund had been warm and concerned with life and love. Only in India, beginning with that first night in Calcutta, had he seemed to lose his grasp of reality. If only they could get away, perhaps they could begin to build a real life together.

The reports that filtered into Patna in the *India Gazette,* which passed on news recorded months earlier in Macao's *Canton Press,* were still mixed. In May, the British had advanced up the Pearl River to the very gates of Canton, demanding a ransom of six million dollars for the city. The Chinese had retaliated by attacking the British ships with fire rafts and all but demolishing the Canton hongs. The British had successfully occupied Hong Kong for several months. But it was a barren, fever-ridden island that would have been useless were it not for its deep water anchorage and fairly friendly natives. Edmund, who had once had a keen interest in politics, seemed unmoved by any of the news, leaving Larissa to worry alone about how events in China might shape their future.

The dry season had returned, and Sean was nearly a year old when something happened that convinced Larissa she had to confront Edmund with his problem before he completely destroyed himself and endangered her and Sean by sinking any further into oblivion.

Since that night when the jackals had approached them in the garden, she had begun carrying a pistol with her whenever she ventured outside and even when she went to the more remote wings of the house. She was not sure she could bring herself to kill any animal, but it was comforting to have the weapon. Raju, one of the Bengali footmen, had taught her to load and use the pistol, and now she was satisfied that she was a fairly accurate shot.

While Sean napped one afternoon, Larissa had taken a stroll in the garden, as always thinking about the stranger Edmund had become. For some time, she had felt plagued by a dull, nagging suspicion of what her husband's problem really was. But the thought was so terrible that she resolutely stifled it, avoiding all impulses to confront him directly. Returning to the house, she could feel the pistol

in the pocket of her cotton skirt. She mounted the
stairs, intending to return the pistol to her bureau drawer,
but she could not resist stopping first in the nursery to
look in on her sleeping son.

Opening the door of the nursery, Larissa smiled to
herself as her eyes fell on the teakwood cradle Edmund
had carved when Sean was born. Soon the child would be
too large for it. Her smile vanished as she approached
the cradle and saw a swaying movement at its foot. A
scream stuck in her throat as she saw a cobra coiled on the
edge of the blanket, only inches from Sean's foot. As she
watched, the snake raised its head over the child, inflating
its hood and hissing ominously.

Larissa's first impulse was to snatch the child out of
the cradle and run. But she knew she could not move fast
enough to avoid the cobra's deadly fangs. If she was not
extremely careful, both she and Sean could be killed.

Slowly, she slid her hand into her pocket and closed it
around the pistol. Forcing herself not to panic, she drew the
gun out of her pocket and aimed toward the cobra's head.
Her hands were shaking so violently she was sure she
would miss and the bullet would rip into her son's flesh.
Through clenched teeth, she drew in a deep breath and
steadied her hands.

The cobra leaned forward, seeming to sway in a weird
death dance over the sleeping child. Its head looked so
thin, so easily missed. Holding her breath, she corrected
her aim. In the last instant, the cobra turned its head
toward her, its beady eyes menacing. Larissa squeezed the
trigger.

The cobra seemed to leap into the air as the bullet hit
its body, sending it hurtling over the edge of the cradle.
The bullet passed through the snake and sped on to shat-
ter a windowpane on the opposite side of the nursery.

Startled from his nap, Sean wailed in fright and confusion. Larissa felt her body swimming in perspiration as
she focused on the limp cobra on the floor beside the
cradle. Dropping the pistol, she gathered Sean into her
arms.

"It's all right, baby," she crooned, "Mama's here. Mama
won't let anything happen to you."

She carried him into the hall, where a group of servants, startled by the gunshot, had already gathered. Mei

Ling hurried to her side. "What happened, madam?" Mei Ling asked. "Is the child hurt?"

"No. There was a cobra in his cradle," Larissa said, surprised at the steadiness of her voice. "I killed it."

She turned to Raju. "Please see that the snake is removed and have the cradle moved to my room. I don't want Sean sleeping alone any more."

"Very well, madam." Raju bowed, and the other servants dispersed, murmuring among themselves.

The commotion in the hall upset Sean even more, and he continued to wail as Larissa carried him into her suite. She paced with him from the sitting room to the bedroom and back again, patting him and crooning to him, but he could not be comforted. As she entered the bedroom with him again, the dressing room door opened, and Edmund stepped into the room. His hair and clothing were badly rumpled, and his face had a haggard look. Once, he would have hurried to take Sean from her, coaxing him to laugh, but now he looked annoyed that the child had disturbed him.

"What's wrong with him?" he asked sharply.

Larissa stared at her husband for a moment, unable to believe his harsh tone. "A cobra almost attacked him in his cradle," she replied. "I had to shoot it."

"Umm," Edmund grunted, as if she had merely commented on the weather.

She shot him an irritated glance "You seem quite unconcerned."

"Of course I'm concerned!" he retorted. "His screaming is giving me a beastly headache." He dug into his pocket and withdrew a small, brown, powdery cake. "Here," he said, thrusting it at her, "give him this. At least it will quiet him."

Larissa's eyes widened, and she drew back in horror, instantly recognizing the substance. Still, hoping somehow to deny this evidence that confirmed the suspicion that had haunted her in recent months, she whispered, "What is it?"

"What does it matter what it is, if it will make him stop wailing? Just give it to him."

"No!" She slapped the cake out of his hand, watching it crumble on the floor. "I'm not going to feed my baby opium!"

"For the love of God, Larissa!" Edmund snorted disgustedly. "Practically all the Indian women give their children small doses to keep them quiet." He stooped and picked up a few crumbs of the opium cake, holding them out to her. "Now, be sensible and stop acting like I'm trying to poison the child. It's not going to hurt him."

Shaking her head furiously, she stepped back, clutching the still-wailing child to her chest. Admitting to herself there was no way to ignore the problem any longer, she threw back her head and demanded hoarsely, "Is that what you thought the first time you took it? That it wouldn't hurt you? After what it's done to you, how can you try to foist that drug on this innocent child?"

Edmund froze. He opened his mouth as if to speak, then closed it abruptly. Quickly stooping to pick up the scattered crumbs of opium, he popped them into his mouth and stormed back to his own suite, slamming the dressing room door.

The argument and the slamming door made Sean scream even louder. Carrying him to the corridor, Larissa called to Mei Ling, who was already running toward the suite, her face showing concern.

Before the maid could ask any questions, Larissa handed Sean to her and instructed, "Take him downstairs and give him some coconut milk. My husband and I have important matters to discuss. Please tell the other servants we are not to be disturbed, no matter what."

Turning back to her suite, she saw Indrani lurking in the shadows of the corridor, smirking in satisfaction. Suddenly remembering the Indian woman's words to her the day she first arrived at the estate, Larissa strode angrily toward her.

"You knew, didn't you?" she hissed. "You knew from the beginning that Edmund had a weakness for opium!"

Indrani tossed her head defiantly. "Yes, I knew! You may recall that I even warned you. Is it my fault you were too stupid to understand my warning?"

"But how could you let him deteriorate to this point? If you really cared for him, and at one time I thought you did, how could you stand by and watch him destroy himself? Why didn't you come to me and help me save him?"

The Indian woman shrugged disdainfully. "Why should I care for him, after he cast me aside like some wretched untouchable? Why should I want to save him so he can make love to you and you can bear more of his brats? I would rather see the drug kill him!"

Blinded by rage, Larissa lunged at Indrani, raking her fingernails down her cheeks. "Get out of my house!" she shrieked. "I never want to see you on this estate again."

Catching her wrists, the housekeeper pushed Larissa backwards, kicking at her furiously as she fell to the floor. "You needn't worry," she said tartly, dabbing at her scratched face. "I am pleased to go elsewhere—somewhere that I can find a real man, one who will not desert me for a useless woman like you!"

Before Larissa could struggle to her feet to attack her again, Indrani was running down the stairs, her sari billowing out behind her. Larissa sat for a moment, regaining her breath, as she watched Indrani storm out of the house. Then, standing up and squaring her shoulders, she walked into her suite, through the dressing room, and pounded on Edmund's door.

"Edmund!" she shouted, "we've got to talk! I can't stand by any longer and watch you destroy yourself." When silence greeted her, she tried the door knob and found that he had locked her out. Pounding harder, she yelled, "Edmund, I'm not leaving until we have a talk! I'll stand here pounding all day and all night if necessary, and then think what a headache you'll have!"

More silence, then she heard the key turn in the lock. Edmund opened the door and gazed at her sheepishly. Looking beyond him, she could see that his room was a shambles, with dirty, wrinkled clothing tossed carelessly over the furniture and on the floor. Obviously, he had not allowed a maid or valet in for weeks.

"Oh, Edmund," she whispered, "what are you doing to yourself? Do you even realize?"

He shrugged. "I warned you I had a terrible secret."

Nodding, she sighed. "And I have allowed you to keep it for too long. Even when I knew it in my heart, I could not bring myself to admit it and confront you with it. I kept hoping I was wrong. But then today I told you our son had almost been killed, and you acted as if it was quite unimportant. Did you even understand what I was telling you?"

Again he shrugged. "I—well—it seemed unimportant.

Everything seems unimportant when I have my drug."

"Even your wife and child?" she whispered.

Nodding miserably, Edmund sank down on his unmade bed and buried his head in his hands. His words were muffled, so Larissa had to strain to hear him.

"I know that sounds terrible, but it's true. I don't even care about my own health. Oh, God, Larissa, what am I going to do?"

Feeling her eyes brimming with tears, she crossed the room and slid an arm around his heaving shoulders. "The first thing you have to do," she said firmly, "is give up the opium."

"But I can't! I need it! I'll die if I don't have it!"

"You'll die if you continue eating it!" she said crisply, "and I'm too young to be left a widow with a fatherless child."

"I know," he shook his head wretchedly. "But it's impossible. I'm much too weak to stop now."

"You are not too weak," Larissa insisted. "Besides, I'll help you. What's become of the strong Englishman I married—the one who killed a man because he threatened to kidnap me on our wedding day? Oh, Edmund, why did you ever let yourself get into this trap?"

"I don't know. I'm still not sure how it happened. I'd eaten it before a few times, before my last trip to China, just to see why the Chinese were willing to pay so much for it. It made me feel pleasant, as if I were in an unreal, happy world all my own. But I didn't use it regularly, and I didn't miss it when I left India, especially after I met you."

"Then why did you start eating it here?"

Edmund shrugged. "I sampled it with friends in Calcutta and Patna, and those occasions reminded me how pleasant it could be. Then, when it became difficult for me to face things here—"

"What was so diffi—" Larissa cut herself off, suddenly realizing what he was driving at. "It was my pregnancy, wasn't it? The fact that I was carrying another man's child?"

Turning his face away, he nodded. "I tried to be so noble about it, saying it didn't matter and no one would ever know. But I couldn't help the way I felt, watching you grow bigger month by month and knowing I couldn't even lie with you when I wanted you so much. God knows I wanted to accept the situation, and when Sean was born, I was so delighted I made up my mind I would not let opium come between us any more. Then—"

He lapsed into silence, and Larissa did not prod him with more questions. She knew what had happened then. Rather than face the agony of repeated failures in their bed, he had once again sought the sweet oblivion offered by opium. She blamed herself for the problem, cursing herself for tormenting him for so many months. Her instincts should have kept her from marrying him, even when he assured her everything would be all right. She sighed to herself, knowing it was too late now for self-reproach. As his wife, she had to help him.

"Edmund," she said firmly, "you stopped before, when Sean was born, and you can stop again—this time for good."

He grimaced. "It won't be that easy. I'm eating far more now than I was then."

"But you do want to stop, don't you?"

He hesitated, battling with his body's dependence on the drug, then nodded slowly. "Yes. Yes, of course I do."

"Then we'll manage. I know it won't be easy, but we'll manage."

Larissa could not have guessed that afternoon just how difficult the task would be. She began by having his suite thoroughly cleaned and instructing the servants to destroy every bit of opium they found. In all, they discovered almost two hundred cakes tucked under his mattress, beneath the chair cushions, in hidden recesses of his bureau and desk, and in the pockets of his clothing.

She soon learned that his craving for the drug far outweighed his desire to be rid of it. If she did not watch him every second, he bribed or browbeat the servants to get him a cake.

Living on an estate where opium was the main product made it almost impossible to avoid contact with the drug. Larissa found herself in the upsetting position of having to tolerate the drug as the source of their livelihood, even when she had seen firsthand just how poisonous it could be. Whenever Edmund rode out to inspect or oversee estate operations, Larissa left Sean with Mei Ling and rode with him, determined not to let him find a new source for his habit.

At night, she slept with him, lying awake when he tossed nervously, holding him and soothing him after his frequent, vivid nightmares or when his body shook with chills. Sometimes, watching him shake as he sat across the dinner table from her, she was filled with so much pity that she almost wanted to give him a cake. Then she thought of how he had calmly shrugged away the cobra attack, and she knew that, for all of their sakes, she had to resist the temptation.

All through those difficult months, Larissa depended more and more on Mei Ling. While Edmund required almost constant surveillance, she knew she could trust Mei Ling to take care of all Sean's needs. Whenever she felt the situation was hopeless, she knew that Mei Ling was there to offer her gentle wisdom. Mei Ling had become more a friend than a servant, and Larissa thanked God daily for her presence.

It was midsummer before Edmund seemed completely recovered. His eyes were bright again, he enjoyed playing with Sean, who was now a cheerful toddler, and he seemed generally concerned about the world around him. Still, Larissa felt uneasy living on an opium estate, fearing that at any provocation, Edmund might succumb to his weakness again. She wanted to get away from the trade entirely but was unsure how. When she suggested they might go to his home in England, Edmund shook his head adamantly.

"And what would we do in England? I'm a trader, darling. I'd be bloody unhappy sitting around in some little shop or office."

"But I hate even to be involved with opium," she said. "After what it did to you, how can you, with a clear conscience, sell it to anyone else?"

"Well, I admit I don't like it, but it's the basis of the company trade with China. You and I can't change that."

"Then perhaps you should leave the company."

"And do what?"

"Well—" She thought for a moment, suddenly brightening. "You could manage my share of the company I inherited from my father! Of course, the *Queen of Cathay* carried opium when I came to China on her. But it doesn't have to. I mean, it's our company, so we would dictate what our ship carries. My Uncle Hiram might give us some trouble, but—"

"No!" he cut her off sharply. "I've always despised men

who live off their wives' fortunes, and I absolutely refuse to become one of them."

"But you wouldn't be living off me if you were doing all the work! Besides, as I've told you before, I don't want to lose everything to my aunt and uncle. When I set off for the Orient, I was too young to fight them by myself. But, as my husband, you can help me get what is rightfully mine."

Edmund sighed patiently. "Darling, I wish you would forget about that Boston business. As I said the first time you told me this story, your aunt and uncle sound like despicable creatures and you ought to be glad to have them out of your life. You don't need that shipping firm. You have a husband and a charming little boy—enough to occupy any woman, I should think. Besides, I wish you would stop thinking of yourself as a Bostonian. As my wife, you're British now."

"My father gave his life to that business," she said sullenly. "I may have put any thought of it aside while I worried about the baby and helped you through your crisis, but I can't simply abandon it."

Frowning in annoyance, Edmund snapped, "Did your mother participate in your father's firm, or did your father inherit the firm from your mother's family?"

"Well, no. Papa founded the firm, and mama was too busy caring for me to give it much thought."

He nodded vigorously. "So, you see, they would both surely understand my position. In fact, I'm certain they would tell you, as I do, to forget about business matters, devote yourself to your family, and allow your husband to worry about your future. You do believe, don't you, that I'm in full control of myself now, and am capable of handling matters?"

Reluctantly, she nodded, biting back any more arguments about Bennett and Barnes and telling herself it was important not to question Edmund's newly recovered confidence. She still felt uneasy about living on the estate, but for the moment she would simply wait and watch, hoping she would not betray her uneasiness to Edmund. She would postpone further discussion about the firm, but she would not forget about it. She would not give up her legacy, even for Edmund.

In September, toward the end of the monsoon season, word reached Patna that the British and Chinese had

signed a peace treaty at Nanking. Though the Chinese still
refused to legalize the opium trade, they had agreed to
cede Hong Kong to the British. In addition, they had
opened the ports of Amoy, Foochow, Ningpo, and Shanghai to British trade, even granting permission for foreigners and their families to set up permanent residences in the
trading cities. Canton was reopened to British trade, but
the restrictions against women in the Canton hongs remained.

Despite the continuing Chinese ban on opium traffic, the
drug trade exceeded its pre-war records within days after
the treaty was signed. Soon the Patna opium factories
were sending massive shipments of the drug downriver to
Calcutta, where it could be picked up by ships on their
way to China.

Other trading news interested Edmund more. Sir Henry
Pottinger, a soldier and diplomat of the East India Company, who had directed the British offensive for the last
year of the war, sent word of a vast, untapped market for
British and Indian cotton goods in the newly-opened Chinese ports. For the next month, Edmund traveled to and
from Patna, conferring with East India Company officials
there and corresponding with more officials in Calcutta.
Late in October, he returned to the estate one evening,
smiling broadly.

"Well, darling," he exclaimed, taking Larissa in his arms,
"we're out of the opium business! The company's sending someone else to take over the estate. You'd better
begin packing, because we leave for China in two days.
You're looking at the head of the East India Company's
new cotton trade headquarters in Shanghai!"

Part Four

�֍

1842-1843

Chapter Twenty

Larissa began to feel her first wave of apprehension as they sailed into Macao harbor aboard one of the new steam frigates from London. They had made a smooth trip from Calcutta in less than two weeks, so now it was only late November.

In the weeks since his announcement, Larissa had been elated by the thought that Edmund was completely cured and opium would no longer have any part in their lives. He had even gained enough confidence to begin making love to her again. Though their unions could never approximate what she had enjoyed with Nathan, at least they were not the dismal failures they had known on the estate, and Edmund seemed contented enough.

Larissa was pleased that their return to Macao would give her the opportunity to make personal inquiries about the status and success of Bennett and Barnes. Whenever she thought of the firm, she had tried to avoid thinking of Nathan. Now she knew that was impossible.

Standing by the rail and gazing up at Macao's terraced hills, her eyes were drawn to the house she had shared with him. In the months when she had been battling Edmund's addiction, she had almost succeeded in closing her mind to those happy months when she had felt like Nathan's wife. But now she could not help wondering if he was wintering in Macao or on his way back to Boston. What would she do if they met on Macao's streets or, worse yet, at some social event when Edmund was at her side?

She felt Edmund's hands on her shoulders, and his concerned voice cut into her thoughts. "You're trembling, darling. Are you upset about something?"

"No," she said quickly, "I suppose I'm just a bit uneasy

—remembering our last day here, when you killed the hoppo and we learned Sun Yuan had hanged himself."

His arms slid down to her waist, pulling her firmly back against him. "I understand. But all that is behind us, and you must try to put it out of your mind. We could have stayed the winter in India, but I knew how anxious you were to get away from everything India has meant to our marriage. And I thought we would be better off here than on Hong Kong. From all I've heard, it's a rather Godforsaken, fever-ridden place, and I wouldn't want Sean exposed to it. Here, we can spend a pleasant winter in my house on the Praya Grande and go north to Shanghai in the spring."

"Of course." She forced a smile. "I'm already over my misgivings. I've always loved Macao, and I'm sure Sean will, too."

Edmund nodded happily. "Mei Ling's just gotten him up from his nap. He'll be dressed and ready to disembark by the time we dock. I'm sure Mei Ling will be glad for the chance to spend a few months in her hometown. Perhaps she can even visit some of her friends, the servants from your old home."

Yes, Larissa thought, perhaps she will, but *I* must resist all temptation to visit old friends and old places.

They had been on Macao scarcely a week when Larissa's resistance crumbled. For the first days, she occupied herself organizing her new household staff and helping Sean become accustomed to his new home. Edmund was away from the house most of each day, conferring with East India Company officials and others who had already visited Shanghai. He returned one evening with disturbing news.

"If our traders aren't careful," he muttered, shaking his head, "we could just end up with another war on our hands. The Chinese specifically said they want no foreign women in Canton, and yet several of our captains took their wives upriver with them."

Larissa frowned. "Is that really so terrible?"

"The Chinese think it is. They don't change their traditions easily. In fact, they rioted and burned down the British flagstaff right in front of the hong. They would have attacked the American factories, too, if the Yankees hadn't held them off with gunfire."

She paled. "How dreadful! Was anyone hurt?"

Edmund shrugged. "They say the American fire killed five Chinese. None of the British were hurt, but I'm not sure about the Americans. I understand the rioting went on for hours. Even the Chinese troops couldn't stop it."

Looking away, Larissa could not help but think of Nathan. Was he still in Canton? Was he on Macao? Had he sailed out of the Orient? Was he safe? She tried to tell herself she should not concern herself with him at all. He was a part of another time in her life, a time that was past and could never be recaptured. She was Edmund's wife, and he was the only person to whom she owed any loyalty. She had to remain true to Edmund. But could she really pretend, even to herself, that she cared nothing about Nathan?

The following afternoon, after Edmund left on business, Larissa tucked Sean in for his afternoon nap, left Mei Ling to watch over him, and called for the carriage. Pretending she was only out for some air, she directed the driver up into the terraced hills, toward the house she knew so well. As they rolled along, she admitted to herself the ride was probably a foolish idea. She dared not knock on the door and inquire about Nathan's whereabouts, so the only way she would know he was there was if she glimpsed him entering or leaving the house. If she saw him, she would know he was safe, but if she did not see him, she could make no assumptions. After all, he could have left the Orient. If she did see him, she would have to be very careful that he did not see her, for she was certain she could not bear to speak with him.

As the carriage neared the house, Larissa directed the driver to slow down. As he did so, Larissa spotted Nathan from the back, walking toward the house. Clinging to his arm was a tall, slim blonde. Larissa felt as if someone had grabbed her heart and twisted it mercilessly. She slid lower in the carriage, watching Nathan escort the woman into his house. As the woman laughed and tilted her head to look up adoringly at Nathan, Larissa realized the woman was Estelle Jamieson. Estelle, the wife of Nathan's friend Lawrence, the woman they had always joked was such a cold, forbidding woman! She looked anything but cold as she rested her head on Nathan's shoulder.

With a sinking feeling, Larissa wondered if their relationship had existed even then, when she was still living with Nathan. Leaning forward, she whispered to the driver, "I'd like to go home now, please."

Sean was still asleep when Larissa stepped into the nursery. Looking up from her silk embroidery, Mei Ling asked simply, "Did you see him?"

Larissa flushed. "What are you talking about?"

"I think you know quite well," Mei Ling replied serenely. "And you needn't pretend innocence to me. I shan't reproach you or run to your husband with tales. But I beg you to remember that, despite all his failings, Mr. Farrell is a fine man. More important, he is your husband."

About to remind Mei Ling that she was still a servant and had no place reproving her mistress, Larissa stopped herself. In their time together, Mei Ling had become far more than a servant. In some ways, she was almost a mother to Larissa. Larissa knew the woman loved her deeply and wanted to protect her from being hurt again. And she could not help loving Mei Ling in return for the concern she had shown her and Sean and for the quiet support she had provided during Edmund's crisis.

Aware that Mei Ling knew her too well to be deceived, Larissa murmured, "You're right, of course, and you needn't worry that I will disgrace my husband or myself in any way. Nathan is part of my past. It's been almost three years since we've seen each other, and I've no intention of renewing our acquaintance."

Mei Ling nodded, but Larissa knew the woman only half believed her.

The servant had good reason to worry. The next afternoon, while Sean slept and Mei Ling watched over him, Larissa slipped out to the stable, saddled a roan mare, and rode alone into the terraced hills. Knowing this excursion was even more foolish than the one the day before, she still felt somehow powerless to resist the force drawing her toward Nathan's home.

To salve her already guilty conscience, she told herself she really hoped to see him with Estelle again. Surely seeing him laughing happily with that obnoxious woman would convince her that he was fickle and unworthy of another thought. Yet, she wondered, could she really accept the thought that he could forget her so easily?

She was nearing the house when she heard the thunder of hoofs behind her and automatically nudged her slower-paced mount to the side of the road. The noise subsided as the other rider slowed his horse beside hers, and a mellow, slightly sarcastic voice interrupted her musings.

"I really don't think it's safe for a woman to ride alone in these uncertain times."

She tensed, using all her willpower to keep from looking at him as she recognized Nathan's voice. Perhaps, faced with her discourtesy, he would simply ride on, and she could relax and return home. But, even as she thought that, he leaned toward her horse, and his voice softened.

"Are you all right, madam? You needn't worry that I'm a highwayman, out to take your money or virtue. Actually, I'm just a chivalrous—" He stopped abruptly as he caught a glimpse of her profile. "Larissa!" he murmured. "I should have known no one else could have quite that shade of auburn hair. What are you doing here? They told me you had gone to India."

Still keeping her eyes averted, she responded simply, "I did."

"Then what are you doing on Macao?" His voice hardened as he asked, "Is your husband here? Does he know that you're out riding alone?"

She took a deep breath before answering. "Yes—and no."

"Then why *are* you out riding? Unless—" He let the word hang as, unable to resist the temptation, she turned her eyes to his. For a moment, their eyes met and held. Then he nodded curtly. "I see. So you were looking for me. Why?"

Larissa adamantly shook her head. "I was not looking for anyone! I was simply out for a ride!"

"And you just happened to choose the road past the house that used to be ours?" He shook his head. "No, Larissa, I can't accept that. I lived with you too long not to know you better. There's a reason for everything you do, and there's only one reason why you would be riding by my house."

Ignoring her pounding heart, she snapped, "Oh! You are as insufferably arrogant as ever!" She dug her knees into her horse's flanks, intending to spur forward, but he leaned toward her and caught the bridle, holding the mare steady.

"They told me you were married and gone," Nathan said coldly, "but that's all anyone told me. Whether you like it or not, Larissa, you're stopping at my house. After all I've been through with you, I think I deserve some explanations."

She knew she should refuse, but she suddenly wanted him to understand. They could have no future together, but she could not bear the thought of him hating her, despising her for deserting him. Meekly, she allowed him to lead her mare to the door of his house, the house that had once been theirs.

Following him into the sitting room, she shook her head distractedly when he offered her tea. He dismissed the curious servants, closed the room's double doors, and turned to her expectantly.

Without waiting for his questions, she began to tell her story, beginning with the day he left for Whampoa and the hoppo came to visit her. He frowned as she told of her two unsuccessful attempts to contact him, but let her continue her story through the point where the Portuguese government placed a guard over the house and she first met Edmund Farrell.

"I must say," Nathan injected dryly, "it took you little enough time to find a new man."

"He was a friend who offered me protection when I was terrified," she insisted. "Besides," she added tartly, "it seems to me you should have little to say when you're consorting with a married woman!"

He scowled, then snorted in amusement. "I see you've been doing more spying than I thought. If you're referring to Estelle, she's no longer married. Larry died of smallpox last spring. Since then, she's become something of a commodity on Macao. If I choose to avail myself of her services from time to time, that's my business. At least she makes no false pledges of love and fidelity." He paused to stare at Larissa meaningfully, anger and jealousy burning in his amber-flecked eyes. "Tell me—why did you decide so quickly to marry this Farrell?"

"As I already said, after you did not respond to my messages, I supposed you no longer cared for me. Edmund offered me security, protection, companionship—" she faltered, but forced herself to add, "love. I needed an escape, and he was there."

Nathan frowned. "You know that I never received those messages?"

She nodded. "But I didn't find out until it was too late

After the wedding, I was in the carriage in front of Edmund's house on the Praya Grande, when the hoppo tried to kidnap me again. Edmund killed him. We drove back here and found the house in an uproar. Sun Yuan had hanged himself. That was when I found out the hoppo had bribed and blackmailed Sun Yuan and Lin Po not to deliver my messages."

Nathan rubbed his chin thoughtfully. "Apparently he had quite an efficient blackmail system. I wondered why you never answered my letters I sent from Whampoa. When I returned and learned you were married, I assumed that was why. But I suppose you never got those letters?"

She shook her head, and he continued on a pensive note. "No one told me about Sun Yuan's suicide," he whispered.

Watching him, Larissa suddenly realized that there was much more no one had told him. She had not mentioned her pregnancy to him, and Mei Ling had been the only servant to know. She would have to guard that secret now. If Nathan found out he had a son, he would surely want to see him, perhaps even to claim him. And that would be devastating to Edmund, who had struggled so hard for both her and Sean. Immersed in her thoughts, she scarcely heard Nathan's next question.

"Do you love him?"

Larissa blinked and looked up at him. "Who?"

"Your husband. Do you love him?"

"Yes. Of course." She wished she sounded more convincing.

Nathan crossed the room and stared down at her where she sat on the watered silk loveseat. His eyes were searching and sad. "You really don't love him, do you?"

Blinking uneasily, she shifted her gaze. "Nathan! What a terrible question! He's my husband, of course I love him." Flustered, she stood abruptly. "I think I'd better be going now."

His hands dropped onto her shoulders, gently restraining her. "If you love him so much, why did you say you found out 'too late' about the hoppo's blackmail? A woman who is happy with her marriage should have no regrets."

She swallowed, biting her lower lip. "Nathan," she

pleaded, "let's leave well enough alone. It's all behind us now. We can't change anything, so what does it matter?"

"It matters," he whispered, "because you and I still love each other."

"No—"

Nathan cut short Larissa's protest as his lips covered hers. Instantly, her knees weakened, her head began to spin, and she threw her arms around his neck to steady herself. Her mind told her she should fight and resist, but her body begged for surrender. Her body, long starved for the touch of true love, easily won.

Whimpering in delight, Larissa parted her lips and accepted his mouth. Her hands roamed over his back, re-acquainting themselves with his firm, strong muscles. She pressed herself against him, straining for the moment when they would be one.

Nathan's lips moved to the hollow at the base of her throat, and he gave a groan of anticipation. With tantalizing slowness, he unfastened the bodice of her green velvet riding habit and continued to undress her, his hands and lips caressing each newly bared inch as her clothing fell away. When she was naked, he stepped back, the amber flecks in his eyes changing to dancing fires of burnt orange as they roved over her body.

"I think you've grown even more beautiful," he murmured. "When I left you here, you were still part girl. But now you are all woman—all beautiful, bewitching woman."

Stepping to his side, she helped him undress, trembling with uncontrollable anticipation. She rubbed her face in the soft, matted fur of his chest, reveling in the scent she had known and loved for so many months. Her arms wound around him, and she closed her eyes. They were together again. He still loved her. For the moment, nothing else mattered.

His lips were on hers again as he lifted her and carried her to the settee. As they lay together, she was gripped by a passion stronger and more demanding than she had ever before known. Sensing her need, he drove into her almost immediately, and she sighed with the sensation of sweet fullness. They moved together in a frenzy of desire, together finding their final, shuddering fulfillment.

Afterwards, they continued to lie together, and she felt

his manhood growing again against her stomach. Smiling blissfully, she slid a hand down to stroke it, then gently guided him into her. Their urgency spent, they moved more slowly this time, each savoring the fullness of the other's love. Slowly, sweetly, he brought her to the peak of sensation, urged on by her soft, ecstatic moans. Again and again she soared to the heights, floating peacefully down in the wake of the small explosions within her.

He had lost none of his stamina and forgotten none of the things that most pleased and excited her. For more than an hour, they were one, locked together by the forces of love. They became the only two beings on earth, striving only to bring each other pleasure and feeling that pleasure returned one hundredfold.

In the drowsy, contented aftermath of love, Larissa propped herself on an elbow and gazed down lovingly at Nathan's face—the crooked nose, the ruggedly chiseled jaw and cheekbones, the mop of chestnut hair. He opened his eyes, and she stared into their amber-flecked gray depths. Sean's eyes, she thought suddenly. All of reality seemed to cave in on her, and she looked away, unable to bear his gaze.

"Larissa?" He caught a lock of her hair, tugging on it gently until her eyes returned to his. "What will we do now, love? Will you tell him about us and leave him?"

Her eyes brimmed with tears, and she slowly shook her head. "I can't. It's impossible."

"You mean it would be too hard for you to tell him? Do you want me to come with you?"

"No! No!" She sat up, her tears tracing patterns down her cheeks and dripping to his chest. "I mean I can't leave him. I pledged my life to him and—he needs me."

He frowned. "Do you suppose for one moment that I don't need you? What about the love you've professed for me? Isn't that also a kind of pledge?"

Turning away, she covered her ears. "Please, Nathan, don't! You're strong, you can survive without me and—" She stopped herself on the verge of declaring Edmund's weakness, her fear that he might return to opium if he lost her. Instead, she blurted, "And we have a son."

"What?" Stunned, he sat up beside her.

"Edmund and I have a son," she said slowly, so there could be no mistaking her meaning. "I can't leave the child, and it would be too cruel to take him away from Edmund."

Pursing his lips, Nathan studied her thoughtfully. "But, you're not happy, are you?"

"I'm—" she faltered, knowing she could not deceive him. "I'm as content as possible. Sean is a darling little boy, and I love him with all my heart. Edmund is very kind, very devoted, and I know he loves me deeply. What more could I want?"

"Someone you love in return."

She sighed, getting up to begin dressing. "I do love you, Nathan. Even if I wanted to, I couldn't deny that. But—"

"I'm not giving you up!" he interrupted. "If I can't have you all of the time, at least let's be together whenever possible. There must be afternoons like today when your husband is away and we can meet."

"No!" she said firmly. "I won't do it to Edmund, and I won't do it to us. How long do you think our love could remain intact while we were torn apart by guilt? Each time we held each other, each time we became one, we could forget, but the guilt would always be there, returning ever stronger after every day we spent together. I know now that I should never have come here today. I'm sorry, Nathan, because now we'll both be tormented by this reminder of our months together. But, in time, that memory will grow more distant, and we'll learn to treasure what we had instead of craving its renewal."

Watching silently as she fastened the last hook of her riding habit, Nathan shook his head. "That was a fine, lofty speech," he murmured, "but I don't think you believe it any more than I do."

She concentrated on pulling on her kid riding gloves. "I have to believe it, Nathan," she said, striving to keep her face and voice impassive, "because, no matter how much I love you, this is the last time I will allow myself to see you."

Chapter Twenty-One

Mei Ling regarded Larissa reproachfully, but did not question her when she arrived home that afternoon. It was obvious where she had been, since a mere glance at her smiling son made her burst into tears.

How, Larissa wondered, could she keep from weakening again, when Sean was always with her, a painful reminder that Nathan lived only a few miles away?

Claiming a headache, Larissa retired to her room and was still there when Edmund arrived home. Hearing him moving around in the adjoining bedroom, she dabbed at her eyes with a handkerchief and tried to put her face and hair in order. But it was no use. When Edmund knocked and entered, he could see immediately that she had been weeping.

"Darling, what's wrong?" he asked, crossing the room to examine her tear-ravaged face. "Mei Ling told me you weren't feeling well, and even little Sean said his mummy was crying. I'm afraid the child is quite upset about you."

She forced a smile. "It—it's nothing, really. I went out for a little ride this afternoon, and I just got a bit melancholy, thinking of how you and I used to ride together."

Edmund looked confused. "Are those memories so painful they make you weep?"

"No, of course not. Those are treasured moments. But you know how we women are—we weep for joy as often as for sadness."

He shook his head, still unconvinced. "Some women are like that, I know. But you have always seemed so strong. You're not—" he paused, almost embarrassed by his question, "with child, are you?"

She stared at him dumbstruck, wondering for the first time if she could be pregnant again. So far, she had no reason to believe she was carrying Edmund's child. For the first time, she thought about the possible consequences of her reunion with Nathan. Was it possible she could have come away from her one afternoon with him nurturing his seed? Would all her resolutions for the future be lost in this one afternoon of weakness? Not daring to think more about that possibility, she shook her head briskly.

Stunned by her reaction, Edmund sighed and mumbled, "Forgive me. I had no idea the thought of carrying my child would be so repulsive to you. I merely thought that sometimes during pregnancy a woman. . . . But of course when you were carrying Sean, you seemed in perfect control of—"

He stumbled in his embarrassment, and Larissa's heart went out to him. Overwhelmed with guilt, both for the afternoon and for her own insensitivity to her husband, she exclaimed, "Darling, you mustn't jump to conclusions! I'd love to bear your child! It's just that I've had no indication, and your suggestion surprised me so. I'm sorry if I've upset you. I just feel a bit under the weather today, but I'm sure I'll get over it."

He nodded, wanting desperately to believe her. "I suppose I've been neglecting you too much. Perhaps you got melancholy thinking about our rides because I haven't taken you riding once since we arrived here. But here's some news that should cheer you—Governor Pinto has invited us to his Christmas ball."

Larissa swallowed hard, struggling to maintain her composure as she realized Nathan would, no doubt, be invited too. "How very kind of him," she whispered, "but of course I can't attend."

Edmund looked shocked. "What do you mean? Of course you can attend! It will be a marvelous party. I understand he's invited quite a large number of prominent traders of all nationalities."

"But I can't leave Sean for the evening," she protested lamely.

"By the time the ball begins, Sean will be sound asleep and won't even know you're gone. And Mei Ling is quite capable of caring for him. Really, Larissa, I thought you'd be more excited at the prospect of reentering society. You're not embarrassed to be seen with me, are you?"

"Of course not! I—it's just—" She sighed, knowing she could not tell him the real reason for her reluctance. "Well, we'll see," she concluded weakly, hoping she could find some plausible excuse during the three weeks remaining before the ball.

Beginning the very next day, those three weeks proved to be even more difficult than the months when she had helped Edmund battle his addiction. Now, she had to fight her own addiction, which had lain in abeyance for almost three years—her addiction for Nathan. And there was no one to whom she could turn for support and guidance.

Larissa was in the nursery with Sean and Mei Ling the morning after her meeting with Nathan, when a package arrived addressed to Sean. Despite her premonitions, Larissa allowed the child to unwrap and open the box, to reveal a delicate china cup with his name printed in gilded letters across the side.

"Pretty!" Sean exclaimed. "Who gave it?"

"Umm, let's see." Larissa watched anxiously as the boy pulled the cup out of the box. Hoping to escape Mei Ling's watchful gaze, she snatched away the note that lay concealed beneath the gift. "It's from one of mummy's old friends, darling," she explained.

"Who?" Sean persisted.

"Someone you don't know, Sean. Her name is Estelle."

Mei Ling's frown told Larissa the maid knew she was lying. Averting her gaze from the older woman, Larissa said, "Mei Ling, why don't you take Sean to the kitchen and fill his new cup with milk for him? I'm sure he's anxious to try it out."

"You come too, mummy," the boy pleaded.

"Oh, I'll be along in a moment," she said. "Now, run along, sweetheart."

Shaking her head disapprovingly, Mei Ling led the child away. As the door closed behind them, Larissa opened the note, sighing as she read:

Dearest love,
  Fearing the sincerity of your farewell, I must, nevertheless, beg you to reconsider. After all we have shared, I cannot believe you capable of turning your back on me, and if you search in your heart, I do not think you can deny that I am right. At this point, I do not know what the solution is, but I do know that I want you and I refuse to give you up so easily. I will be at the house this

afternoon at the same time we met yesterday. Please, my love, find a way to come to me. I need you, and I do not think you want our separation any more than I.

I shall await you most impatiently,

Your loving Nathan

The words seemed to swim on the paper as tears welled in Larissa's eyes. She thought how difficult it must have been for Nathan to write such a note. Of course she did not want to be separated from him, but her desires were secondary now. She had to think of Edmund and of Sean. She could not allow herself to succumb to the temptation.

Crumpling the note, she took it to her room and burned it over a candle. She ached at least to send Nathan some message of explanation. But she smothered the desire to do even that. What could she say that she had not said yesterday? Besides, if she replied, even to say she would not meet him, he would be encouraged to approach her again. It would be better not to reply at all. Let him think her harsh and unfeeling if necessary. At least she would be spared the anguish of seeing him or hearing from him again.

But he did not give up so easily. In the next several days, more gifts arrived for Sean—toys, clothing, even an intricately carved and painted rocking horse—all accompanied by notes begging Larissa to meet him again. Larissa would have turned the gifts away, but Sean was always there when they arrived and seemed so excited that she could not deny him the pleasure of opening them. Fortunately, Edmund was so immersed in his work that he did not notice the numerous additions to the nursery. But Larissa lived in fear that Sean would mention the gifts to him.

Two weeks after she had said goodbye to Nathan, Larissa was enjoying a late breakfast in bed when a note arrived for her. Surprised that it had not been concealed within another gift to her son, she tore it open immediately and scanned the terse lines:

Larissa,

Since you refuse to do me the courtesy of accepting my invitations or even of replying to them, I find that I must deliver an ultimatum. If you do not consent to visit me this afternoon, I will be forced to call on you at your

home—perhaps about seven o'clock in the evening, when
you and your husband are at dinner. As always, I await
your pleasure.

                                                    N.

Larissa's heart seemed to jump into her throat. Nathan
was reckless and headstrong enough to do just as he
threatened. But Edmund must never know who her lover
had been. He must never suspect that she had seen him
since their return to Macao, that she still loved him.

In her haste to get up and dress, she overturned her
breakfast tray, spilling tea and juice on the counterpane.
Without even bothering to right the cups, she hurried to
her armoire, chose a simple brown riding habit, and
slipped into it. Opening her door to the hallway, she met
a startled Mei Ling, her hand raised, about to knock.

"I was coming to help you dress," Mei Ling said, "but
I see that won't be necessary." Her eyebrows raised quizzically as she looked beyond Larissa to the overturned
breakfast tray.

"I was anxious to go out riding," Larissa explained
quickly, "so I dressed myself. I had a slight accident with
my tray. Please see that it is cleaned up while I'm gone."

She brushed past Mei Ling and hurried down the hall,
appearing to ignore the servant's warning to be careful.

Riding toward Nathan's house, Larissa's sense of urgency was gradually replaced by rage. Who did Nathan
think he was, threatening to go to her husband? If he loved
her as much as he claimed, he would want to protect her
from any scandal, even if it meant sacrificing his own desires. But he was obviously too selfish to think of anything
except satisfying his own passions.

By the time she reached his house, she was livid. Dis-
mounting, she pounded furiously on the door until Nathan
himself answered.

He stood in the doorway, one brow cocked, as he smiled
in amusement. "A bit early, aren't you?" he quipped. "I
believe our appointment was for this afternoon."

"We have no appointment," Larissa snapped, "and I'm
in no mood for your sarcasm, Nathan Masters! Just who do
you think you are, threatening to visit me when Edmund
is at home?"

He shrugged. "What does it matter? The threat brought
you here, did it not?"

Her eyes flashed in rage. "Do you mean you wouldn't have come? That it was all a ruse?"

Again, he shrugged. "Who can say what I might have done? Desperation drives a man to do strange things. But as I said, what does it matter? You're here. That's all that is important."

Nathan reached out, taking Larissa's hands to draw her into the house, but she shook him off roughly. "Don't touch me, you scheming, deceitful, selfish beast! I'll come in, but only for a moment, and only because I want to avoid a scene within view of the street." She stepped past him into the house, pushing the door closed behind her.

"Shall we go to the sitting room or perhaps to the veranda?"

She stiffened at the undertone of laughter in his voice. "That won't be necessary. I have little enough to say, so I can say it right here."

He sighed and brushed a stray curl away from her face, his fingers lingering on her cheek. "Why don't you admit it, Larissa, you want to be here—otherwise you would not have come."

"I do *not* want to be here!" she snapped. But tears brimmed in her eyes, and she fought the quivering caused by his touch. "Don't you understand, Nathan, that what *I* want, what *you* want, what *we* want doesn't matter one whit? There are times when one must put honor and obligations before personal desires. Can't you admit that this is one of those times?"

Nathan shook his head slowly. "You've grown up more than I would have wished, Larissa. What's happened to the girl who impulsively stowed away on the *Queen of Cathay*? Or the girl who damned the risks and bribed Jonathan Dillard to take her ashore at Smyrna? Has your stuffy British husband tamed you so thoroughly?"

She tossed her head defiantly. "He hasn't tamed me at all! But when I left Boston I had only myself to think of. Now I have responsibilities to others. I have to think of Edmund and Sean."

"What about your responsibilities to me? You've told me you love me. Doesn't that give me the right to demand some allegiance?"

"No!" she said sharply. "You didn't marry me—even when—" She stopped herself, on the verge of saying, "even when I was carrying your child." Again, she reminded herself that he had not known, did not know, and must never know that Sean was his son. "Even when you knew I wanted it," she finished lamely.

"So, that's it!" Nathan snarled, suddenly angry. "Is marriage more important to you than love? Now who's the selfish one? I told you there were good reasons why I would not marry, but my feelings made no difference to you."

Throwing up her hands, she turned toward the door. "I knew I shouldn't have come. It's impossible for either of us to talk sensibly. You know as well as I that I would have stayed with you indefinitely, even without marriage, if only I thought you cared. But when you didn't respond to my messages—"

"Through no fault of my own," he cut her off sharply, "since I never received them. Must we go over the same ground again? Can't we forget that? Do we have to be punished for the rest of our lives by the scheming of that evil hoppo?"

He caught her by the shoulders, turning her to face him, his eyes filled with pleading. "I love you, Larissa. Doesn't that mean anything to you? For the sake of your son, I'm willing to admit I can't have all of you. But can't I have at least some part of you?"

Quickly, before she succumbed to his pleading gaze, she shook her head. "You can have the memories of the time we shared. The same memories I will treasure for the rest of my life. Anything else, any liaison we might arrange, would soon become sordid, soiled by deceit and guilt. No matter what you say, I know you're too honorable to take what belongs to another man. And I could not live with myself, knowing what I was doing to Edmund."

Sighing, Nathan tightened his grip on her shoulders. "Don't you think," he asked softly, "that you will someday find memories are not enough to satisfy you?"

Larissa tensed, thinking how, already, she was dissatisfied by the way Edmund failed to stir her passions. Closing her eyes, she shook her head. "No!" she insisted, surprising herself by the firmness of her tone. "Memories are all I need. Now all I ask is that you leave me alone."

Nathan's hands dropped away from her suddenly, as if he had been burned, and Larissa knew that his eyes must be filled with hurt. Fearing her resolve might crumble, she did not look at him. Eyes downcast, she turned and let herself out. She stumbled on the front walk as tears clouded her vision. She might have turned to beg Nathan to forget all she had said, but she had gone no more than a few steps when the door slammed behind her, underscoring the grim finality of their separation.

Sean received no more gifts, and Larissa received no more notes. Trying to forget Nathan, Larissa concentrated on preparing for Governor Pinto's ball, which she now admitted she could not escape attending. Together with Mei Ling, she designed an original ball gown that combined Chinese and European styles.

The gown was emerald green silk with a modest décolletage. Fitted over the bosom, it fell loose to the floor, without a waistline. A line of elaborate gold satin frogs trimmed the front, left of center. The sleeves were wrist-length and flowing, and Mei Ling labored for days to complete an exquisite silk embroidery pattern on the back. On each side, the gown was slit to the knee, revealing a pale green silk underskirt.

The evening of the ball, Mei Ling spent almost an hour arranging Larissa's hair in an elaborate French roll, then attached tiny silk butterflies above each temple and in the back.

When, at last, Larissa went to meet Edmund in the salon, he smiled appreciatively, "You look stunning, darling, I wager I'll be the most envied man at the ball tonight."

Cocking her head, she surveyed his green brocade waistcoat and impeccable black evening attire. "And I will be the most envied woman. How splendid you look, Edmund!"

Beaming at her compliment, he took her arm and steered her toward the door. "Now, aren't you glad I wouldn't listen to your nonsense about staying home with Sean? Any mother as devoted as you deserves an occasional evening out."

"I suppose you're right," she mumbled, but already her mind was wandering. Would Nathan be at the ball? Would she be able to face him with the same cool exterior she had somehow managed to maintain when they had parted?

The governor's mansion was already crowded when they arrived. Standing outside the ballroom, waiting to be announced, Larissa stared at the polished marble pillars and intricately tiled dance floor, afraid to lift her eyes and survey the other guests.

His hand on her elbow, Edmund bent to whisper solicitously, "You're shivering, darling. You're not becoming ill, are you?"

She shook her head distractedly. "No, I must just have gotten a bit chilled in the carriage."

"Well, no doubt you'll warm up once you begin dancing. You look so exquisite that I'm sure the men won't give you much chance to stand idle."

Indeed, she did not miss a single dance, but moved from partner to partner, acknowledging each with a smile, but scarcely hearing their compliments as they danced. Inside, she felt like a tightly coiled spring that might unwind at any moment. She scanned the crowd, vacillating between relief and despair when she did not see Nathan.

It had been more than a week since their last confrontation, and already she was beginning to doubt the wisdom of her decision. How had she managed to turn away when she could have embraced at least a part of the happiness they had once shared? How could she manage to live the rest of her life without him? When she thought about it objectively, she knew it was best not to see him —especially here, where Edmund would be sure to detect the depth of passion they shared. Still, it was impossible to squelch the desires burning within her.

The evening was more than half over when, while the orchestra stopped to rest, Edmund escorted her to the veranda for a breath of fresh air. They strolled along the balustrade, gazing out over the Pearl River. Lost in thought, Larissa did not notice until too late that they were walking toward Estelle Jamieson and her tall, dark escort.

"Larissa!" Estelle exclaimed with false warmth. "What a pleasure to see you!" She clung to her escort's arm, just as Larissa had seen her clinging to Nathan the day she glimpsed them entering his house. "This is my dear friend, Sir Rodney Drake," she bubbled. "Won't you introduce me to the handsome gentleman accompanying you?"

"The handsome gentleman," Larissa replied icily, "is my husband, Edmund Farrell."

"Ah, your husband." Estelle eyed him curiously, then continued. "Speaking of handsome gentlemen, I've some news that might interest you about a certain one."

Larissa stiffened, feeling Edmund tense beside her. "Really, Estelle, I hardly think I'd be interested. Since my marriage, I've confined my interest in men to my husband."

"Is that so?" Estelle's eyebrows shot up doubtfully. "Then perhaps you wouldn't care to know that Nathan Masters has left his house on Macao and moved to the British colony of Hong Kong."

"Oh." Larissa tried to keep her voice expressionless. "Why would he want to do that? Edmund tells me Hong Kong is a dreadful place."

"So I've heard. But he seemed quite set on locating in the most dreadful place imaginable. I've heard his decision had something to do with a woman. Something about a broken-off love affair. But I can hardly believe dear Nathan would take a matter of the heart so seriously, can you?"

"No—no I can't. But, of course," Larissa added quickly, "I really didn't know him that well."

"Oh?" Estelle paused meaningfully, then laughed lightly. "Well, I knew him most intimately, and I must say I'm most surprised at his behavior. But mark my words— in no time he'll recover his old spirit. No woman can hold that man's heart for long. Well, dearie"—she reached out to squeeze Larissa's arm—"I can't tell you how nice it was to see you. Do stop in at the house sometime, so we can relive old times."

Frowning, Edmund watched Estelle and her partner move away. "Who is that woman?" he asked.

"Estelle Jamieson. She's the widow of an American trader. We attended the races together a few times before I met you."

"Oh. From the way she spoke, one would think you and she had been close friends."

"Not at all. Estelle is rather a superficial person. Actually, we never got along too well." Inwardly, she sighed in gratitude that Sean had never told Edmund about the gifts she claimed came from Estelle.

"And who was this Masters she spoke of?"

"A mutual acquaintance. A trader from Boston, I believe." Casually, she added, "I think he was one of Estelle's former lovers."

"Hmm," Edmund chuckled, "no doubt she was not the one who sent the man into exile. A woman must be very special to cause a man to give up his home." Pausing, he stared at Larissa pensively. "Someone like you, for example. If you were ever to leave me, darling, I don't know what I'd do."

Forcing a light laugh, she averted her eyes. "Well, I don't think you need to give the possibility much thought, as I fully intend to stay with you for life!"

Chapter Twenty-Two

With Nathan gone from Macao, Larissa found it easier to devote herself to her husband and son. Though her heart still ached to be near him, she accepted the fact that he was out of reach and strove to lose herself in her everyday duties as a wife and mother. Frequent invitations to balls hosted by members of the British community also helped her to forget, at least for a little while, the ecstasy she had rejected.

Soon after the New Year, she began to suspect that she might have more than memories to remind her of her brief reunion with Nathan. By February she was sure she was carrying another child. Of course, she consoled herself, in all likelihood this child was Edmund's. Their marital relations had fallen into a regular pattern, so it was much more likely the child had been conceived on one of those occasions, rather than on the single afternoon with Nathan. Still, every time she looked at Sean, who grew more like his father every day, she felt gripped by a certainty that Nathan had also fathered the child growing within her.

When Larissa finally confided her condition to Edmund, he was elated. He insisted that they host their own ball to celebrate the coming event, and Larissa found herself powerless to refuse him. Dressed in pale blue moire, she graciously greeted each guest and danced with each gentleman who asked her, all the time praying that her husband's great expectations would not be disappointed.

Though he had always treated Sean with all the love and attention due from a father, it quickly became obvious that Edmund would prize the new baby as his own firstborn. He would never deny Sean either his affection or the right to what he owned, but he felt a special pride, believing he had helped to create the child Larissa was carrying. Before her pregnancy had even begun to show, he became so solicitous that his attentions were almost bothersome. Forcing a laugh, Larissa reminded him that she had survived a monsoon and a boatwreck while carrying Sean, and the child was none the worse for the experiences.

Edmund's attentions greatly underscored Larissa's fears. Suppose, she worried, the child looked exactly like Sean? Would Edmund know then that the same man had fathered both children? Would he realize she had been unfaithful, for however short a time? And if he did, what would that realization do to him? He had been more than generous in accepting Sean and presenting him to the world as his own son. Could she expect him to accept a second bastard so graciously?

Spring came, and Larissa began to wonder why her husband did not seem more anxious to depart for Shanghai to assume his position as head of the company cotton trade. At breakfast one morning in April, she asked casually, "Should I have Mei Ling begin packing for the trip north?"

Edmund frowned into his tea and cleared his throat. "I'd like to begin the trip immediately. Goodness knows," he said, gazing at her growing middle, "if we delay much longer, you'll be in no condition to travel. And I really should begin to set up the company office there."

"Well, then when is the next ship north? Sean, Mei Ling, and I can be ready whenever you say."

He smiled indulgently. "I'm sure you could be, but I'm afraid that's not the issue." He hesitated, then plunged ahead. "There are reports of smallpox in the Shanghai region, and I can't bring myself to endanger your life, Sean's, or the baby's. But, if I don't go soon, I'm afraid the company will find someone else to handle their textile trade."

"But they can't expect you to endanger *your* life!" she protested.

"No," he said simply, "but my superiors know I would not be endangering my life. You see, I've already had smallpox and, having survived, am immune to further attacks."

She stared at him incredulously. "You've had smallpox? But there's no indication."

"You mean my skin is not pitted? I was one of the fortunate few who escaped without scars."

"And you're certain it would be safe for you to be exposed now?"

"Quite certain. The doctors assured me I need never again fear the disease."

"Then you must go on to Shanghai without us," she said firmly.

Edmund pushed his chair back from the table, stood up, and began to pace. "That's out of the question. I can't leave you in your condition. I have to be with you when the baby is born. I saw how you suffered with Sean, and I'd never forgive myself if I left you to bear all that pain—pain that I caused—without my comfort."

Larissa winced, wondering for the thousandth time whether Edmund or Nathan had fathered the child. "But I wouldn't be alone," she quickly assured him. "Mei Ling will be here and all the other servants. I won't deny you were a great help when Sean was born, but no matter how much I miss you, I'm sure we could manage."

Still, he shook his head. "It's unthinkable. What if something should happen to you during the birth?"

"Nothing will happen. I'm strong as an ox. But perhaps—" she paused to think, "we could go with you, after all. We could get vaccinated—I heard it was done in Boston during a smallpox outbreak some years ago."

"No." Edmund held up a hand to stop her flow of words. "I won't hear of it. Some physicians say this vaccination works, and others say it does not. Perhaps, if we were in an area where you were already threatened by the disease, I might consider it. But it hardly seems wise to take unnecessary chances. Besides, we can't guess how a vaccination might affect the unborn baby."

"I suppose you're right. But if you won't go yourself and you won't take us with you, I can think of only one other solution to the problem."

He stopped pacing to stare at her expectantly.

Swallowing, Larissa forced herself to go on, before she lost the nerve to suggest it. "Let the company send someone else to Shanghai. You can stay here and take over my share of Bennett and Barnes. No doubt the ship is—"

"I believe we've discussed this before," he said, cutting her off sharply, "and I thought I made myself clear at that time. I refuse to live off my wife's inheritance."

Larissa sighed, more from relief than from frustration with his stubbornness. Dealing with the company would demand contact with Nathan, and now, of all times, she knew she could not bear even to see him. She still had not abandoned hopes of someday claiming her inheritance, but now that she was pregnant, she was quite willing to put off the task. Perhaps, in time, Nathan would leave the company, making her eventual dealings with Bennett and Barnes less emotional. In the meantime, Edmund must not know her relief or the reason for it.

"Well," she stated flatly, "since you insist on being so stubborn about my father's business, you had better start thinking more seriously about the other two alternatives. I assume that if you lose your position with the East India Company our wealth will be greatly curtailed—unless of course you have some independent source you've never disclosed to me?"

He shook his head.

"Then the only logical course is for you to go to Shanghai alone." Seeing he was about to protest further, she hurriedly added, "It would only be for a few months, Edmund! By the time you establish the cotton trade office and find us suitable living quarters, the smallpox scare may have passed, and we can all join you there. In fact, if you travel by steamer both ways and encounter no business difficulties in Shanghai, you may even be back on Macao before the child is born."

"I suppose that might be possible," he agreed quietly. Then, crossing the room to put his arms around her, he gazed into her eyes and asked, "You're sure you wouldn't feel I was deserting you? I mean, I'd make every effort to be back here in time, but I can't be sure of what I might find—what conditions might delay me."

"I understand," she said, smiling. "And even if you can't be here when the baby is born, we'll all still be here whenever you do return." Secretly, she thought that the rest of her pregnancy might be easier to bear without Edmund underfoot. And if the child was born while he was still gone and did resemble Nathan, she would have more time in which to consider what to do.

Perhaps only her condition made her think so, but summer seemed excessively hot and sultry that year. With Edmund gone and her stomach growing larger every day, Larissa graciously declined whatever social invitations she received, preferring to stay at home with Sean.

Estelle Jamieson dropped in uninvited one day to inform her that Nathan had stopped on Macao before going north to Canton. "It was such a thrill to see him," she remarked cattily. "He seemed to have survived the winter on Hong Kong without ill effects, and I daresay he's gotten over whoever it was he was pining for."

She gazed at Larissa pointedly, staring longer than necessary at her distended belly. "I couldn't help mentioning to him how we'd met at the governor's ball and what a charming, handsome husband you have. And, of course, I just had to mention the coming blessed event."

"Of course," Larissa replied coolly. "But really, Estelle, I don't know why you should bother him with details about me. We have separate lives now, and I'm sure neither of us is particularly concerned about the other."

"Well," Estelle said haughtily, setting aside her lemonade and rising, "it did seem evident to me that he was not particularly interested in what I had to say about you. By the way, when is the baby due?"

"Late August, I believe."

"I see." She motioned for Larissa to remain seated as she walked toward the terrace door. "For some reason, Nathan asked. I'll have to tell him the next time he visits me. Don't disturb yourself, I'll see myself out."

Larissa sank back on her lounge, contemplating Estelle's words. If Nathan didn't particularly care about her, why did he ask when the child would be born? Did he suspect that he might be the father? No, that was absurd, she told herself. He thought he had never impregnated her in all the months they had lived together, so he would not suspect it now, after their one time together. No doubt his question had been no more than a casually dropped remark, and Estelle, sensing that she still cared, intended to torment her with it.

She was still thinking about Estelle's visit that night as she tried to fall asleep. She could hear the mosquitoes buzzing around the netting that swathed her bed. They all slept under netting to avoid the insects, which seemed especially pesky this summer.

Trying to push Nathan from her mind, Larissa turned her thoughts to other things. One of the servants had returned from the market that morning with reports of malaria in the city. The news did not especially worry her, since she and Sean remained relatively isolated in the house on the Praya Grande. Since they did not breathe the swamp air present in some of the more unsavory sections of the city, which everyone knew caused the illness, they were unlikely to be threatened by it.

"Mummy! Mummy!" Sean's sharp cry cut into her thoughts. She pushed aside her sheets and netting, wondering what could be alarming the child. Before retiring less than an hour ago, she had checked on him, and he had been sleeping peacefully. Wearing only her thin lawn nightgown, not bothering to slip into a dressing gown, she hurried to his room.

"Here I am, darling," she called. "What is it?"

In the moonlight, she could see her son sitting up in bed, sobbing. "Mummy, is it really you?" he asked, "Are you all right?"

"Of course I'm all right, darling." She crossed to the bed and gathered him into her arms. "What's the matter?"

He huddled against her. "I don't know. I just woke up and thought you were gone away." He paused and drew a long, sniffling breath. "Mummy, when the new baby comes, you'll still be my mummy too, won't you?"

Larissa smiled tenderly, remembering how many of Edmund's married friends had warned her that the first child was always very jealous of a new baby. "Of course, darling," she soothed. "I'll always be your mummy. And in another month or so, the new baby will be born, and papa will be coming back from Shanghai, and we'll all be a nice, happy family."

"Are you sure?" he asked, sniffling.

"Of course I'm sure. Now, you lay back down and go to sleep."

Obediently, Sean lay back, but he still clutched her hand. "Will you stay here, mummy, until I go to sleep?"

"If you wish." She pulled his covers around him and adjusted the netting over his bed. In a few minutes he was asleep again, and she tiptoed back to her room.

As she was about to climb back into her own bed, Larissa felt an itch on her left forearm. Scratching, her fingers found a small, raised spot. So, she thought absently, one of the mosquitoes had found its target. Well, the bite would be a nuisance, but it would be gone within a few days. Yawning, she pulled her covers over her and readjusted her netting to avoid any more bothersome bites.

Ten days later, Larissa had long forgotten that isolated mosquito bite. Almost all her thoughts were now concentrated on speeding the next few weeks so she could deliver her child and return to feeling normal.

Sitting on the terrace, while Sean played at her feet, she watched the assortment of junks, sampans, and clippers gliding on the Pearl River. She was thinking of going indoors for a bit, for the hot sun made the terrace unbearably bright, and she was developing a severe headache. In fact, she did not feel at all well, and she supposed she had stayed out too long for a woman in her condition.

She was so large now that she felt uncomfortable no matter what she did. She could neither sit nor stand for any length of time. She shifted position in her chair and smoothed her gown. Her hand brushed her bare forearm, and it occurred to her that her skin felt quite cool, despite her time in the sun. Suddenly, she began to shiver with cold. The shivering increased until her whole body seemed to be shaking with chills.

Struggling to her feet, Larissa stumbled toward the doors leading into the house. She was shaking so violently and her head was pounding so insistently that she could scarcely focus her eyes. She felt a tugging at her hand and looked down to see Sean staring up at her, wide-eyed.

"Mummy, what's wrong?" he asked in alarm.

She shook her head. "I'm not sure, darling, but mummy feels very ill. Run and get Mei Ling for me. Hurry!"

Leaning weakly against the door frame, she closed her eyes and listened to the boy's running footsteps as he went to find her maid. Chills continued to wrack her body, and she felt as if she would surely collapse if she tried to take another step. Hours seemed to pass before Mei Ling, accompanied by one of the male servants, bustled to her side. Together, they half-dragged, half-carried her to her bed.

Buried beneath a mound of comforters, Larissa continued to shiver and shake for almost two hours. Then, as the shivering stopped, she felt her body growing gradually warmer, until she was throwing off all her covers in an attempt to cool down. Her heart thudded rapidly, and she begged for glass after glass of water, feeling as if her thirst would never be quenched. Drifting on the edge of delirium, she could hear Mei Ling talking to someone.

"Yes," said a man's voice with a pronounced British accent, "it's malaria, all right. A severe case, from all indications. Keep the boy away from her and call me again if she seems to get any worse. I'll send some quinine over. See that she takes some three times a day."

Hours later, her body was drenched with sweat, and the fever gradually subsided. In the dim light of a candle, Larissa could see Mei Ling sitting beside her bed, looking worried.

"How could I have malaria?" Larissa asked weakly.

The servant shrugged. "Who can say how? We know only that it is so. I have seen the disease many times before, and the doctor confirmed my suspicions. Now, you must rest while you can, for I fear the fever is far from finished with you."

On awakening the next morning, Larissa was sure Mei Ling had been wrong. She felt rested and stronger and would have gotten out of bed if Mei Ling had not insisted that she stay there.

"No, no," Mei Ling said. "In your condition, you must rest all you can. Believe me, the worst is not over yet."

By afternoon, Larissa was again wracked by chills, followed by fever, delirium, sweating, and finally, exhausted sleep. Somehow, Mei Ling managed to force the bitter quinine down her throat three times a day, but its effects seemed minimal.

The pattern was repeated on the third day. On the fourth day, a new dimension of suffering was added. As her body moved from the chill to fever stage, Larissa felt a sharp cramp in her stomach. She tried to ignore it, concentrating on the time when the fever would subside and she would again sink into blessed sleep. But the pain came again and again with a regularity and insistency, until at last the realization swept over her—the baby was coming!

In the next hours, as she drifted between delirium and acute awareness, the pains increased until they became almost unbearable. She screamed and sobbed, digging her fingernails into Mei Ling's hand. At last, she heard a baby's cry, and again she drifted into delirium.

She did not wake again until morning, when the fever had broken again and she felt rested but weak from her ordeal. Squinting in the harsh morning light that flooded the room, she slowly remembered the events of the day before. Sometime while she burned with fever and ached with thirst, she had heard a baby cry. Her baby had been born!

"Mei Ling!" she called, struggling to sit up. "Mei Ling!"

The door opened, and Mei Ling entered, looking haggard from a sleepless night. "Forgive me, mistress. I had intended to be here when you awoke, but I had expected you to sleep a while longer."

"Never mind." Larissa waved away her explanation. "Where is the baby? Will you bring him to me?"

Mei Ling hesitated, and a shadow passed over her strained face. "I'm afraid that's not possible," she whispered.

Larissa frowned in annoyance. "Not possible? Why not?" Then she smiled in sudden understanding. "Oh, I suppose he's sleeping, and you don't want to disturb him. Well, never mind, I'll go myself and have a look at him." She swung her legs from the bed and began to stand up.

"No!" Mei Ling gave a strangled cry.

Sinking back on the edge of the bed, Larissa flashed her maid a puzzled look. "Mei Ling, what is wrong with you? Surely I can be allowed to see my own son. Or is it a daughter?"

"A girl," Mei Ling whispered.

"Well, Edmund should be pleased. We can name her Victoria, for the queen." She slipped on her dressing gown and stood to tie its sash, swaying a bit on unsteady feet.

"Please," Mei Ling moaned. "You can't see the baby."

"I won't wake her, but—is it the malaria? Does the doctor think she could catch it?"

"No, no," Mei Ling wrung her hands in despair. "Please sit down. Please!"

Perplexed by her maid's earnest pleading, Larissa did as she asked. Suddenly, a wave of fear enveloped her. "Mei Ling," she demanded, quietly but firmly, "is something wrong with my baby?"

Mutely, Mei Ling nodded, her eyes swimming with misery.

"What is it? Why can't I see her?"

"Because she's—she's—" Mei Ling stammered, then forced herself to say, "—She's dead."

"No!" Larissa paled and held onto the mattress for support. "You're wrong! I know you're wrong! I heard her cry when she was born!"

"How I wish it was not so!" Mei Ling sobbed. "She did cry at birth, but she lived less than an hour."

"And where is she now?" Larissa asked in a hollow voice.

"The Episcopal priest was here only minutes ago to take her for burial."

"Before I even saw her?"

Mei Ling looked down. "I thought it best. If you saw her, you would only be haunted by the memory of her for the rest of your life. This way, it will be easier for you to forget—and you must forget, for your own peace of mind."

Larissa's eyes snapped. "It was not your place to make the decision! She was my child. I carried her for almost nine months. I had a right, at least, to see her."

"Someone had to attend to matters," Mei Ling said quietly, her voice heavy with hurt. "There was nothing more anyone could do for the baby, so I had to think of your well-being."

For a long moment, Larissa was silent. Then she whispered, "I'm sorry, Mei Ling. I know you were only thinking of me. It's just so hard to accept what happened. Can you tell me, at least, what she looked like?"

Mei Ling shifted uneasily. "With a newborn baby, one cannot really say."

Larissa stared at her maid, and she knew, instinctively, without asking more, exactly how the child must have looked. She was more sure than ever that the baby had been Nathan's. The death would spare Edmund the pain of ever learning the truth, but for her it would be eternal punishment for the one day she had betrayed her husband.

Chapter Twenty-Three

The malaria continued to ravage Larissa's body for another ten days, during which she alternated between delirium and lucidity. In her most delirious ravings, she damned Nathan for his power over her and damned herself for giving in to him so easily. In her more clearheaded moments, she mourned her lost baby and agonized over how Edmund would receive the news. At times, when the fever gripped her, she almost wished that it would claim her life, too.

She was in a half-conscious state of mounting fever when she became aware of Mei Ling's voice raised in heated argument outside her bedroom.

"No!" the maid said firmly, "You must not see her! It would be very bad for her, very bad!"

"Don't be absurd," a male voice responded. "How can it be bad for her to know someone cares about her?"

"She knows that already," Mei Ling insisted. "I care. Her son cares, her husband cares—"

"But her husband is not here."

"Here or not, he is still her husband, and he is the only man with rights to her bedchamber."

"For God's sake, Mei Ling, you ought to know me well enough to trust me not to molest a sick woman! I just want to see her!"

"No!"

There was a muttered curse, and then the door flew open, and Nathan strode into the room. He stopped at the edge of the bed, stunned by Larissa's gray, haggard face. "Larissa," he whispered, gently taking her hand, "it's Nathan. Can you hear me, love?"

She nodded, struggling to focus on his chestnut hair.

The amber flecks of his eyes seemed to burn through the haze of her delirium. "Nathan," she repeated dully.

"Yes. I heard you were sick, and I had to see you. The *Queen of Cathay* sails for Boston tomorrow, and I'm going with her. I'd like to take you along. You could bring your son, too, of course."

Slowly, his words penetrated her consciousness, setting off a struggle within her. Part of her wanted to say yes, why not, but another part insisted it wasn't possible. Fighting her weakness, she whispered, "My husband—"

"Your husband isn't here," Nathan interrupted sharply, "which ought to be some indication of how much he cares for you. What sort of man would go away and leave his wife when she's pregnant and there's malaria around?"

"He didn't know about the malaria," she protested weakly. "And his leaving was no worse than you—" She swallowed the end of the sentence, unable to think clearly.

Nathan's face clouded as he tried to imagine what she had intended to say. He could only suppose she was referring to her current pregnancy. "Oh, my God, Larissa," he breathed, "are you trying to say—do you mean you're carrying *my* child? Why didn't you let me know?"

Suddenly, she could see and hear him clearly, and all the bitterness and grief that had built in her since the baby's birth and death exploded. "Look at me!" she shrieked. "Do I look as if I'm carrying a child?"

His eyes moved over her form, hidden beneath the comforters. "It's hard to tell beneath all those covers." He hesitated, then paled. "You're not trying to tell me you lost the baby?"

"No. I bore her. A girl they tell me. But she died before I even got to see her."

"Oh, Larissa!" He sank down beside the bed, burying his face in the comforters beside her. "How terrible for you! I wish I could have been here to—"

"You should have been!" she snapped. "You should have been here, because it's all your fault!"

His head jerked up, and he stared at her with hurt, glistening eyes. "You don't mean that, love," he whispered. "It's just the fever talking."

"I do mean it! It's your fault I was pregnant, your fault my baby died. I wish you would leave me alone, Nathan Masters! Just when I thought my life was going smoothly, you had to come back and cause me trouble!"

Standing, Nathan stepped back from the bed. "You're not making sense, Larissa. You're delirious now, and you just can't think straight. I'll wait until the fever passes, and then perhaps we can talk sensibly."

"No! I don't want to talk to you! I don't want you ruining any more of my life! I just want you to go away and stop bothering me!"

He stared at her incredulously, opening his mouth to speak.

"Please," she sobbed, "please just get out of my life!"

For a moment he stared at her. Then he nodded, turned abruptly, and strode from the room.

Larissa opened her mouth, desperately wanting to call him back, but the words would not come. The door closed, and the fever claimed her again.

Hours later, when the fever had passed, she opened her eyes to see Mei Ling sitting beside the bed. Her eyes roamed the room frantically, then returned to her maid's dark, sorrowful gaze. "Nathan?" she asked weakly.

"Gone," Mei Ling replied simply.

Larissa turned her head so Mei Ling would not see the tears that sprang to her eyes. She waited a moment before speaking again, hoping her voice would not betray her emotions. "Did he leave any message?"

"No. I'm sure he felt there was no need to. You screamed at him to leave you alone, and so he did."

"Yes," Larissa said slowly. "I remember that—but I thought perhaps it was a nightmare caused by the fever."

Mei Ling drew a long breath. "You were right to send him away, you know, no matter how much you love him. Before you married Mr. Farrell, I warned you he was not the man to make you happy. But you made your decision, and you must abide by it. In your heart, I'm sure you know you could never be happy if you forsook your husband."

"No. I couldn't be. And I told Nathan once that the guilt would only drive us apart. But, oh, Mei Ling, I don't know how I can live the rest of my life without him!"

"You can, and you will," Mei Ling said sharply. "You have your son, you have your husband, and you have me. In time, no doubt, you will have other children to love. Your Nathan is gone from your life now, and you will learn to manage without him, just as you did in India. It will not be so difficult now, when you know he is not near and you need not fear a chance meeting."

"I know you're right," Larissa said, then sighed, "and I've told myself the same thing countless times. But even knowing our separation is for the best cannot make it any easier to bear."

"No," Mei Ling replied. "Only time can make it easier." They were silent for a few moments, and then she drew a letter from her pocket. "This arrived for you while you were suffering from the fever."

Recognizing Edmund's script, Larissa broke the seal and read:

Darling,
I hope to be reunited with you soon after you receive this note. I cannot tell you how anxious I am to hold you again, to play with little Sean, and—has the new member of our family arrived yet?

At that, Larissa dropped the letter into her lap, blinking rapidly to dispel her tears. Poor Edmund! He had so looked forward to this child! She remembered how he had beamed when she told him she was pregnant, and she wondered how she could bear his crushing disappointment. Swallowing her tears, she picked up the letter and resumed reading:

Trade possibilities here seem quite favorable, but I'm afraid the living quarters afforded foreigners are most deplorable. I am, of course, making arrangements to have a house built for us, but in the meantime, I hesitate to bring you, Sean, and the new baby here. However, we can discuss the problems at length after we are reunited. Fortunately, the smallpox reports were little more than a scare—a few isolated cases, but nothing approaching a general outbreak.
I sincerely hope, my darling, that you are well. The separation has been difficult for me, but I must assure you I have never once considered returning to the crutch of opium. You have saved me from that fate, my dear Larissa, and I will never disgrace your faith and understanding by succumbing again.
Well, dearest, I shan't write more, since the mail ship is soon due to depart. Expect me soon.
                                        All my love, for eternity,
                                        Edmund

Avoiding Mei Ling's gaze, Larissa carefully refolded the letter. Whatever misgivings she might have had about sending Nathan away dissolved in the face of Edmund's message. Edmund loved her and needed her. And even if she never tasted the fulfillment she craved with him, she could never forget he had pledged himself to her at a time when she desperately needed his love and protection.

Free at last from the daily bouts of fever, but still weak and pale from her long ordeal, Larissa was sitting on the veranda five days later when she saw a ship dock in the harbor. A short time later, she heard Sean's shrill, exuberant cry of "Papa!"

Turning in her chair, she saw Edmund framed in the doorway, hugging Sean, who had abandoned his toys on the terrace floor to run to him. Smiling affectionately, Larissa thought he looked tanned and healthy. As she started to rise, he hurried to her side, setting Sean on his feet as he bent to kiss her.

"Hello, darling. I thought you might be out here, so I came here directly." He stepped back, his eyes filled with warmth as they traveled over her. "It's wonderful to see you. But I must say, you look a bit tired. Was it a hard labor for you again? Is the baby inside sleeping now?"

Larissa cleared her throat uneasily as she saw Sean about to blurt out the awful news. "Sean, darling," she said quickly, "run and tell Mei Ling that your papa has arrived, and you might tell her I said you could have a treat. Papa and I have to talk a bit."

"All right." Nodding importantly, the boy hurried inside.

Larissa sank back in her chair, and Edmund pulled another chair close to hers. Taking her hands, he gazed into her eyes and asked gently, "It was hard for you, wasn't it?" Without waiting for her reply, he added, "I knew I should have gotten back sooner."

Smiling sadly, she squeezed his hands. "You mustn't chastise yourself, darling. There's nothing you could have done for me. If I look a bit haggard, it's because I only recently recovered from malaria."

His mouth dropped open, and he muttered, "Oh, God! And the baby?"

Larissa looked away, afraid to see the pain in his eyes. "The baby—" She choked on the sentence and began again. "She's—I mean she—" Her chest heaved with sobs, and she could not go on.

Suddenly, Edmund was kneeling beside her chair, peering

up into her tortured, tear-blurred eyes. "What is it, darling? Is something wrong with the baby?"

Larissa nodded, then blurted in a wrenching sob, "She died."

Watching helplessly as the color drained from his face, she felt as if she had plunged a knife into his heart. That moment, seeing his pain and disappointment, was worse punishment than when she herself had learned of the death. If only she had not succumbed on that one afternoon with Nathan, Edmund might have been spared the soaring hopes and terrible despair. "Oh, Edmund," she sobbed, "I'm so sorry. I failed you. I'm so terribly sorry!"

Without quite knowing how, she found herself seated in his lap, her head cradled against his warm, strong chest. "Hush," he soothed, stroking her hair. "It's not your fault, darling. You've suffered enough already, and you mustn't torment yourself more. Surely you don't think I would stop loving you because God chose to take our child?"

"No," she sniffled, "but it's my fault. I know it is."

"Larissa!" he said sharply, "I won't have you talking like that!" His tone softened as his fingers massaged her back. "We have a long life together ahead of us, darling. I know it hurts to lose a child after you nurtured it within you for so many months, but blaming yourself will only make it worse. We have Sean, and we'll have other babies. For now, you must concentrate on regaining your strength."

Swallowing further sobs, Larissa wondered if he would be so understanding if he knew the full reason for her guilt and sorrow. It would ease her conscience to tell him everything, but for his sake she kept silent. It was better for her to suffer alone than to hurt him. Vowing she would never again allow herself to betray him, she snuggled closer to him.

"Edmund," she whispered, "I want to leave Macao. When can we go to Shanghai?"

He cleared his throat. "As I told you in my letter, darling, living conditions there are rather deplorable. And I doubt that our house will be completed before next spring."

"But I don't want to spend another winter here. It's too depressing, too filled with haunting memories."

"I understand. But in Shanghai you'd have to live in a place that's little more than a crude hut. Perhaps I ought to send you and Sean to England for awhile. You've had to suffer in the Orient too long, and I'm sure you'd enjoy some time in a more civilized country."

"Don't you want me with you?"

"Of course, darling. But I want you to be comfortable, too."

"Then you'll take me to Shanghai with you—soon. I'm your wife, and I belong with you. I'm not some fragile flower who can't survive a bit of privation."

He sighed. "No, I suppose you're not. You proved that in India. But we'll see, darling. Give yourself some more time to recover your strength, and we'll see."

Part Five

✿

1843-1845

Chapter Twenty-Four

They arrived in Shanghai in October, and the first month was more miserable than Larissa had dared to imagine. The area the Chinese had allotted for British residents was a dismal stretch of marshland along the Whangpoo River, just outside the city walls. In Edmund's absence, the workmen had neglected even to begin construction on the house he had commissioned, so Larissa, Sean, Mei Ling, and Edmund were forced to move into a shabby, two-room shack.

The first time it rained, water streamed in through the torn paper windows. Shanghai was a good deal cooler than Macao, and Larissa felt as if she were perpetually chilled. But thinking of how she had begged to come and had ignored all Edmund's protests, she refrained from complaining and concentrated on keeping Sean healthy and happy.

Hardly more than a handful of Englishmen had yet arrived in Shanghai, and none of them had brought their wives or families. On Macao, where Europeans had lived for centuries, the Chinese treated them matter-of-factly. But here in Shanghai, white men were still an oddity, and some Chinese even believed they were malicious foreign devils. As the only white woman in the small foreign community, Larissa became a special object of curiosity. Whenever she stepped out of the shack, she was surrounded by curious women and children, and she soon learned to ignore the hands that reached out to finger her clothing or hair.

Despite the horrible conditions in the British quarter, Larissa was impressed by the old, walled city. Almost daily, she and Mei Ling went to the markets to purchase vegetables and other foods. The long, narrow paved streets were lined with small, neat shops and stores and large, ornate temples. Some of the streets in the more affluent

sections featured lovely teahouses with red tiled roofs, surrounded by ponds and gardens. Chinese dignitaries traveled
through these sections of the city in richly painted and
draped sedan chairs, carried by overburdened coolies.

One afternoon late in November, Larissa ventured out
alone. Edmund was out trying to hasten construction of
their home, and Mei Ling was suffering with a cold. Not
wanting Mei Ling to become more chilled, Larissa assured her she could do the necessary marketing, using sign
language to make the shopkeepers understand her.

It had rained all night, and now a mixture of rain and
slushy snow was falling. The streets of the settlement oozed
slick mud. Holding her skirts carefully above the mud,
Larissa picked her way through the rutted street, anxious
to reach the smooth, paved streets of the inner city. She
walked with her head bent, her bonnet shielding her
face from the miserable weather. She was still some distance from the city walls when she felt a sucking sensation
around her ankle and realized she had lost her slipper in the
mud. Bending to retrieve it, she was startled by a friendly
voice.

"Might I be of service, madam?"

Looking up, Larissa saw a dark-haired stranger on a
horse. "No, thank you. I'm afraid the mud just robbed me
of my slipper." Managing to jam her foot back into the
shoe, she smiled, "But I don't believe we've had the pleasure of meeting, sir."

The man dismounted and bowed graciously. "Forgive
me. I am Captain George Baskins, formerly of the Madras
Artillery, now Her Majesty's consul to Shanghai. And who
might you be, madam?"

"Larissa Farrell. My husband, Edmund, is here representing the East India Company."

Captain Baskins frowned. "Surely you don't mean to say
you live in this—this—squalor?"

She nodded. "I'm afraid so. Edmund is having a house
built for us, but it's far from completed. The Chinese officials told us there were no vacant houses in Shanghai in
which we could live."

"I'm sure they did. They informed my party of the same
thing when we arrived a few days ago. But a Mister Yao, a
prosperous local merchant, has put his house at our dis-
posal. I would be honored if you would consent to share it."

"That's very kind of you, captain, but I assure you we can manage until our house is completed."

He shook his head. "No. I insist. It's bad enough that any British citizens should suffer the indignities of living in this swamp, but it's unthinkable for a woman to have to endure such privation."

She hesitated. "But there are four in our household—my husband, myself, our young son Sean, and my maid. We wouldn't want to inconvenience or crowd you."

Captain Baskins smiled indulgently. "My dear lady, you're hardly likely to crowd us. There are only four in my party—myself, an interpreter, a surgeon, and a clerk—and Mister Yao's house has fifty-two rooms. Now, I think you'd best agree to my suggestion, so we can end this mindless standing in the rain."

By evening, they were installed in Mister Yao's house, snug within the city walls, on one of Shanghai's main streets. The house was truly magnificent, with each of the fifty-two rooms lavishly furnished in teak, sandalwood, bamboo, silk, and velvet. The upstairs bedrooms were rather cold, since they were not equipped with fireplaces, but they were infinitely more comfortable than the shack in the marshlands. Captain Baskins' ship had arrived laden with wine and groceries, so the meals served by the Chinese servants in the huge dining room were hearty British fare.

But even living in the huge house did not free them from Chinese curiosity. For the first few days, Larissa felt as if the house were a museum and she were one of its main exhibits. Chinese men, women, and children arrived early each morning, wandering from room to room to observe the foreigners in their daily tasks. They even came upstairs to watch when she bathed Sean or when Mei Ling arranged her hair. They stayed until all hours, not even leaving during meals or when one of the residents went to bed.

Finally, Larissa complained to Captain Baskins that she felt like some oddity on display and that the natives were thoroughly disrupting Sean's schedule. The captain relayed her complaints to Mister Yao, who reluctantly agreed to limit future visits to his close friends and relatives. After that, the disruptions were less frequent, though they were by no means eliminated.

When winter set in, Larissa found herself more than willing to bear the stares of Mister Yao's family and friends in return for the snug comfort of a house. While men in the British settlement complained about the wreaths of snow that decorated the floors of their leaky shacks, she and Sean could enjoy the snow—the first she had seen since leaving Boston and the first Sean had ever seen—knowing they could always run inside for a cup of hot tea or chocolate beside a fire.

Captain Baskins and his men treated her with utmost courtesy, and as the only white woman in the house, she began to feel almost like a queen. At Christmas, the captain invited the entire British community to the house for roast goose and plum pudding, and Larissa presided over the celebration as hostess.

After the agony of their first month in Shanghai, Larissa found the succeeding months were the happiest of her marriage. Secure in his new position and confident he could build a prosperous trade with the cities connected to Shanghai by the Yangtze River and the Grand Canal, Edmund was more warm and loving than ever. All of the secretiveness of his opium-eating days and the anxiety of the first months on Macao, when he had worried about his new position, were gone. He was affectionate, indulgent, and a perfect father to Sean.

In return, Larissa felt her affection for him growing. She had long ago reconciled herself to the fact that he would never evoke in her the kind of passion Nathan had. But as she watched him growing ever stronger and more confident in his work, the pity she had felt for him on the Indian estate was replaced by respect, love, and pride that he was her husband. With Nathan removed from her life, she felt she was finally at peace in her marriage.

By mid-spring, Edmund announced that enough of their house was completed to make it habitable, and so they moved from the consul's house back to the foreign settlement.

Larissa was pleasantly surprised to find several of the marshland shacks had been replaced by half a dozen imposing white stone buildings set some distance back from the riverfront. Architecturally, they were more serviceable than elegant, all being built on the same, square, two-storied design, but they were spacious and comfortable. Both floors were fronted by columned verandas.

Leading her to the door of one of the buildings, Edmund

explained that the others doubled as hongs and living quarters, with offices on the first floor and bedrooms on the second. Their home, however, would be a residence only, and he would do his business at the nearby East India Company hong.

Larissa looked perplexed. "It seems terribly extravagant for us to occupy a whole house when the others must live above their working quarters," she said. "Can we really afford such luxury?"

"Of course we can," Edmund assured her. "You mustn't worry about financial details. My salary is quite generous, so you have no reason for concern. Besides, it would never do to thrust you and Sean into the midst of all those men. And when Sean's little brothers and sisters begin arriving—" He paused and cleared his throat. "You haven't had any sign yet of another baby?"

She shook her head. "Not yet, darling. But in time—"

"Yes, of course. No doubt you still need more time to recover your strength. I suppose I'm just overanxious. Sean is growing so fast he's hardly a baby any longer."

Larissa smiled. "Don't worry, Edmund, we'll have more babies to fill this house."

But to herself she wondered. Had her last pregnancy, coupled with the malaria, left her barren? Could she ever bear Edmund's child? Indeed, did she even want to risk carrying another child and then losing it, as she had her daughter?

She worried about those questions as spring moved into summer and still she did not become pregnant. Edmund did not mention the problem again, but she sensed that he thought of it often, and on several occasions she imagined that she saw him gazing wistfully at her flat stomach.

During the summer, more hongs and houses were built, and ship after ship arrived in the newly opened port, bringing more and more British traders to Shanghai. A number of steamers brought the wives of established traders, some from as far away as London. Most of the women were older than Larissa, extremely refined, and rather horrified at the prospect of life so far from civilization as they knew it. They immediately set about establishing some semblance of proper society, segregated from the "Chinese savages."

Shanghai's residents, who had first been curious, then

friendly to the newcomers, quickly changed their attitude when faced with the regimens of the British ladies. The Chinese withdrew into their own areas, from which they excluded foreigners, and the British did the same. Except for the large staffs of Chinese houseservants and the merchants who did business at the hongs, the two groups had little contact with one another.

Since their servants handled all the household chores and their husbands were busy all day building a prosperous trade, most of the women found themselves with little to occupy their time. To amuse themselves, they hosted daily tea parties and planned lavish dinner parties and balls. Larissa would gladly have avoided the evening affairs, but she knew Edmund took great pride in taking her out in the gowns made from the exquisite fabrics he was constantly presenting to her. For his sake, she also endured the tea parties, learning early that those who did not attend were the subject of vicious gossip.

The pretentiousness of the parties never ceased to amaze her. The women spared no expense on sumptuous feasts, and each hostess tried to outdo the last. On one sultry summer night, the meal began with a glass of sherry and a rich beef soup. Champagne followed, accompanied by mutton. The next course featured curried rice and ham and was followed by custard and more champagne. Cheese, salad, bread, and butter, served with glasses of port wine, made up the final course before dessert, a selection of figs, raisins, and walnuts.

Sipping a glass of claret and nibbling on a few raisins, Larissa sighed to herself over her uncomfortable, bloated feeling and the usual boring dinner conversation. The gentleman to her left made her even more uncomfortable with his constant staring at the fashionably low neckline of her gown. For once, she was anxious to adjourn with the other ladies for tea, leaving the men to enjoy their strong coffee and cigars. But her interest in the conversation was rekindled when she heard a gentleman at the other end of the table commenting on American trade in the Orient.

"Mark my words," he said. "Before the year is out, Shanghai will be overrun with Yankee traders."

"Why do you say that?" Larissa inquired, blushing as all eyes at the table turned to her.

The man smiled indulgently. "Because, my dear lady, I received word only yesterday that the Americans have signed a new treaty with China, permitting them to trade at the very ports that we opened! It hardly seems fair," he snorted, "that they should reap such handsome benefits when we had to fight for the rights to trade here."

"But surely there is sufficient business here for all who wish to participate."

Edmund cleared his throat in embarrassment and shot Larissa a distressed look. "You must forgive my wife," he said quickly. "I'm afraid she is not very well-informed on political affairs, and her sympathy for American traders dates back to her childhood in Boston. On occasion, I find I must remind her that she is British now."

Shocked by her husband's public rebuke, however mild it might have been, Larissa flushed and lowered her eyes. Several woman tittered, obviously pleased to see her embarrassment. Their husbands coughed and frowned at them disapprovingly. The moment might have become unbearable if one of the men had not remarked that anyone as charming as Mrs. Farrell could be permitted an occasional error in political judgment.

Biting back a retort that she had made no error, Larissa rose meekly at her hostess's suggestion that the ladies adjourn to the salon.

While the other women sipped their tea and gossiped among themselves, Larissa sat alone in a corner of the salon, the teacup and saucer shaking in her hands. She was angry with Edmund for treating her like a child, but she was even more agitated with herself, for her inner reactions to the news of the Americans. Almost a year had passed since Nathan had last visited her on Macao, and she had tried desperately to block him out of her mind. She had even put off sending a messenger to Macao to inquire about Bennett and Barnes, much as she still wanted to claim her inheritance, because she knew she had to avoid any contact with Nathan. But her first thought on hearing about the new treaty had been that Nathan might be coming to Shanghai—and the worst thing was, she wanted him to come. No matter how she tried to deny it, she actually wanted to see him again. For that very reason, if he did, somehow, turn up in Shanghai, she would have to force herself to keep away from him. She couldn't risk having everything start again.

Larissa moved through the rest of the evening in a daze, unable to push Nathan from her mind. As Edmund escorted her home, she tensed, sure that he would bring up the scene at the dinner table. If they had disagreed about any other subject, she would have renewed the argument herself, berating him for the way he had treated her in public. But she was quite relieved that he did not mention the scene. Perhaps, she thought later as she drifted into sleep, there would be no further problem. Even if Nathan did come to Shanghai, the British seemed so opposed to American trade that she would be unlikely to meet him at any social events, and she simply would not permit herself to see him privately.

American traders began arriving in Shanghai that fall, and at first Larissa's assumptions proved correct. Still indignant about the ease with which Americans had won the right to trade there, the British refused to entertain them. But the coolness between the two groups gradually wore away as both realized they had a common adversary in the Chinese. Before too many months passed, Americans were receiving invitations to the British balls and parties and were extending invitations to the British in return.

Everytime Larissa attended a ball or party, she was filled with apprehension. She cultivated a cool, aloof attitude so that if she did meet Nathan she could appear restrained but at ease. When night after night passed and she did not see him, she began telling herself she had been foolish to suppose he might come to Shanghai. Even assuming he was still engaged in the China trade, he could choose any of the five other opened ports or remain in Canton. Why should he appear in Shanghai?

She had almost convinced herself that she would never see Nathan again when she spotted him across the room at a ball one night. Estelle Jamieson was on his arm, looking more dazzlingly beautiful than ever. Her silver blonde hair was swept back by a narrow band of appliquéd lace, and she had blood-red roses tucked behind one ear. She wore a blue- and white-striped silk gown with a low, pointed waistline and an off-the-shoulder neckline that also swept in a low point, emphasizing her tiny waist. Too late, Larissa realized she had stared far too openly, for Edmund, following her gaze, was bending to whisper in her ear.

"I say, isn't that your friend Estelle Jamieson from

Macao? I wonder what brings her to Shanghai? Do you suppose she's married the chap accompanying her?"

Larissa stiffened but struggled to keep her voice level. "With Estelle, one never knows what to suppose."

"Shall we go over and greet her?"

"Oh, Edmund, I'd really rather not. As I told you on Macao, she was never one of my favorite persons."

"Come now," he chided, "surely you wouldn't wish to snub one of your former countrywomen. Besides," he added, winking, "you might pick up some juicy tidbit for tomorrow's tea party."

Before she could protest further, he was steering her toward them. Rather than arouse unnecessary suspicion, Larissa gave in graciously. Estelle beamed as they approached, offering her hand to Edmund.

"What a pleasant surprise," she chirped. "It seems we're always running into each other when we least expect it." Squeezing Nathan's arm possessively, she said, "But, Mr. Farrell, perhaps you've never met my dear friend, Nathan Masters."

"No, I haven't." Edmund extended his hand, and Nathan shook it, surveying the other man impassively.

"Mr. Masters," Edmund said, "may I present my wife, Larissa?"

"Oh, they've met before," Estelle announced pertly.

"Indeed?" Edmund's eyebrows raised as he turned to Larissa for confirmation.

As she opened her mouth to explain, Nathan cut in smoothly, "Yes, I believe we did meet some years back on Macao. No doubt it was long before the lady became your wife."

"Ah, yes," Edmund murmured thoughtfully, "I seem to recall Mrs. Jamieson mentioning you to my wife on Macao."

"Nathan, dearest," Estelle said, tugging on his arm, "the music is beginning, and you know how I love to dance."

He sighed. "Yes, I know, but I'm really much too tired to dance at the moment."

Estelle became petulant. "If you were so tired, you shouldn't have brought me here! It's not fair to make me stand on the sidelines and watch others enjoy themselves."

"I hardly think that's likely," Nathan retorted. "I'm sure you could find other dance partners."

"Of course I could. In fact, I'm sure Mr. Farrell

wouldn't refuse me so heartlessly as you. Would you, sir?"
She turned to Edmund, batting her eyelashes appealingly.

"I—well—" he stuttered, eying Larissa. "The fact is, I
usually reserve the first dance for my wife."

"I'd be happy to entertain your wife for a few moments
if you wish to dance with my friend," Nathan put in.

"Oh, go ahead," Larissa said, a trifle irritably, suddenly
feeling she couldn't bear another moment standing between
Edmund and Nathan. "I don't mind if Estelle is so set on
dancing, and I won't disappear while you're on the dance
floor."

"You're sure?" Edmund looked a bit sheepish as Estelle
slid her arm through his.

"Yes, yes. Now go ahead. I believe I'll get a glass of
champagne while you're gone."

As Estelle and Edmund moved away, Larissa turned to
Nathan. "Now," she said coolly, "suppose you explain to
me why you staged that little scene to dispose of my husband?"

One corner of Nathan's mouth curled in a smile. "You
seemed more anxious to be rid of him than I. Anyway, despite what you may think, I did not plan to have Estelle
spirit him away. You ought to know that she wouldn't
cooperate in any such plan. Nevertheless, I do want to
talk with you and had intended to seek you out sometime
during our stay in Shanghai."

She stiffened at the way he said "our stay," realizing
that she still felt a pang of jealousy. But she managed to
keep her voice cool as she said, "I suggest that you seize
the moment and say whatever it is you have to say."

"What I have to say will take more than a few moments. Is there sometime I can call on you at your house?"

Lowering her eyes, she replied, "I don't think that's ad-
visable."

"For God's sake, Larissa," he muttered through clenched
teeth, "I'm not going to try to seduce you. Do you think
I've forgotten what you said on Macao? If you're so convinced that I've ruined your life, I've no wish to entangle
myself with you again."

"Then I fail to see what remains for us to discuss."

Nathan raised his brows. "Am I to understand you are
no longer interested in the firm of Bennett and Barnes?
I once believed business affairs were your only reason for
coming to China."

"You know they were," she snapped. "And you might have told me at once that that was what you wished to discuss."

"Then you are still interested?" His tone was mocking.

"Of course I am! What sort of news do you have for me?"

"As I said before, it's nothing I could tell you in a casual moment or two, and I'm afraid we might arouse a bit of gossip if we disappeared into the rose garden for a longer talk. Besides, I'll be damned if I'll let myself be challenged to a duel for doing a good deed—unless your husband is not the jealous type."

She sighed in exasperation. "All right. You've made your point. Come tomorrow at two. Sean will be napping then, and Edmund will be occupied at the hong."

His amber-flecked eyes danced. "You mean you think it's safe to entertain me while your husband is away?"

"You've already made it clear your intentions are quite honorable," she replied tartly. "Besides," she added, "I'd prefer that Edmund not know of this meeting just yet. He doesn't approve of my interest in business matters." Still, she could not help wondering if it was not a mistake to agree to see Nathan again, for whatever reason.

Chapter Twenty-Five

Larissa paced in the spacious salon, fidgeting with her lace collar as the clock in the hall chimed two. Mei Ling had been quietly disapproving as she helped Larissa dress in one of her best day gowns, made of opalescent pink silk and trimmed with maroon velvet ribbon.

"So, you've decided to attend Mrs. Matheson's tea party after all?" Mei Ling asked as she fastened the hooks at the back of Larissa's gown.

"No. I'm staying home this afternoon, but I'm expecting a guest."

"Ah." The maid said no more, pressing her lips firmly together, but Larissa sensed that she knew, somehow, exactly who her guest would be.

Now she waited, wondering again if it was wise to see Nathan. But she would be careful to remain cool, distant, and in complete control of herself. She had dressed in her finest only to show Nathan how well-off and at ease she was as Edmund's wife. And if she had instructed Mei Ling to take special pains in arranging her hair, it had only been to give herself an extra measure of confidence.

"Madam," the butler's voice drew her attention to the door of the salon, "Mr. Masters is here to see you."

The servant stood aside to let Nathan enter, then backed out of the room, discreetly closing the double doors behind him. Staring at Nathan, Larissa saw that he, too, had dressed carefully for the occasion. His tightly fitted fawn trousers contrasted sharply with his chocolate brown frock coat and embroidered gold silk waistcoat. He returned her gaze, his eyes crinkling merrily.

"Well, aren't you going to ask me to sit down?" he asked, the old mocking tone returning to his voice.

"Yes, of course." She motioned to a tall wing chair, and seated herself in a matching chair opposite it.

As he crossed to the chair, he continued to gaze at her, and his voice softened. "You look uncommonly lovely, Larissa. Life here must suit you very well."

She cleared her throat impatiently. "I believe you came to discuss business?"

"Very well, I'll get right to the point. I am no longer involved with the firm of Bennett and Barnes, and, as far as your aunt and uncle are concerned, neither are you."

Larissa's jaw dropped open, and she gripped the arms of her chair. "As far as my aunt and uncle were concerned," she said slowly, "I was never involved in the firm. But that cannot change my right to my father's share."

"Theoretically, no. But unless you return to Boston and assert that right, you may find it to be quite meaningless."

"What do you mean?"

"Your aunt and uncle are acting as if you no longer exist. In fact, since they've heard nothing from you in five years, they are proceeding as if you were dead. They've already changed the firm's name to Hiram Barnes, Ltd."

"They tried that before, when they hired Captain Clinton," she said calmly. "But that still doesn't change the fact that I own half the shares."

"Perhaps not—but now they've made the change of names official. All of Boston has accepted it."

Springing from her chair, Larissa began to pace angrily. "But they have no rights to my father's shares—my inheritance." She stopped to stare at him, her eyes narrowing. "Didn't you, at least, tell them I was quite alive?"

"Of course I did, but they absolutely refused to believe me. Furthermore, your friend Captain Clinton refused to admit he'd ever carried you to China on the *Queen of Cathay*. Your Aunt Harriet accused me of making up stories, just so that I could keep your share of the profits. When I persisted in arguing, your Uncle Hiram promptly released me from my position with his company."

She stopped pacing and stared at him apologetically. "Oh, Nathan! I never thought you'd lose your job on my account."

He waved aside her apology. "It doesn't matter. Your aunt and uncle sicken me so much that I might have quit anyway. I wouldn't give Bennett and Barnes another thought if I weren't so concerned about your interests."

Larissa nodded, once again consumed with anger at her aunt and uncle. "Wasn't there anything you could do? Couldn't you have gone to someone else—a lawyer or a judge, perhaps?"

"Do you really think that my word would be accepted over that of a well-known, respected Boston business-man?"

"If you were telling the truth, they'd have to believe you, wouldn't they?"

He frowned. "I would have thought after all you've experienced since leaving Boston, you would be a bit less naive. Even in the so-called courts of justice, money and influence often count for far more than truth."

"What would you suggest I do?"

Nathan shrugged. "If your father's business is as important to you as it once was, you have no choice but to return to Boston and claim what is yours. You're old enough now that your aunt and uncle can no longer claim to be holding your share as your guardians. Of course, if you no longer care—"

"Oh, I care!" She stopped pacing and chewed nervously on her lower lip. "Every time I think of them stealing all that papa worked for, I feel as if I'll boil over with rage. But how can I go to Boston now? Edmund can't leave Shanghai when he's just getting the cotton trade built up. And what about Sean?"

"I believe you and your husband would have to work out the details between you. But he seems like an understanding enough fellow. Surely he would permit you to visit your hometown. It's not so unusual for ladies of quality to travel without their husbands, provided, of course, that they are well chaperoned. And you could take your son with you."

She shook her head distractedly. "You don't understand. Edmund knows Uncle Hiram and Aunt Harriet are my only living relatives and that I despise them, so he would never believe I want to make a pleasure trip to Boston. As for papa's business, every discussion we have about it seems to end in argument. He insists that I let him worry about business matters, and he seems to think that accepting my inheritance would mean I was supporting him in some way. It's a point of honor with him, and I can't seem to sway his attitude."

Nathan frowned. "But surely he can understand how important this is to you?"

"He does, but he is still inflexible." She paused, then sighed. "Believe me, Nathan, he has his reasons for being so defensive about his position as family provider. They date back to something that happened while we were in India. I can't tell you more, except to say I do understand. Perhaps in a few years he'll be willing to consider the problem again. I won't give up hope of claiming what is mine, but for now there seems nothing I can do."

"But in a few years," Nathan said quietly, "there may be nothing left of Bennett and Barnes for you to claim. If you'll permit me to say so, your aunt and uncle are fools when it comes to business. They were fortunate with that opium shipment, but the other ideas they discussed before my untimely dismissal showed they had little grasp of the situation here. Of course," he added, shrugging, "they may be lucky enough to hire a new agent with enough intelligence to keep the firm afloat."

He paused, and Larissa turned away from him, not wanting to hear anymore about her birthright being stolen and squandered. How strange, she thought, that her desire to preserve her father's interests had shaped her destiny. It had been her whole reason for coming to the Orient. And now it seemed she might lose that inheritance after all.

She strolled to the piano, idly striking a few keys and musing about how piano sales had been one of the foolish, golden dreams of British traders. Never considering the fact that Chinese music was nothing like their own music, they had flooded the new trading ports with grand and baby grand pianos. A few mandarins had purchased them as novelties, but most had been sold at an enormous loss to British families in the trading ports. Still others rotted in Hong Kong warehouses. Perhaps, Larissa thought, her hopes had been like the British piano sales—founded only on silly dreams and doomed now to die.

Engrossed in her thoughts, she did not hear Nathan come up behind her. His hands on her shoulders startled her, but they also felt warm and familiar, and she did not shake him off.

"I think," he murmured, "that I greatly underestimated you on Macao. Or perhaps I overestimated myself. At any rate, I was sure you could not love your husband because you were still so much in love with me. Now I see that I was wrong. Obviously, something very strong exists between the two of you. Not passion, perhaps, but a kind of love founded on respect and honor. You have a sort of protective attitude towards him, and at the ball last night, I sensed that he felt the same for you."

Larissa turned to face him, her eyes brimming with tears. Slowly, she nodded. "I'm glad you understand, at least a little bit." Thinking of Sean and of the terrible months battling Edmund's opium addiction, she added, "There's so much you don't know—so much I can never tell you—about why I married Edmund and what has passed between us in our marriage. We owe each other a great deal, and there are very strong bonds between us. One afternoon on Macao, I forgot those bonds for a while, but I'll never do it again, even if, in the end, I have to sacrifice my own desires."

Nathan smiled tenderly. "When I met you, Larissa, you were a wild, impetuous girl. Today you seem more like a serene, wise woman." He was silent a moment, then gently touched her cheek and then her neck.

Larissa wondered if he could feel her pulse pounding beneath his fingertips. Her eyes were drawn to his, and she trembled at the familiar smoldering she saw in their amber depths. All the tension she had controlled until that moment unleashed itself. Her lips parted, her breath became ragged, and she had all she could do to keep from screaming, "Nathan, hold me! Kiss me! Take me!"

Abruptly, his hand dropped away. She could see the muscles in his face tense, and when he spoke, his voice was strained and husky. "I promised not to seduce you, and I've said all I came to say, so I'll be going now. You'll have to do what you and your husband think best." Pausing, he cleared his throat. "For all of our sakes, I don't think I'll be seeing you again."

Impulsively, she grabbed his hand, squeezing it while she gazed at him imploringly. How many times had she told him goodbye on Macao? And hadn't she always insisted it was for the best—hadn't she almost said as much moments ago? But this time she knew in her heart the goodbye was really final. There would not be a next time, so could it really hurt to linger for a moment?

Her musings were interrupted as the salon doors opened and Edmund stepped into the room. Instantly, she dropped

Nathan's hand, but not before her husband noted the furtive movement. He hesitated, cocking an eyebrow in question, then strode briskly toward them, extending his hand in a friendly greeting.

"Mr. Masters, I hadn't expected to see you again so soon." His eyes darted around the room as Nathan shook his hand. "Is the lovely Mrs. Jamieson here, too?"

Nathan cleared his throat. "No, I'm afraid she wasn't feeling up to visiting today."

"What a pity. I'm sure Larissa would have enjoyed hearing the latest news from Macao." Edmund slid an arm around Larissa's waist, drawing her close to him. "You're looking a bit flushed yourself, darling. I hope you're not coming down with some sort of fever."

Larissa laughed nervously. "No. I'm quite all right. I'm probably just excited since Na—Mr. Masters was telling me about Boston. At the ball last night, he mentioned that he'd traveled there last year. Naturally, I was anxious to hear news of my old hometown, so I invited him—and Estelle, of course—to tea. Perhaps I neglected to mention the plans to you."

Inwardly, Larissa grimaced, ashamed at the facile way she was lying to her husband. Still, she consoled herself, it was the best way to avoid hurting him, and she and Nathan had not done anything wrong that afternoon.

"Perhaps you did," Edmund agreed, "or perhaps my thoughts were so occupied by work that I did not hear you. At any rate, I'm glad you had a pleasant afternoon. But I hope that Mr. Masters' tales didn't make you too homesick. I'm afraid my work precludes any trips to America for a while. And I couldn't bear to have you go and leave me behind."

She smiled. "Well, you must know there's little chance I'd do that. But we can talk more in a moment, dearest. Mr. Masters was just leaving."

Frowning, Edmund turned to Nathan. "Couldn't I induce you to stay for dinner? Larissa seldom has the chance to chat at any length with one of her countrymen. And I must confess I'd enjoy hearing any news you've brought from Macao."

"You're very kind," Nathan said smoothly, "but I really couldn't impose upon you. My impression of Shanghai society is that there is a constant round of parties, so I'm sure you and your wife must treasure your rare evenings alone together."

"I assure you, Larissa and I will still find time to be alone together." Edmund winked meaningfully and nudged Larissa. "Darling, tell Mr. Masters he would not be imposing."

"Of course you wouldn't be," she said quietly, in a flat, convictionless tone.

Nathan hesitated, searching his mind for another excuse.

Taking Nathan's hesitancy for consent, Edmund clapped an arm around his shoulders. "Splendid."

He turned to Larissa. "Darling, why don't you go and tell the cook we'll have a guest for dinner? In the meantime, Mr. Masters and I can go to my study and sample some of the excellent whiskey that arrived on the last ship from England."

On her way to the kitchen, Larissa wondered how she could survive the tension of the next few hours. She felt tempted to plead a headache and retire to bed, but she knew she would be in agony, wondering what the two men were discussing. She wondered how much Edmund suspected. She was sure he had seen her drop Nathan's hand, but might he simply assume Nathan had been kissing her hand in a gracious farewell? Surely he would not have insisted that Nathan stay for dinner if he thought he had any reason to be jealous. Still, the whole situation made her uncomfortable.

Her thoughts flew back five years, to her first dinner with Nathan. She had been uncomfortable then, too, fearing that somehow Aunt Harriet and Uncle Hiram would sense what had transpired between them. How ironic that her relationship with Nathan, despite all that had happened in the years between, should begin and end on so similar a note.

Larissa stopped for a few moments to see Sean, who was having dinner with Mei Ling in the nursery, then hurried to join the men in Edmund's study. As they walked to the dining room for dinner, she mentioned that Sean had asked that Edmund be sure to tuck him in later.

"But you should have had him dine with us," Edmund exclaimed. "I'm sure Nathan would like to meet him."

Larissa stiffened at the suggestion, knowing Nathan could not mistake Sean's resemblance to him and wondering suddenly if Edmund had noted it yet. "Oh, Edmund," she protested, "Sean's only a small boy. With all the adult conversation, he'd start fidgeting in no time."

"But I'd be delighted to meet your son," Nathan put in graciously.

"You're very kind," she said smiling, "but I detest people who force their children on their guests. At any rate, he and Mei Ling were already having dinner when I looked in. No doubt by now she has him undressed and into his bath."

"Well," Edmund said as he seated his wife, "perhaps next time."

"Perhaps," Larissa replied offhandedly, praying that there would be no next time.

The meal was as strained as Larissa had feared. Conversation remained light, but she found it impossible to relax with Edmund seated across the table from her and Nathan seated to her left. One would never know he was the father of her son, while the other proclaimed himself the father, though he knew he was not. She loved them both in different ways and for different reasons. But she could have only one, and she had no choice as to which it would be. She could never forget that her life belonged to Edmund, though Nathan would always own her heart.

Nothing in Edmund's conversation indicated that he suspected her real relationship with Nathan. Yet, from time to time, she could feel him gazing at her curiously, then shifting his gaze to Nathan.

Under Edmund's questioning, Nathan revealed that he had once worked for a small trading firm in Boston, but had recently purchased his own clipper and was exploring the trade possibilities in the newly opened Chinese ports.

"And are you impressed with what you've seen?" Edmund inquired.

Nathan shrugged. "It's hard to say just yet, but at any rate I don't think I'll be locating my headquarters in Shanghai. I plan to stay here a few days more, then sail south to explore the possibilities at Ningpo."

Edmund nodded thoughtfully. "And will the stunning Mrs. Jamieson accompany you?"

Again, Nathan shrugged. "It's difficult to say. If she wishes to accompany me, she is welcome to, but Estelle does as she pleases."

Edmund's brows raised curiously. "Then, forgive me for

asking, but am I to assume the two of you are not betrothed?"

Laughing, Nathan shook his head. "We most assuredly are not. Long ago, I made up my mind never to marry—for personal reasons. And Estelle, charming as she might be, is hardly the person to change my mind."

"Well," Edmund said, "no doubt you feel your decision is well-founded. But I, for one, think marriage is the best thing that ever happened to me. When I look back at the years before I found Larissa, I see nothing but a wasted void."

"I can understand that," Nathan said softly, raising his eyes to gaze at Larissa. "A woman like your wife could probably induce me to marry, despite my misgivings. But she seems a rare jewel indeed, and I doubt that another woman quite like her exists in all the world."

Listening to him, Larissa coughed, almost choking. Now, when it was too late, he was saying he would marry her! If only he had done so on Macao before that last trip to Whampoa, she would not be in this position now—feeling herself torn between two men, worrying every moment that her husband would discover he was dining with her past lover.

Alarmed, Edmund hurried around the table to pat her back. "Are you all right, darling?"

"Yes." She reached for her glass of claret and took a sip.

Edmund looked unconvinced. "Are you sure you're feeling all right? I noticed you've hardly eaten a thing, and you usually have such a hearty appetite."

She flushed. "Really, Edmund, I'm fine."

"Nevertheless, perhaps you'd best go up and lie down. I'm sure our guest will understand."

Nathan slid his chair back from the table and stood. "Please, madam, if you're not feeling well, don't let me detain you. I'll have to be leaving quite soon, anyway."

Larissa's gaze traveled from Nathan to Edmund and back again. Quickly deciding she could only make the situation more awkward by protesting, Larissa rose and smiled weakly. "Perhaps I should lie down, after all. Thank you both for being so understanding."

She squeezed Edmund's hand, then turned to Nathan. "Mr. Masters, it's been a pleasure chatting with you. Please give my best to Estelle."

He nodded. "The afternoon and evening were delightful, Mrs. Farrell. I'm sure I shall treasure this day as a very special memory of Shanghai."

Their eyes locked for only an instant before Larissa continued toward the door of the dining room.

Behind her, Edmund called, "I'll look in on you in a short while, darling."

"All right," she answered automatically. But she hardly heard him as her mind fastened on the fact that this final moment with Nathan would have to last her the rest of her life.

Chapter Twenty-Six

A whole lifetime seemed to pass before Larissa finally heard Edmund mount the stairs and enter the bedroom adjoining hers. Actually, she had lain in bed less than an hour, waiting for Nathan to leave, to walk out of her life forever. On Macao, she had wept each time they had said goodbye, but now she lay dry-eyed, incapable of tears. The ending had been inevitable.

But what about Edmund? How much did he know? Or suspect? She could not avoid being hurt, but she did not want him to be hurt because of her.

Listening to him pacing in the next room, Larissa lay tensely, wondering when he would join her in bed. They slept together almost every night now because Edmund was anxious for her to conceive, and she was just as anxious to please him. The minutes stretched on, and still he did not come through the dressing room connecting their bedchambers. Finally, unable to bear the agony of listening to him pace, Larissa slid out of bed and put on her dressing gown.

Opening the dressing room door, she saw that the door on the other side leading to Edmund's room was ajar. Dim lamplight spilled from the room. Tiptoeing through the small connecting room, Larissa stood in the doorway and watched her husband for a few moments. He had cast aside his navy blue frock coat, but otherwise he was still fully dressed. His hands were shoved into his trouser pockets, and his shoulders were slumped.

"Edmund," she asked gently, "is something wrong?"

Whirling, he saw her for the first time. "No," he whispered quickly, "nothing's wrong."

"Then why don't you come to bed?"

"Well—I—I thought I'd sleep in here tonight. I thought you weren't feeling well."

"I'm much better now, but I won't sleep a wink if I continue to hear you pacing all night." She walked to him, took his hands, and gazed earnestly into his eyes. "Won't you tell me what's wrong?"

He looked perplexed as he returned her gaze. "Don't you know?"

She shook her head, biting her lower lip to keep from blurting out her fears. Of course she had some idea of what was bothering him, but she didn't want to tell him more than he already suspected. It would be difficult enough to allay whatever suspicions he had, and she didn't want him hurt more than necessary.

Sighing, he turned away from her and sank down on the edge of the bed. "If you don't know, then I must have been imagining things."

The room seemed to echo with silence as he covered his face with his hands. Lifting his head, he stared at her for a long moment. "But it seemed so obvious. I could sense something the moment I entered the salon. Oh, darling, forgive me for asking, but is it possible you and Nathan Masters had more than just a passing acquaintance on Macao? Did he really come here today only to talk about Boston?"

Larissa hesitated, tempted to lie. But something told her she would be a most unconvincing liar, and her lies would only cause Edmund to assume the situation was worse than it really was. Slowly, she shook her head. "No, he did not come here merely to talk about Boston. He came to tell me the newest scheme of my Aunt Harriet and Uncle Hiram. You see, Nathan was once the agent for Bennett and Barnes."

He frowned as he tried to digest the information. "But why didn't you tell me that to begin with? Why did you feel it necessary to make up a story about wanting to hear about Boston?"

"Because I know how strongly you are opposed to my interest in business matters. I knew you would not approve of my even discussing the firm, and despite what I learned from Nathan, I had no intention of getting involved with Bennett and Barnes again—at least not until I was sure I could get your approval. For that reason, knowing how the subject always upsets you, I thought it better to avoid discussing it."

Edmund nodded pensively. "I see. But I'm still puzzled as to why you didn't tell me at once how you had met him—that he was employed by your father's firm. At the ball last night, you led me to believe you had only a casual acquaintance on Macao. And when we met Estelle at Governor Pinto's Christmas ball and she mentioned Nathan Masters, you acted as if—"

Larissa winced as his voice trailed away, knowing he was remembering exactly what Estelle had said—that Nathan had left Macao to forget an ill-starred love affair. Edmund stared at her, his eyes pleading for denial.

His voice seemed hollow and distant as he whispered, "All evening I was plagued by a vague, nagging awareness. There was something hauntingly familiar about his face, but somehow I couldn't decide what it was. Now I know! It's the eyes! Nathan Masters has Sean's eyes! That man is Sean's father, isn't he?"

Tears blurred her vision as Larissa nodded. "Yes. But you must believe me, Edmund, that's all over. Nathan really did come here today strictly on business. He knew how important it was to me to preserve my father's interests, and he wanted to tell me what he'd learned in Boston."

Running to the bed, Larissa sank to her knees and buried her head in Edmund's lap. "There's nothing between Nathan and me now, Edmund. There hasn't been for years. I'm your wife, that's all that matters."

"But you loved him once, didn't you?"

"Edmund, don't," she sobbed. "My relationship with Nathan is in the past, and it would be unfair to all of us to dredge it up again. When you asked me to marry you, you said the past didn't matter. Have you changed your mind now?" She lifted her head and stared into his glassy, blue eyes.

"I—no—that is—" He slammed his fist into his palm. "It's a damn sight harder to be so rational when you meet your rival face to face. I'd be deceiving myself if I didn't admit he's handsome and charming and—"

"Edmund!" she cut him off sharply. "Nathan Masters is *not* your rival! Do you really think me so fickle and immoral that I would consider looking at another man when I'm married to you?"

"No, but whether you admit it to yourself or not, there's still something between you two. I sensed it the moment I entered the salon."

Her brow wrinkled. "Then why on earth did you insist he stay to dinner?"

"Because I wanted the chance to prove myself wrong. I thought that if we talked a while the feeling would pass, and I would never have to confront you with it. Instead, it grew stronger as the evening progressed. There was no mistaking your tension—or Nathan's." He fell silent for several minutes, then asked hoarsely, "Does he know Sean is his?"

She shook her head. "No. And he will never know. No one but you and I will ever know, and in time perhaps even we can forget. Sean is your son, darling. You're the only father he has ever known or ever will know. I could never ask for a better, more loving father for my son."

Edmund sighed. "Our lives seemed to be going so perfectly. I should have known something would have to ruin our happiness."

"Nothing has ruined our happiness!" Larissa protested. "You heard Nathan say he would only be staying in Shanghai for a few days. We'll probably never see him again. You knew before we married that another man had touched my life—considering my condition, I could hardly hide that fact. The only difference now is that you know that man's identity."

"But how could you even allow him in the house, knowing what he had done to you?"

"I told you, I had to find out about papa's business. Besides, I thought he'd be gone long before you arrived home. I knew you'd be hurt if you found out who he was, and I didn't want that to happen. Oh, Edmund, can't you understand that I love you and I wouldn't do anything to jeopardize our marriage?"

Rising to her feet, Larissa pushed Edmund down gently on the bed. He stared at her with wide, vacant eyes as she slowly unbuttoned his waistcoat and ruffled shirt. Sitting beside him on the bed, she massaged his chest, coaxing him to forget all the tension of the last hours. It was strange, Larissa thought, to be seducing him, since Edmund had always taken the initiative in their lovemaking. But she could think of no stronger way to show her love and stop him from fretting about Nathan.

While one hand continued to stroke his chest, the other

slid down to open the sash of her dressing gown and untie the ribbons of her flannel nightdress. Pulling open the garments to expose her breasts, she slid one leg over his waist and sat on him. Leaning down, she drew the tips of her breasts back and forth over his chest until he began to moan with desire. She lay full-length atop him, pressing her body to his and caressed his lips with her own. Her tongue darted into his mouth, tasting the brandy he had drunk after dinner.

She could feel his rising hardness beneath her groin, and she murmured, "Take me, darling. Love me, my dearest husband." Her hand slid between their bodies to open his trousers and free him. She inched her nightdress higher and squirmed against him, caressing his rigid maleness with her smooth, soft belly.

His arms swept around her, pressing her to him. With a groan of suppressed desire, he rolled her to her back and slid between her thighs. Seeming not to notice that, despite the fact she had initiated their lovemaking, she was not ready for him, he drove into her with a violence foreign to his usual gentle manner. Larissa bit back a cry of pain as he took her forcefully, as if to prove to both of them that he possessed her. The moment seemed to stretch interminably, until at last he reached his culmination and collapsed, sweating, on her.

Several minutes passed before he finally slid off of her. Larissa turned her face away from him, not wanting him to see the tears brimming in her eyes. She wondered if she had been wrong in encouraging that lovemaking, for she had never felt more distant from him than at that moment. In the past, though he could never stir her passions like Nathan, he had always shown some concern for her when he had taken her. But this time he had treated her almost as he would a whore. Had just learning about Nathan changed their relationship so much?

Trying to push her misgivings out of her mind, she decided to try to sleep. Sleep could block out their problems, and tomorrow they would both be able to think much more rationally. She was just drifting on the edge of sleep when Edmund's voice assailed her consciousness.

"Larissa? I'm sorry, darling. I don't know what got into me to treat you so roughly. Are you all right?"

She reached out to pat him reassuringly. "Yes. Don't worry. Go to sleep now."

He got up to finish undressing, extinguished the lamp, and got back into bed, pulling a comforter over them. His arms cradled her against his chest, and she thought he was asleep when he expelled a long sigh and asked, "Darling? Are you still awake?"

"Yes," she said, sighing. "What is it?"

"I can't sleep. I keep wondering—at Governor Pinto's ball, why did Estelle say Nathan had just then left Macao in despair? Had you—" he hesitated, then plunged ahead, "seen him since we returned from India?"

Larissa tensed and chose her words carefully, not wanting to give him more to worry about. "We met one day when I was riding. He asked to see me again, and I told him that was impossible."

"But hadn't he already adjusted to that fact earlier, when he returned to Macao and learned you were married and gone?"

She sighed. "I don't know, Edmund. All I can tell you is that any relationship Nathan Masters and I had is quite over. Nathan and I both accept that fact, and I wish you would, too. Nothing happened between us today, and nothing will ever happen between us again."

"Of course," he murmured. "Forgive me, darling, for being such a foolish, jealous husband. I just love you so much I can't bear to think of life without you."

"But I'll never leave you, Edmund, so it's pointless even to consider that possibility."

In the darkness, he groped for her cheek, stroking it gently, then rising over her to deliver a tender kiss. "Thank you for being so understanding, darling. You've put my mind at ease, and now I feel sure I can sleep peacefully."

Within moments, he was asleep beside her. But Larissa lay awake, thinking of the afternoon on Macao when she had been unfaithful, the afternoon when she was sure her second child had been conceived. With a twinge of guilt, she vowed that that was one secret she would always keep from Edmund. He had suffered enough just learning of Nathan's role in her past. There was no need to supply him with further details.

For the first week after Nathan's visit, Larissa thought that her marriage could continue as before. There was some tension between Edmund and her, but she assumed that time and understanding would dissolve it. They attended balls together, went to the English community's small church, and made love every night in the gentle way she had come to expect of him.

At one of the afternoon tea parties, Larissa learned that Nathan had left Shanghai the morning after their meeting. He had become terribly drunk that night and caused a commotion in the community's only hotel when he attempted to force his attentions on a Chinese waitress. Apparently, the same Chinese girl later softened toward him, since she was seen on the deck of his clipper as it sailed out of Shanghai. Estelle Jamieson had remained in Shanghai a few more days, eventually leaving on a British steamer bound for Bombay.

One of the matrons at the tea party clucked her tongue in disapproval. "Such a handsome young man, but obviously a scalawag where women are concerned. Of course, I've heard it said before, these Americans are just barbarians when it comes to proper courtesy." She paused and shot Larissa an apologetic glance. "Pardon my bluntness, my dear, but even you must agree, since you chose to marry an Englishman rather than one of your own countrymen."

"I married Edmund because he is an extraordinary person," Larissa replied coolly, "certainly not because I prefer Englishmen to Americans."

The matron raised her brows as if she were offended. "But certainly you would not condone the actions of this Mr. Masters?"

"I think," Larissa said quietly, uncomfortably aware of the color staining her cheeks, "that it is not our place to approve or disapprove. On the face of things, I would say that Mr. Masters behaved rather badly, but we can hardly guess what prompted his actions."

"Hmph," the woman snorted. "I think you are defending the man simply because he is American. You would do well to remember you've become British by marriage."

Larissa smiled sweetly. "You may think whatever you wish, but my position remains the same. Now, if you ladies will excuse me, I really must get home to prepare for dinner with my husband."

On the way home, Larissa regretted having been so blunt. It would have been better to have ignored the woman's remarks. Now she worried that the old matron would relay her comments to her husband, who in turn might mention them to Edmund. Then Edmund's doubts would begin all over again, since he would assume her attitude meant she still cared about Nathan. Of course, she *did* still care about him, but, considering the gossip, she supposed she was better off without him. If he could move so easily from one woman to another, could he ever have been completely true to her?

Reaching the house, she went upstairs to her room, intending to have a bath and change her gown before dinner. There were no balls or dinner parties scheduled that night, and so it would be her first dinner and evening alone with Edmund since Nathan's visit. She felt a bit apprehensive, wondering if Edmund would be thinking back to that evening. She would have to be sure to keep the conversation moving so that their thoughts could not dwell on the past. Perhaps she would even have Sean join them, instead of having him dine earlier in the nursery as he usually did.

After bathing and dusting herself with lemon verbena, Larissa chose a bright green and gold floral-printed woolen gown, with forest-green piping trimming the bodice seams. The bodice was open at the neck to reveal a white lace chemisette. She slipped a green velvet ribbon around her neck, crossed it in front, and was just securing it with an engraved gold brooch when Mei Ling entered.

"A messenger boy just arrived with this," the maid said, holding out a crisp white sheet of stationery, folded and sealed.

Puzzled, Larissa took the note, broke the seal, and read:

Darling,
I hope you can forgive me, but a new load of cottons arrived from Bombay not an hour ago. I'm afraid I must stay late at the hong so we can inventory the shipment and send it on its way inland before winter sets in and hampers transportation. I fear I will be extremely late, so I suggest that you proceed with dinner and do not wait up for me. If I do not see you tonight, I look forward to sharing breakfast with you.

Your loving husband,
Edmund

Frowning, she dropped the note in her lap. Was it possible, she wondered, that Edmund was just as apprehensive as she about this evening? Had he simply invented the shipment as an excuse to avoid being alone with her?

"Madam," Mei Ling said, breaking in on Larissa's thoughts, "the boy is waiting for your reply."

"Oh, yes, of course. I'll go down and take care of it." She descended to the main floor, nodding to the young Chinese boy waiting in the foyer. In Edmund's small study, she took a leaf of paper and penned a short reply.

> Dearest Edmund,
> I will be lonely without you this evening, but, of course, you must do what you think is best for business. I will try to wait up for you, darling. Please don't overtax yourself.
>
> > Your devoted wife,
> > Larissa

Giving the boy the note, she sent him back to the East India Company hong. As she closed the door behind him, she wondered again about Edmund's note. Why would he have to inventory the shipment? Wouldn't the ship's captain have a manifest accurately listing all it contained? Even if it were necessary to check the manifest, weren't there clerks—"griffins," the traders called them—to handle such menial details? Of course, she didn't know precisely what Edmund did at the hong. Firm in his conviction that women should not be involved in business matters, he still refused to discuss his work with her. Shrugging to herself, Larissa went back upstairs to share dinner in the nursery with Sean and Mei Ling.

After dinner, Larissa read to Sean from a storybook illustrated with lovely color paintings, then tucked him in and retired to her own room. She passed several hours leafing through the various fashion journals that had recently arrived from England. Sometime after midnight, she fell asleep in her chair over a copy of *World of Fashion*. She did not hear Edmund come in and retire in his own room at two in the morning and did not wake until late morning, when Edmund stood over her chair, gently shaking her.

"Are you going to have breakfast with me, darling?"

She jolted awake, feeling stiff all over, and looked up into his laughing blue eyes. "Breakfast? Goodness, is it really morning already?"

He nodded. "You really ought not to sleep in a chair."

"I must have fallen asleep waiting for you."

Edmund frowned. "I thought I told you in my note not to wait up. I got in rather late, so I slept in my own bed rather than disturb you." He turned toward the door. "I'll be waiting in the breakfast room whenever you care to join me."

Entering the breakfast room a few moments later, Larissa squinted at the bright morning light flooding the room. She bent to kiss her husband's cheek, then seated herself opposite him and cracked her soft-boiled egg. "You must have worked very late," she commented. "Did you at least finish with everything?"

Sighing, Edmund shook his head. "I'm afraid not. And there are rumors of another shipment arriving today, so I may well be detained again tonight."

"You know we've accepted an invitation to the Spencers' soiree tonight?"

"I know, but I must put business matters first. If I'm detained, you'll have to send our regrets—or attend without me, if you wish."

Larissa grimaced. "I'd rather stay home than go alone."

"Well, do as you please. I'll try to get home of course, but I'd hate to think of you missing all the fun if I have to work."

She finished her egg and pushed aside the plate. "Just what is it you have to do?" she asked curiously. "I mean, could no one else handle it?"

Edmund shook his head. "No. No one else could handle it. But I'd only bore you if I tried to explain. You shouldn't clutter your head with business matters."

"Well, I hope you'll manage to finish everything before the end of the week. Remember, we're hosting our own party three nights from now."

"Umm," he grunted noncommittally. He got up from the table, then brushed his lips across her forehead. "I really must be going, darling. If I can't get home in time for the Spencers' party, I'll send a message."

The messenger arrived at four that afternoon, and again Edmund did not return home until long after Larissa was asleep. He looked tired at breakfast the next morning and seemed rather distant, as if he did not really hear most of what Larissa said. When she inquired about his work, he became evasive and almost hostile, but she convinced herself that he was simply overtired.

The same events were repeated that evening and the following morning. When the messenger arrived again on the fourth evening, Larissa decided to take Edmund's advice and attend that evening's ball without him. She was bored staying home every night. Though she did not look forward to the company of any of the prim matrons at the ball, she supposed she could at least lose herself in the music and dancing.

Dressed in a patterned silk gown of opalescent blue, with a modestly high round neck and pointed waist, Larissa asked the butler to order her a sedan chair. When she arrived at the Beale mansion, she was greeted at the front door by her hostess, who looked surprised to see her alone.

"I hope Mr. Farrell is not ill?" Mrs. Beale said.

"Not at all. But he was detained at the hong and insisted that I attend without him."

"How very kind of him. We missed you at the Dents' gathering last night and at the Spencers' the night before."

Mrs. Beale smiled knowingly, and Larissa winced, wondering what sort of gossip was already circulating about her and her husband. No doubt her appearance alone tonight would begin all sorts of rumors about an impending separation and divorce.

By the time the first hour had passed, Larissa was thoroughly sick of explaining to people where Edmund was, and she decided to go home. As she made her way toward the door, a young East India Company griffin named George Wilcox stopped her and asked her to dance. Thinking that a few more moments' delay could not matter, Larissa agreed.

As he led her onto the dance floor, she said, "At least *you* won't be asking me where Edmund is."

George Wilcox looked surprised. "As a matter of fact, I was just about to ask you. Of course, you might say that's none of my business—"

Larissa frowned. "Surely you are jesting, Mr. Wilcox! You must know that Edmund is still at the East India Company hong, as he has been every night this week. I only wonder why you aren't there helping him."

Wilcox blushed uncomfortably. "Your pardon, madam, but I live upstairs at the hong, and there was no one downstairs in the working quarters when I left this evening."

"You must be mistaken! Who is taking care of the cotton shipments that came in this week?"

"Cotton shipments? As far as I know, no new ships have docked here all week." Suddenly realizing that he was exposing the deception of one of his superiors, Wilcox cleared his throat and tried to regain his composure. "But the fact is," he said quickly, "I don't generally have much to do with the textile trade. No doubt I'm just not aware of what's come in or who's working on it."

Larissa's eyes narrowed. "But you did say there was no one at work when you left this evening?"

"I—well—I suppose I could have been mistaken. I mean, I didn't actually walk all through the warehouse looking for anyone."

"I see." Fighting the realization that Edmund had lied to her all week, Larissa suddenly felt sick. "I think we'll have to finish our dance some other time, Mr. Wilcox," she said in as steady a voice as she could muster. "I think I'd like to go home immediately."

George Wilcox paled. "Lord, I hope I didn't say something to upset you! Can I order a sedan chair or a carriage for you?"

"No. No thank you. I think I'd prefer to walk." Tearing away from him, Larissa bolted through the Beales' front door and rushed down the streets of the settlement toward the hongs. In her haste to leave the ball, she had forgotten her cloak, but she hardly noticed the cold or the scattered snowflakes.

As she ran, she clung to a wild, unreasonable hope that George Wilcox was mistaken. Edmund simply would not lie to her. He had never lied to her or deceived her about anything, except when he had been ruled by his opium habit, and that was now years past. He had pledged never to be tempted by the drug again, and she had no reason not to trust him.

But what was the explanation? She could understand his hesitancy to have dinner alone with her three nights ago, but why had he also missed their social engagements when he had always seemed to enjoy them so much? Was it possible he had become involved with another woman? Had seeing her with Nathan, knowing that Nathan had once been her lover, made him feel the need for another woman's caress?

Even before she reached its door, Larissa saw that the East India Company hong was dark. Nevertheless, she pounded on the door for several minutes, hoping that somehow Edmund might be inside and would come to open the door. When her fists ached from pounding, she walked around the huge, square structure, seeking some sign of light within. Even then she did not give up hope, but raced home, telling herself Edmund had probably finished his work and gone home, expecting to find her.

"Edmund! Edmund, darling, are you home?" she shouted as she pounded up the stairs to the second floor.

Mei Ling stumbled sleepily from her room beside the nursery, her eyes widening in shock as she noted Larissa's disheveled state. Without realizing it, Larissa was shivering now from the penetrating cold.

"What's happened to you?" Mei Ling exclaimed. "Come by the fire and warm yourself immediately."

Ignoring her maid's concern, Larissa demanded, "Is Edmund here?"

"I don't believe so. I retired only a few moments ago, and I haven't heard him come in."

Before Mei Ling finished speaking, Larissa threw open the door to Edmund's room and rushed inside. He was not there, and nothing in the room had been disturbed since it had been cleaned that morning. Whirling in despair, she saw Mei Ling standing in the doorway, a concerned expression on her face.

"Is something wrong that you must see him immediately?" Mei Ling asked anxiously. "Should we send a messenger to the hong?"

Larissa shook her head helplessly. "No, no. That wouldn't do any good. You see, that's the problem—Edmund is not at the hong. I've just come from there, and there's no one there. He lied to me, Mei Ling!"

Mei Ling's mouth dropped open, and she shook her head. "No. You must be mistaken. Calm yourself and try to think more clearly. Mr. Farrell is a good man. He would not deceive you. Unless—" She hesitated, shifting uncomfortably. "Do you think he has fallen under the spell of that evil drug again?"

Only minutes earlier, Larissa had discounted that possibility, not wanting to remember that dreadful period, which she thought had been forever shut out of their lives. But now, when Mei Ling asked, she felt forced to consider the possibility more seriously. In fact, his attitude the last few days *had* been very similar to that of his opium-eating days in India. When they had breakfast together, he seemed withdrawn, detached, and disinterested in anything she said. He had not asked about Sean in days, and he looked tired and haggard. She had attributed all of these symptoms to overwork. But now, knowing he had not been working every night, she had to find some other explanation.

Still, after their struggles to conquer his addiction, it was hard to imagine Edmund would go back to using the drug for any reason, she thought. Unless meeting Nathan and learning precisely who he was had been more difficult for him than she had imagined. Despite all her explanations and all her reassurances, had that knowledge been eating away at him until he felt forced to seek escape? While she convinced herself that the tension between them would pass, had he found a more pleasant way to suspend reality?

Remembering suddenly that her maid was still waiting for an answer, Larissa whispered, "I don't know, Mei Ling. I pray that he has not turned to opium again, but I don't know. Perhaps we'd better check his room while he's still gone."

They spent more than an hour going through his drawers and checking all the hidden places the maids would not notice in their routine cleaning, but they found no sign of opium. A thorough search of Edmund's study also yielded nothing.

"But he could keep a supply at the hong or even somewhere else in Shanghai," Larissa said, then sighed. "I guess there's nothing for me to do but confront him with the fact I know he has not been at work these nights and ask him point-blank if he's back to eating opium." Smiling ruefully, she said, "Thank you for your help, Mei Ling. You can go back to bed now. I'll have to handle this alone."

As her maid went back upstairs, Larissa went to the parlor and settled down to wait for Edmund's return.

Chapter Twenty-Seven

Larissa waited in the parlor all night, but Edmund never came home. In the morning, Larissa drank a cup of hot, bitter coffee and then went to look for him again at the hong.

It was not yet nine o'clock, and most of the hong personnel did not begin work until ten. But the doors of the East India Company were unlocked, so Larissa let herself in. Because of her husband's stubborn belief that women should not be involved in business, she had never even visited the building. Curious, she made her way through the large warehouse area to the group of small offices in the rear. The door to one office was half-open, and she could see Edmund slumped over his desk. Knocking briskly, she entered the office and closed the door behind her.

Edmund lifted his head drowsily, squinting in disbelief as his eyes focused on her. His frock coat was thrown haphazardly over a chair, his waistcoat was only partially buttoned, and his shirt was rumpled.

Gazing at him sorrowfully, Larissa said simply, "You didn't come home last night."

He cleared his throat. "No—I—I worked through most of the night, so I thought I'd just nap a bit here."

She shook her head. "There's no need to lie to me, Edmund. I know you didn't work last night. And I know there haven't been any new cotton shipments."

His eyes widened in shocked dismay. "What are you talking about, and"—his gaze flicked over her ball gown, which she had been too upset to change—"why are you dressed that way?"

"I'm dressed this way because I went to the Beales' ball last night. On the way home I stopped to see you, but you weren't here. In fact, no one was here. I went home and sat up all night waiting for you."

Edmund's tone became defensive. "That was a foolish thing to do when I've warned you before not to wait up. As a matter of fact, I had to go to the home of one of my Chinese clients last night."

"And did you have to stay all night?" she asked in a hurt, quiet voice.

He bristled. "Why are you asking me all these questions? What's the matter—have you stopped trusting me and started to find me lacking since you renewed your acquaintance with Nathan Masters?"

"Edmund!" she cried. "Nathan has nothing to do with this! Anyway, he's been gone from Shanghai for days."

"Oh, really? How do you know? Did you personally see his ship off?"

"Now who's acting untrusting! Of course I didn't see his ship off! I heard about it through idle tea party gossip. And the reason I'm asking questions is because I care about you. You're my husband, and I don't want anything to happen to you. That's why I have to ask you—" She hesitated, then blurted the question that had plagued her all night, "Are you using opium again?"

For an instant, he paled. Then he answered indignantly, "Opium? Of course not! Where did you get such an absurd idea?"

"From you—because you've been acting just as you did in India when you were eating opium."

"That's ridiculous! I've been acting tired, which is precisely what I am. Now I think you'd best go home so I can continue my work."

Unconvinced, she stood staring at him. "Will you at least promise to be home this evening?"

He shrugged. "I'm not sure. I'll let you know."

"Edmund, I have to know now. Have you forgotten we're hosting a soiree tonight? Only a few weeks ago, you insisted upon it. It would be most embarrassing for both of us if you were not present at your own party."

"Oh, all right," he sighed irritably. "I'll be there. Now, leave me, so I can get some work done."

All day Larissa worried about Edmund. She had found no sign of the drug, and he had strongly denied using it, but all his denials could not allay her doubts. She hoped that the evening's party would induce him to come home on time, since he always took special pride in the affairs he hosted, but she still feared that something would keep him away.

At five o'clock, two hours after the usual time for work at the hongs to cease, Edmund still had not returned home. Larissa summoned Li Tong, one of the house servants, and directed him to go to the East India Company hong in search of her husband.

"If he is in his office," she said, "you must convince him to come home immediately. If he is gone, you must find out if anyone knows where he has gone, and then you must find him. Do you understand?"

Li Tong nodded. "Yes, madam."

Watching the servant depart, Larissa felt a bit guilty, as if she were having someone spy upon Edmund. But any guilt was quickly overcome by her heartfelt concern for her husband. She had given him ample time to fulfill his promise to come home, and she would have gone looking for him herself if she did not have to begin preparing for their party. If Edmund was late, at least she could be on hand to greet their guests and cover his absence. Besides, he had seemed rather unmoved by her pleas that morning. Perhaps having a servant come after him would touch his pride and induce him to come home immediately.

She dressed slowly, listening for Edmund to enter the adjoining room. In her nervousness, she spilled her perfume on her gown, leaving a dark stain that forced her to choose another gown.

At seven, when she descended to wait for her guests, neither Edmund nor Li Tong had returned, and Larissa was becoming increasingly agitated. She forced a smile as the guests began arriving and directed them to the salon, where tables of champagne and appetizers had been set up. She tried to ignore the knowing looks of her guests when they inquired about Edmund, and she assured them he had simply been detained and would be joining them in a short time.

After the first hour of strained entertaining, her head was throbbing unbearably, and she began to wish she had cancelled the whole party, claiming illness in the family.

She had just been cornered by Mrs. Beale and was wondering how much longer she could keep up pretenses, when Li Tong burst into the salon and pushed his way to her side.

Oblivious to the curious guests, he blurted breathlessly, "Madam, I've found him!"

The guests quieted, and all eyes turned to the servant. Larissa froze, feeling Mrs. Beale's eyes boring through her and the rest of her guests closing in around her. Summoning some composure, she smiled weakly and said in a quiet, surprisingly steady voice, "Please, continue with your conversations. It appears my servant and I must speak privately." Taking Li Tong's elbow, she guided him out of the salon to Edmund's study.

"What do you mean, you found him?" she demanded as she closed the study door against her curious guests. "Where is he? Why didn't you bring him home with you?"

Li Tong squirmed uncomfortably. "There is not time to explain right now. I think you must go to him."

"But where? At the hong?"

The servant shook his head, wringing his hands despairingly. "No. Oh, believe me, madam, I tried to bring him home, but he would not come. There is a sedan chair waiting outside for you. I beg you, come immediately!"

Nodding, Larissa rushed from the study, grabbed a velvet coat, and hurried outside. On the street, she climbed into the sedan chair Li Tong had hired. After giving instructions to the carriers, Li Tong also climbed in, huddling in a corner and hoping to escape further questioning.

Larissa leaned forward, pulling aside the shabby velvet curtains to watch as they raced through the settlement. They entered the walls of the old city and moved on to a fairly well-to-do section of Shanghai. She knew instinctively what was wrong but would not believe it until she asked Li Tong. "It's something to do with opium, isn't it?"

The servant nodded glumly, shrinking further into the corner of the seat.

The chair stopped before a spotless red-tiled building surrounded by peach trees, sculptured cedar trees, and a small brook with a curving bridge. Larissa cocked an eyebrow as they got out. "A teahouse?"

Li Tong shook his head. "It only looks like a teahouse. It is an opium house, and it is here that I found the master."

Without waiting to hear more, Larissa pushed open the bamboo gate and ran up the walk to the front door. She threw open the door, pushing past the two astonished men standing guard at the entrance. The proprietor, a small man in black trousers and jacket, his forehead shaved in the style of the Manchu dynasty and his remaining hair dangling down his back in a long queue, hurried to greet her.

Bowing, he said, "We are privileged to be visited by so fine a lady. Did you wish to sample our fine products?"

Shaking her head, Larissa struggled to keep from choking in the smoke-filled room. "No. I'm looking for my husband, Edmund Farrell."

The man smiled ingratiatingly. "I am very sorry, but of course we do not disclose the identity of our clients."

"I don't care about your other clients. I just want my husband, and I know he's here."

Standing on tiptoe, Larissa surveyed the room. Men, most of them Chinese, were reclining on dingy mattresses ranged along the walls in three tiers. Each man had a pipe, a stylet, and a lamp over which to heat his opium dose. She realized then what she should have realized the night before—Edmund did not have to keep a supply of opium cakes at home for eating. In China, it was customary to smoke the drug at places like this instead of consuming it in one's own home.

She watched in horror as some of the clients heated the drug over the lamp, others inhaled the drug deeply, and still others lay back, apparently enjoying the effects of the drug. Pushing aside the proprietor, Larissa moved closer to the men, trying to find Edmund, still hoping that Li Tong had been mistaken and she would not find him here.

As she moved from mattress to mattress, trying to ignore the leering expressions of some of the men, the proprietor caught her arm. "Unless you have come to smoke," he said firmly, "I cannot allow you to stay. You are disturbing my clients."

She shook him off roughly as her eyes flicked to the next mattress and she caught sight of the blue silk waistcoat Edmund had been wearing that morning. Falling to her knees beside the mattress, she grasped his hand and bent over him. His eyes were closed, and he seemed to struggle for every breath.

"Oh, Edmund," she sobbed, "why, why? After all we've been through, how could you turn back to opium?"

His eyes flickered open, and he squinted in the dim light, seeming to take an eternity before he recognized her. Finally, he grimaced and shook his head weakly. His words came in short, painful gasps. "Couldn't face you after met him—tried, but couldn't do it. I—know—you loved him. Never loved me."

"Edmund," she pleaded, "you mustn't say that. You know I love you! I wouldn't be here right now if I didn't!"

Again, he shook his head. "Not the kind of love I wanted—but not your fault—you warned me before we married." He choked, and his chest shook as he tried to draw in more breath.

"Edmund, darling, please, you mustn't talk like that! Come home with me now, darling, I do love you! I need you! Sean needs you."

He drew in another long, racking breath. "Sean—his child. I couldn't even give you a baby—what a failure!"

"No, Edmund. I won't listen to any more of this! Just come home with me." She tugged on his arm, and when he did not respond, she shook him. Still, he did not respond, and for a horrified instant, she thought he had died. Despite the hot, smoky atmosphere in the room, his skin felt cold and clammy. "Edmund!" she screamed hysterically.

"Here!" the proprietor barked as he and one of his guards hauled her to her feet. "You can't behave like that in here! You're disturbing all my customers!"

"You've killed my husband!" she shrieked. "You and your filthy drug have killed him!"

"Nonsense," the man snarled. "Your husband was simply foolish enough to take too much. No one forced him to do so. In time, he will sleep it off. As for you, I'll have no more of your yelling in my establishment!"

Larissa felt herself roughly propelled through the room, then shoved out the door. Turning angrily, she charged back toward the door, yelling, "I won't leave without my husband!"

A huge arm shot out to bar her way, and the owner barked a command to two more of his employees. The next moment, she was shoved brutally back onto the front path, and Edmund's body was flying through the air to land beside her.

The shock of being thrown from the opium den seemed to have no effect on him. His body was limp, and his skin still felt cold and clammy. Pressing her ear to his chest, Larissa could detect a slow, very faint heartbeat.

She looked up and saw Li Tong standing on the street near the waiting sedan chair. "Li Tong," she cried, "help me quickly! We must get Mr. Farrell home!"

Obediently, the servant helped her load Edmund into the sedan chair. Since the chair had room for only two passengers, Larissa instructed the servant to run for a doctor while she and Edmund went directly home. All the way back to the settlement, she shook her husband in a vain attempt to rouse him and listened frantically for his feeble heartbeat.

At home, she was relieved to learn that all her guests had left, gossiping among themselves about her strange disappearance and her husband's probable whereabouts. The gossip did not concern her at all, as her whole being was concentrated on reviving Edmund. Mei Ling helped her drag him into his study and lay him across the divan. In the light, she could see that his pupils were no larger than pinpricks and his lips were a sickly blue-gray color.

Within minutes the doctor arrived. He strode into the study, glanced at Edmund, and then looked at Larissa. "Opium, am I right?" he asked curtly.

She nodded. "I don't know what to do! He talked to me when I first found him, but now he doesn't seem conscious of anything."

Frowning, the doctor grasped Edmund's wrist, feeling for a pulse. "How long since he smoked it? And how much?"

She shrugged helplessly. "I don't know. All I know is the owner of the den said he had too much. I got him home as quickly as possible."

"You might have done better to get him on his feet. Now it may be too late," the doctor said. Looping one of Edmund's arms around his neck, he dragged him to his feet. "Have you any smelling salts?" he demanded.

"Yes. I'll get them immediately."

"You might also tell someone to brew a pot of hot, strong coffee."

Nodding, Larissa ran from the room to do as the doctor asked. When she returned with the smelling salts a few moments later, the doctor was pacing back and forth, pulling Edmund's unresponsive body with him. With shaking hands, Larissa held the smelling salts beneath her husband's nose, but still he did not respond.

"Slap him!" the doctor ordered.

"What?" She stared at him unbelievingly.

"Slap him—all over! We've got to stimulate his skin!" In example, he delivered a stinging blow to Edmund's face. Grimacing, Larissa did the same. They were both slapping him and dragging him around the room when Mei Ling entered, carrying a pot of coffee.

Sighing, the doctor said, "We might as well try to force some of that down his throat. Nothing else seems to be working."

Together, they pulled him to the divan and propped him up in a sitting position. While Mei Ling poured the coffee, the doctor groped for Edmund's pulse. His face clouded, he dropped Edmund's wrist, and moved his fingers to his throat. For a moment, he was silent. Then he cleared his throat and lifted his eyes to Larissa.

"Perhaps you'd best sit down and drink that coffee yourself, Mrs. Farrell." He hesitated, clearing his throat again. "I'm afraid it will be of little use to your husband. There is no delicate way to put it—the man is dead."

"No!" she whispered. "That's not possible!"

"I'm afraid it's quite possible," the doctor replied calmly. "His heart has simply stopped beating. It appears that he partook of a quite lethal dose."

"No! No! No!" Larissa rushed to Edmund's limp form, shaking him roughly in a vain attempt to revive him. Grabbing the cup of coffee Mei Ling had poured, she opened his mouth and tried to pour it down. The coffee spilled down his chest, staining his shirt and burning her hands. Staring at Edmund's lifeless face, she dropped the china cup, and collapsed in tears against his chest.

Sobbing, she recalled Edmund's last words. Had he sought only a temporary escape from a world in which he saw himself as a failure, or had he actually intended to commit suicide?

Unable to accept the thought of suicide, she looked up
at the doctor and mumbled, "He must have been poisoned.
He would know better than to take too much. In India he
—he ate opium. So he knew how much it was safe to take.
I'm certain he would not take too much."

The doctor frowned. "Perhaps not deliberately, but his
mind may have already been so blurred by early doses
that he did not quite realize what he was doing. Then, too,
I understand that the smoking dose is considerably larger
than the normal eating dose—and produces a much more
rapid and marked effect. Perhaps your husband did not
realize that fact."

"Perhaps." She shrugged. "But I still wonder—isn't it
possible he was poisoned? It's no secret that at least some
of the Chinese hate the British, and the proprietor of the
opium den was rather reluctant to let me in. Couldn't
someone have given him something other than opium?"

"It's possible, but not likely. First of all, people do die
from too much opium—it is a definite poison. If your husband was at the opium den, he must have gone there on
his own free will—at least you've made no mention of him
being tied to the mattress like some kidnap victim." He
paused, raising his brows in question.

When Larissa shook her head, he continued. "The Chinese pay exorbitant fees for their opium, so they in turn
charge outrageous fees to smokers. I doubt that the proprietor would willfully destroy a paying customer. Furthermore, the use and sale of opium is still illegal under the
Manchu dynasty, so I doubt that the proprietor would wish
to draw attention to his establishment by deliberately
poisoning a foreigner."

"Not even if he thought his crime might be hidden behind the guise of the victim's own weakness?"

The doctor sighed. "My dear young lady, I find your
imagination altogether too fertile. The fact, as I see it, is
that your husband consumed a lethal dose of opium smoke.
For your own peace of mind, I advise you to accept that
fact. Of course, you may find it somewhat embarrassing,
but a wife can hardly be held responsible for her husband's
actions. Now, if you'll excuse me, there really is nothing
more I can do here."

While Mei Ling showed the doctor out, Larissa sank
back on the divan and stared at Edmund's lifeless form.
"A wife can hardly be held responsible for her husband's

actions," she repeated to herself. But she wondered—if the doctor knew everything, would he still say she was not responsible? Or would he think, as she did at that moment, that by marrying Edmund, even by consenting to see him again after their first meeting on the Praya Grande, she had ruined the life of a good, though weak, man?

Chapter Twenty-Eight

The entire foreign settlement turned out for Edmund's funeral. The women murmured polite though strained condolences before moving off to whisper behind their fans. The men were quietly gallant, but Larissa had the feeling they were all assessing her body, wondering which of them would win the right to call her mistress. Even Captain Baskins, the consul who had so generously shared his home with them during the first months in Shanghai, seemed more solicitous than necessary.

No one inquired about the cause of Edmund's death, but Larissa sensed it was common knowledge. She wondered if the doctor had blurted out the secret or if someone had simply managed to surmise it. Leaving the church, she could not help overhearing the whispered comment of one gentleman.

"I hear he once ran one of the largest opium estates in India—and you know the seaman's proverb; those who prosper in the opium trade are doomed to die an atrocious death. What could be more atrocious or more ironic than to die from opium itself? Pity he left such a young and lovely wife, though."

"Is it really such a pity?" another man chuckled. "I should think that depends on how one looks at it."

The funeral was the last time Larissa saw most of the people in the settlement. After her husband's death, the women stopped inviting her to their tea parties, and it was out of the question to include an unattached woman at their evening social events. Besides, they told their husbands sharply when a few ventured to suggest inviting her, Larissa Farrell was in mourning and would surely refuse any invitations.

Only one man persisted in inviting Larissa to dine with

him—Captain George Baskins. At first, she politely declined all his invitations, relieved to be free of all social pressures. But after a few weeks, as loneliness began to assail her, she relented, agreeing to dine with him at the newly built British consulate at the junction of the Whangpoo River and Soochow Creek. Recalling the complete respect with which the consul had always treated her, Larissa convinced herself she had only imagined his overly friendly attitude at Edmund's funeral. Besides, for some time she had considered discussing with him her theories about Edmund being poisoned. She had gradually come to accept the fact that Edmund might have returned to opium, but she still found it hard to believe he had taken too much. If anyone could help prove her theory and see that the culprit was punished, it was the British consul.

To her chagrin, Captain Baskins merely greeted her theory with an indulgent grin. Leaning back in his chair, he sipped his after-dinner brandy and murmured, "I realize it's difficult for you to accept the fact that your husband had this weakness for opium. But you mustn't allow your embarrassment to make you imagine the Chinese are such sinister creatures. No doubt the poor proprietor would shudder at the thought of scandal being connected with his establishment. Let me assure you, Mrs. Farrell, in all my dealings with the Chinese, I have never had reason to suspect they might poison anyone."

"Then you won't investigate the case?" she asked lamely.

The consul shrugged. "What is there to investigate? Your husband took more opium than his body was able to handle. I'm not about to stir up hostilities because of his foolishness. And I shouldn't think you would want to publicize the fact that he was in an opium den. My advice to you is to forget the whole incident."

"Forget?" Larissa cried. "You expect me to forget my husband's death? For as long as I live, I'll remember the ghastly smell of the smoke in that place."

He smiled almost condescendingly. "Of course I can understand your feeling that way right now, but in time, surely, you will learn to forget. You must think of yourself and of your son. Any man who was weak and foolish enough to turn to opium does not deserve to be mourned for long."

Scowling, Larissa slammed down her claret glass and pushed herself away from the table. "You have no right to judge my husband!" she snapped. "How could you even begin to presume what problems may have driven him to the drug?"

The captain's eyes widened. "Indeed? Am I to understand all was not well between you and Edmund? Do you mourn him more from guilt than love?"

Larissa felt her face redden, but she managed to hold her voice steady. "Captain Baskins, you assume far too much! Now, if someone will get my cloak, I think I'd best be going home."

She whirled away from him and marched toward the dining room door, freezing suddenly as his words followed her. "You must forgive me if I've offended you. I'm afraid I've never been very good at courting. What I've been trying to say is, you're going to need someone to take care of you and Sean. My position with the government gives me a certain amount of security, and I would feel privileged to become your husband."

Turning slowly, Larissa stared at him in disbelief. "You can't actually be proposing?"

He nodded calmly, and something about his calm self-assurance made her explode indignantly. "You, sir, are being worse than presumptuous! My husband has not yet been dead a month, and you suppose that I shall simply fall into your arms."

"Well, after all," the captain said quietly, "it's not as if you were madly in love with the man, and I really don't expect you to profess undying love for me."

"Edmund's and my personal relationship is not your affair," Larissa snapped, "but I'm sure you will be surprised to learn that we did, indeed, love each other. Furthermore, nothing could be further from my mind than remarriage. I assure you, I'm quite capable of taking care of myself and my son. Edmund built a prosperous textile trade in Shanghai, so I'm sure I won't be suffering any financial problems."

"Are you really so sure?" Captain Baskins asked knowingly. "Perhaps you ought to consult with the East India Company officials before you make any rash decisions."

"What do you mean?" she asked coldly, trying to convince herself he was only trying to sway her. Still, she wondered just how financially secure she really was. Edmund had never discussed finances with her, except to assure her he kept an adequate reserve in the company accounts. He had always supplied more than ample funds to run the household and had been most generous with his gifts, so she assumed they had no worries. But she had also assumed he would never go back to opium.

Seeing her confidence begin to waver, Captain Baskins smiled. "Perhaps you really should talk to someone at the company. Randolph Davis would, I believe, be the man to see. And in the meantime, remember that my offer has not been withdrawn."

Larissa slept very little that night, and when the East India Company hong opened at ten the following morning, she was there to see Randolph Davis. She had met him briefly at a number of social events, but now, standing in the doorway of his office, she noted with surprise how young he was—at least ten years younger than Edmund.

He smiled weakly as Larissa entered the room, nodding her into a chair while he rearranged some papers on his cluttered desk. Finally, he shifted his eyes to meet her gaze.

"Mrs. Farrell, I must say I've been expecting this visit. In fact, I had been thinking of calling on you later this week. I assume you are interested in your late husband's financial status?"

She nodded, and he sighed, turning to reach for the account books on a shelf behind him. "I hope you are not expecting a large inheritance, because I'm afraid the news is rather bleak. As a matter of fact, Edmund Farrell died with scarcely more than a penny to his name."

Larissa gasped. "But that's not possible! He told me he kept a healthy account with the company, and with the success of the textile trade, I'm sure—"

Davis cut her off with a sharp clearing of his throat. "Apparently he did not tell you that the textile trade has not been nearly as successful as he had hoped. It seems Sir Henry Pottinger's assessment of the situation was grossly inflated. The Chinese have their silks and a fair supply of their own cottons, so they are only mildly interested in cottons and woolens from England and India. Even so, Edmund did a creditable job, one that should have allowed any man to live decently. Unfortunately, he chose to live far beyond his means."

Pursing his lips thoughtfully, he continued, "At one time—when you first arrived in Shanghai—he did have quite a sizable account, one that reflected his years of service to the company, particularly the years when he was involved in the more lucrative opium trade. However, he withdrew large sums to build your house, hire and keep the servants, and—well, I'm sure you know better than I what the money went for. In addition, during the last week or two of his life, he made several large drafts on his account, which I can only assume went to support his—opium habit."

Swallowing hard, Larissa asked, "Mr. Davis, how much money is left in the account?"

He shook his head sadly. "If you're frugal, I would guess enough to see you through the winter. In consideration of your husband's years of service, I feel certain the company will provide you with free passage to England in the spring. Edmund had relatives there. Certainly they would not hesitate to take in his wife and son."

Frowning, she shook her head adamantly. "I know no one in England, and I've no desire to become a burden to someone I've never met."

"Well"—he moistened his lips as his eyes traveled over her—"I can think of another alternative—one that would enable you to stay in Shanghai, in your own house. Of course, I have a wife, but—"

"Mr. Davis!" she cut him off sharply, rising and turning toward the door. "You needn't outline the rest of your suggestion! I prefer to find my own alternatives. I'll inform you when I wish to draw on Edmund's account."

All the way home, she fumed to herself about the presumptuousness of both Randolph Davis and George Baskins. Both thought she would be only too willing to run to them when she discovered her financial condition. But neither realized she was not as poor as they thought. She still had her share of Bennett and Barnes—or Hiram Barnes Ltd., as her uncle now chose to call it. All she had to do was find a way to claim it. That wouldn't be easy, but she was determined to manage. In recent years, she had put off pursuing her inheritance, partly in deference to Edmund's wishes and partly because she was afraid of becoming involved with Nathan again. But now Edmund was gone, Nathan was no longer connected with the firm, and that inheritance seemed her one hope of surviving with her honor intact. She would not live on charity, and she would not demean herself as some man's mistress. Somehow, she would force her aunt and uncle to give her what was rightfully hers.

Her thoughts turned back to Nathan, and for an instant, she wished he were there to advise her. He knew better than she just what the company's assets were and what Aunt Harriet and Uncle Hiram intended to do to keep them from her. His years of business dealings had given him a shrewdness she did not possess. But Nathan had been gone almost two months, along with his little Chinese mistress.

Shaking her head, Larissa decided it was probably best that Nathan was gone. If he were near enough to help her, she would no doubt find it impossible to deny her love for him. And, even with Edmund gone, she was not free. They could never go back to the carefree months on Macao, because now she had Sean to worry about. Knowing Nathan's views on marriage, she could not subject her son to society's barbs by living with her lover—even though he was the real father of her son. Besides, even if she and Nathan were reunited, how could she be sure he would not discard her in time, as quickly as he had tired of Estelle Jamieson?

In the past, they had loved each other deeply, but they had also caused each other incredible pain. Whatever the explanation, she wondered if Nathan could ever fully forgive her for marrying another man and leaving Macao in his absence. And could she forgive him for flaunting his recent affairs so openly?

If Nathan were there, it would be so easy, at least for a time, to rely on him. But she was not willing to pay the price of the hurt that might come in the end. It was better to face and solve her problems alone.

By afternoon, Larissa had decided what to do. It was already late December. There would be no more ships out of Shanghai that winter. But in the spring, she and Sean would take the first ship east, toward Boston. Only by confronting her aunt and uncle face-to-face could she finally claim her inheritance. Besides, nothing remained to tie her to Shanghai. Even in the settlement, she felt like an outsider, and she was anxious to start a new life among new people.

In the meantime, she was determined not to depend on the questionable wisdom of Randolph Davis to dole out the funds to see her through the winter. The less often she had to deal with him and his lewd suggestions, the better she would like it. Before the afternoon was over, she sent Li Tong to the East India Company hong, requesting that Mr. Davis immediately release to her all funds remaining in her husband's account. Within minutes, Li Tong returned, followed by Randolph Davis.

"My dear lady," Davis exclaimed as he entered the study, "I wonder if you have any idea what you are asking? I beg you, at least allow me to counsel you in financial matters. If you spend all you have now, in one lump sum, you'll have no way of supporting yourself in the coming months—"

His voice trailed away as Larissa looked up, scowling, from the desk where she had been reviewing the household accounts. "Mr. Davis," she said coldly, "I am hardly such a simpleton that I am unaware of the need to budget. I am perfectly capable of deciding for myself how my funds should be spent, and I have no intention of exhausting them all at once."

"Then," he replied calmly, "I fail to see why you should desire all the funds at this time. If you'll forgive me for saying so, women are notorious for their empty-headedness in business matters. But then—" he paused, his eyes widening in sudden comprehension, "perhaps you actually wish to speed your inevitable destitution. Might I suppose that the proposition I offered you this morning appeals to you? As long as you have some money, I suppose you might feel guilty accepting my offer. But if you were destitute and had to find some way to provide for your son—"

Angrily, Larissa stared at him. "Mr. Davis, I beg you kindly spare me any further analysis of my motives. It really is none of your business, but to satisfy your curiosity, I'll tell you why I want all the money now—so I won't be forced to deal with a despicable worm like you during my remaining months in Shanghai!"

Davis's jaw dropped open, and he stared in stunned disbelief. Then he slowly moistened his lips and whispered, "The money will be sent by messenger first thing in the morning. I think, Mrs. Farrell, that there is nothing left for us to say to one another. Good day."

Randolph Davis had been gone less than an hour when Mei Ling entered the study to tell Larissa she had another visitor. Moving her eyes beyond her servant, Larissa saw George Baskins framed in the doorway. She rose stiffly and walked toward him.

"Captain Baskins," she said coolly, "I don't recall that we had an appointment today."

"We didn't," he replied. "But I assume that by now you have seen Randolph Davis, and so I thought you might be prepared to continue our discussion from last night."

"I see." Larissa nodded dismissal to Mei Ling and paused while the servant left the study. Turning nonchalantly, she strolled to the settee and seated herself, leaving Baskins to stand awkwardly near the door. "As a matter of fact, I did confer with Mr. Davis this morning—and again this afternoon. But I fail to see how that can have any bearing on my relationship with you, captain."

Baskins' eyes widened. "Didn't Davis tell you your husband left you only the most meager funds?"

"He did," she nodded.

"Then might I be so bold as to inquire how you intend to support yourself?"

"I fail to see that that is any of your affair, but I can assure you I shall manage quite nicely."

Baskins' expression darkened, and he took a step toward her. "It's Davis, isn't it? I always knew he wanted you. He's younger than I am and better looking too, I suppose. But let me remind you that he is also married. He can't offer you an honorable relationship, while I—"

"Captain Baskins," she cut him off irritably, "must *I* remind *you* that I am not currently interested in *any* relationship, honorable or not. As a matter of fact, Randolph Davis did offer me a proposition, but I turned him down, just as I turned you down last night."

"Then there must be someone else! Who is it?" Baskins demanded, stepping closer. "What did he offer you? From the first moment I saw you in the muddy settlement streets, I knew you were a slut. No lady would have come to Shanghai in those first months, even to be near her husband. Oh, you acted highhanded and prissy enough while you were living in my house, but I knew you weren't really so pure, and I promised myself, even then, that one day I would possess you!"

Stunned by his words and by the undisguised lust burning in his eyes as he advanced toward her, Larissa shrank back against the settee. He was only a step away when she recovered her wits and jumped to her feet.

"I think it would be best for you to leave now, Captain Baskins," she said in a cool, detached voice. "In the future, my servants will be instructed not to admit you to my home, and of course I will not accept any future invitations you might send."

As she tried to move past him to the study door, he grabbed her shoulder. His fingers pinched her flesh through her woolen dress, and he growled, "You won't brush me off so easily. I've wanted you too long to be denied now." His other arm swept around her waist, pulling her roughly to him, and his mouth came down hard over hers.

Larissa squirmed, struggling to free an arm, but he tightened his hold, pulling her more firmly against him. Jerking her wrists behind her back, he grasped them both in one hand while his other hand slid upward to squeeze a breast. He pushed her back toward the settee, stumbling in his haste. That brief stumble threw their bodies apart just long enough for Larissa to drive her right knee up hard into his groin while she screamed for help.

Baskins' pained howls drowned out her screams as he released her and fled the room. Larissa fell back on the settee as she heard the pounding of feet in the hall. A moment later, Li Tong, followed by a frightened-looking Mei Ling, burst into the room

"Madam," Li Tong panted, "two of the staff have detained Captain Baskins in the hall. Has he hurt you? Do you wish me to go for help?"

She smiled weakly and shook her head. "No, release him and show him out. I don't believe he'll bother me again."

The following day, at midmorning, a messenger arrived from the East India Company hong. As she counted out the few pounds Edmund had left her, Larissa sighed regretfully. Randolph Davis had not exaggerated when he warned she would have to be frugal to survive the winter. And she would still have to find money for passage to Boston.

Seeing she would need to scrimp wherever possible, Larissa began by calling together the servants and telling them the majority of them would be dismissed. She wrote letters of recommendation for each of them, and within

two weeks only Mei Ling and the cook remained with her.
Still, she knew what little she saved would hardly be
enough to pay two passages halfway around the world, and
so she began to sell the extravagant furniture on which
Edmund had squandered so much of their money.
Wealthy Shanghai mandarins were eager to purchase the
strange English furnishings, but they were too shrewd to
pay more than a small fraction of its worth.

Watching the rooms of his home slowly emptying, Sean
asked Larissa gravely one day, "Mummy, are we poor
now that papa's gone?"

She hesitated, then smiled bravely. "Of course not, darling. We're just getting ready to move again, and we can't
take everything with us. Besides, we shall always be very
rich, so long as we have each other."

Frowning, he persisted, "But we don't have very much
money, do we?"

"No," she said, then sighed, "we don't have very much
money. But we'll manage, Sean. I promise you, we'll manage just fine."

By mid-February, with more than half the furniture sold
at an incredible loss, Larissa was satisfied she had enough
money to pay for her trip to Boston. The only thing that
really pained her about leaving China was the thought of
leaving Mei Ling behind. In their years together, the woman who had begun as a maid had become a companion,
nurse to Sean, confidante, even a mother at the times Larissa most needed advice.

Only Mei Ling knew just how much she had suffered
and agonized over her love for Nathan and her obligations
to Edmund. Mei Ling alone had known from the beginning, even before she herself imagined it, that she was
carrying Nathan's child. Even when she had disapproved of
Larissa's actions, she had remained devoted and loving.
She had become an integral part of her life, and Larissa
knew she would miss her terribly. Still, she did not think
she could ask her to leave the Orient and travel with her
to the United States. Much as she regretted it, she felt it
best to send Mei Ling back to her home on Macao.

Mei Ling, however, had different ideas. When Larissa
told her her plan, the old woman's eyes widened and glistened with tears. "You mean you do not want me with
you?" Mei Ling murmured. "You mean to dismiss me like
the other servants? How have I offended you?"

"Offended me?" Larissa repeated incredulously. "Mei Ling, you must know how I've cherished your presence, your support, and your love for all these years. It's because I love you so much that I can't take you away from your homeland."

"Have you forgotten that I went with you to India?"

"Of course not. How could I forget what a help you were there? But Boston is not so near as India. It's halfway around the world, and life there is so different from anything in China or in India."

"I could adjust," Mei Ling said softly. "I've passed more than half my years in foreign communities, so I've learned a great deal about how you Americans must live."

"Can you really say you don't want to go back to Macao —to your own home and people?"

Mei Ling nodded. "I have no more relatives on Macao, and I have no home there. My home is with those I love —with you and Sean, wherever you may go. Of course, if you do not want me, I cannot force myself upon you. Perhaps I can find a place elsewhere. Perhaps another family will need me—"

"Mei Ling," Larissa interrupted tearfully, "*I* need you. And Sean needs you. If you're certain you want to come, I mean certain beyond a doubt, we'll find a way. After all, I still haven't sold the rest of the furniture or the house."

Beaming, Mei Ling embraced her. "I knew you wouldn't leave me behind," she murmured, her voice husky with tears. "And I promise you, you will never regret taking me with you."

Part Six

�֍

1845

Chapter Twenty-Nine

Larissa lifted Sean to the rail for a last glimpse of Shanghai as the *Ocean Maiden* glided up the Whangpoo River toward the Yangtze, which would take them to the Pacific Ocean. Mei Ling was below in their cabin. On boarding, she had insisted that she wanted to put the cabin in order immediately. Larissa, sensing her maid felt a bit sentimental about leaving China, had decided it was best to leave her alone.

Now, as Shanghai's pagodas receded in the distance, Larissa felt herself becoming nostalgic, too. Despite all the heartache she had suffered in the Orient, she had also known more joy there than anywhere else on earth. She had become a woman there, and for a few months on Macao, she had been happier than she had ever dreamed she could be. Yet now she was returning to Boston, not because of any great love for the city or her relatives there, but because it was the only way to protect what was hers and gain her independence. Once she was sure of receiving her share of the business profits, she had no intention of staying there, though she had no idea where else she might go.

Sean interrupted her thoughts. "Mummy, how many days till we get to Boston?"

Setting him on his feet, she replied, "Not days, darling, months. Probably about three, which would get us there in the middle of July. The captain says we'll be stopping off in the Hawaiian Islands for a few days."

"Will the islands be like China?"

"I don't know, Sean. I've never been to the Hawaiian Islands."

"But you have been to Boston, haven't you?"

"Of course I have. Don't you remember I told you I grew up there?"

He nodded gravely. "Does that mean we'll be staying in Boston forever?"

Larissa smiled absently. "We'll see, darling." For the first time, she wondered if she would be doing her son a disservice if she moved him to Boston and then uprooted him yet again. In his less than five years, he had already lived in three homes, all of them far too temporary for a growing child. But it would be at least three months before they reached Boston and she was forced to consider the problem more seriously. Bending down, she swatted his rump affectionately. "You ask too many questions, little boy, and I think it's time I took you below for your nap."

"Oh, must I go?" His lower lip protruded in an appealing pout, and his amber-flecked eyes glistened pleadingly.

For an instant, Larissa's eyes clouded, and she saw Nathan during a playful moment in their bedroom on Macao. Shaking her head briskly, she pushed the image out of her mind and bent to take her son's hand. "Yes, you must. Now, come along and don't make a fuss."

The first week aboard the *Ocean Maiden* passed peacefully. Sean, who had been too young to remember much about his first shipboard adventures, kept Larissa occupied with constant questions about the ship. She was grateful for the boy's curiosity and chatter, for it kept her from thinking too much about her first voyage between Boston and China.

But she still had to contend with the nights, when both Mei Ling and Sean were asleep and she lay awake beside her sleeping son. Sometimes, when moonlight flooded the cabin, she would doze fitfully, waking to imagine that Nathan, not Sean, lay beside her. Without surprise, she realized that after all their months apart she still wanted him, and she could not help wondering if, somewhere in the world, he, too, was lying awake, wanting her.

In the middle of the second week, Larissa began to notice a change in Mei Ling. The servant had never adapted very well to ship travel, but she seemed to be suffering more than her usual amount of seasickness. She picked at her food, forcing down only a few bites at each meal, and she dragged herself around the ship as if every movement pained her. Day by day, she seemed to grow weaker and more lethargic, until Larissa became quite concerned about her.

As they stood at the rail one afternoon while Sean napped below, Larissa studied her servant, noting the hollows beneath her eyes and the slight flush to her cheeks. "No matter what you said," she murmured, "I should never have taken you away from China."

Mei Ling stared at her in surprise. "Why do you say that?"

"I've never known you to seem so strained and weak. It's obvious to me you're pining for your homeland."

"Nonsense," Mei Ling smiled weakly. "I've hardly given China a thought since we left Shanghai. I'm just a bit tired. I'll never be able to understand how anyone can sleep on a pitching ship. And you know I always suffer from a bit of seasickness."

Larissa shook her head. "I think it's more than seasickness. This has been an unusually calm voyage, yet your symptoms are more pronounced than on our rocky crossing to India."

Impulsively, she reached up to touch Mei Ling's forehead. "Your forehead is flaming!" she exclaimed. "I think you'd better lie down immediately."

Mei Ling turned away abruptly. "Of course my face feels hot—I've been standing in the sun. I tell you, I'm perfectly well."

Larissa was unconvinced, and she became even more concerned the next day when Mei Ling looked no better and admitted she had a slight headache. "No doubt the sun has caused it," Mei Ling said casually. "I must remember to wear a bonnet when we come on deck. For now, I think I'll go below and rest until my head stops throbbing."

Larissa nodded agreement and turned to greet Captain Henderson, the ship's master, who was passing on his way to the quarterdeck. A stifled gasp behind her made her turn back to Mei Ling, just as the older woman collapsed on the deck.

The captain knelt beside Mei Ling, carefully feeling for her pulse, touching her forehead, and opening her mouth to examine her tongue. Without a word, he picked the woman up in his arms and strode below to Larissa's cabin. Perplexed and worried, Larissa followed.

Without waiting for Larissa, Captain Henderson kicked open the cabin door and carried Mei Ling to the empty bunk. Awakened by the commotion, Sean stirred sleepily on the other bunk. "Mummy," he asked, "what's wrong?"

"Nothing, darling," Larissa reassured him, going to sit beside him on his bunk. "Mei Ling just isn't feeling too well. She'll feel better after she rests a bit."

"I'm afraid it's not that simple," the captain said. "It may be weeks before she feels better—if then."

"What are you trying to tell me?" Larissa asked, alarmed. "What's wrong with her?"

He sighed. "I'm afraid it's the fever—typhoid, I've seen enough cases to be fairly certain." His gaze shifted to Sean, and he sighed again. "I suppose you'll want to nurse her yourself, but I suggest you let me take the boy into my cabin. It wouldn't be wise to keep him in the same cabin. Have no fear—I'll see that he's well cared for."

Larissa nodded numbly. "You're very kind, captain."

The captain shrugged. "You may change your opinion when you hear what else I have to say. I must insist that you and your maid remain confined to your cabin. I can't risk infecting anyone else."

"That seems reasonable enough."

He held up his hand, indicating he was not finished. "And when we reach the Hawaiian Islands, I must insist that your entire party leave this ship."

"But we can't do that! We must go on to Boston, and I've already paid you for our passage."

"Under the circumstances, I'll be happy to refund the unused portion of your passage, but I simply cannot allow you to remain aboard. If anyone so much as suspects we have typhoid on board, it could throw my crew and passengers into a panic. Besides, think of your maid. She'll be much more comfortable on dry land."

"Suppose Mei Ling recovers before we reach the islands?"

He shook his head. "It won't happen. Typhoid takes weeks—sometimes even more than a month—to run its course. We'll reach Hawaii next week, and you'll have to get off. There'll be other ships to Boston later in the year. Now," he said, moving toward the door, "if you'll excuse me, I have to get back to running my ship. I'll send my cabin boy down to collect your boy and his belongings."

"Thank you, captain," Larissa said stiffly, "you've been most helpful."

Within five minutes, the cabin boy, a red-haired youngster of about thirteen, knocked on the door. Sean hung back, watching uneasily as his mother handed the boy a bundle of his clothing. "I don't want to go, mummy!" he cried.

"Nonsense," Larissa said briskly. "It's a great honor to be invited to the captain's cabin."

"But I want to stay with you!"

"And I want you to stay, darling, but it's just not possible. I have to take care of Mei Ling, and I don't want you getting sick, too."

Seeing tears begin to cloud his eyes, she clutched him to her and murmured, "Oh, Sean, don't make this more difficult than it already is. Remember on Macao when I was sick and Mei Ling took care of me? Now it's my turn to take care of her, and when she's feeling better, we can all be together again. In the meantime, you can have a wonderful time exploring the captain's cabin."

"All right." Nodding bravely, Sean sniffled and took the cabin boy's hand.

As she closed the door after her son, Larissa turned to meet Mei Ling's doleful gaze. The servant shook her head weakly. "I promised I would cause you no trouble, and already I am disrupting all your plans. Perhaps it would be best for you to leave me in Hawaii and go on to Boston without me."

Larissa shook her head adamantly. "That's out of the question. How could I desert you after all the years you've cared for me?"

"But if it's so important for you to get to Boston at once—"

Larissa was embarrassed at how selfish she must have sounded arguing with the captain. "It's not so important. I was just worried about the money. If Captain Henderson hadn't offered to refund our passage, I don't know how we would have managed. But, I can wait to get to Boston. There's no one there I care about. You mustn't worry about anything but resting and getting well."

"Thank you." Mei Ling closed her eyes and smiled weakly. "I promise that I'll make it up to you."

By the time the *Ocean Maiden* reached Honolulu harbor a week later, Mei Ling was suffering from a constant fever. Hot and uncomfortable, she thrashed on her narrow bunk, sometimes lapsing into delirium. Larissa sat beside her day and night, bathing her with cool water and coaxing her to eat small amounts of porridge and drink some water. She watched helplessly as violent tremors possessed Mei Ling's body and the skin on her chest and belly became covered with rose spots.

Both Larissa and Mei Ling had fallen into a fitful sleep when the clipper docked in Honolulu, so neither was aware they had reached their destination. A knock on the cabin door awakened Larissa almost two hours after they had anchored. She opened it to a concerned Captain Henderson.

"We're here," he said simply, his eyes moving past Larissa to Mei Ling's prostrate figure. "I've been ashore already and found you a place to stay. I also took the liberty of installing your son in another house."

Larissa's face clouded as she thought of how much she had missed Sean in the days since Mei Ling had become ill. "You mean he won't be staying in the same house with me?"

"It wouldn't be wise," Captain Henderson said evenly. "As long as you're nursing your maid, you'll be too busy to care for him. And you'd have a hard time finding a nurse to do it for you."

"So you've given him to some stranger?" Larissa asked dubiously. "How could you do so without even consulting me first? How do I know I can trust these people?"

"Oh, you can trust them, all right. Dr. Judd and his wife are medical missionaries here, well respected by both the natives and foreign population. In fact, the doctor is so well respected that the Kingdom of Hawaii has appointed him a sort of unofficial prime minister. A number of years ago, the queen regent even entrusted her own daughter to the care of the doctor and his wife."

"I see." Larissa sighed in resignation. "Then I suppose it is best for Sean to stay with the doctor and his wife. Did you, by chance, ask this Doctor Judd if there is any way he can help Mei Ling?"

The captain nodded. "I did, and though he thought there might be little he could do, he promised to look in on you." He crossed to the bed and took Mei Ling in his arms, tucking the blanket tightly around her. "Gather up your belongings, and I'll take you to your house."

Larissa was silent as Captain Henderson took them ashore. She stared at the grove of coconut palms along the beach, the lush green hills behind them, and beyond the hills, the blue-veiled mountains. Under different circumstances, she would have found the view breathtaking. But now she brooded about Mei Ling's fate. What did the doctor mean by saying there might be little he could do?

She focused on the city, noting with surprise that it was a thriving, cosmopolitan community, not at all the primitive, tropical village she had imagined. The streets were wide and lined with rows of palm trees. Though there were many grass huts, there were also a large number of impressive stone houses and stores. Captain Henderson hired a carriage to take them to their house. On the way, he explained that Honolulu boasted more than nine thousand residents, one thousand of whom were foreigners. The king, Kamehameha II, employed many of the foreigners in his government in an attempt to build his nation into a thriving, competitive, modern country.

The carriage rolled past the king's coral palace, past a few more impressive stone residences, then stopped before another spacious stone building. After assessing the building through the carriage window, Larissa turned to the captain, feeling a mixture of embarrassment and confusion.

"Surely this can't be the house you acquired for us?"

He nodded, his brown eyes dancing. "It is, indeed. Don't tell me you find it unsuitable?"

"No, I—" she stammered, "I do appreciate your kind assistance, captain, but the fact is I can't possibly afford to pay for anything so grand."

"What makes you think payment is necessary?"

"You didn't—I mean, you—"

"No," he cut her off crisply, "I didn't pay for it. Mrs. Judd made the arrangements. It seems the house belongs to a member of the royal family. A few weeks ago, her sister died here, and since then she has refused to occupy the house, claiming it is haunted by ghosts." He paused to study her carefully. "I assume that you are not afraid of ghosts?"

Larissa glanced at Mei Ling, sleeping fitfully, seeming so near to death herself. "It depends. What did the woman die of?"

"From what I understand, old age. They say she was close to ninety."

"All right." Larissa nodded briskly. "After the trouble you and Mrs. Judd have taken, I would be most ungracious to reject your kindness. If you'll just help me get Mei Ling settled, I won't trouble you further."

After they had installed Mei Ling in one of the three bedrooms, Captain Henderson took Larissa on a brief tour of the house, pointing out the store of food already waiting in the kitchen.

As she walked him to the door, Larissa said pensively, "You must know, captain, how grateful I am for all you've done. But I must admit, I'm also curious. Why did you do it? Do you treat all your passengers so well?"

He shrugged. "Perhaps I did it for your son. He's a fine lad, one I'd be proud to call my own. Or perhaps," he said, pausing to slide a hand beneath her chin, then lifting it to look deep into her eyes, "I did it because I've wanted so badly to see a smile on that lovely face. From the moment you boarded my ship, I sensed an urgency, a determination, and also a sadness, in you, that constantly beclouded your features. I knew from the first that I could never make you laugh, so I thought at least I might lighten your load and make you smile."

Touched, she blinked back her tears and forced up the corners of her mouth. "Thank you, captain," she said, smiling and crying at the same time. "I wish I could give you some real token of my gratitude, but I'm afraid I have nothing."

"Hush," he said softly. "That smile is all the thanks I seek. Goodbye, Mrs. Farrell. I'm pleased that our lives touched, even for so short a time. I'm sure you'll get to Boston and that you'll accomplish whatever you are so set upon." Quickly, he bent to brush his lips across her cheek. Then he strode away from the house and out of her life.

As promised, Doctor Judd arrived to look in on Mei Ling the next day. Obviously overworked, the man was thin and gaunt, with large, dark circles beneath his eyes. It occurred to Larissa that he could probably use a doctor himself. After examining Mei Ling, the doctor advised Larissa to continue nursing her, but admitted he could give her little aid.

By the time Mei Ling's illness wore into the third week with no sign of a break in the fever, Larissa felt herself on the verge of collapse. As much as she missed Sean, she was glad he was not with her, for she had all she could do to care for her maid. Mei Ling seemed to become more

emaciated every day. Her tongue was brown, and she
suffered almost constant abdominal pains. Worse, her moments of delirium became much more frequent than her
times of lucidity. She imagined herself back in China and
begged for people Larissa could only assume were her relatives. Most of the time, she chattered in Chinese, so Larissa could not even understand her. She sat helplessly beside
the bed, bathing Mei Ling and trying to calm her.

Late one afternoon, as Larissa sat in a stupor beside
the bed, Mei Ling suddenly sat upright and grasped her
stomach. Her face contorted with the intensity of her pain,
and she stared at Larissa as if she were a stranger.

"Mei Ling!" Larissa cried frantically. "What is it? How
can I help you?"

Mei Ling continued to stare with unseeing eyes, clutching her stomach, and then she began to vomit. For several
minutes her body heaved uncontrollably, before she collapsed against her pillows. Consumed by despair and wishing desperately that Doctor Judd was there to advise her,
Larissa hurried to get clean linens and fresh water to
bathe Mei Ling.

The woman's breathing seemed heavy and labored as
Larissa struggled to remove the soiled linens. Her eyes
were closed, but her mouth hung open awkwardly. After
changing the linens and bathing Mei Ling, Larissa took the
soiled sheets and dirty water from the room. Returning a
moment later, she wearily slid her chair close to the bed
to continue her vigil. Since their arrival in Honolulu, she
had slept only in snatches, and now she was so exhausted
she could hardly focus her eyes. Even so, glancing down
at Mei Ling's still form, she sensed immediately that something had changed. Leaning closer, she realized that Mei
Ling's chest no longer heaved with her labored breathing. She dropped her head to the older woman's chest,
hoping to hear a heartbeat.

The room seemed suddenly silent, filled with the suf-
focating stillness of death. In that agonizing instant, Larissa
realized she had lost her beloved Mei Ling. "Oh, Mei
Ling," she whispered, "forgive me. I should never have
brought you here!" Hurtling into a dark well of oblivion,
Larissa collapsed over Mei Ling's form.

Larissa awoke in another room in another house. A tall,
brown-haired woman in her early forties was leaning over

her. The woman smiled as Larissa opened her eyes. "Ah, it's good to see you looking better. For a few days, we feared we would lose you, too."

Larissa blinked and looked around. "Where am I?"

"In the prime minister's residence. I'm Laura Judd, Doctor Judd's wife. The doctor found you when he stopped to look in on Mei Ling. We brought you here to care for you."

Feeling confused, Larissa asked, "Did I have typhoid?"

"I don't believe so. More than likely, you simply collapsed from lack of sleep and the shock of losing your friend."

Slowly, Larissa began to remember. "Mei Ling's dead, isn't she?" she asked weakly.

"Yes." Mrs. Judd nodded sympathetically. "But you mustn't worry more about her. Her soul is at rest. We gave her a Christian burial."

Larissa stopped herself on the verge of declaring Mei Ling had not been a Christian. Swallowing the words, she decided it didn't matter. Surely Mei Ling's gods would understand the Judds' good intentions. Her eyes roamed the room again, and she asked, "My son—is he here?"

"Yes. Sean is here, healthy and anxious to see you. Tonight we can all say a prayer of thanksgiving for your recovery."

The Judds made her feel thoroughly welcome in their household, which included among its distinguished boarders John Rictor, a lawyer who had been appointed attorney general soon after his arrival from New York. From their first meeting, Larissa knew that the tall, dark, attractive, young lawyer found her intriguing. But, though she could not deny he was handsome, she could not return his feelings.

Larissa soon found there was an emptiness in her life without Mei Ling. Mei Ling had shared with her the most intense years of her life, the years in which she had become a woman, a wife, a mother. Besides herself, only Mei Ling and Edmund had known the true identity of Sean's father. Now both of them were gone, and she vowed to keep the secret forever locked in her heart. Only Mei Ling, by turns understanding and reproving, had known the intensity of her passion for Nathan. Larissa knew she would mourn Mei Ling for the rest of her life.

Except for an occasional bout of loneliness for Edmund

and Mei Ling, Sean seemed more contented and healthy
in Honolulu than he had ever been in China or India. He
thrived on the varied diet of taro root, sweet potatoes,
pineapple, coconut, and roast pig, beef, and fowl. Playing
outdoors in the sun each day, he grew almost as brown as
the native children. He especially delighted in taking Larissa on long walks outside of the city and into the countryside, where the Hawaiians still lived in grass huts and
dressed in colorful *kapa* cloths, tied around their waists,
leaving their chests proudly bare.

Sean seemed in no hurry to resume their journey and
never mentioned Boston, so Larissa continued to put off
the trip, even when ships called at Honolulu harbor on
their way to the United States. She told herself it was best
not to disrupt Sean's life again. But in her heart she knew
she was becoming less and less anxious to return to her
aunt and uncle and resume the sordid battle for her inheritance. If she did not feel so desperate to secure Sean's future and preserve what her father had built, she might have
been tempted to forget about Bennett and Barnes entirely.
She had already lost so much that money could never replace, beginning with her father, her husband, Mei Ling
—and Nathan, who was lost to her as surely as if he, too,
were dead.

When she watched the sun rise over the verdant hills
in the morning, ran with Sean on a clean, deserted beach,
glimpsed a waterfall plummeting hundreds of feet down
a red-brown cliff face, or listened to the night breezes
ruffling the coconut palms, she always felt herself longing
for Nathan. No place on earth could have been more perfect for their love to grow and prosper. The happiness they
enjoyed on Macao would surely become infinite ecstasy in
Honolulu. Day after day, she struggled to push all thoughts
of Nathan from her mind, telling herself they had no future
together and that they never could have had, considering
the ease with which he moved from one woman to another.

At dusk one evening, Larissa stood on the balcony of
the Judds' house, watching the blue of the interior hills
deepening to purple. Sean was already asleep in his own
room, worn out by a long day of play and exploration. She
had heard that day that an American clipper, the *Columbia*,
had docked in the harbor, and she supposed that she
really should inquire about passage to Boston. It would be
easier to ignore the ship, as she had ignored at least half a

dozen others, but she could not rely on the Judds' hospitality forever, and even with the money left that would have paid Mei Ling's passage, she could not expect to support herself and Sean in Honolulu for long. Still, she wavered in her decision, telling herself it would not really matter if she waited a few more weeks, or even a month.

"It is a spectacular view, isn't it?"

A soft voice behind her startled Larissa, and she turned to see John Rictor standing in the shadowed doorway of the room adjoining hers. He stepped closer, smiling in mild amusement. "You must forgive me for startling you, but for some time I've been wanting to speak with you privately, and the opportunity has never seemed to present itself."

She frowned. "And what could you have to say to me that could not be said in the presence of the Judds and their other guests?"

Rictor grinned lazily. "I think you must have some idea. You strike me as an extraordinarily intelligent woman."

She shook her head innocently. "I'm afraid I don't follow you, Mr. Rictor."

"Why not call me John?" He was standing beside her now, and he reached out to take her hand. "I'm thirty-two, Larissa, and I'm a healthy, normal man, with all the normal, healthy urges of a man. My work here, drafting and testing laws for a foundling nation, is stimulating, but I require other stimulation as well. As a young widow, I suspect you may have the same needs."

Snatching her hand away from his, Larissa turned away. "I'm afraid you are mistaken, Mr. Rictor. At this moment, I can think of nothing I require. I have a very active young son, who provides all the stimulation I can handle."

"We both know that isn't so," Rictor said softly. "And if you believe it, you're only deceiving yourself. Think about it, Larissa. You came to Hawaii unintentionally, on your way to another port. Yet, you've made no effort to continue your journey. I think that's because you're looking for something—something I could give you."

"You think very highly of yourself, Mr. Rictor," she said acidly.

"I think very highly of both of us."

He reached out and began stroking her back, and Larissa shivered despite herself. Too many months had passed since she had known a man's tender touch. In Shanghai, after Edmund's death, she had thought herself immune. But now she had to struggle to keep her voice level. "Please—John—I don't want—"

"You don't want this?" He turned her in his arms and brought his mouth to hers. His lips were firm, sweet, sending tremors unbidden down her spine. "Or this?" he murmured, sliding a hand up to cup her breast.

"No!" She pulled back but was still held prisoner in his arms.

"Why are you so afraid? I assure you, I can be discreet. Indeed," he said, chuckling, "the God-fearing Doctor Judd would probably dismiss me from my post if he thought I was dallying with someone beneath his very roof. But I want you, Larissa, and your kiss was not that of a woman who has no desires of her own."

"I'm not staying in Hawaii," she said quickly, anxious to change the subject.

"Nor am I indefinitely," he countered. "Oh, I'm content here for the moment, but before many more years pass, I'm sure I'll be struck by wanderlust again. I've already lived all over the United States, from New York to Louisiana to Oregon, and I've every intention of visiting the rest of the world. You could come with me, if you wished."

"Along with my son?" she asked, her voice tinged with sarcasm.

Rictor shrugged. "I suppose I could arrange that."

"No, thank you, Mr. Rictor," she said crisply. "Your suggestion does not suit me, and I doubt that it would suit Sean."

"Then consider the present. At least we could share something while you remain in Hawaii."

"I'm afraid not. I understand the *Columbia* docked in the harbor is bound for Boston, and I intend to be aboard."

Dropping his hands from her shoulders, John Rictor said, "You're running away, Larissa. And you may be able to run away from me, but you won't be able to run away from yourself. There are dozens more men who will approach you as I have. Eventually, you will capitulate—and you may find the bargain worth far less than what I offer you." Turning abruptly, he strode off.

Larissa remained on the balcony, mulling over his words, guiltily recalling the response evoked by his touch. It would have been so easy to let him make love to her, and she supposed that he had sensed as much. She knew he was right about other men. Already she had been approached by George Baskins, Randolph Davis, and, in a more honorable way, even Captain Henderson. Something about her made men not only desire her, but consider her available, and she could not deny that she, too, desired a man. But her pride and self-respect would not allow her to accept just any man, under any circumstances.

Damn Nathan Masters, she thought with sudden venom. Everything was his fault! He had made her experience what it was to really want a man. And he had left her unable to find happiness and satisfaction with anyone else.

Silently, she thanked John Rictor for one thing. He had, however unintentionally, convinced her that she must leave on the *Columbia*. If she ever hoped to be free of leering men with devious propositions, she would have to secure her financial independence. And the only way to do that was to confront Uncle Hiram and Aunt Harriet and wrest from them her share of Bennett and Barnes.

Chapter Thirty

To her despair, Larissa found the next morning that the *Columbia* had no room for additional passengers. No matter how she pleaded with the captain, he remained firm in his stand.

"There simply are no passenger cabins available," he said. "I'm sorry, but there's nothing I can do for you."

"We don't even need a cabin," she pleaded, as he maneuvered her to the main deck and toward the gangplank. "We'll gladly sleep on deck if you'll just grant us passage."

"Not on my ship, you won't," he snorted. "Now, off with you. I've work to attend to."

Larissa stood her ground, determined not to be pushed away. Remembering the money that would have paid Mei Ling's passage, she blurted, "I could pay you very well, captain. Much more than the average payment for passage."

"That, madam, does not interest me in the least. Now, I suggest that you leave my ship, before I have you thrown off." As he started to turn away, a woman's voice stopped him.

"Captain Sinclair, I'd like a word with you, if you please."

Both Larissa and the captain turned their attention to a tall, buxom woman with honey blonde curls. She was immaculately dressed in a blue and white silk gown, a blue silk bonnet, and white kid gloves.

Irritated, the captain raised his brows. "What is it, Mrs. Kingsbury?"

She smiled, showing deep dimples in both cheeks. "I'm afraid I could not help overhearing your conversation. If the lady so desperately desires passage, I'll be pleased to share my cabin with her."

"You, Mrs. Kingsbury? As I recall, you already have rather crowded accommodations—a single cabin with only one bunk."

She shrugged. "True enough, but there are enough blankets to make an extra pallet on the floor. The truth is, I dearly crave the company of another woman."

Larissa smiled hesitantly. "You're very kind, but perhaps you do not understand my situation. I'm not alone. My son will be traveling with me."

The other woman's face softened, and her eyes became cloudy. "Your son, you say? How old is the boy?"

"Almost five years old."

"Five years old," she said quietly. "Steven would have been—" She stopped herself, shaking her head, then smiled broadly. "Well, I can't see that a five-year-old boy would take up much room. My offer still stands. What do you say, captain, will you relent now and let the lady on your ship?"

He shrugged. "If you want to travel with three people jammed into one small cabin, far be it from me to argue with you. But"—he turned an icy stare to Larissa—"I will still expect full payment for both yourself and the boy, and I will not tolerate any squabbles about your close quarters."

As he strode away, the blonde woman made a face. "Ships' captains! They're all in love with power. But don't let him scare you. He's mainly bluster."

"That's a relief," Larissa said. "I've dealt with some who are every bit as harsh as they sound." She turned her attention away from the captain and surveyed her hostess. The woman was a few years older than she, with a definite air of independence. "I really don't know how to thank you for what you've done. You've no idea how desperate I was to leave Hawaii. But it's just occurred to me, we haven't been introduced. I'm Larissa Farrell." She extended her hand, and the other woman squeezed it in her own gloved hand.

"I'm very pleased to meet you, Larissa. I'm Alicia Kingsbury. And there's no need to thank me. As I said, I've been dying for some female companionship, since there is not a single other woman on this ship. If you can abide me, I'm sure I'll be overjoyed to have your company. Why don't you go and collect your son and whatever belongings you have, and we'll get you settled in the cabin."

By the time the *Columbia* sailed two days later, Larissa felt completely at ease with Alicia Kingsbury. Sean adored the woman, and she doted on him, insisting that he call her Aunt Alicia. She also insisted that he sleep in the bunk each night, while she and Larissa alternated sharing it with him.

"You're so wonderful with him," Larissa commented one night as she and Alicia strolled on deck after tucking Sean in. "I'm afraid some women would resent sharing their quarters with another woman's child."

In the moonlight, she saw Alicia's sad smile, and she was surprised to see tears glistening in her eyes. "Your Sean is very special to me," Alicia said softly. "You see, he reminds me so much of my own son. Even his hair is the same color. My Steven would be almost six years old now, but he was only three when he died from smallpox."

Larissa shivered. "I'm sorry. I never imagined—but what a painful experience it must be to have Sean with you now as a daily reminder. If I'd known, I would never have accepted your hospitality."

"Nonsense." Alicia patted her arm reassuringly. "I feel it's a great privilege to have Sean with me. Sometimes I even pretend to myself that he's my little boy. Of course," she added sorrowfully, "I'll never have other children."

"But of course you will!" Larissa exclaimed.

"No," Alicia said firmly. "After Steven died, I was so distraught I could not bear to stay in New York, so I went to Foochow, where my husband was engaged in the tea trade. Four months after I arrived, he died—cholera. So you see, I'm a widow, with no prospects of having more children."

"But you're young, beautiful—you could marry again."

"I'll never marry again. One marriage was enough to teach me not to trust men. I had thought that Jason and I had a good, happy marriage, so you can imagine my surprise when I arrived in Foochow and found him less than pleased to see me. I later discovered he had a pretty little Chinese mistress, and I had upset his relationship with her."

Larissa thought of Nathan leaving Shanghai with his own Chinese mistress. "Well," she said lamely, "men have certain appetites that demand satisfaction, I guess. Most times, these incidental mistresses mean nothing to them."

"Ha!" Alicia snorted. "That's precisely what Jason tried

to tell me. I suppose your husband fed you the same story?"

"No—I—" she stumbled. "Except for a few months when he first went to Shanghai, Edmund and I were never separated during our marriage, and I'm certain he did not have any affairs. Oh, he knew other women before we were married," she said, wincing as she thought of Indrani, "but afterwards, he was true to me." He was true, she thought, but I was not.

"So," Alicia said, "I suppose all marriages do not hold the same disappointments as mine."

Larissa was silent for a moment, thinking of the disappointments she had borne in marriage—learning of Edmund's addiction, realizing he had weakened and returned to opium after his years without it, lying with him night after night without any hint of the physical fulfillment she had found with Nathan.

"All life has disappointments," she said softly. "If we don't learn to live with them, we might as well die." Die, she thought, as Edmund died when he realized I still loved Nathan.

Alicia's hand tightened on her arm. "I'm sorry, Larissa. I can tell that's a lesson you learned through experience. I'm afraid sometimes I become so immersed in my own bitterness that I forget other people suffer as well. Still, you do have Sean. If I still had my son, I'm sure I would find it much easier to be philosophical about my life."

In the next days, Larissa watched somewhat uncomfortably as Alicia became more and more attached to Sean. She could not fault her in her treatment of the boy, and, knowing about Steven, she did not begrudge her the love Sean freely gave. Still, she wondered how both Alicia and Sean would react to their inevitable separation when they finally reached Boston.

For the moment, that separation lay far in the future. The *Columbia* was scheduled to stop in the Mexican port of San Francisco before heading south and rounding Cape Horn. From the grumbling of the crew, Larissa learned the stop in San Francisco could involve some problems. In recent months, the Mexican government had become increasingly wary of foreign ships docking in its northern ports. They feared the United States, which already had designs on the Republic of Texas, intended to extend its borders to the Pacific Coast, taking over the Mexican lands in Alta California. As a result, all foreign ships,

especially those from the United States, were carefully in-
spected, and passengers were not encouraged to disembark
in any Mexican port.

Larissa supposed the reports were greatly exaggerated,
since sailors who had just spent the last several months in
the Orient could hardly know the current situation in
Mexico. Sean, who was developing into a rugged, high-
spirited child, found the prospect of trouble intriguing.
Alicia greeted the reports indifferently. In the end, they never learned what type of reception the *Columbia* would
have had in San Francisco.

About three days before they would have reached the
port, Larissa was strolling on deck with Sean. The weather
had been extraordinarily pleasant since they had left Hawaii, but that afternoon it had become suddenly chilly.
Pulling her woolen shawl more tightly around her, Larissa
glanced at the ominous dark clouds that had been building
all afternoon. It was midafternoon now, but already the
sky was as dark as at dusk.

"Come along, Sean," she said calmly. "It's going to storm
soon, so I think we'd better go below."

Sean's face puckered in disappointment. "Oh, mummy,
can't we stay up here a while longer? It's not raining yet.
Besides, you know Aunt Alicia has a headache. And it's
so crowded down there."

Larissa sighed, bending down to button his jacket and
turn up his collar against the increasing wind. "Oh, very
well. I don't feel much like being cooped up in a stuffy
cabin, either. I suppose we can always make a run for
the ladder when the rain finally starts."

"Hooray!" Sean jumped up and down excitedly. "I've
never seen a storm at sea." Pointing to the quarterdeck, he
said, "Let's go up there so we can watch everything better."

Dubiously eyeing Captain Sinclair, who was standing
at the ship's wheel, Larissa followed her son. "All right,
Sean, but we'll have to stay well out of the captain's way.
Soon he'll be giving orders to trim the sails, and we can't
be interfering with the sailors' work."

By the time they had climbed to the quarterdeck, the
wind had whipped most of the pins from Larissa's hair.
Her auburn tresses swirled around her face, obstructing
her view. Realizing it would be impossible to repin it in the
stiffening wind, she let her hair blow free, reveling in the

sudden feeling of freedom that surged through her with
each new gust. Although Sean clutched her hand for balance, she could sense that he, too, was enjoying the experience. Together they faced the wind, laughing with exhilaration.

Far out at sea, a jagged shaft of yellow-orange suddenly cracked the sky. The clipper reverberated with the
roar of thunder, and then it began to rain. Larissa knew
they should run for the companionway leading to the
cabins, but she stood for a few moments, allowing the
rain to soak through her clothing, transfixed by the power
of nature.

Lightning flashed and thunder crackled all around them,
suddenly triggering in Larissa the memory of another terrible storm. Her thoughts flew back to that afternoon on
the Ganges, when their Bengali guide had been struck by
lightning, and she realized that she had to get Sean to
safety. Shielding him with her body as much as possible,
she pushed the boy toward the main deck. She swayed
and caught the rail to steady herself as the ship lurched in
the violent waves.

Passing Captain Sinclair, she stopped in surprise as she
noted his calm, pleased smile. Suddenly, she realized he
had not given a single order during the intensifying storm.
None of the sails had been trimmed, and the ship was
running with the wind at breakneck speed.

Unable to contain herself, Larissa asked, "Aren't your
men going to trim the sails?"

Continuing to smile, he said, "Whatever for?"

"The storm," she shouted above the wind. "It's so fe-
rocious. If the wind gets control of the ship, won't it be
wrecked?"

"*I* am in control of my ship, madam," he bellowed back.
"The wind is simply a tool. Clipper ships' captains are
not afraid of the wind. They use it, both in sunshine and
storm. It's my job to get this ship to its destination in the
shortest time possible, and this storm could get us to San
Francisco a full day or more sooner than I had anticipated."

"And you'll sacrifice safety for speed?" she cried incredulously.

Captain Sinclair shrugged. "That's my job. I should
think you would have known the reputation of a clipper
before you begged to travel on the *Columbia*. But don't

worry. I've ridden out storms before. I'll deliver you safely
in Boston. For the moment, I suggest you take the boy,
and your worries, below."

The storm raged for another two hours, and Larissa,
Alicia, and Sean huddled restlessly in their cabin. Larissa
tried to convince herself a ship, being much larger than the
boat she had ridden up the Ganges, was much more capable of withstanding the fury of a storm. But that logic was
little comfort, since it followed that the ocean, being mil-
lions of times larger than the Ganges, was correspondingly
more treacherous. In addition, she could not help thinking
of how her father had perished at sea. Of course, the typhoon in which he had been killed must have been infinitely more violent than the storm she was now experienc-
ing. But there would be a certain grim irony to her aunt
and uncle winning full rights to the firm if she, too, perished
at sea.

A violent lurch and a terrifying cracking noise interrupted her thoughts. Just an extra strong gust of wind,
Larissa tried to reassure herself. And the noise was simply
thunder, a bit nearer than before. But when she heard
running feet on the decks above her and in the passageway
outside their cabin, she knew that it was useless to delude
herself. With fear-stricken eyes, Sean had run to clutch at
her skirts. Alicia sat on the edge of the bunk, chewing
nervously on her lower lip. None of them spoke.

They sat silently for a few moments, staring at each
other, afraid to speculate about what had happened. Finally, pushing Sean gently away from her, Larissa rose
and went to the cabin door. She opened it to a young
sailor, panting with exertion, his hand poised to knock.

"Captain sent me after you, ma'am. Says you'd better
come topside immediately. We've run into something in
the storm, and it looks like we're sinking fast."

Pressing her lips together, Larissa suppressed a scream.
She nodded numbly and reached for Sean's hand. Alicia
ran to her trunk and began rummaging for something.

"There's no time for that now," Larissa said sharply,
trying to pull her away.

Alicia shook her off roughly and continued to search,
coming up with a flat jewelry case. Nodding triumphantly,
she followed Larissa and Sean into the passageway.

On deck, the crew was scrambling to launch the *Columbia*'s lifeboats. The small boats bobbed helplessly in the

storm-swept ocean, looking far too small and weak to survive the fury of the waves. Pointing to a Jacob's ladder dangling over one of the boats, Captain Sinclair shouted, "You women, take the child and get in!"

Larissa balked. "It hardly looks safe."

"Madam, the *Columbia* is sinking. Would you prefer to stay aboard and go down with her?"

She glanced over the side again, to the sailors waiting in the boat to help her. The ladder flapped angrily in the wind, and Sean clutched at her hand, his eyes darting around in terror. As the ship lurched again, she made her decision. "All right," she said, "I'll go first, and you must follow very close to me, Sean. Aunt Alicia will follow you."

Alicia nodded, and Larissa stepped over the side to the first rung of the ladder. The ropes were treacherously slippery. Gingerly she stepped down two more rungs, holding out a hand to steady Sean as Alicia lifted him over the rail and set him on the top rung. Watching him clamp his small hands around the rope sides of the Jacob's ladder, she shouted, "It's very slippery, darling, so you must hold on very tightly. I'll help you, and we'll go down very slowly."

She backed down another rung, holding on with one hand as she helped her son with the other. She could feel him trembling through his jacket. "Come on, Sean," she soothed. "We'll make it. I'll help you."

Slowly, carefully, they continued to back down the ladder. The *Columbia* shifted again as it sank lower, and in the same moment a violent gust of wind tore into the ladder, sending it flying out from the side of the ship.

"Mummy!" Sean screamed in terror. "I'm going to fall!" His little feet slid off the slippery rung, and he hung by his arms, flailing his legs helplessly as he struggled to find the rung again.

Horrified, Larissa reached up with both hands to catch him, bracing her feet against the ladder's flimsy rope sides. As her hands left the ropes, another gust of wind attacked the ladder. Before she could think of what to do, she was tumbling backward through space. Her head cracked against the side of the boat as she landed in its bottom. Unable to focus her eyes, she struggled to sit up. "Sean," she gasped. "My baby! Someone catch my baby!"

From somewhere above her, a man's voice rang out. "We've got him, lady! He didn't fall!"

A moment later, Sean threw his arms around her waist, sobbing, "Oh, mummy, I'm so sorry. I'm all right, though. Will you be all right, too?"

"Yes, of course," she mumbled, ignoring the hammering pain in her head and fighting to remain conscious, knowing even as she did so that the effort was in vain.

Just before she passed out, Larissa heard Alicia's soft, consoling voice. "Don't worry, Larissa. I'm sure you'll be all right. And don't trouble yourself about Sean. I'll take care of him, just as if he were my own son, for as long as necessary."

Chapter Thirty-One

Blinking, Larissa looked around the small, adobe-walled room. She was lying on a narrow bed, covered by a rough woolen blanket. A crude, straight-backed wooden chair and a small night table were the only other furnishings in the room. Late afternoon light spilled through the single, high window, highlighting the carved wooden crucifix hanging above the closed door.

Slowly, she sat up, looking at the voluminous cotton nightgown she wore. Her head throbbed as she tried to recall where she was and how she came to be there. But the last thing she could recall was sinking into unconsciousness in the *Columbia*'s lifeboat. She stretched and looked around her, searching for further clues. Obviously, they had reached land somewhere, and someone had seen that she was cared for. But where were the others? Where was Sean? And Alicia?

For a few moments, she sat on the edge of the bed, straining her ears for some familiar voice. Except for the birds chirping outside her window, there was silence. Getting to her feet, she went to the door, opening it to step into a short hallway. At the end of the hallway was a large sitting room, where a woman stood sweeping the red and black Mexican carpet. On legs weak from her days in bed, Larissa staggered toward the room.

At the sound of Larissa's approaching feet, the woman looked up, giving her a beaming smile. She had long, straight, black hair tied at the back of her neck, dark skin, and dark, almost black, eyes. Dressed in a coarse white blouse and brightly woven skirt, the woman appeared to be about forty years old.

Returning her smile, Larissa asked, "Where am I? Is my son here?"

347

The woman squinted and cocked her head.

"Sean," Larissa persisted, "is Sean here? My little boy." She gestured to indicate a small child beside her. Seeing that the woman still did not understand, she crossed her arms and rocked them as she would rock a baby. "My baby," she said. "Where is my baby?"

Shrugging, the woman mumbled something in Spanish, a language Larissa neither spoke nor understood. She sighed in exasperation, then started for the door to look for Sean herself. The woman held up a hand, gesturing for her to wait. Hurrying to her side, she led Larissa to a velvet chair and indicated that she should sit. Sighing again, Larissa complied. She watched impatiently as the woman bustled from the room. Hours seemed to pass, and she was just about to get up to resume her search when the woman returned, followed by a Franciscan padre dressed in a black wool robe. He was quite thin, and his dark brown hair was tonsured.

"Praise be to God!" he exclaimed in a gentle voice as he entered the room. "You've recovered!"

Larissa stood uncertainly, unsure of how one should receive a priest.

"Sit down, child," he said kindly as he crossed the room to sit beside her. "That must have been quite a blow to the head you received. You've been unconscious for more than a week, and we've all been praying for you most fervently. I myself have been beside you most of the time, but I had gone to the church just now for evening prayers."

She smiled, trying to control her anxiety. "I'm most grateful for your kind care. Did the others all escape injury?"

The padre frowned. "I'm afraid I know of no others."

"The others who were in the boat with me," she cried, feeling a stab of panic.

He smiled. "Ah, how charitable you are to think first of others when you yourself have just recovered from injury and illness. But, again, I must say I know of no others."

"But there *were* others—several others! We escaped from a sinking ship, and my son was one of the group! Do you mean to tell me he is not here?"

The padre looked pained, and he spread his hands helplessly. "I was told nothing about a child. You were brought here by Don Armando Estrada nine days ago, and he asked us to care for you. He said only that he had found you on the beach, badly in need of proper care."

Larissa's thoughts raced, and her heart pounded with fears for her son. Had he perished somehow while she lay unconscious? Had he disappeared? Thinking of Alicia's promise to care for him, she demanded, "Do you know anything about a woman named Alicia Kingsbury? She was with us in the boat."

When the padre sadly shook his head, she thought of another possibility. "This Don Armando Estrada—is he still around here? Could I speak to him?"

"Most assuredly. He calls at the mission every evening to inquire about your health. I'm sure he will be most pleased to learn you have recovered."

"Then I must speak to him as soon as he arrives. I must find out about my son!"

"Of course," the padre said calmly. "But you mustn't overtax yourself with worry. It can't be good for your health. No doubt the child is quite safe somewhere, and Don Armando simply neglected to mention him to me."

Larissa stared at him, desperately wanting to believe him, but certain that, however well-intentioned his remark, he was probably wrong.

Sensing her disbelief, the padre coughed uneasily. "Incidentally, it seems in my excitement over your recovery, I neglected to introduce myself. I'm Padre Carlos, and this is the Dolores Mission of San Francisco."

Nodding absently, she replied, "I'm Larissa Farrell. When do you think Don Armando will be arriving?"

Padre Carlos frowned. "Within the hour, I suspect. But, my dear, you cannot greet him so attired." He gestured at her nightgown. "I'll have Carmela bring you some more suitable clothing, as well as something to eat, and I will summon you the moment Don Armando arrives."

Back in her room, Larissa could only pick at the plate of paella the Mexican woman named Carmela brought her. Her stomach was churning nervously, and she could not stop worrying about Sean. What had happened to him, to Alicia, and the others? Had they all perished trying to reach the shore? If they had reached safety, surely they would not have abandoned her, unconscious, on the beach.

With shaking hands, she put on the undergarments and the calico dress Carmela brought. The dress, made for a tinier woman than she, was too tight in the waist and

bodice. She managed to button it, but she feared that if
she breathed too deeply the seams would surely burst.
A hairbrush and comb lay on the nightstand, so she occupied herself with brushing her hair while she waited for
Padre Carlos to fetch her. The room had no mirror, so she
could not arrange her hair and left it flowing down her
back and over her shoulders.

When the padre knocked, Larissa was at the door instantly. He smiled gently, and for the first time she noticed
there were lines of perpetual sadness etched around his
grayish-brown eyes. "He is here, my child," he said simply.
"You may speak with him in the receiving room."

He led her down the hall to the room where she had
first met Carmela. It was dark now, and so the room was
lit by flickering candles and a glowing fire in the grate. A
man of medium height stood in the shadows, staring out
the window. He turned at the sound of their footsteps, and
his teeth flashed white against his tanned face. Striding to
meet them, he took Larissa's hand lightly in his and bent
to kiss it.

"Señora Farrell, I was most pleased to be informed of
your recovery." He spoke English with a soft, lilting Spanish
accent, and his smile flashed again as he looked at her. "I
cannot tell you how happy I am to see you looking so well."

He spoke it as a gallant understatement, and Larissa
blushed, sensing that he meant to say, "You are quite beautiful." She met his gaze levelly, surprised to note the deep
blue eyes that contrasted sharply with his dark hair, mustache, and tanned face. He was shorter than most men she
had known, with strong, broad shoulders and narrow waist
and hips. His frilled white shirt and expertly tailored black
trousers told her he had at least some degree of wealth
and was accustomed to fine things. Though his face was
weathered from long hours of riding, she supposed he was
no more than thirty years old.

Suddenly realizing she had been staring and had not
yet spoken a word of greeting, Larissa flushed again. "It
seems I am much in your debt, Señor Estrada. I will be
forever grateful to you for bringing me here. But," she
rushed on, "at the moment, I am most concerned about
the fate of my son."

Padre Carlos cleared his throat and interrupted quietly, "Perhaps I should take my leave and let you discuss
matters alone. I have a number of chores to perform be-

fore retiring. I trust, Don Armando, that you will not keep our patient up too long."

Don Armando nodded, and the padre shuffled from the room. Indicating a crystal decanter of wine on the table, Don Armando asked, "Would you care for refreshment, señora?"

Larissa shook her head. "My son, señor. I want to know about my son."

Raising his brows, the man went to the table and poured himself a glass of claret. He took a sip, rolling it around on his tongue before replying. "Señora Farrell, I'm afraid I may be unable to help you. There was a child in the group on the beach, but I assumed he belonged to the other woman."

Her eyes narrowed. "So there *were* others with me when you found me! The child—was he about five years old, with hair just a shade darker than mine?"

Don Armando nodded. "It's possible, though I must admit I paid scant attention to him. He was asleep at the time, and I was much more concerned with getting you to the mission."

Larissa sighed. "Well, then the woman—do you remember her?"

He smiled and nodded. "Indeed. I'm not likely to forget an attractive woman. She was tall, extremely shapely, with hair the color of honey. One of the most tempting women I've encountered in a long time—though not," he added, pausing to watch the firelight dance on Larissa's auburn hair, "nearly so beautiful as you."

Ignoring the compliment, Larissa continued questioning him. "This woman, did she say anything about the boy—about where she might be staying with him?"

"Not precisely." He took another sip of claret and motioned her into a chair. "Perhaps you'd best sit down, so I can begin at the beginning."

Impatiently, Larissa threw herself into a straight-backed chair near the fire. Don Armando poured a second glass of claret, handing it to her. "You might find this will have a calming effect," he said.

She took the glass but shook her head. "How can I be calm when my little boy is missing?"

Holding up a hand to silence her, Don Armando began. "Ten days ago, I had just arrived in San Francisco from Monterey. I had taken my horse for an early morning run on the beach when I saw a small boat approaching the shoreline. I had a great deal of time to pass before my first appointment of the day, so out of curiosity I waited and watched. The boat eventually beached some distance down the shore from me, and I watched perhaps ten people climb out. One of them, the honey-haired woman, was holding a child, whom she laid down on the sand and covered with her cloak. Then she and one of the men returned to the boat and lifted out a limp form, which I soon learned was you.

"Sensing that they might need some help, I cantered down the beach to offer my assistance. The men all looked to be burly sailor types, well capable of caring for themselves. The woman looked bedraggled but unharmed, and she asked where she could find help for you. Immediately, I offered to bring you to the mission, and she agreed that would be the best course. When I inquired as to whether I might also escort her and the child to the mission, she declined, saying she would not dream of troubling the padres more than necessary. She said she had salvaged her jewels before leaving the sinking ship and could use them to pay for food, clothing, and housing for herself and the child. Naturally, I assumed then that the child was hers—"

"No! The boy was my Sean, and the woman was Alicia Kingsbury, a friend of mine who has no children of her own. She and Sean adored one another, and just before I passed out in the lifeboat, she assured me she would care for him as long as necessary."

Don Armando smiled. "So, then you see, you have nothing to worry about. Your son and your friend are probably snug in a San Francisco inn right now, just waiting for you to recover and call on them."

"I suppose you're right," Larissa agreed hesitantly. "But why didn't she leave word with you of where I could find her? Surely she would know I'd be frantic with worry for my son."

He shrugged. "That's not so hard to understand. In the first place, she was quite worried about you and anxious to have you cared for. No doubt her mind was too occupied even to consider such details. Secondly, she did not know San Francisco, so she could not possibly know where she would be staying. But I'm sure she assumed that any problems would be resolved in the end."

Larissa pursed her lips thoughtfully. "But you did tell her where you were taking me, did you not?"

"Of course. Why do you ask?"

"Doesn't it seem strange she hasn't called at the mission to inquire about my health?"

"Not especially," Don Armando replied quickly, but Larissa thought she detected a note of uncertainty in his voice. "She was most concerned about not disturbing the padres, so she may not want to come here. Or she might be concerned about the effect on the child of seeing you lying helpless. No doubt she expected the mission, or even myself, to send her word when you had recovered sufficiently to receive visitors. It probably never occurred to her that she neglected to tell me her name, and even if she did think of it later, she probably assumed that you, yourself, would ask for her in due time."

When Larissa remained silent, he sighed. "I'm free tomorrow, so I'll be happy to go to the inns and inquire about your friend and son."

"I'll go with you," Larissa said quickly, "but I want to go tonight."

Don Armando frowned. "I think that would be most imprudent. We've already established that the child is in good hands, so you have no need to worry. At this hour, I would imagine that he is already asleep—an example that you would do well to follow. I wouldn't want the good Padre Carlos to accuse me of overtaxing you the first day you are back on your feet."

"But I must see my son!" she protested.

"You'll see him tomorrow, I promise you."

"You'll call for me and take me with you to the inns?" she asked hopefully.

Don Armando nodded. "If you will promise to go and rest now. I would be most dismayed if, after all my efforts to save you, you were to have a relapse. Come now," he chided, "drink up your wine. It will help you to sleep."

Obediently, Larissa downed the contents of her glass and allowed Don Armando to escort her to her door. "I'll call for you tomorrow at ten," he said.

"Nine?" she pleaded.

He sighed. "How can I argue with so devoted a mother? Nine it shall be. Until tomorrow, señora." He kissed her hand and left the mission for the night.

Despite the wine and the general fatigue she felt from

her slow recovery, Larissa slept very little that night. Over and over she admonished herself to relax, telling herself Sean was in capable hands and she would soon be reunited with him. But, somehow, she could not believe that. She felt certain the morning would hold some terrible discovery, bringing her no closer to her son.

She was up and dressed in the calico gown long before eight o'clock. In the receiving room, Carmela brought her hot chocolate and a light breakfast of bread and fruit. She nibbled a bit, then paced, waiting for Don Armando. He did not arrive until half past nine, and she knew the moment she saw his face that something was terribly wrong.

Without regard for the early hour, he strode directly to the table and poured a glass of claret. He swallowed it in two gulps, then refilled it. He began to raise the glass to his lips again, then hesitated and slammed it down on the table. The fragile crystal stem splintered and the glass toppled off, spilling claret across the table. His chest heaved as he searched for words that would soften the blow of his news. Failing, he blurted out, "They're gone! Señora Kingsbury and your son are gone!"

Larissa stared at him, openmouthed, but less shocked than he had imagined she would be. The sense of foreboding that had assailed her all night had prepared her for the news, so that now she needed only the details. "How do you know?" she asked quietly.

Don Armando began to pace, running his hands through his hair. "I thought to save you the trouble of riding from one inn to another this morning, so I made some inquiries before coming here. I had supposed that I would find out where Señora Kingsbury and the child were staying, and then I could take you directly there."

"And instead you found that they have gone?"

He nodded. "At the third inn the proprietor distinctly remembered them. He said the boy was a charming little lad who called Señora Kingsbury Aunt Alicia and kept babbling about the things he would do when his mother got better. At any rate, they left yesterday morning. She didn't say where they were going, but a few days ago, the innkeeper overheard her in conversation with a sailor who told her she'd have a better chance of getting a ship out in Monterey."

"A ship out!" Larissa gasped. Suddenly, as she thought again of her shipboard conversations with Alicia, she real-

ized the reasons for her sense of foreboding. Alicia Kingsbury wanted another child, but without the complications
of a husband! She had even admitted that she sometimes
thought of Sean as her own son.

"My lord," she gasped, "that woman has kidnapped
my baby! I've got to get to Monterey and stop her from
sailing away with him!"

Don Armando nodded grimly. "I'm afraid I've come to
the same conclusion, so I've a carriage outside, waiting to
take us."

"No," she shook her head adamantly. "No carriage. We'll
make better time on horseback, and we've got to remember
Alicia has a one-day headstart on us."

He frowned. "You are right, of course, but are you
up to a trip by horseback? Some of the terrain between
here and Monterey is rather rugged, and in your condition——"

"There's nothing wrong with my condition!" she cut him
off sharply. "I'm an experienced rider, and I see no reason
why I should not travel by horseback! After all, it's not as
if I've really been ill. I've just been unconscious for a
few days."

Shaking his head, Don Armando headed for the door.
"Well, already, I think I know better than to argue with
you. I'll just see that two of the horses are fitted with sad-
dles, saddlebags, and blanket rolls."

He was almost to the door when Larissa remembered
something. "Señor Estrada?" He turned, raising his thin
dark brows in question. "You don't have to go to all this
trouble. I mean, why should you accompany me to Monterey? Sean means nothing to you."

His teeth flashed white against his face. "But perhaps his
mother does. After all, I had a hand in saving you, and
I should hate to see my efforts wasted."

She flushed. "I'm afraid I have no money and no valu-
ables with which to pay you. And I can hardly ask you to
make the journey at your expense."

His eyes traveled over her slowly, and his tongue flicked
out to moisten his lips. "Señora Farrell, my home is in
Monterey, so I would be returning there at any rate. As
to costs and payments, I have an idea that everything will
even out in the end."

Chapter Thirty-Two

Within the hour, they bid the padres goodbye and started south toward Monterey. Immune to the discomfort of riding astride a horse that was not equipped with a sidesaddle, Larissa immediately spurred her mount to a full gallop. But Don Armando soon convinced her to slow down to avoid wearing out the animals before they had completed even half a day's journey.

Intent on reaching Sean, Larissa could think of nothing else as they traveled south. She noticed neither the serene beauty of the shoreline, nor the stupendous majesty of the towering redwood forests to the east. For the moment, all the untamed beauty of California represented only added obstacles and added miles between her and Sean. She would have ridden all night, ignoring her fatigue and using the stars for light, if Don Armando had not insisted that they stop soon after dusk descended.

"It's foolish to wear out both ourselves and the horses," he said simply. "Traveling as light as we are, we're sure to catch up with the señora and your son soon enough."

Larissa wanted to argue but found she hadn't the strength. In fact, she found she was too stiff and tired even to swing herself from the saddle. She sat silently for several moments, embarrassed to admit her plight, until Don Armando realized her problem. Reaching up, he planted his hands firmly around her waist and lifted her from the saddle.

Even when her feet touched the ground, he did not release her. His touch had a tender yearning that made Larissa shiver. For the first time since their departure that morning, she thought of how he had looked at her and his comment about being repaid in the end. Suddenly, she realized how foolish she had been to embark on a journey with a man she hardly knew. But what choice had there been? She could have gone alone, but that course would have placed her in an even more precarious position. She had to find Sean at all costs, and if the price was being raped by this man in this deserted stand of pines, she would have to pay.

Sensing her uneasiness, Don Armando reluctantly withdrew his hands. Silently, he turned away from her and busied himself gathering wood for a fire. Feeling her cheeks burning, Larissa turned toward the shoreline, lulled by the comforting sound of lapping waves. Then Don Armando's voice interrupted her thoughts.

"The night air is becoming chilly. Come sit by the fire, warm yourself, and eat a bit of the mutton the good padres packed for us."

Larissa walked slowly into the circle of firelight and dropped to her knees on the blanket he had spread for her. "I'm not hungry," she said dully.

"Nevertheless, you must eat, or you won't feel strong enough to continue tomorrow."

Without further comment, she took the portion of meat and bread he handed her and accepted the canteen of water, warm from their day of traveling. She ate without tasting the food, conscious of him watching her across the fire. A breeze ruffled the pine needles above them, and she shivered, aware now of the damp cold that permeated her being.

Don Armando smiled like an indulgent father. "Roll up in your blanket and go to sleep now. You've had a long day, and tomorrow promises to be no easier."

Gladly, she followed his suggestion, but even the wool of her blanket could not stop her shivering. Watching her pensively, Don Armando said, "You're still cold, aren't you?"

"N-no." The chattering of her teeth betrayed her.

"Of course you are," he said gently, moving around the fire to spread his blanket beside hers.

Larissa tensed. She could fight him, of course, but it wouldn't do to alienate him now. She hadn't the slightest idea where they were, and she needed him to get to Monterey—to find Sean. He lay down beside her, sliding an arm beneath her and pulling her close against him.

"Relax," he whispered, "I'm not going to hurt you, but I learned long ago that the heat of another person's body is the most effective way to combat the night's chill."

She swallowed, not quite believing him. But his arms remained wrapped around her in a chaste embrace, never straying to explore the contours of her body. Within a few minutes, his relaxed, slow breathing told her he was asleep. Only then did she, too, relax, admitting to herself that it was a blessing to have his shared warmth.

She felt more relaxed with him the next day, more trusting and less afraid he would demand something she was not yet ready to give. There was no question that she felt indebted to him, and now she admired him more than ever for his gentlemanly restraint when he so obviously wanted her. Again, they rode until dusk, and again they slept side by side.

Late in the afternoon of the third day, they began to encounter the twisted cypress trees that Don Armando told her were peculiar to the Monterey peninsula.

"My rancho is a short distance north of the town, if you'd like to stop—"

Larissa shook her head, cutting him off. "No. If you are anxious to be home, don't let me detain you. Just give me directions into town. I shan't rest until I'm reunited with my Sean."

Don Armando nodded. "I expected you would say that, and so I will continue with you, to aid you in your inquiries."

Smiling, she accepted his company. It was comforting to have him with her, to know she could depend on his strength and resourcefulness, if necessary.

As they rode into Monterey's central plaza, Larissa looked around curiously. "Where are the inns?"

He smiled. "Monterey has none. The people here are so hospitable that any visitors are taken directly into our homes."

"Then how will we ever find Sean and Alicia? Must we knock on every door and disturb every family?"

"I think not. I suggest we begin our search there." He pointed to the harbor beyond the customhouse, where a ship lay at anchor. Even without seeing its flag, Larissa could tell by its streamlined hull that it was an American clipper.

"Oh, yes!" she exclaimed. "I'm sure it's an American

ship, and if Alicia and Sean are in Monterey, they're certain to be aboard."

He nodded. "We'll see soon enough." He dismounted, swung her from her saddle, and led her inside the custom-house, the only building on the harbor side of the plaza. They spoke briefly with the agent, who told them the ship was the *Artemis*, bound for New York. As they walked back outside, Don Armando said, "We'll row out and have a talk with the captain about her passengers."

The young sailor on watch reluctantly permitted them on board, grumbling that the ship's passenger cabins were already filled. While they waited to speak with the captain, Larissa looked around impatiently. Hearing the sound of feet on the nearby companionway ladder, she assumed it was the captain, but her face lit with joy when a tousled auburn head emerged above deck.

"Sean!" she screamed ecstatically, rushing toward the companionway.

At the sound of her voice, his head swiveled around, and his face lit up with happiness. "Mummy, mummy!" he screamed, flying into her arms.

For a long moment, she held him, her tears of joy mingling with his. When at last he pulled away, he was still beaming. "Oh, mummy, I'm so glad to see you! Aunt Alicia said you were very sick and you would not be able to meet us until after we get to New York. But you're better now, aren't you, mummy?"

Larissa brushed away her tears with the back of her hand. "Yes, darling, I'm much better now. And having you hug me makes me feel absolutely wonderful!"

Squeezing him again, she looked over his shoulder and saw Alicia, flushed with guilt, retreating down the ladder. "Alicia!" she said sharply, "I'd like a word with you, if you please!"

Alicia hesitated, then slowly dragged herself to the deck.

"I must thank you for taking such good care of Sean," Larissa said dryly. "He seems in perfect health. However, I wish you had had the courtesy to notify me before leaving San Francisco with him."

Alicia paused to wet her lips nervously. "Well, I—when I heard nothing for so many days, I naturally assumed you had—succumbed. You were in a very bad way when we landed, you know. I didn't want the child to have to face that, so I thought it best to take him away. Then, too, I had heard so much about the Mexicans being hostile to Americans that I feared for our safety if we remained too long in California."

"I see." Larissa nodded slowly. "And did you have any indication that the Mexicans were, in fact, less than hospitable to you?"

"Well, no, I—"

"And did you ever think to send word to the mission, to inquire about my condition?"

Alicia shrugged helplessly. "I suppose it's quite useless to try to deceive you. It's obvious you know why I brought Sean here—why I sought passage on this ship. But you must know I've done nothing to harm him. I love the boy to distraction, Larissa, and after a few days of caring for him alone, I was certain I couldn't bear to live without him. I couldn't give him up to you, and so I had to bring him here."

Feeling sad, Larissa shook her head. "I've never doubted your affection for him, Alicia. But if you loved him so much, how could you have schemed to hurt him by taking him away from me—his mother—forever? What would you have told him when I never appeared in New York? Would you have hurt him more then by telling him I was dead or that I had deserted him?"

Sobbing, Alicia covered her face with her hands. "I don't know," she wailed. "I just don't know. I suppose I had hoped that by then I could have replaced you in his heart."

"Larissa." Don Armando's gentle touch on her elbow startled her. It was the first time he had not addressed her formally. She looked up into his grave blue eyes.

"I can arrange to have her prosecuted, if you wish. California parents consider their children their jewels, and they see kidnapping as one of the most heinous of crimes."

Looking first at the sobbing woman, then at Sean, who had observed the whole scene round-eyed, not quite understanding what was happening, she shook her head. "No. Alicia will suffer the rest of her life, remembering what she did and knowing she has lost Sean forever. Once I had considered remaining close to her when we reached the United States so that she and Sean could enjoy each other's company. But now I think it's best that she never see him again. As for Sean, he seems to have suffered little from the incident, not really knowing what Alicia intended. I would prefer that he forget it all as quickly as possible, so I'd rather not prolong the fuss."

Don Armando nodded understandingly. "In that case, I suggest that you, Sean, and I return to my rancho immediately."

"To your rancho?"

"Of course. We've already learned that there are no cabins available on this ship. And, even if there were, for the boy's sake it would be better not so sail on the *Artemis* with Señora Kingsbury. As I've already told you, Monterey has no hotels, so I insist that you allow me to show you a bit of California hospitality."

Relieved at having Sean back and genuinely grateful for Don Armando's role in the reunion, Larissa smiled warmly. "Sean and I are delighted to accept your invitation, Señor Estrada."

"Please," he smiled, offering his arm, "call me Armando. I think by now we know each other well enough to use first names." The flash in his eyes told her he wished to know her far better.

"Ahem." The captain loudly cleared his throat, to attract their attention. They turned to see a short, stout, blustery man standing at the head of the companionway ladder. "Might I be so bold as to demand why I've been summoned from my—um—siesta?"

Don Armando laughed lightly. "You might, but it seems, captain, that while you were rousing yourself, the problem had resolved itself. Briefly, you'll be carrying one less passenger to New York. The boy will not be sailing with you."

The captain raised his eyebrows at Alicia, who lifted her swollen, red-eyed face to nod quickly.

"Well," he said, starting back down the ladder, "it makes no difference to me."

Larissa bent to take Sean's hand. "Come along, darling. We're going to stay at Don Armando's house for a few days."

Sean nodded, then his expression became serious. "Mummy, would it be all right if I kiss Aunt Alicia goodbye?"

She smiled faintly. "Of course, darling. And thank her for taking such good care of you."

Dropping to her knees, Alicia enveloped the boy in her arms. Looking up at Larissa, she sniffled and mouthed a thank you. Sean pulled away from her a moment, then planted a resounding kiss on her lips. "Don't cry, Aunt Alicia," he counseled, with the peculiar perceptiveness of young children. "Maybe someday you'll have a little boy of your own."

"Maybe," she murmured, squeezing him again quickly, then pushing him toward Larissa and Don Armando.

· The sun was setting by the time they arrived at Don Armando's rancho. Don Armando had immediately won Sean's admiration by carrying him in front of him on his saddle. In the setting sun, Larissa was awed by the sight of his house. It was a sprawling adobe structure, painted white, with a red-tiled roof. The front facade was decorated by colored stones and pebbles, pressed into the adobe in the intricate design of a Mexican quetzal bird. A wide veranda stretched across the front of the house.

As Don Armando dismounted and helped Larissa and Sean down, the heavy carved redwood door swung open, and several servants hurried out to greet them. Don Armando greeted them affectionately, then issued a string of orders in Spanish. A groom led away their horses, and the women servants hurried back inside to prepare rooms for Sean and Larissa. Swinging Sean into his arms, Don Armando took Larissa's hand and led her into the house.

The interior was even more spectacular. Every room opened onto a central patio, surrounded by a red-tiled veranda. A fountain splashed gaily in the center of the patio and was surrounded by palms, shrubs, giant ferns, and a solitary cactus plant. Beds of sweet peas, hollyhocks, lilies, roses, pinks, and jasmine gave the area a sweet fragrance.

"It's enchanting, Armando," she murmured. With a stab of pain, she remembered a similar reaction to the gardens on Edmund's Indian estate. How many years ago had that been? Only five? It seemed a lifetime when she thought of all the heartache suffered in the span.

Sensing her melancholy, Don Armando gently interrupted her thoughts. "You must be tired from all the travel and the strain of worry. I've instructed Juana to prepare baths for you and your son. Perhaps, afterward, you will join me for a late supper."

He led her to the adjoining rooms given to her and Sean, then disappeared into the shadows as she and Sean went inside. The rooms were spacious and airy, painted white, with redwood floors and redwood rafters. The doors and windows were framed with the same wood.

In the room assigned to Sean, Juana was setting out a cold supper for him. By the time he finished eating, his bath water was ready. Larissa helped him undress and then bathed him gently, thinking again what a miracle it was to be reunited with him. Juana produced a white nightshirt belonging to one of the servants' children. Larissa helped him into it and tucked him into the wide bed.

As she bent to kiss him, he slid his arms around her neck and whispered, "Mummy, I love Aunt Alicia, but I love you much more. I'm glad I didn't have to go to New York without you."

Blinking back fresh tears, she lay her head on the pillow beside his. "I'm glad, too, darling," she murmured. "Go to sleep now, and tomorrow we can spend the whole day together."

Exhausted from his travels and from the excitement of the reunion, the little boy was asleep within minutes. Larissa lifted her head to gaze at him, smoothing his hair and planting a tender kiss on his forehead. Carefully, not wanting to disturb him, she rose, extinguished the lamp, and went into her own bedroom.

A copper tub filled with steaming water awaited her. She gratefully stripped and slid into the bath, luxuriating in its warmth and in the delicately scented lavender soap Juana had provided. Glancing toward the bed, she saw that a fresh gown of pale pink crepe awaited her. Beside it on the bed lay a white cotton petticoat and other necessary undergarments. White satin slippers were on the floor at the foot of the bed.

Larissa soaked in the tub until the water became cool, washing her hair and letting it drip down her back. Finally, she stepped out and enfolded herself in a voluminous bath sheet. She dressed slowly, enjoying the feel of fresh clothing against her skin. The gown and slippers were almost a perfect fit, making her wonder where Don Armando had acquired them. The gown was ruffled at the hemline and a few inches below the waist, and tiny ruffles formed cap sleeves that just covered her shoulders.

As she sat down at the dressing table, Juana knocked shyly, entering to arrange her hair. Parting it in the middle, she pulled it back from her face and formed a loose roll at the base of her neck. At the crown, she attached a white, mother-of-pearl comb. She chattered gaily in Spanish all the while, and though Larissa could not understand her, she appreciated her warmth. After she had finished arranging Larissa's hair, Juana led her to the parlor, where Don Armando waited.

Looking up from the book he was reading, he smiled broadly. "I had begun to think you had decided not to join me."

Larissa looked down at the floor, keenly aware of his gaze traveling over her. "I'm sorry. I was so absorbed in enjoying my bath I quite forgot the time."

"No matter." Don Armando waved away her explanation as he rose to take her hands. "I'm glad you had some time to relax."

As he bent to kiss her hands, Larissa noted that he, too, had bathed and changed. Over his white, frilled, open-necked shirt, he wore a short black silk jacket. His black velveteen trousers were slit open below the knee and laced with gold cord. Around his waist, he wore a red silk sash.

Stepping back, Don Armando surveyed her again. "I must say, you were well worth the wait. You are the picture of loveliness, Larissa."

"You look very fine yourself," she replied. "And, no doubt, the clothes are responsible for my appearance. How fortunate that you had things so near to my size."

"Yes, isn't it?" He smiled mysteriously. "But then, as I've told you before, we Californians pride ourselves on being exceptional hosts. If that means clothing our visitors, we are only too pleased to do so. Now then, shall we go in to dinner?" He offered his arm and led her to the dining room.

The long dining table was set for two, with Don Armando's place at the head and Larissa's to his right. A silver candelabra provided the only illumination as they dined on Spanish rice, chicken, and rich red wine. Thinking contentedly of Sean sleeping in another room, Larissa thoroughly enjoyed the meal. As the servants cleared away the dinner dishes and Don Armando refilled her wineglass for the fifth time, she smiled at him drowsily.

"I can never thank you enough for your help in finding my son or for the way you have opened your home to us."

He returned her smile, and in the candlelight, she saw a hint of sadness in his eyes. "There is a way to thank me, but under the circumstances, I would be decidedly ungallant to ask it. Besides, what I desire is something to be given freely from shared desire, not as a form of repayment. I must admit I began to want you from the moment I first saw you, when I carried you to the mission. Then, perhaps, I would have let lust rule my actions. But now I have seen so much more of you—your devotion to your child, your kindness to Señora Kingsbury when most people would have thought of revenge. Now I respect you too much to take you, or even to ask."

Later, Larissa would wonder if it was the wine that made her respond, her overwhelming sense of gratitude, or a secret aching for a man who would treat her with respect and tenderness. Twirling her wineglass in her hand, she murmured, "What if I were to say my desires are the same as yours?"

She heard Don Armando's breath catch in his throat. His hand reached across the table to close over hers and coax her to look up at him. "Let's stroll a bit on the patio, shall we?" he whispered.

Nodding, she let him help her to her feet. He put a serape around her shoulders, and sliding his arm around her waist, he led her outside. For a few moments, they strolled silently, listening to the fountain's cascading water. Applying gentle pressure to her waist, he pulled her against him and brought his lips to hers. At first his kiss was shy, but it quickly increased in ardor as she wound her arms around his neck. His hands moved gently down her form, exploring as if she were a fragile piece of porcelain.

Slipping the serape from her shoulders, he spread it carefully on the ground. He lifted her in his arms, then knelt to lay her on the makeshift bed. Slowly, with infinite care, he undressed her and took the comb and pins from her hair. Then he sat back on his heels to gaze at her creamy skin, shining in the moonlight.

For an instant as Don Armando undressed, Larissa thought of a similar night in a garden in India. Somehow, she knew this encounter would prove much more satisfying.

Don Armando was a gentle, considerate lover. He treated her like some fragile goddess he was privileged to know intimately. Nothing in his touch made her burn with passion or ache with desire. Yet when it was over, she felt drowsily content and drifted easily into relaxed sleep.

Chapter Thirty-Three

Larissa awoke alone in her room. In her first, drowsy moments of awakening, she imagined that the scene in the garden had been a strange dream brought on by drinking too much wine. Her head ached from her wine consumption, and she had no recollection of coming to bed. Yet she knew instinctively that she had not dreamed the incident. Don Armando must have carried her here and dressed her in the chaste lawn nightgown she now wore.

At first she felt embarrassed, wondering what Don Armando must think of her and certain she could not remain in his house. Thinking back, she admitted somewhat guiltily that the experience had been enjoyable, though not the ecstatic kind of union she had shared with Nathan. Still, she did not want Don Armando to expect her to continue such a relationship.

She respected him, enjoyed his company, and would always be grateful to him, but she did not love him. And to continue to give herself without love could only be a sort of prostitution. If she had wanted that, she could just as easily have accepted the propositions offered her in Shanghai or Honolulu. No matter how much she appreciated Don Armando's thoughtfulness, she had compromised her principles last night, and she must not let it happen again.

As a knock sounded at the door, she sat up, calling a greeting. Juana entered, carrying a tray with hot chocolate and pastries. A single pink rose, the color of the gown she had worn last night, lay across the tray. Beaming, Juana set the tray across Larissa's lap and went to open the curtains, allowing the morning sunshine to spill into the room. As Juana left, Larissa noticed a folded piece of white paper tucked beneath the chocolate pot. She slid it out and opened it to find a note in Don Armando's bold scrawl:

Good morning, my love!
I hope you will enjoy this simple fare. When you have eaten, Juana will bring fresh clothing for you and Sean. If you will meet me then on the inner veranda, I will be most pleased to take you both on a tour of my rancho and the environs.

Your humble host,
Armando

Pursing her lips, Larissa stared again at his salutation, and her sense of guilt began to grow. Not only had she compromised herself, but she had misled and encouraged Don Armando.

Before she had time to consider the problem further, Sean stumbled in from the adjoining room. Sniffing the air, he said sleepily, "I smell chocolate."

Larissa laughed, overjoyed at having her son to share the morning with her. Pushing her guilt to the back of her mind, she said, "Indeed you do, darling." She patted the bed beside her. "Come and share some breakfast with me."

Sean climbed up onto the bed and eagerly accepted a cup of chocolate and some pastry. Slowly sipping her own chocolate, Larissa gazed at her son tenderly. Unable to resist the urge, she reached out to tousle his auburn curls, bringing his amber-flecked eyes up to stare at her curiously.

"I like this place, mummy," he said. "Are we going to stay here long?"

She shrugged, as always seeing Nathan's eyes in her son's. "Oh, for a few days, I suppose."

"Oh, let's stay a long time!" he pleaded. "This is much better than Boston!"

She laughed, tousling his hair again. "How would you know that, imp? You've never been to Boston."

"I know it, anyway," he giggled. "It just is."

At that moment, Juana knocked and entered with the promised fresh clothing. For Larissa, she brought an emerald-green velveteen riding habit, and for Sean an outfit exactly like the one Don Armando had worn the previous evening, complete with a broad-brimmed black hat trimmed with a red satin ribbon.

When Don Armando met them on the veranda, he did not mention the evening before, but his eyes seemed to hold a special tenderness Larissa had not noticed before. She cringed, again realizing that her behavior last night had given him the wrong impression. Now she would have to find a way to undo the damage without causing him unnecessary pain.

Leading them to the front of the house, Don Armando inquired, "You don't mind riding again today? I mean, perhaps you are too exhausted from three days in the saddle."

Larissa shook her head. "No. It will be a pleasure to ride for relaxation, with no need to hurry anywhere. I'm afraid I was rather immune to the magnificent scenery yesterday. But now, with Sean with us, I'll be able to enjoy it so much more." The ride, she thought, would give her a chance to sort out her feelings and find a way to avoid future compromising situations.

Don Armando helped her mount a roan mare, then lifted Sean into the saddle of a palomino and swung up behind him. He began with a short tour of the rancho. Casually, he informed them that he kept ten thousand head of cattle, over a thousand horses, and a few hundred sheep. When Larissa expressed amazement at the numbers, he shrugged, assuring her many ranchos were much larger, that his was only average in size.

Leaving the boundaries of his rancho, they rode into the forest overlooking the shore. There the Monterey pine ruled supreme, surrounded by buckeye trees, wild lilac, and the colorful shrub called manzanita. As their horses picked their way back toward the shore, they came upon more of the strange, twisted Monterey cypress trees, which, even in her agitation, Larissa had not failed to notice the afternoon before. In the springtime, Don Armando informed them, golden-flowered California poppies covered the bare spots between the cypress, pines, and oaks. Larissa shivered, for poppies, even this harmless kind, would always remind her of Edmund's weakness.

They sat for a few moments on a rocky cliff overlooking the hammering waves below, then rode down to a sandy stretch of beach to enjoy a picnic lunch of boiled eggs, chicken, tongue, and wine.

Afterwards, as Don Armando lifted him back into the saddle, Sean remarked, "I wish I could ride my own horse, like you and mummy."

"Then tomorrow we shall begin teaching you to ride," Don Armando assured him. "After all," he added, turning to help Larissa mount, "most Californians are well on their way to becoming excellent horsemen by Sean's age."

"But he's hardly more than a baby," she protested, "and besides, he's not a Californian."

"But he could become one," Don Armando said, swinging into the saddle behind the boy. Larissa greeted that remark with silence, turning away at Don Armando's veiled proposal. If only she had not given herself so willingly last night, perhaps he would not assume that she cared for him more than she did.

At the rancho, Larissa took Sean to his room for a nap, then paused in her own room to change out of her riding habit. A white blouse, embroidered with colorful red and yellow flowers, and a full red skirt were spread across the bed, waiting for her. Dressed, she stepped to the dressing table to brush her hair.

As she picked up the hairbrush, she noticed several coins lying on the dressing table. She picked them up curiously, wondering where they had come from. They had not been there yesterday when Juana had arranged her hair, nor this morning when she had arisen. Then the thought struck her—Don Armando was paying her for her services of last night, paying her like some common whore! No wonder he had such a large selection of women's clothes on hand. He probably entertained women regularly and considered her just one of his conquests.

And to think she had felt she had wronged him by leading him on! His initial gentility, his speech about how much he respected her, even his kindness to Sean had obviously all been an act, to lull her into submission. He was no different from the other men she had met since Edmund's death.

Enraged, she scooped the coins into her hands and rushed out to the patio. Don Armando was lounging in the shade of the veranda, sipping a cool drink. He looked up in surprise as she stormed toward him and hurled the coins at his feet.

"Keep your filthy coins," she shouted. "Do you really think you can buy me?"

He stared at her with hurt, bewildered eyes. "I don't understand," he murmured. "The money is yours, to do with as you please. If you don't want it, you needn't take it, but I see no reason to become so violent about it."

"Don't you?" she snapped. "Do all your other women guests accept your payment more casually?"

Suddenly comprehending, Don Armando's face twisted in a grim smile. "The money has nothing to do with last night, Larissa," he said calmly. "I would have given it even if we had shared nothing more than dinner. It's a custom here in California to leave money in the rooms of one's guests. It saves them the embarrassment of asking for it if they find themselves low on funds. While you are my guest at my rancho, you will not need money, since I will see to all of your needs. Still, I thought you might find it comforting to have at least a few coins you could call your own."

Larissa stared at her feet, embarrassed and unable to speak. "I'm sorry," she whispered at last. "I didn't know, and I've had too many experiences with men who think—" She broke off lamely. "What must you think of me, behaving so rudely?" Contrite, she stooped to pick up the scattered coins.

"It's all right," Don Armando said mildly. "I was wrong to assume you would know our customs. Will you take a glass of lemonade? It's very refreshing, cooled with ice imported from your New England."

Gratefully, she took the glass and sank into a chair beside his. She was silent, groping for something to say, wondering how she could ever reestablish the easy companionability that had developed between them on their trip from San Francisco.

"You know," Don Armando said softly, reaching out to squeeze her hands, "I meant it when I said Sean could become a Californian. I'd like you both to stay here forever—as my wife and my son."

With an effort, Larissa forced her voice to remain calm. "How kind you are. But I cannot accept. It would be so unfair to both of us. We hardly know one another."

"I know all that I need to know. But your true reason is more profound, I think. Perhaps I have been presumptuous in proposing so soon. As a widow, I suppose you think still of your departed husband, and so you do not feel free to marry another."

"Yes, that's it," she said quickly. It *was* partly because of Edmund, but not in the way Don Armando must think. She was convinced she had ruined Edmund by marrying him without love, and tempting though he might be, she could not bring herself to do the same to Don Armando.

Looking into his deep blue eyes, she whispered, "You're a fine man, Armando, one any woman would be proud to call her husband. I will always feel honored that you proposed to me, but I do not think I will ever marry again. As for last night—"

"You needn't explain," he interrupted. "Last night existed in its own time, for its own reason. I believe we both derived enjoyment from it, so there is no reason to examine the experience in the harsh light of afternoon."

"Thank you." She sighed. "I suppose you will want me to leave your rancho now. It's wrong for me to occupy your home and your time when you should be free to pursue other women."

He shook his head. "When I asked you to be my guest, I did not stipulate that you had to marry me, and, at the moment, there is no one else I wish to pursue. Besides, you can't leave now. I've promised Sean I'd teach him to ride, and we mustn't disappoint him."

He stared at her silently for a moment, then added, "I think you could use a bit of rest and relaxation. I sense that you've suffered much in the last months—not just in the shipwreck or in losing your husband, but before—perhaps even years before."

Stunned by his perceptiveness, Larissa nodded meekly. "I wasn't aware I bore my heartaches so obviously. You're right, I could use a rest. I have business in Boston, but it's already waited for six years, so a bit more time can hardly matter."

"Good." He smiled, but his eyes remained serious. "Larissa, there's something I wish you would think about while you're here."

"Of course."

He grasped her hand, and his eyes became even more serious. "It's admirable to be devoted to a memory—at least for a time. But a memory can never satisfy all your needs or those of your son. If you consider it selfish to think of yourself, think of Sean. Then perhaps," he said, smiling wistfully, "I will still have a chance in your heart."

Looking into his pleading blue eyes, she hadn't the heart to tell him he had no chance. Nor could she tell him the memory that haunted her most was of a living man, the father of her son.

Monterey, it seemed, had a constant succession of rodeos, barbecues, picnics, and fiestas. Don Armando took Larissa and Sean everywhere, and everywhere the people accepted them most graciously, never hinting at the growing hostility between the governments of Mexico and the United States. The days stretched into weeks, then into months, and Larissa rarely thought of leaving that enchanted land.

If the strict Catholic matrons and their daughters' stern duennas thought it strange that Señora Farrell resided so long at the home of Don Armando, they never indicated as much. Indeed, Larissa and Armando's relationship was quite innocent. Since that afternoon on the patio, he had never touched her in any but the most casual, friendly fashion.

On the few occasions when Larissa did think regretfully of continuing her journey east, she changed her mind quickly enough when she looked at Sean. For his fifth birthday in November, Don Armando had presented him with a handsome pinto pony, which he rode with an expertise that astounded Larissa. Sean was brown and healthy from his hours in the sun, his hair bleached an appealing strawberry blond, and Larissa could not bear to uproot him for the cold and grime and the vicious arguments she knew awaited in Boston.

In truth, she was enjoying California tremendously herself. The natural friendliness of the people made social functions more enjoyable than the priggish, formal affairs of Shanghai or Macao. And even with the mission's important influence on life, the people lacked the strained morality enforced by the missionaries in Hawaii.

Most of all, she loved the frequent fandangos, or general dances. They were held outdoors, with a wooden dance floor laid beneath the shelter of overhanging trees. Pitchpine torches atop slender poles lighted the dance floor. The guitar music always began slowly, then accelerated to a wild pace as the evening wore on. If she had found it easy to lose herself in the staid waltzes of English society, Larissa was utterly absorbed by the rhythm and passion of Mexican dancing. She learned the steps quickly, delighting Don Armando and his friends with her abilities.

Sometimes the floor was cleared of dancers, and a few of the men performed on their horses, strumming guitars and singing tender love ballads, while the well-trained animals stepped in time to the music. At other times, the activity was less disciplined, as young men broke eggshells filled with lavender and perfume over the heads of the girls of their dreams. An atmosphere of gaiety pervaded.

In late November, Larissa witnessed the pageantry of a California wedding. It began with a wedding cavalcade from the bride's home to the San Carlos Mission Church. The bride, in a white gown of lace and satin, rode before her father on a single, ornamented horse. One of her satin-slippered feet rested in a loop of gold braid dangling at the horse's side. Don Armando explained that the bride's satin slippers had been made by the groom, according to custom, a few weeks before the wedding.

The groom and other members of the wedding party followed the bride's horse to the church. There they and their guests went inside for the ceremony, which lasted nearly two hours. Larissa, who had begun to learn a few words of Spanish, listened attentively. She was particularly intrigued when the padre wound a silk tasseled cord around the shoulders of the couple kneeling before the altar, symbolically binding them together for life.

After the ceremony, the entire wedding party and guests formed a cavalcade back to the bride's parents' home for a lavish feast and hours of energetic dancing. The music and dancing were still continuing when Armando and Larissa left after midnight. In all likelihood, the celebration would stretch into the next several days, but they had left Sean in Juana's care, and Larissa was still hesitant to leave him for more than a day.

As their horses cantered toward his rancho, Don Armando whispered, "It was a wonderful day, wasn't it? The love of a husband and wife is very special, very sacred."

Something in his voice compelled her to look at him. Even in the moonlight, Larissa could read in Don Armando's eyes all the tenderness, love, and passion he had expressed when he had first asked her to become his bride. Despite her refusal, despite the fact she had not consciously encouraged him in all those months, he had not lost his desire for her. He had only masked it to avoid frightening her away, to give him more time to wear down her resistance to his obvious charms.

A lump rose in Larissa's throat, and she looked away. She was very fond of Don Armando, and she realized now that she had been unfair to him to remain in his house so long. Before, she had sometimes felt guilty about the money he had spent on her and Sean when she had no means to repay him. Now, she realized she was more guilty of spending his emotions, allowing him to hope when there was no hope. She should have known that day in the garden when he had first proposed to her and cautioned her that memories could not suffice forever. How could she have assumed he would turn off his emotions, simply because she was incapable of feeling the same as he did? She had refused to marry him, but as long as she remained in his house, he would not seek happiness with another. Her presence was ruining him just as surely as it had ruined Edmund Farrell.

For the remainder of the ride, Larissa was silent, thinking only that she had to leave quickly and hope that Armando would still be able to forget her. After helping her dismount, Don Armando asked, "Will you have a glass of brandy with me before retiring?"

She shook her head, averting her eyes. "Thank you, but no. I'm afraid I already drank far too much wine at the wedding. I've a bit of a headache, so I think I'd best retire immediately."

Without waiting for his reply, Larissa fled to her room. Tiptoeing into Sean's room, she stared for a long moment at his still, sleeping form. Oh, my darling son, she thought, I hope you can forgive me, but I must uproot you yet again. Perhaps it would have been better for you, too, if we had gone sooner, before you became so attached to this land, this way of life, this man. But now I know we must surely go before our staying here destroys us all.

Back in her own room, she undressed, without bothering to light a lamp, and slipped a nightgown over her head. She slid into bed but, though weary from hours of dancing, could not sleep. She was thinking of riding into Monterey the next day to inquire about passage to the United States.

The melancholy strains of a strumming guitar, accompanied by a rich, low voice, drifted to her on the night breezes. The music seemed to begin far away but gradually moved closer, until it came from beneath her window. Straining her ears, Larissa recognized the words of a poignant Spanish love ballad. And she recognized the voice as Armando's. The wedding of his friends had rekindled all the emotions he had stifled for so many months, and now he was wooing her as hundreds of other California rancheros wooed their lady loves.

The music tugged at her heart until she could no longer bear to listen. Hiding her head under her pillow, she tried to staunch the tears flowing noiselessly down her face. And she wondered, was there any way now that she could avoid breaking Don Armando's heart?

Chapter Thirty-Four

At breakfast, Don Armando announced he would spend the day inspecting his stock and asked if Larissa and Sean would care to accompany him. Sean was elated by the prospect, but Larissa declined.

"I'm still rather exhausted from all the dancing," she said, "so I don't fancy spending the day in the saddle. Sean can go, if you're sure he won't be too much trouble to you, Armando."

"No trouble at all." Don Armando grinned. "It's time he learned something about raising prime cattle. Who knows, someday he might inherit a rancho."

Larissa tensed, uncomfortably aware of Don Armando's implications. Since she had not shooed him away from her window last night, did he assume she was wavering in her decision?

The moment Sean and Don Armando were out of sight, she went to the stable, saddled the roan mare she had come to consider her own, and rode toward Monterey. She felt a bit guilty about deceiving Don Armando about her intentions for the day, but she knew he would undoubtedly have tried to dissuade her. If she told him only after her passage was assured, she would be less likely to listen to any arguments.

As she galloped toward Monterey, she admitted to herself that even if there was an American ship at anchor, she might still be denied passage. Since the shipwreck, she had only the small amounts of money Don Armando had given her, nowhere near enough to pay passage to Boston for herself and Sean. She could not bring herself to ask Don Armando for the necessary funds, so she was forced to hope the captain would accept her story that she was a shipping heiress and could pay him promptly when they arrived in Boston.

In the plaza, she looked toward the harbor, catching her breath as she recognized the distinctive shape of an American clipper ship. The customs agent confirmed that the ship was American and said it was named the *Lorelei*. Without asking any questions, he delegated one of his assistants to row her out to the ship.

To her utter amazement, the man who helped her over the side of the *Lorelei* was Jonathan Dillard. They stood opposite one another on deck, both blinking in disbelief. Then Jonathan gave a whoop of joy and threw his arms around her, squeezing so hard she thought her ribs would crack.

"Larissa Bennett!" he exclaimed, stepping back to look at her. "I never thought to see you in Monterey!"

"Nor I you," she replied warmly, "but it's Larissa Farrell now."

"Oh yes, I'd forgotten you're married."

"Widowed," she said quickly, still too dazed at seeing him to wonder how he knew of her marriage. Seeing his eyes cloud with sorrow, she added hastily, "It's been a year now, so I think I've weathered the worst."

Surveying Jonathan, Larissa thought he had matured considerably in the years since they had last seen one another. He still had the same boyish good looks, though his skin had become weathered, particularly around the eyes. But, in the past, he was nervous even being near her and would never have embraced her so heartily. Obviously, the years had taught him to be less self-conscious about his feelings for women.

"What brought you to Monterey? And what brings you aboard the *Lorelei*?" he asked.

Larissa sighed. "It's a long story, one I hope to have days to tell you in the future. Tell me—is the *Lorelei* by any chance bound for Boston?"

He nodded eagerly, anticipating her next question.

"And do you suppose there might be room on board for me and my son?"

Again he nodded, his eyes beginning to glow. "I would suppose so, but of course, you'd have to ask the captain. He's on board now. Why don't you go down and talk to him personally? I think you should remember a clipper's layout well enough to find your way."

She hesitated. "You don't think he'll be angry at my disturbing him?"

Jonathan grinned. "On the contrary. I think he'll be more than pleased. Now go ahead. I've got duties to attend to."

As she made her way to the companionway, Larissa felt vaguely concerned about Jonathan's last statement. How could he be so certain that the captain would be pleased to see her? It occurred to her that she should have asked the captain's name, but since she was already outside his cabin she supposed she might as well knock and let him introduce himself.

At the very instant she knocked, some part of her brain realized who the captain was. Even before a mellow baritone voice said, "Come in," Larissa knew precisely how the voice would sound. She froze in the doorway, unable to force her hand down to turn the handle.

On the other side of the door, she heard a chair being pushed back, and then she heard measured, slow steps approaching the door. How many times had she lain in a darkened bedroom on Macao, listening to those same steps approaching her bed? But no, she had to be imagining things. What had he told Edmund in Shanghai? Only that he had purchased his own small clipper. But surely he would not be the captain. What did he know about sailing?

The door opened, immediately erasing all her suppositions. Nathan stood staring at her, his eyes mirroring surprise, pleasure, and tenderness, as if, after all these years, they still belonged to each other. Her heart thumped against her breast, and she struggled for breath. Her mouth became too dry to speak, but even if she could have spoken, she would not have known what to say.

For an instant, she was overwhelmed by the realization that for the first time since he had left her in their house on Macao, they were together with no barriers between them. She had no husband now, acting as a weight on her conscience, keeping them apart. And yet, she realized with crushing suddenness, there *were* still barriers—the barriers they had built themselves. She could remember as if it were only yesterday his declaration that he would never marry. And she knew she could accept that as she once had, were it not for Sean. But Sean was hers, even if Nathan himself would never make the commitment to become fully hers.

Sean was hers, and she had to protect him at all costs. Nathan had hurt her too much over the years. Perhaps she had hurt him, too, though he had seemed resilient enough, finding solace with other women. But no matter what had passed between them, neither of them must be allowed to hurt Sean. Sean must not suffer because she still wanted Nathan.

He was still staring at her, his brow creased slightly. "Hello, Larissa," he said with deliberate coolness. "Won't you come in and sit down?"

She wanted to accept his invitation, wanted desperately to be able to talk with him again, to feel the warmth of their old bonds. Even more, she wanted what would inevitably come after the conversation. But she was afraid. Afraid for herself. Afraid for Sean. Afraid she would lose herself again to Nathan's power.

Larissa wavered for a moment, remembering what he had said in Shanghai, at dinner with Edmund. He had said someone as special as she could make him forget his misgivings about marriage. But could she really believe that, or did he say it only because she had belonged to someone else and could never hold him to that statement? He had had ample opportunity to marry her before, on Macao, and had managed to avoid it. Perhaps now he had changed his attitude. She could bear to take the chance with her own future, but not with Sean's—never with Sean's.

Forcing out a strangled "No," she shook her head and bolted for the companionway ladder.

Stunned, Nathan watched her disappear up the ladder. Then he recovered his senses and rushed after her. "Larissa!" he yelled helplessly, "come back!"

Nathan reached the main deck in time to see Larissa climbing over the side to her waiting rowboat. "For God's sake, Larissa, will you wait a minute?" he bellowed. "If you didn't want to see me, why in heaven's name did you board my ship and come to my cabin?"

Without looking up at him, Larissa continued down the Jacob's ladder. She could feel him start down the ladder after her, and she was shaking so badly she could hardly hold onto the ropes. But she managed to settle herself in the rowboat and directed the assistant to the customs agent back to shore, leaving Nathan dangling alongside his ship.

Jonathan Dillard watched the scene with amused interest. As first mate of the *Lorelei*, he had great respect and loyalty for Nathan. But he had an equal amount of affection for Larissa and was glad to see that she seemed as spunky as ever. Suppressing a smile as Nathan climbed up the Jacob's ladder, he inquired, "Shall I order the gig lowered, sir?"

Nathan scowled as he hauled himself back up on deck. "No, dammit! I'm not chasing after some pigheaded woman. If she wants to talk to me, she can just come back again!"

"Aye, aye, sir !" Jonathan muttered with a touch of sarcasm.

Nathan regarded him darkly, considering whether to say more, then shook his head and barked, "If you can wipe that smirk off your face, Jonathan, you can come below with me for a drink of rum!"

Larissa arrived back at the rancho long before Don Armando and Sean had returned from their rounds. Leaving the stablehands to care for her horse, she went directly to her room, where she threw herself across her bed and finally released the flood of tears she had held back all the way from Monterey.

Now what was she to do? She couldn't go to Boston, at least not aboard the *Lorelei*. Just seeing Nathan had been painful enough. If they spent the next few months on the same ship, she would be sure to capitulate to his charms again. On the other hand, it was clear she could not remain on the rancho, allowing Don Armando to serenade her and woo her when she had no intention of marrying him. She had to remove herself permanently from his life. She had to be kinder to him than Nathan had been to her, forever popping up in her life, tempting her with that which she could never have.

She blamed Nathan completely for ruining her life. The role the hoppo had played, as well as Edmund and his needs, had diminished in her mind. She traced everything to that morning on their veranda on Macao when Nathan had insisted he would never marry and had sidestepped her questions about having a child. If only he had answered differently! Perhaps she could have trusted him, even when their letters went astray. Perhaps when he returned to Macao and found her pregnant, he would have married her, and then Sean would have known his real father.

But it did no good to think bitterly of the past. Her job was to plan for the future—a future that could not include Nathan. She supposed there was a chance, even now, that Nathan would marry her if he learned about Sean. What man could resist claiming such a strong, active, healthy, handsome boy? But she didn't want him on those terms. She didn't want to spend the rest of her life thinking he wanted the boy more than her. Surely such a situation would not be good for Sean either, for the boy could always seem to sense her unhappiness or discontent.

It seemed she would have to stay on at Don Armando's rancho for at least a few more days, until another ship came into port, bound for the United States. Since Monterey had no inns, there was nowhere else she could go. Don Armando's friends all treated her well, but she did not feel close to any of them, and she doubted that any would be pleased to take her in. Besides, seeking shelter elsewhere, even at the Mission San Carlos, would cause Don Armando unnecessary embarrassment. Surely it could not hurt him too much if she stayed there a few days more, especially since she vowed to herself not to lead him on in any way.

She was sitting up and drying her tears when Sean burst into the room, radiating excitement. "Mummy, mummy," he exclaimed, "it was wonderful fun out there! Don Armando says you should come out to the veranda with us and have some lemonade now." He tugged insistently at her hand, for once not noticing her distress.

"All right, darling," she said, forcing a smile. "You run along and tell Don Armando I'll join you in a moment."

While Sean ran back outside, Larissa went to the basin and bathed her eyes in cool water. Then she combed her hair and put on a broad-brimmed straw hat, which she hoped would shade her face and conceal her swollen eyes.

As she stepped through the door, Don Armando rose from the stone bench where he had been sitting with Sean and walked toward her. "I hope you had a pleasant rest," he said, smiling. "Your son is truly amazing. In no time at all, he'll become a model ranchero."

He stopped before her, his smile fading to a frown. "My dear Larissa, you've been weeping! Has something upset you today?"

Larissa shook her head mutely.

Don Armando's eyes softened. "Then perhaps *I* upset you by my behavior last night?"

"Your behavior was very touching," she whispered. "It's just that I—I guess I'm becoming homesick at last."

"After all these years, homesick for Boston? From what you've told me, you left very little there for which to be homesick."

"I know." She couldn't meet his piercing gaze. "But it's not right for us to depend on your hospitality forever."

"If you married me, you would not need to feel you depended on my hospitality. You could say with conviction, 'mi casa es su casa'—my house is your house."

Larissa looked past Don Armando to Sean, who was sitting on the stone bench idly swinging his legs as he stared at the fountain. "Perhaps it would be best to postpone this discussion. Sean tells me he's had a wonderful day, and I wouldn't want anything to spoil it."

Flashing a smile, Don Armando offered her his arm. "As usual, your mother's instincts are correct. Come then, let us entertain the child. For the moment, at least, his happiness is more important than ours."

A week passed, and Don Armando did not mention marriage to Larissa again. In fact he spoke to her very little, instead taking Sean out for long rides each day. But there was little he could have said to compare with the way Sean glowed returning from each day's adventures and anticipating the next day's. What Armando did have to say, he spoke in song beneath her window each night, promising the most tender love any woman could wish.

Larissa continued to mope about Sean's and her future. Then midway through the week, it occurred to her that marriage to Don Armando would be nothing like marriage to Edmund. The two men were completely different. In the months she had lived at the rancho, she had observed no weaknesses in Don Armando. Even when she rejected him, he had not responded with anger, bitterness, or dejection, but had continued to wage a steady, silent campaign for her heart.

She realized also that not only were the men different,

but the situation was also different. Knowing she loved another man and had borne his child, Edmund had felt hurt, jealous, and inadequate. When he had finally met Nathan, those feelings were more than he could bear. Armando, on the other hand, assumed that Scan was the product of her marriage. Knowing her husband was dead, he had no reason for jealousy. He adored Sean and, like her, seemed to put the child's happiness above all else.

The more she thought about it, the more the reasons for staying in Monterey outweighed those for leaving. No matter where she went, she could never fully escape the memories of Nathan. But at least here she felt more content than anywhere since Macao. As long as she stayed away from the town on the rare occasions when the *Lorelei* might be in port, she could probably save herself the pain of ever seeing Nathan again. After the way she had acted on his ship, she was sure he would be too proud ever to seek her out, so Armando would never know about him, and Sean would be protected from him as well.

Sean was certainly the most compelling reason for reconsidering Don Armando's proposal. He was thriving on the rancho and under the strong male influence of their host. Compared to this, what could Boston offer him? The chance, perhaps, to inherit a lucrative firm, but little else. He wouldn't find the fresh air, open spaces, and amiable companionship of the rancho in Boston. Experience had taught Larissa there were always men eager to entertain her, but she doubted she would ever meet another with the character of Don Armando or the willingness to accept her child.

Even if she married Don Armando, she wouldn't have to give up her claim to Bennett and Barnes. Don Armando was an understanding man. Surely at some convenient time he would help her to pursue the claim. Sean could have the best of both worlds—the pastoral serenity of California and the financial rewards of a Boston shipping firm.

Still, she put off changing her mind, wondering if she could bring herself to marry a man she liked but did not love. Of course, just as her first marriage, this one would not be entirely loveless. Don Armando's nightly serenades convinced her of his deep emotions, and she could not help caring a great deal for him after all the consideration he had shown her and Sean. But was it fair to marry him, knowing she could never fully return his love?

Thinking of the many months she had already shared his home—months in which he had seemed quite happy—she began to think that it was fair. After all, marriage would not entail many changes, except that she would also share his bed and perhaps bear his children. Remembering their first night on the patio, she could not feel upset by that prospect.

A week after her visit to the *Lorelei*, Larissa was strolling on the patio, trying for the hundredth time to sort out her thoughts and reach a final decision, when Sean rushed onto the veranda. She stepped behind the fountain to observe him without him seeing her. Even from several feet away, she could see his cheeks were flushed, his eyes were sparkling, and his chest was heaving excitedly from the joy of his last ride. The door from the dining room opened, and Don Armando stepped out. In one easy motion, he grabbed the boy from behind, lifting him high in the air, then settling him comfortably on his shoulders. Sean squealed with delight, mussing his host's hair and making him laugh, too. In that moment, seeing their relaxed intimacy even when they thought no one was watching them, Larissa knew what her decision would be.

Larissa waited until she had tucked Sean into bed that night before approaching Don Armando in his study. He looked up in surprise as she entered. In the last week, afraid to be alone with him, she had always retired right after Sean. Pointing to a soft velvet chair beside the fire, he smiled encouragingly and waited for her to speak.

"Armando," she began hesitantly, "I've been thinking a lot this week about the things you've said."

He nodded. "Yes, you have been quite pensive."

Pausing, she stared at the fire for a long moment, then continued. "I mean, about 'mi casa, su casa,' and about Sean becoming a ranchero." She lifted her gaze to see his half-smile, encouraging her to go on. "I've been thinking I would like that very much and so would Sean."

Rising, he walked to her chair, then fell on his knees before it. He took her hand and held it to his cheek. "Are you saying that you've decided, at last, to become my wife?"

She nodded. "If you still want me."

His blue eyes beamed with the intensity of his desire for her, but he spoke carefully, watching her for the slightest hint of hesitancy. "Of course I still want you, dearest, but you must be very, very certain. You realize you'll have to sign an oath of allegiance to Mexico?"

She laughed lightly. "Whatever for? I assure you I have no intention of overthrowing the government!"

"Of course you don't. It's a silly regulation, but there's been so much talk about the United States wanting to take over California that the government requires the oath from all permanent residents."

She shrugged. "All right. I'll sign it."

"There's one other thing." He hesitated. "You'll have to become a Roman Catholic. The government requires that, too, and of course, the church would never permit me to marry someone of another faith."

"Well, Catholic or Protestant, I'll still be worshipping the same God, so I can't see any objection to that."

Don Armando sighed and smiled broadly. "Then there is no reason why we cannot proceed with our plans at once. Tomorrow morning I'll ride to Mission San Carlos and bring back a padre to begin instructing you in the faith."

Rising, he drew her to her feet and cradled her against his chest. "Ah, Larissa, you've no idea how I've longed to do this through all the months just passed." He lowered his head, catching her mouth with his own. Larissa surrendered to the feeling of security that overcame her, pushing her last bothersome doubt to the back of her mind.

Chapter Thirty-Five

While Larissa grappled with her future, Nathan Masters sat in his cabin aboard the *Lorelei*, brooding about the fickleness of women. Day after day he scarcely moved, trusting Jonathan as first mate to oversee the cargo loading and any other necessary chores. By the fourth day, all the cargo had been loaded, and the crew was becoming anxious to begin the last leg of their voyage home to Boston. Still, Nathan sat and brooded, cursing the day he had met Larissa, wondering what had possessed her to board his ship, then flee without even speaking to him.

On the morning of the eighth day, Jonathan Dillard knocked on the cabin door, barging in when Nathan refused to answer. Taking one look at Nathan's unshaved, uncombed appearance, he said curtly, "She's not going to come back, you know."

Nathan's head jerked up, his eyes blazing. "What makes you think I want her to?" he growled.

Jonathan shrugged. "It's not like you to lay idle in a harbor when your business is completed. Even the crew has begun to comment on your strange behavior. It's obvious you're waiting for something—or someone."

"So what if I am? What makes you so sure she won't come back?"

Sighing, Jonathan flopped into a chair. "I think I know her almost as well as I know you—at least well enough to know she's every bit as stubborn and has every bit as much pride as you. I don't know what you ever did to her, Nathan, but it must have left a powerful impression to make her run like she did."

Smacking his fist into his open palm, Nathan stood and began to pace. "That's just it! I never did anything to her!

She's the one who did all the hurting—running off and getting married when I left her on Macao for a few months. And then when her husband finally died, she didn't even have the decency to stay put in Shanghai and wait for me! Didn't she know I'd be back for her?"

"How could she? Why don't you stop degrading her long enough to admit you love her?"

"Of course I love her! She knows that! I must have told her a hundred times when we were living together on Macao!"

"Then why don't you tell her now?"

Nathan stopped pacing and stared at Jonathan with narrowed eyes. "How in hell can I tell her anything when she isn't here?"

Jonathan smiled calmly. "You could talk to her. I've taken the liberty of making some inquiries in town, and I've learned she's staying at the ranch of one Don Armando Estrada, just a few miles north of Monterey."

"I don't suppose you went to the trouble of finding out her relationship with this Don Armando?"

Jonathan shrugged innocently. "If you care enough, you'll ride out and find out for yourself."

"And what if I find out she's become this man's mistress?"

"We both know that's highly unlikely."

"Is it? She was my mistress once, you know."

Jonathan bristled. "She was more than that, and you know it! She loved you, and I think she fancied herself your wife, even if you were too pigheaded to speak the vows!"

Nathan smiled sardonically. "You've become quite the philosopher, quite the judge of human character, haven't you? Whatever happened to the naive young lad who shipped out on the *Queen of Cathay*? If I were you, I'd be a bit more careful how I addressed my captain."

"I can't be careful, I care too much about both of you! Sure, I've grown up in six years. I've had a lot of time to observe things. And I can tell you one thing, *Captain* Nathan Masters—if you ship out of here without Larissa, you're nothing but a damned fool!"

"Enough!" Nathan thundered, turning away from him. "Get out of my cabin! And count yourself lucky you still have a job on this ship!"

Jonathan left. But he could not resist a smile of self-satisfaction half an hour later when Nathan came on deck, shaved and dressed in fresh clothing, and ordered the captain's gig lowered.

The first person Nathan saw as he approached the Estrada rancho was a small boy perched on a pony, trying desperately to twirl a lariat. Even from a distance, he recognized the auburn hair and knew the boy must be Larissa's son, Sean. Strange, he thought to himself, but in all their meetings on Macao and in Shanghai, she had never even described the boy to him. In fact, that evening in Shanghai when he had dined with her and Edmund, she had seemed particularly anxious to keep Sean away from him. Of course, he might have imagined that. After all, they had both been very agitated that night.

So intent was he on twirling his lariat, Sean did not even look up as Nathan dismounted before the house. Captivated by the child, Nathan stood watching him for a moment, putting off the inevitable confrontation with Larissa. Sean was dressed in the black, short-jacketed suit so popular in California. A broad-brimmed black hat bounced against his back as he moved. His skin was tanned from riding, and, except for his mop of auburn hair, he could easily have passed as the son of a ranchero.

Stepping closer to the pony, Nathan asked, "You're Sean, aren't you?"

The boy's head jerked up, and he grinned at the stranger. "How did you know? Did Don Armando tell you?"

Nathan tensed, wondering just how close Don Armando was to Larissa and her son. "No. I'm a friend of your mother's. I knew her in China, and she used to talk about you sometimes." Nathan stared at the boy's eyes, wondering why they looked so familiar to him.

"Oh," Sean responded, turning his attention back to the lariat. "Well, I'm glad we're not in China now. I think California is much more fun. Do you know how to twirl a lariat?"

"I'm afraid not. We don't have much need for lariats aboard ship."

"You mean you're a sailor?" Sean looked at Nathan again.

He nodded, still studying the boy's eyes. They were nothing like Larissa's. Her jade green eyes would haunt him the rest of his life. And if he remembered correctly, Edmund Farrell had had light blue eyes. He shrugged, wondering why he should care about the boy's eyes anyway. Then it struck him. Sean's eyes were identical to the eyes that had stared back at him from the mirror as he shaved only hours ago. Sean had *his* eyes!

"How old are you, Sean?" he asked quickly. "I mean, when is your birthday?"

"I'm five. My birthday's in November. Don Armando gave me this pony."

Nathan hardly heard the last statement as he figured rapidly in his mind. Five years old. That would mean the boy was born in 1840, November of 1840. When had he left Macao that year? Early March? Eight months before? He was sure Larissa had not been untrue to him when they were living together, which could only mean. . . . Studying Sean's amber-flecked gray eyes once more, he asked, "Is your mother home, Sean?"

The boy nodded. "She's inside."

Feeling a strange mixture of anger, hurt, resentment, and elation, Nathan strode toward the front veranda. He was a few steps from the door when Larissa appeared in the doorway. She froze momentarily, then looked past him, acting as if he were not even there. "Sean, darling," she called, "you know I don't want you to ride when no one is watching you."

Sean sighed. "Well, I wasn't really riding, just sitting here while I try to throw the lariat."

"But you could fall so easily, darling. You should have asked Juana or me or one of the stablehands to stay with you. I thought you were on the patio all this time, and I just now discovered you'd disappeared. I was worried about you."

"Larissa," Nathan cut in impatiently, "aren't you going to speak to me?"

Her eyes flitted to his face, then back to her son. "Hello, Nathan. But I really don't believe there's anything for us to talk about."

"Oh, yes, there is!" There was an undertone of steel to his voice. "For one thing, there's Sean, and if you won't take me inside to discuss him, I'll shout out everything here and now, in front of the child."

Larissa blanched and whispered hollowly, "What do you mean?"

"You know," he nodded, his eyes showing grim determination.

Turning abruptly into the house, she called, "Juana!" As Juana bustled toward her, she quickly instructed her to watch Sean and to see that she and her guest were not disturbed. She led Nathan to the patio, trying to appear casual and unconcerned. "Would you like some lemonade or perhaps a cup of tea or coffee?"

Shaking his head, he grabbed her by the shoulders and turned her to face him. His fingers dug into her flesh, and his eyes flashed with rage. "Why, Larissa?" he whispered. "Why did you keep my son from me? What right did you have to hide him from me all these years?"

Larissa stiffened, throwing back her head as her own eyes flashed in answer. "*Your* son, you say!" She laughed bitterly. "How strange that you should want to claim him now that you see what a fine boy he is! I didn't realize you wanted a son, Nathan! Once, when I asked you what would happen if I bore a child, you pushed the question aside as if it didn't matter."

His gaze became tortured. "But I didn't think, Larissa! You didn't tell me! I thought you were simply speculating."

"At the time, I was. But you made your views clear enough, so when I did learn I was carrying a child, I saw no reason to bother you with the fact."

With a vacant stare, he nodded. "So that's why you married Edmund Farrell. I always knew there were more reasons than you told me."

Releasing her, Nathan was silent for a moment. Then he asked in an anguished tone, "But when Edmund died, why didn't you wait for me in Shanghai? Why didn't you try to send word to me? You could have told me everything then. With Edmund dead, no one would have been hurt."

"No one?" She stared at him meaningfully. Uncomfortable, he shifted his weight.

"Oh, Larissa! Surely you don't think I would have done anything to hurt my own son—or the woman who bore him! Can you really imagine I wouldn't have welcomed you both into my life?"

She shook her head slowly. "No, I never imagined you would cast us aside. I always knew you would want Sean if you ever found out. But I didn't want it that way, Nathan. I didn't want you to accept me just because you wanted him."

"But I've always wanted you first! Why do you think I rode out here today, when I should have sailed for the Horn five days ago? It wasn't because of Sean, you know. I didn't even know he was mine until I saw him."

Tears brimming in her eyes, she cried, "He's not yours, Nathan! He's mine! My son. I've raised him and loved him and rescued him from kidnapping. Don't say he's yours, because, even though you fathered him, you can't have him!"

Nathan's eyes narrowed, and he caught her wrist as she started to turn away from him. "Not even if I say I want you both?" he whispered.

Shaking her head, she lifted green, glistening eyes to his. "No matter what you say. It's too late."

"What do you mean, too late? You haven't gone and married this Don Armando character, have you?"

Larissa caught her breath, feeling a stab in her heart as his amber-flecked eyes dulled with hurt. "Not yet. But I've promised myself to him. He's gone to the mission this morning to bring back a padre so we can make our plans."

"Then it's not too late! If you haven't spoken the vows, you can still be mine."

He paused, waiting for her to agree, but she only stared at him in desperation. Did she dare to suppose he was proposing to her? Or did he expect her to begin again as they had lived on Macao? Was it possible his views on marriage really had changed, or did she only imagine that because she wanted him so much? She did want him, but not at the expense of Sean's happiness and security.

Clearing his throat, he prodded her. "Larissa, did you hear me? I said it's not too late. Unless—" he swallowed, searching her eyes for an answer, "—do you love him?"

Wrenching herself from his grasp, she turned and took a few steps away from him. "Oh, Nathan!" she sobbed. "Why must you even ask that question when you surely know the answer? Do you insist on hearing it from my own lips? All right, I'll tell you, and I hope my answer will satisfy you enough that you'll go away and leave me alone. Of course I don't love him—"

Hearing a sharp gasp behind her, Larissa stopped and turned to face him again. But her eyes went beyond Nathan to the veranda, where Don Armando stood with a short, plump padre. Closing her eyes, she felt her face turn crimson. How much had he heard? After all he had done for her, how could she bear to look at him and read the hurt in his eyes?

She heard the click of his boots on the patio stones and then his painfully controlled voice as he approached Nathan. "Sean and Juana told me we had a visitor. I am Armando Estrada, and this is Padre Alvarado from Mission San Carlos."

Nathan introduced himself in a cool, controlled voice, and Don Armando turned his attention to Larissa, who stood with her eyes still tightly closed, swaying dizzily. "My dear Larissa, you're looking quite faint. I think you'd better sit down."

Opening her eyes, she allowed him to lead her to a stone bench. When he was satisfied that she was settled, he spoke to Nathan. "Señor Masters," he said smoothly, "one cannot mistake your resemblance to Sean. Your eyes, especially, seem identical. Were you, perhaps, related to the boy's father?"

Nathan's gaze traveled from Don Armando to Larissa and back again before he replied, "I *am* Sean's father."

For a moment Don Armando's expression was puzzled. Then he sighed and smiled sadly. "Ah, now I understand."

Taking Larissa's hand, he said gently, "You do not love me because you love this man, isn't that so?"

Larissa lifted her tormented eyes to his, wanting desperately to deny it, to spare him any hurt. But she read such infinite understanding in his gaze that she felt compelled to nod slowly. "But I didn't know—I mean, I didn't think—"

"Hush." He ran a finger gently down her jawline. "You needn't explain. I think I know enough. Even last night when you finally agreed to marry me, I knew in my heart you did not love me, at least not in the way I would have liked. So, while part of me rejoiced that you would finally be mine, another part grieved that I would never have all of you. I knew I could never bring you all the joy you would bring me, for your heart belonged to someone else. And I grieved even more, thinking the man you loved was dead. At least now I will have the consolation of knowing he is alive and can bring you the full happiness I never could."

She stared at him, tears streaming down her face. How could he speak with such compassion and self-control, when his own heart must be twisting in pain? Looking up, she saw Nathan standing frozen beside the bench and was shocked to see his eyes glistening with unshed tears.

Forcing a bright smile, Don Armando turned his attention to the padre, who was standing to one side, looking as if the events had thoroughly confused him. "Well, padre," Don Armando said heartily, "you came to plan a wedding, and instead it seems you will be performing one! In my opinion, this couple should not have to wait even one day more to be married."

Staring at him in surprise, Larissa blurted, "But I'm not sure Nathan wants—"

"Hush, woman," Nathan interrupted. "I think it's time we had a proper union, for your sake as well as for our son's."

She swallowed, afraid to believe him. "But how can I take Sean away from here? He's happy. He adores Don Armando—"

"But he belongs with his real father and will surely adore him even more," Don Armando assured her. "And since we had not yet told him of our marriage plans, he will be spared that confusion."

The padre glanced from one to the other nervously. "I'm not sure I understand. The boy outside is your son, is he not, Señora Farrell?"

Larissa nodded.

Turning to Nathan, Padre Alvarado asked, "But am I to understand he is your son as well, Señor Masters?"

Nathan nodded.

The padre shook his head. "Oh, dear, and neither of you married to the other! The poor child was obviously conceived in sin!"

"Which is all the more reason why you must right the situation and marry them immediately," Don Armando pointed out.

"But how can I? You've already told me Señora Farrell is not a Catholic, and as for this gentleman—"

"I am not Catholic, either," Nathan put in.

"Then the situation appears to be completely out of my hands," the padre said excitedly. "How can I marry them when neither is Catholic?"

Smiling in amusement, Don Armando shrugged. "You must, of course, be guided by your own conscience, padre. But if you refuse to marry them, I'm afraid they'll have to continue living in sin, at least until they've left California and found a place where the Catholic Church does not rule supreme. And, of course, that means the boy will continue to be subjected to this questionable moral influence. But, if you wish to be responsible for such a thing—" He shrugged, again leaving the sentence unfinished.

"All right!" Padre Alvarado threw up his hands in resignation. "For the child's sake and for the sake of their immortal souls, I'll perform the ceremony. But I'm not at all sure my superiors would approve."

Still smiling, Don Armando positioned Nathan and Larissa before the fountain and directed the padre to prepare for the ceremony. He sent another servant to replace Juana in the front yard with Sean so that Juana could witness the marriage with him. Within a few minutes, Padre Alvarado was beginning the ceremony, his voice droning on about the responsibilities of marriage.

Larissa stood dazedly beside Nathan, her thoughts a wild jumble. After all the years she had despaired of it ever being possible, were they really exchanging marriage vows now? Did she dare believe they would be united for all eternity? That they could share Sean, and perhaps other children, as she had always hoped?

She felt a dim rush of surprise when Nathan produced a ring—a wide, rose-gold band, engraved with trailing primroses. But why shouldn't he have a ring ready for the occasion? It was all so dreamlike anyway. In an hour or two, she would probably awaken and find herself sitting on a stone bench, receiving instruction from Padre Alvarado, while Don Armando stood by.

The padre's droning ceased, and then Nathan was leaning over her, enfolding her in strong arms, as he bent his head to press his lips to hers. The fiery spark that had lain dormant for so many years ignited, jolting her being with a force that told her it was not a dream after all. Beyond Nathan's shoulder, she saw Don Armando's eyes, glistening with unshed tears that celebrated her happiness while mourning his loss. Those deep blue eyes, which she would remember for the rest of her life, confirmed the fact: she was Nathan's wife now—now and for all time.

Part Seven

�֍

1845-1846

Chapter Thirty-Six

At last they were alone and free to engage in the most intimate form of reunion. Jonathan Dillard, mumbling something about newlyweds needing privacy, had immediately offered to entertain Sean, assuring them he would be delighted to share his cabin with the boy.

Larissa had been relieved at how quickly Sean had accepted her marriage and agreed to leave Don Armando's rancho. He seemed to sense her happiness and required no further explanation. He had, of course, regretted leaving his pony, and for a moment he had clung to Don Armando, weeping pathetically. But Nathan, showing boundless paternal understanding, had gently pulled him away, assuring him that they might return to visit Don Armando sometime in the future.

Now, as the waning light of dusk filtered in through the cabin ports, the *Lorelei* began to move slowly out of Monterey harbor on the evening tide. Turning to Nathan, Larissa smiled and whispered, "Shouldn't you be on deck, directing the sailing of your ship?"

He shook his head. "Jonathan is perfectly capable of handling everything. I have more important business to detain me right here—unless, of course, you mean to say you don't want my company."

"Oh, Nathan!" She threw her arms wide in welcome. "How can you even say that?"

He smiled. "Well, you didn't give me much of a welcome on the rancho, you know. And you didn't seem too pleased to see me the first time you came to this cabin."

"Forget about all that," she said quickly. "I married you, didn't I?"

"Indeed you did." He advanced toward her, his eyes

burning with their old, familiar fire. "And I intend to hold you to all the obligations of a wife."

Watching his advance, Larissa felt strangely shy, as if, even after all the times they had shared love, this time was really the first. Realizing this was their wedding night, she suddenly felt as flustered as a young, innocent virgin. But all shyness vanished as his arms enfolded her and his lips lowered to claim hers. The past, laden with all the hurt and confusion they had ever caused one another, fell away as they strained toward the instant when they would become one again.

Nathan fumbled with the hooks at the back of her gown. Failing to open them quickly enough, his hands moved to her neckline, and he ripped her bodice wide.

"Nathan," Larissa gasped, as his head lowered to her throbbing bosom.

"Forget about the dress," he murmured. "I'll buy you a hundred more to replace it."

Giggling, she slid her hands beneath his shirt, moving them upward to massage his chest, delighting as the buttons popped off and his shirt opened. His arms tightened around her, drawing her closer, until their bared flesh seemed to fuse. His mouth met hers again as his hands moved downward, loosening the rest of her clothing. Unembarrassed, she continued to undress him, too, her desire mounting as she felt each newly bared inch of flesh beneath her fingers.

By the time they were naked, Larissa felt as if she could not wait a moment longer to feel him inside her. Overwhelmed by her craving, she moaned, "Take me, Nathan! I want you so much!"

His desire matched hers as he lifted her from her feet and swiftly carried her to the spacious bunk. The moment her body touched the bed, he was over her and in her. Her head fell to one side, and she panted with appreciation as his pulsating maleness filled her. Together they moved, oblivious to all but the delicious urgencies of their twin desires.

Having at last surrendered to the destiny of their love, they were caught in a raging fury, unleashing all the passion they had kept locked inside during the years of their separation. At last, Larissa admitted the slow starvation her heart and soul had suffered, and she wondered, fleetingly, if they could ever fully make up for those lost years.

Then all thought became a blur as her body soared to the heights of sensation that only true love could bring. Locked in love, they rolled from side to side, and for a time she found herself on top of him. Then he rolled her to her back again, and she clung to him as they both shuddered in the final glorious moments. Physically and emotionally drained, they still clung to one another as they drifted into sleep.

It was dark when Larissa awakened. She lay still for several moments, not wanting to disturb Nathan. Even now, she could scarcely believe that they were really husband and wife. She squeezed together the fingers of her left hand, reassuring herself that she was, indeed, wearing Nathan's wedding band. His hand moved down to stroke hers, and she could see the amber flecks of his eyes glowing in the moonlight.

"I didn't mean to wake you," she whispered.

"I've been awake for some time," he replied, touching his lips lightly to her cheek, "marveling that at last we are together for good."

Nuzzling his neck, she teased, "Now that you've had time to reconsider, do you regret your haste in marrying me?"

Nathan laughed softly. "Haste, you say? I've only had six and a half years to think about it! No, love, I suspect I'll never regret it."

She was silent for a moment, hesitant to bring up old problems. At last she sighed and said, "Yet, on Macao, you always insisted love was enough. You said then you would never marry. Why?"

He expelled a long sigh, stroking her hair as he rolled to his back and settled her more comfortably against his chest. "As a child, I saw how marriage could hurt a man, and I swore that I would never let it happen to me. When I was nine, my mother left my father—ran off with another man. My father adored her, and when she deserted him, he became little more than a hollow shell. He lived for nine years after that—but you could say he didn't live at all. Sometimes I thought I felt his pain as deeply as he. I was sure that all women were fickle, and so I decided I would never fall into the trap of committing myself in marriage. As I got older, I realized I didn't want to deny myself the comforts a woman could provide, but I still vowed not to make the commitment."

"So," she asked slowly, "what finally made you change your mind?"

"You, of course. That first spring and summer, when I left you on Macao, I realized what a fool I was being, punishing both of us for the sins of my mother. I would have married you the moment I returned. Only I returned to find you were already married and gone. I thought then that my views on women and marriage had been right all along."

"Strange, isn't it," she mused, "how we always hurt ourselves because we're afraid of someone else hurting us? On Macao, I held back just a bit, because I was sure you'd never marry me, and I was so afraid you'd desert me. Later, when I was carrying Sean, I wouldn't write and tell you, and I wouldn't wait for you because I was so afraid of what you'd say or do. Of course, the hoppo had a hand in determining our futures then, too. But even later, when the hoppo was dead, and then Edmund died, too, I wanted you so badly, but I was afraid to look for you. I deliberately avoided seeing you, because of silly pride and fears."

"I know," Nathan said, then chuckled. "When you left my ship a week ago, I swore I wouldn't go after you, no matter how much I wanted you. It took Jonathan to convince me what a fool I was being. Still, I think I always knew we would be reunited one day. That's probably why I always carried the ring—as a sort of good luck talisman."

"What do you mean?"

"Here, I'll show you." He sat up and lit the bedside lamp, then drew her left hand into the light and gently pulled off the wedding band. "Read this," he said, pointing to the inscription inside.

Larissa gasped as the light fell on the engraved letters. "N.M. to L.B." she read aloud, then looked at him. "How long have you had this?" she breathed.

"I brought it back from Whampoa in the fall of 1840. When I learned you were gone, I damn near threw it into the Pearl River. But something made me keep it. And after the first time I saw you again on Macao—when you had returned with Edmund and Sean—I put it on my key ring, and I've carried it ever since. I knew that first time I saw you again that you still loved me, and something in me felt that we'd be together again one day."

"Oh, Nathan!" she cried, touched beyond words.

"There's something else I want to tell you, though you may have guessed it by now. The *Lorelei* was named for you."

"Lorelei?"

"Well, I couldn't very well have called it the *Larissa*, could I? Can you imagine the flapping tongues if I'd sailed into Shanghai in a clipper named for another man's wife?"

Larissa giggled, thinking of the staid British matrons on Shanghai's foreign settlement. She had never fit in very well with them, and she imagined they would have dearly loved some juicy gossip about her. Her laughter stopped abruptly as she realized Nathan was staring at her, his eyes smoldering with rekindled desire.

He smiled sheepishly. "It's been a long drought, Larissa. Can you blame me if my thirst is not quenched so easily?"

Returning his smile, she opened her arms to him. "How can I blame you, Nathan, when I am just as parched as you?"

Pushing her lovingly down on the bunk, he left the lamp burning, so he could drink in all of her beauty. Before, consumed by passion, they had moved quickly, in the dim light of dusk. Now, as light flooded their bodies, they moved more slowly, each savoring the other's touch, feel, smell, and appearance. He kissed her all over, letting his lips fall randomly, burning her soft, sweet-smelling flesh, making her skin erupt in gooseflesh as his mouth tickled and teased. Her fingers roamed his body, becoming reacquainted with every ridged muscle, every small hollow, every bit of fur. She moaned, breathing in short, frantic gasps, as his mouth closed over a breast, nibbling tenderly at the nipple.

His hands slid beneath her buttocks, as he guided himself into her, and her mouth found his. She arched upward, willing him closer, deeper. Her arms pressed him to her, and she surrendered to ecstasy that was far sweeter than anything she had ever before experienced. This time, she thought rapturously, their joy would not be fleeting, for they were pledged to one another for all time.

The voyage to Boston was a perfect honeymoon. Even the chill gale winds that buffeted the *Lorelei* as she rounded Cape Horn could do nothing to dispel Larissa's good spirits.

With Nathan's gentle encouragement, she shared with him all that had happened to her in the years they had been apart. He agreed that as soon as they reached Boston they should call on her aunt and uncle, settling once and for all her claim to her father's firm.

Giving Larissa a wry grin, Nathan quipped, "It seems our lives have been linked since the beginning of this controversy, so it's only fitting that I should be present to see its final resolution."

Larissa sighed. "After all these years, it might be easier not to bother. You have the *Lorelei,* so I suppose we don't need the money. But I still can't bear to think of them reaping all the profit from papa's work."

"Not to mention my work," Nathan added grimly. "I was your father's assistant for four years and agent of the firm for four years after that. When I finally lost my position, your uncle seemed to have committed the oversight of forgetting to pay my back wages. I would say we all have a stake in this controversy—including Sean. I won't stand by and see my son cheated of his just inheritance."

"Well," she said firmly, "they can't deny our claim when I finally present myself to them. I'm twenty-four years old now, so they can't make up any stories about holding my share in trust for me."

"No, they can't," Nathan agreed. "But knowing your aunt and uncle, I feel certain they'll think of something."

For the remainder of the voyage, Larissa, determined to enjoy her honeymoon, pushed the problem to the back of her mind. She delighted in watching Nathan and Sean together, marveling at the easy companionship that developed almost instantly between them. She was fearful, however, when Nathan encouraged the daring child to climb the rigging or perform other dangerous feats, but Nathan laughed away her concern.

"He's a boy, Larissa! You can't coddle him all his life. He's got to get a few bumps, bruises, and scratches, and you can rest assured he's too precious for me to allow him to do anything that might seriously hurt him."

It was obvious that Nathan did treasure the boy, so Larissa swallowed further protests and let her two men enjoy themselves together. Watching Nathan, it occurred to her that he was innately more suited to being a ship's captain than to being a businessman tied to an office desk. When she mentioned that fact to him one evening, he seemed pleased.

"By the time I purchased the *Lorelei*, I'd observed enough seamanship to know what to do. Also, I was fortunate enough to take on Jonathan in Boston, right after I made the purchase. I'd always liked him, and he was thoroughly sick of Captain Clinton and wanted a change. For my part, I'll have to admit I'd gotten a bit tired of managing other people's business, always being on the fringe of things, never really making the important decisions. With the *Lorelei*, I'm both captain and agent. I can't compete with the major firms of Boston and New York, perhaps, but I do well enough for myself, and—" he paused and grinned, "well enough to support a wife and son. The best part is the independence—deciding for myself what I'll carry and where I'll put into port."

"I hope your cargo has never included opium."

He laughed, playfully swatting her rump. "Not a particle of the stuff has ever touched my ship, since a certain lady in my life heartily disapproves of the opium traffic."

Despite the grumblings of his crew, Nathan extended the honeymoon somewhat by putting in at several ports on both the west and east coasts of South America. But the idyll finally ended early in April, when the *Lorelei* glided into Boston harbor and tied up at India Wharf. For Larissa, the docking evoked no glad feelings of homecoming, only anxiety and grim determination to put the inevitable, ugly scene with her aunt and uncle behind her. She had been gone almost seven years, years spent in four different countries, but she could still hear her Aunt Harriet's sinister, gleeful chuckle in the library the night they learned of her father's death.

As the crew prepared to begin unloading cargo, Larissa turned to Nathan. "I think I'll go ahead to the house on Pearl Street," she said. "I can't bear the anticipation. The sooner I see them the better."

Nathan frowned. "I wish you wouldn't, love. Just give me an hour or so to get things arranged here, and we'll both go. I don't imagine your aunt and uncle will be too pleased to see you, so I'd rather you wouldn't go alone."

"But if I go ahead now, I may have the whole business completed before you even finish here. Besides, if I go alone, Sean can stay with you. I'd really prefer not to expose him to Aunt Harriet and Uncle Hiram. I'm sure I'll be perfectly safe. They may not be pleased to see me, but I doubt that they'll do anything violent."

Shrugging, Nathan kissed her cheek and turned to direct his men. "Well, have it your own way, then. If I've learned one thing in the years I've known you, it's that you're a very stubborn woman, and I'd be wasting my breath to argue with you. Go ahead, if you must, but I'll still be following within the hour. Jonathan can take over here and keep an eye on Sean as well."

Adjusting her black silk bonnet, Larissa ran down the gangplank and hurried along the quay toward Pearl Street. Her heart pounded with anxiety. Yet, she asked herself, what could possibly go wrong? Her aunt and uncle would have no choice but to surrender her interests to her.

As she bustled down High Street toward Pearl Street, she did not notice the tall, dark-haired man staring at her from a shop doorway. Keenly, he watched her approach, instantly recognizing the flushed cheeks and the auburn tresses slipping from beneath her bonnet. Seven years had dulled neither his memory of her nor his desire for revenge for the way she had humiliated him before all of Boston.

Looking up and down the street, he nodded with satisfaction as he noted it was deserted. And even if someone did chance to see what he did, who would question him, one of the richest, most powerful, most respected lawyers in Boston? His carriage waited outside the shop doorway. As Larissa stepped between the carriage and the shop, he stepped in front of her, making a sweeping bow.

"Good day to you, Mistress Bennett."

Larissa glanced up sharply, not recognizing the voice. But she recognized the speaker as he straightened, and her eyes widened in shock. It had been years since she had even thought of him, and she had certainly never imagined she would encounter him her first hour back in Boston. "Andrew—" she said lamely.

Before she could say more, his hand clapped over her mouth, and he dragged her into the carriage. Still holding her, he leaned out the window to give his driver instructions. Then he settled back in the carriage, smiling wickedly as he held her pinioned between his knees, one hand still covering her mouth.

"Well, Larissa, I must say this is a pleasant surprise.

After all these years, you've finally come back to me, eh?"

Her eyes flashed with fury as he finally withdrew his hand. "I hate you, Andrew Allerton, just as I always did!" she cried. "Where are you taking me?"

He shrugged. "Somewhere where we can be alone and get reacquainted. It's been a long time, Larissa. But I think I'll enjoy picking up where we left off."

"Oh, no you won't!" she screamed. "I'm not going anywhere with you!" She lunged for the carriage door, but Andrew grabbed her and pulled her back to the seat beside him. He gave her cheek a stinging slap.

"That's for screaming, my dear. Do it again, and you'll suffer worse. It seems to me you've got a great deal of suffering due you—as payment for deserting me. You must have had a good laugh, thinking how humiliated I was when my bride did not even show up at her own betrothal party."

"I did!" she replied spitefully. "But it was your own arrogant fault if you suffered. I never promised myself to you, no matter what you or Aunt Harriet or your parents thought. You've had seven years in which to nurse your pride, Andrew. By now you should be fully recovered, so why don't you just let me go?"

"Oh, no." He shook his head savagely. "You're going to pay, and, who knows, in the end you may just decide to marry me, after all."

"You're wasting your time! I'm already married, and even if I weren't, nothing could make me marry you."

"Well, we'll see, my dear." He settled back contentedly as the carriage rolled into a stable. Climbing down, he offered her his hand. "Come along, Larissa. I'd like to show you my house. *Our* house actually, since it was to have been our wedding gift from my parents."

Docilely, Larissa let him help her out of the carriage, deciding that the moment they left the stable she would scream and kick until the neighbors came to her aid. From the carriage, she had recognized the area as Beacon Hill, and she assumed its wealthy residents would rush to help a lady in distress. Her plans were thwarted immediately, however, as Andrew pointed to a hatch in the floor.

"An ingenious invention, don't you think? It leads to a tunnel connecting to the house. Allows me to come out to the stables for any reason, in rain or snow, without being subjected to the elements."

Without waiting for a response, Andrew pushed her down the stairway to the tunnel and followed behind her. Carrying a lantern to light their way, he steered Larissa into the house and pushed her up the servants' stairway. At the top of the stairs, he shoved her into a bedroom, slamming and locking the door behind him.

As he set down the lantern and advanced toward her, Larissa gritted her teeth and held back a scream. She realized it would do little good to scream, since none of his servants would dare dispute his power in his own house, and so she refused even to give him the satisfaction of trying.

Smiling, he asked, "Has the fight gone out of you so soon, Larissa? Or have you decided you would like to sample what I have to offer, after all?"

She stared at him sullenly, waiting for him to come within kicking range. But he hung back, playing with her, taunting her. His eyes raked her body. "In appearance, at least, you are as desirable as ever. A touch fuller in the breast and hips, perhaps, but, of course, now you are a mature woman, more capable of giving pleasure than the girl I knew." He paused, imagining the coming moments. He would make them worth all the years he had waited.

"You may yet regret not marrying me," he said offhandedly. "I'm a prosperous attorney now. I have everything I desire. You could have shared all I have if you had not been so stubborn."

"I have my own prosperity," she answered acidly. "It is measured in love instead of possessions, and it is far more valuable than anything you might offer me. And as an attorney, sir, you must know it is unlawful for you to detain me here or to harm me in any way."

Andrew raised his brows in mock concern. "Is it now? And who will ever prove that I broke any laws? Who will dispute my word? I think no one, not even you, Larissa. It would be an easy matter, once I am finished with you, to dump you in the back bay area. Who would miss you after you've been gone from Boston seven long years?"

"My husband would," she said staunchly. "And he will never rest until he finds me."

"Indeed? Then I fear the poor man may never rest again." He yawned elaborately. "This conversation bores me. Take off your clothes!"

She glared at him, refusing to move.

Raising his hand to strike her, Andrew moved a step nearer. "I said, take off your clothes! We're not playing one of your coy, old-fashioned games on your aunt and uncle's widow's walk now, Larissa! I want you, and I will not be thwarted!"

Still she stared at him defiantly, not a flicker of fear in her eyes.

"Damn you!"

He strode toward her, and when he was only two feet away, Larissa kicked, aiming for his groin. But he had anticipated her move. Catching her foot deftly in one hand, he twisted cruelly, bringing her tumbling to the floor. He was atop her before she could regain her breath, clawing at her clothing, determined to have his way. At that moment, all he could think of was revenge. He could taste its sweetness even before he had forced his legs between hers. Exhilaration filled him as, finally, a ragged, desperate scream tore from her throat.

Chapter Thirty-Seven

Larissa had been gone less than half an hour when Nathan gave in to his worries about her. Sighing, he left Sean in Jonathan Dillard's care and directed Jonathan to see to the unloading. He had already started down the gangplank when he stopped and went back to his cabin. Without quite knowing why, he took his pistol from his desk drawer, checked to see that it was loaded, and tucked it into his belt.

The Barnes residence seemed curiously quiet as Hannah, the downstairs maid, let him in. "Mr. and Mrs. Barnes are in the library," she said. "Shall I announce you?"

"No," he replied, "I know my way." He strode down the hall to the library. Throwing open the door, he stepped into the room. To his surprise, Larissa was not there.

Harriet and Hiram Barnes looked up abruptly from their account books as Nathan strode into the room. "Just what is the meaning of this intrusion?" Harriet demanded haughtily.

Ignoring her question, Nathan asked, "What have you done with Larissa?"

Harriet's face registered genuine shock. "Larissa? You know as well as I, Nathan Masters, we haven't seen Larissa in seven years. For all we know, she's dead."

"Don't try my patience, woman," Nathan growled. "Larissa is my wife, and we all know she is not dead. She left my ship for your house not forty-five minutes ago."

Hiram's mouth dropped open, and he stuttered, "Larissa? Alive? Here?"

"Yes, dammit, and you can both stop acting so surprised and innocent! It's no secret you've tried to cheat her out of her inheritance, and I don't doubt you'd go to any lengths to keep the firm all to yourselves." His hand toyed with his pistol butt. "Now, for the last time, what have you done with my wife?"

Watching Nathan's hand, Harriet moved closer to the desk and carefully opened a drawer. "He's lying, Hiram, can't you see? He wants us to believe Larissa's alive and he is her husband just so he can force us to give him a part of Hiram Barnes, Ltd. I always knew he was an ambitious fellow, but this is little better than blackmail. Married to Larissa, indeed!"

"I'm warning you," Nathan said, in a low, tightly controlled voice. "if you've done anything to harm her, you'll pay dearly—with your lives if necessary."

As he moved across the room toward them, Harriet's hand darted into the open drawer. She withdrew a pistol and, raising it and steadying it with both hands, pointed it directly at Nathan's chest.

"Come one step closer, Nathan Masters, and you may be the one to pay with your life. You can't fool me with your idle threats and your senseless prattling about Larissa. Of course she's not here! She never was here. And how could she be married to you when you told us yourself, the last time we met, that she had married an Englishman?"

"Her first husband died," Nathan replied, calmly removing his own pistol from his belt. "Now, I think you've stalled quite long enough. Where is Larissa?"

With trembling hands, Harriet cocked the pistol, keeping it aimed at Nathan's chest. "Out!" she hissed. "Get out of my house before I shoot!"

Nathan advanced another step, and Harriet's finger tensed on the trigger. Beside her, Hiram gasped in alarm.

"Harriet," he said in a pleading tone, "let us not have senseless bloodshed in our home! Give me that pistol." He grabbed her arm, turning her toward him.

"No!" she shrieked. "You can't stop me, Hiram. This man is an intruder in our home, and I have a right to get rid of him!"

She tried to shake off her husband's grasp and to aim the pistol at Nathan again. Hiram struggled with her, trying to knock the weapon from her hand. As his hand moved toward it, Harriet instinctively tightened her grasp. Before she realized what she had done, she squeezed the trigger, and a bullet burst out of the gun and into Hiram's chest. His white shirt exploded in a deep red splotch as he sank, groaning, to the floor.

For an instant, Harriet stared at him, unable to believe what had happened. She stood rigidly, watching the blood seep through her husband's shirt. Dropping his own pistol, Nathan rushed to kneel beside the dying man, ripping off his own shirt to staunch the flow of blood. Still, Harriet stood, seemingly uncaring, while her husband struggled for his last breath. Slowly, her eyes focused on Nathan, and her lips curled in a thin, vicious smile.

"Murderer!" she screamed.

As she screamed, the library doors opened, and several servants, alerted by the shot, rushed in. Assessing the situation in one glance, three of the men pounced on Nathan, pinning him to the floor.

Harriet turned to Hannah, who stood quivering by the door, and commanded crisply, "Hannah, go to the constable's office and tell him to send someone at once. There's been a murder committed here."

Hannah hesitated, blinking at her mistress. "But, ma'am—"

"Go!" Harriet cried. "I want this murderer removed from my house as soon as possible, so I can mourn poor Hiram in peace."

Andrew Allerton raised himself momentarily to gaze at Larissa. Her dress lay in tatters around her, and her chest heaved from the exertion of screaming. She was silent now, her green eyes boring into him with certain hate. But in a moment, he was sure, she would be whimpering as he pressed into her. Dropping back down on her, he guided his shaft toward her secret recess and began to force his way in, aware, and pleased, that he was hurting her. Just then, there was a knock at the door.

He refused to acknowledge it, and the person knocked again. Then, a woman timidly called, "Mr. Allerton, sir, I know you don't want to be disturbed, but there's a messenger here with a most urgent message from Mrs. Barnes."

"What the devil does she want?" Andrew muttered, more to himself than to the servant.

"She wants you to come to her house at once. Says Mr. Barnes has been murdered and she needs your assistance."

Larissa flinched, suddenly remembering Nathan's promise to follow her to her aunt and uncle's. Without thinking, she murmured, "Oh, dear God, not Nathan!"

Andrew looked at her sharply. "What do you know

of this? Is Nathan your husband? Did he plan to murder your good uncle for some reason?"

Larissa shook her head in alarm. "No! No! I don't know what made me say that. Just worry, I suppose—knowing he would be worried about me. Of course he wouldn't harm Uncle Hiram—" She stopped abruptly, realizing she was making no sense and confused by her irrational thoughts. Why was she possessed by this certainty that Nathan was somehow involved?

Pushing her roughly aside, Andrew got to his feet. He shot her a wistful glance as he fastened his trousers. "I can deal with you later, my dear. I trust you won't mind waiting for my return. Perhaps," he said, laughing evilly, "I can bring you word of your husband."

Turning, he strode from the room and slammed the door. Larissa's heart sank as she heard the lock click.

Ten minutes later she was standing by the window, staring hopelessly at the steep drop to the ground, when she heard the lock click again. Whirling, she saw a small, middle-aged woman enter the room. Eyeing Larissa's tattered remnants of clothing, the woman clucked and shook her head.

"I don't know what possessed Mr. Allerton to do that to you," she said sorrowfully. "He has his women often enough, but they always seem to come willingly, him being the fine-looking man he is. I don't say I approve, but it's not my place to tell the master what to do. I heard you scream a while back, and it chilled me to the marrow of my bones. But what could I do?" She paused, her eyes narrowing as she studied Larissa. "Perhaps he fancied you were the girl who jilted him. Sometimes, when he gets in his cups, I hear him muttering about an auburn-haired girl and how much he wants revenge. At times, he seems to become quite mad with the idea, although he is really quite a brilliant lawyer and a witty, good-natured man most of the time."

Larissa shivered, thinking just how close he had come to extracting his revenge. Then, with alarm, she realized he could still have an even more terrible revenge than he had first planned. If Nathan was in any way involved with the incident at her aunt's house, Andrew would surely contrive to take him from her forever.

Unsure just how loyal the woman might be to Andrew, Larissa did not tell her that she was, indeed, the girl who had jilted her master. Instead, she blurted, "Please, could you find me a dress? I must get out of here before Mr. Allerton returns."

The woman nodded. "Yes. I think you're about Rachel's size. I'll get you one of her dresses. I don't ordinarily interfere in Mr. Allerton's affairs, and I suppose he'll be terribly angry when he finds out I did, but I must admit I sympathize with you."

A quarter of an hour later, dressed in a drab brown cotton dress, Larissa raced down Beacon Hill toward Pearl Street. By the time she reached her aunt's house, she was breathless. She burst in without knocking, then stopped in the foyer to collect her thoughts. Voices carried to her from the library, and she tiptoed down the hall to where the door stood ajar.

"I don't care so much about Hiram," Harriet was saying blandly. "The man was a bumbling fool, and I'm well rid of him. I had a constant struggle getting him to follow my business advice. Now I'll be able to run the firm as I see fit."

"Of course," Andrew agreed. "And with Masters available to take the blame, no one can suspect you had any part in your husband's death. You're sure no one witnessed the scene?"

"Absolutely. Hiram, Masters, and I were the only ones in the room. Masters burst in here making a scene about Larissa being missing. Claimed she was his wife and we had done something to her. Of course, I'm sure it was all a hoax. Obviously, he was trying to blackmail us."

Andrew cleared his throat, quickly deciding there was no reason to reveal Larissa's whereabouts. "Obviously," he said quietly. "And I'm sure the attempted blackmail will help convince the jury of his guilt. No doubt the man wanted your money and was willing to go to any lengths to get it. Murder was the natural outcome of his greed." To himself, Andrew thought how sweet it would be to see Nathan Masters hang, knowing how it would make Larissa suffer.

Larissa wanted to burst in and attack them for their scheming, but she realized how foolish that would be. She had to concentrate on saving Nathan. If there had been no witnesses to her uncle's death, the conversation she had overheard might well be the only bit of evidence in Nathan's favor. For the time being, it would be best if

Andrew and her aunt did not even suspect she had heard. In their desperation, they might easily decide to do away with her so she could not defend Nathan. Holding back her sobs, Larissa tiptoed out of the house.

On the street, she paused only a moment before running frantically toward India Wharf. The wharf was still bustling with men unloading the *Lorelei*'s cargo. Brushing past the startled workers, Larissa rushed on board and grabbed Jonathan Dillard.

Jonathan looked at her quizzically, noting immediately that she was dressed differently from when she left the ship. "Larissa, what's wrong?" he demanded.

"Oh, God, Jonathan," she sobbed, "everything's wrong! I don't know exactly what happened, but my uncle's dead and Nathan's been accused of the murder. Only I'm sure he didn't do it. In fact, I think Aunt Harriet did!"

He shook her gently. "Larissa, you're not making much sense. I think we'd better sit down so you can get a grip on yourself and try to explain things more clearly."

Looking around, he was relieved to see Sean standing some distance away, engrossed in watching the cargo unloading, oblivious to their conversation. "Atkins," he called to the second mate, "take over here and keep an eye on the boy. I'm going below for a bit."

In Nathan's cabin, Jonathan handed Larissa a glass of brandy, directing her to drink it, then begin at the beginning. She told him the whole story, glossing over the most intimate moments with Andrew. By the end, Jonathan was pacing in the cabin.

"Well," he said, "we'll have to see about visiting Nathan and getting him a lawyer—though I'm not sure what good it will do. A man is dead, and there were no witnesses. It's Nathan's word against your aunt's. The fact is, Nathan did take a pistol with him when he left the ship. I know as well as you he'd never use it, but—" He stopped abruptly, as he glanced at Larissa and saw her anguished expression.

"Don't worry," he said with more conviction than he felt. "If he's innocent—and we know he is—no jury in Boston could find him guilty."

Chapter Thirty-Eight

Jebediah Halsey, the attorney hired to defend Nathan, was less optimistic about the chances for acquittal. Sitting with Nathan and Larissa in the damp jail cell, he shook his head and sighed. "What it comes down to, Mr. Masters, is your word against Mrs. Barnes's. She's a respected citizen here, and you aren't as well known. If only we had a witness."

"What about what I heard in the hallway?" Larissa pressed. "My aunt practically admitted to Andrew Allerton that she killed Uncle Hiram."

"Practically admitted is not the same as admitted," the lawyer said. "Besides, you did not actually witness the killing, you just heard about it secondhand. On top of that, you're married to the defendant, so the jury would be less likely to believe you. I mean, what wife wouldn't defend her husband?"

"Aunt Harriet," Larissa replied grimly.

Halsey waved away her statement. "We'll let you testify, of course, but I'm afraid we're going to need more substantial evidence to be sure of saving your husband."

"What about the fact that my aunt and uncle cheated me of my inheritance? Wouldn't that prove that Aunt Harriet is dishonest and throw some doubts on the validity of her testimony?"

The lawyer frowned. "Probably. But I think you're grasping at straws. For one thing, there's no proof they cheated you. At the time of your father's death, you were too young to take over his interests. Since you disappeared soon after that and have been gone for seven years, they were within their rights to assume you were dead. This is a trial to establish guilt or innocence in a murder, so I doubt that the judge will allow me to spend any length of time debating the question of your inheritance. And even if he does, the jury just might believe the situation furnished Nathan with a perfect motive—finding no other way to collect your due, he decided to murder the man who stood in your way."

Larissa stared at him, dumbfounded. "But that's preposterous! Nathan wouldn't do that! You do believe he's innocent, don't you, Mr. Halsey?"

He nodded. "I do. But the important thing is to make the jury believe it." He turned to Nathan, who had sat silently through the whole discussion. "You're sure you told me everything, Nathan? Exactly as you remember it?"

Nathan nodded.

Sighing, the lawyer rose. "Then there's nothing for me to do but go back to my office and try to prepare a case. I might interview some of Mrs. Barnes's servants to see if any of them heard or saw anything, but I doubt that we can expect much help from that quarter." He paused at the cell door, waiting for a guard to come and let him out. "If all else fails, we might try establishing that the circumstances involved the heat of passion, rather than calculated premeditation. At least then you'd be spared the gallows, though you'd still have to face life in prison."

"No!" Nathan said sharply. "I didn't kill the man, so there's no way I'm going to take the blame!"

Halsey shrugged. "You may have no choice. But we'll see."

For several minutes after the lawyer left, Larissa and Nathan were silent. Sitting, he turned away from her, his shoulders slumped in dejection. Larissa was consumed by guilt, and could not bear to look at him.

Finally, she walked to him and put her hands on his shoulders. "I'm sorry, Nathan," she whispered. "It's all my fault. If I hadn't been in such a hurry to go to Uncle Hiram's without you—" Her voice caught, and tears began to stream down her face.

Turning, he pulled her into his arms. "For God's sake, Larissa, don't cry!" he said in a husky voice. "And don't start blaming yourself, either. Who knows what might have happened if we'd gone there together? Perhaps something even worse."

She shook her head, clinging to him as if for the last time. "What could be worse than this? Oh, Nathan, what are we going to do?"

He laughed bitterly. "We don't seem to have many choices. I'm going to stand trial, and we're both going to hope and pray the good citizens of the jury can distinguish truth from lies."

Hugging him silently, Larissa searched her mind for some surer way to win his release. As much as she hated to admit it, her mind kept returning to one possibility. "Nathan?" she ventured weakly, "perhaps there is something else we can do—or at least that I can do."

He lifted his face from her hair and stared into her eyes. "What can you do, love?"

Swallowing hard, she struggled to keep her voice steady. "I—I could go to Andrew Allerton. I understand he's become very powerful in Boston, and he—he still wants me. If I give him what he wants, perhaps he could secure your release."

Nathan's eyes widened in horror. "Larissa!" he said gruffly, "you are my wife, and I can't allow you to give yourself to any other man—least of all to that swine Allerton!"

"But what good will it do to be your wife if they hang you?" she cried. "At least this way, even if I'm forced to spend the rest of my life with Andrew, I'll know that you're alive."

Releasing her, he strode to the far end of the cell and faced the wall. "Alive?" he said through clenched teeth. "Would you call that living—knowing the only woman I ever loved has sacrificed herself to a despicable creature like that?" Whirling, he faced her, his eyes flashing. "Think a minute, Larissa! Do you really believe you could save me that way? Allerton would tell you you could, just so he could have you, but I seriously doubt that he has the power to release a man charged with murder."

Larissa stared at her hands, biting her lip and fighting back tears. Andrew had been the only salvation she could think of, and now her plan seemed foolish indeed.

Nathan watched her a moment, then knelt beside her and buried his face in her lap. "Larissa," he said gently, "you're the most precious thing in the world to me, and I couldn't bear the torment of thinking you in Allerton's power. Just hearing what he did to you tears me apart. And think of our son. What would happen to him if you gave yourself to Allerton?" Pausing, he raised his head, his amber-flecked eyes filled with pleading. "Promise me you won't even think of such a thing again."

She nodded slowly. "I promise. It was a foolish thought, anyway."

Smiling with relief, he added, "And I don't want you out on the streets alone again. There's no telling what Allerton, or for that matter your Aunt Harriet, might attempt."

"I've already thought of that. Jonathan is picking me up here at three."

"Then you'd better call the guard to let you out."

Nathan stood, pulling her to her feet and cradling her against his chest. "Don't worry, love," he said lightly, "if you haven't lost me in seven years, a little trial can't get rid of me. We're bound to win. Truth is always stronger than lies."

Gently, he tipped her chin up and kissed her lingeringly. She tried to smile, but she could not help thinking of that afternoon in Shanghai, when he had told her that money and influence often counted for more than truth. As she turned toward the cell door, Larissa blinked back fresh tears, for despite his optimistic words, his kiss tasted of fear and uncertainty.

The trial began three days later. A few Bostonians, who made it their practice to attend every trial possible, were present, but the courtroom was nearly empty. Having left Sean in the care of Timothy Atkins, the *Lorelei*'s second mate, Jonathan Dillard accompanied Larissa to the courtroom.

Harriet Barnes, looking properly mournful in a black crepe dress and bonnet, sat in the front row, accompanied by Andrew Allerton. Both turned when they heard Larissa and Jonathan enter the room. Since Andrew had never told her that Larissa was in Boston, Harriet's eyes widened in shock. But she quickly recovered her composure and bent her head to consult with Andrew. When he informed her that Larissa was, indeed, Nathan Masters' wife, she looked back at her niece and hissed, "How unfortunate that you will soon be a widow, too, dear niece."

Ignoring her aunt, Larissa stared straight ahead as a bailiff led Nathan into the courtroom. Nathan lifted his eyes to hers, and she mouthed the words, "I love you."

His own lips formed an answer before he turned to sit in the chair indicated by the bailiff.

It took only two days for both sides of the case to be heard. Nathan, Harriet, and Larissa were the only persons to testify. All delivered their testimony with equal assurance. Watching the members of the jury carefully, Larissa could not detect whether or not they believed either side more readily than the other. At the end of the second day's testimony, the judge announced that the court would convene again at ten o'clock the next morning, at which time he would instruct the jurors in their duty and dismiss them to determine the guilt or innocence of the defendant.

Larissa hardly slept that night, and in the morning her stomach was a mass of knots. For a few moments, she considered not even going to the courtroom that day, sure she could not control herself if the jury, somehow, found Nathan guilty. But she knew she had to be there, giving him assurance by her presence, no matter how unsure she felt inside.

For the first time in her life, she doubted the effectiveness of the United States court system. How many times in the last seven years had she naively told Nathan the courts would have to give her her fair share of Bennett and Barnes, simply because she was entitled to it? Now Nathan's life, immeasurably more important and precious than a family business, lay at the mercy of the courts, and she was not at all sure the twelve men would make the right decision.

As she sat down in the courtroom, Larissa felt Andrew turn and appraise her, as if he were sure Nathan would lose the case and she would eventually turn to him for help and solace.

Shaking her head in defiance, she turned her gaze to Nathan. He sat erect, staring out at the courtroom with the same self-assurance she had noted in him the first time they met. She smiled grimly to herself, remembering how she had once compared him to Andrew in that respect. But oh, how different the two men had turned out to be! Nathan owned her, body and soul and heart and mind. No matter what happened, he would always own her, though it seemed he had never really tried to exert such power over her. Andrew, on the other hand, had always claimed her, calling her his betrothed when she had never promised herself to him, nursing the grudge of a jilted lover for seven long years.

The judge began to give his instructions, but Larissa hardly heard him. She was fighting a wave of guilt as she realized she, more than anyone else, was responsible for Nathan being there, accused of murder. She could trace her guilt back to when she first stowed away in Nathan's cabin and entangled him in her life and problems. For the moment, it didn't matter that he had chosen to remain entangled in those problems, that he loved her enough to suffer anything for her. For the moment, all she could feel was the oppressive weight of guilt.

"So then," the judge droned on, "it is your most serious duty to adjourn to the jury room and there to decide, based solely on the testimony presented in this courtroom, whether or not this man, Nathan Masters, is guilty of the crime of murder."

A door opened suddenly at the back of the courtroom, and the judge looked up, frowning, from the papers before him. Silently, all eyes turned to observe the young, brown-haired girl who stood uncertainly in the aisle.

Pursing his lips in annoyance, the judge said, "If you wish to observe proceedings in this courtroom, young lady, please be seated, so I may continue with my instructions to the jury."

"No—I—" the girl faltered as she noted Harriet Barnes's angry glare. Clearing her throat, she threw back her head and began again. "I wish to testify, your honor, sir."

The judge scowled. "Testimony was completed yesterday. We've heard the closing arguments of both attorneys. Why should you be permitted to speak now?"

"Because a man's life is at stake," the girl said clearly.

Her words seemed to ring in the courtroom, making the jurors turn and whisper among themselves. Sighing, the judge waved the girl into the witness chair beside his desk. "All right, young lady, this is highly unusual, but we'll hear what you have to say."

He motioned to the bailiff, who swore her in, then leaned forward to question her. "Suppose you begin by telling us who you are, and then tell us precisely what you know about this case."

Nodding gravely, the girl looked toward Nathan and

smiled shyly. "My name is Hannah Samuels, and I work for Mrs. Barnes as a maid. Five days ago, Mr. Masters came to the Barnes residence and asked to see my employers. I guess he had been there before, because he knew his way to the library without my showing him. Well, I couldn't resist following him." She paused, blushing slightly. "I mean, he's such a handsome man I just wanted to watch him for a bit. So, I bent down and watched through the library keyhole." Her blush deepened as she heard the jurors chuckling.

Clearing his throat ominously, the judge shot the jurors a warning glance. "Go on, Miss Samuels."

Moistening her lips, Hannah continued softly. "I only meant to look for a moment, but when they started arguing, I got so interested I couldn't tear myself away. Mr. Masters kept asking about his wife, someone named Larissa. At the time, I couldn't understand who he was talking about. I've only worked for Mrs. Barnes for two years, and I never remembered her talking about anyone named Larissa. Anyway, Mrs. Barnes kept insisting she hadn't seen Larissa, and Mr. Barnes seemed quite upset at the idea that Larissa was in Boston. Then Mrs. Barnes pulled a pistol out of the desk and pointed it at Mr. Masters."

"She's lying!" Harriet Barnes shouted, jumping to her feet. "She's already told you she was attracted to Masters. No doubt she hopes to win his favor by defending him."

"I do not!" Hannah insisted, tossing her head indignantly. "I'm not the sort of girl who sets her cap for a married man!"

"All right," the judge interrupted. "Let the girl continue, Mrs. Barnes. And I must warn you, if there are any more outbursts, I'll be forced to expel you from my courtroom."

Angrily, Harriet settled back in her chair. Hannah continued. "Mrs. Barnes told Mr. Masters she'd shoot him if he didn't leave her house. Then Mr. Barnes got worried and tried to take the gun away from her. Mr. and Mrs. Barnes had a struggle then, the gun went off, and Mr. Barnes fell down on the floor, with blood running all over his shirt."

"And what was Mr. Masters doing all this time?"

"Just standing there, watching them, sir."

"Can you say, with certainty, that he did not fire the shot that killed Hiram Barnes?"

"Oh, yes, sir. I saw the smoke come out of the gun Mrs. Barnes was holding. Mr. Masters had a pistol, but he never fired it."

"More lies!" Harriet hissed.

Silencing her with a scowl, the judge asked Hannah, "Is there anything else you saw or heard, girl?"

"Well, sir, after Mr. Barnes fell down, Mrs. Barnes just stood there staring at him and at Mr. Masters. Mr. Masters tried to help Mr. Barnes, and then Mrs. Barnes started screaming that he was a murderer. That's all I know, sir."

The judge nodded. "Thank you, Miss Samuels. Just out of curiosity, what made you come forward today?"

The girl shrugged. "I don't know. I was afraid before about what Mrs. Barnes would do if I admitted spying on her. But then I thought about Mr. Masters being hanged for something he didn't do, and I felt I had to come."

In her seat, Harriet scowled and would have jumped up to speak if Andrew had not restrained her. As Hannah stepped down, the judge turned to the jurors. "Gentlemen, you have your instructions, so I believe it would be best for you to retire to the jury room at this time." Nodding, the twelve men stood and solemnly filed out.

They were gone for less than ten minutes, during which Larissa stared straight ahead, twisting her hands in her lap. Hannah's testimony had been a godsend, but she still could not help feeling apprehensive.

As the other jurors filed in and took their seats, the jury foreman remained standing. He spoke in a crisp, clear voice. "Your Honor, we have reached a verdict. It is clear to all of us that Nathan Masters is totally innocent of the murder of Hiram Barnes."

With a shriek of outrage, Harriet Barnes jumped to her feet. "You fools!" she spat. "How could you believe the word of a lovestruck servant girl over that of a respected citizen?"

The judge pounded his desk angrily. "Mrs. Barnes, need I remind you again that I will not tolerate such outbursts?" He paused and shot her a meaningful glance. "It seems this court may be forced to turn its attention to the question of perjury."

Harriet whitened, then shook her head defiantly. "I will not stand here longer and listen to this slander! But I warn you, you'll all be sorry for this!" Motioning Andrew to follow her, she flounced from the courtroom.

Larissa had no time to ponder her aunt's words, for in the next moment, Nathan was beside her, pulling her from her chair and cradling her against his chest. "See, love," he murmured, "didn't I tell you truth is always stronger than lies?"

Caught up in the joy of reunion, they did not talk more about pursuing Larissa's inheritance until late that evening. Lying beside her, Nathan traced a finger along Larissa's cheek and whispered, "I suppose you'll want to visit your aunt tomorrow and get everything resolved at last."

Larissa sighed. "It still might be easier to forget it. Even after today, I'm afraid she won't give in easily. She'll find some way to thwart us."

Nathan's voice hardened. "After what she's put us through, I won't even consider forgetting it. Besides, if she gives us trouble, we'll threaten to take her to court. With a perjury charge hanging over her head, it should be an easy matter to defeat her."

"I suppose you're right, but I don't want to endanger your life again. It seems I've made a habit of doing that over the years."

Chuckling softly, Nathan pulled her closer. "True enough, but I assure you, the rewards have always been worth the risks. Still, I don't think we need to worry too much about your aunt. She'd be a fool to threaten us now."

The following day, Larissa and Nathan went to visit Harriet. As an extra precaution, they had informed Jonathan Dillard of their destination and asked him to follow if they had not returned within the hour.

Mounting the front steps, they knocked. When no one answered, they knocked again. After the third unanswered knock, they tried the door and discovered it was open. The house was deadly quiet, and Larissa could not help recoiling a bit as they walked into the foyer. Seeing that the parlor was empty, they continued down the corridor toward the library. They were no more than five paces from the room when the door opened, and Andrew Allerton stepped into the corridor.

Closing the door behind him, he motioned with his

chin. "I wouldn't go in there, if I were you. It's not a very pretty sight."

Larissa's hand tightened on Nathan's arm. "What do you mean?"

"It appears your aunt shot herself in the head earlier this morning. By the time one of her servants summoned me, it was too late."

Larissa stared at him, unbelieving. "You're lying! It's just one of your new plans to keep my inheritance from me!"

Shrugging, Andrew threw open the library door. "If you don't believe me, see for yourself."

Larissa glanced into the room and gasped in horror. Harriet, clad in a deep purple dressing gown, was sprawled across the Persian carpet, her gray-brown hair loose and matted with blood, her face shattered by the force of the shot.

Turning to Nathan, Larissa swallowed the acrid bile rising in her throat and buried her face in his chest. "Poor, misguided Aunt Harriet," she sobbed. "Why would she do such a thing?"

"Why, indeed?" Andrew cut in sarcastically. "Surely you must know after you goaded her and threatened to steal her livelihood!"

"I didn't!" Larissa protested. "I only wanted what was mine! Mine and my father's!"

She felt Nathan tense as he held her. He spoke for the first time since entering the house. "Get out of this house, Allerton," he said in a steady, measured voice. "If we were alone, I'd be strongly tempted to give you the punishment you deserve for the suffering you've caused my wife. But Larissa's seen enough blood for one day, so I'll spare you this time. But you'd better pray to God we never meet again."

Andrew stared at Nathan for a long moment. Then, shrugging, he strode past the couple and out the front door.

Nathan held Larissa a few moments longer, giving Andrew time to disappear. Then he whispered, "Let's get out of here before the stench of death overcomes us."

In the privacy of their cabin aboard the *Lorelei,* Nathan led Larissa to their bunk and sat down with her. "Well," he said at last, "it appears that you shall finally have your inheritance. I don't think anyone will stand in your way now."

"No," she sniffled. "But I never wanted it at the expense of anyone else. All I wanted was papa's share."

"I know," Nathan soothed, "but I suppose your aunt was too greedy to bear the thought of sharing the firm. After her years of scheming, she must have become quite obsessed with the idea of full ownership. When she realized that all her plans had failed, I suppose death looked to her like a pleasant escape. Then, too, she might have been feeling a bit of guilt at last for your uncle's death."

"But she didn't actually murder Uncle Hiram, did she? You and Hannah both said it was an accident."

"An accident, yes. But a convenient one for her. She certainly did nothing to save him."

Larissa sighed. "I just wish there could have been a less violent end to everything. I hate having both their deaths tied to my inheritance."

Pulling her closer, Nathan kissed her forehead lightly. "But you're not responsible, and I won't allow you to dwell on it. Your aunt and uncle brought it all on themselves. I would like to see Andrew Allerton punished, though. I had all I could do to contain myself when we met him at the house."

"Never mind," she cut him off. "It's obvious he's been punishing himself all these years with his bitterness. And now he'll have to live the rest of his life, knowing his revenge failed."

"I suppose you're right," Nathan said. He was silent for a moment, then asked, "What shall we do with the house on Pearl Street? I imagine you'll inherit that, too."

"Sell it," she replied flatly. "With all of its horrible memories, I never want to set foot in it again."

"And the servants?"

"You decide, Nathan. I should think most of them can find other positions. But perhaps we could keep Hannah with us. I'll always be grateful to her, and I do believe Jonathan is quite taken with her."

Nathan laughed. "Next thing, I'll have to expand his cabin to make room for a wife!" Becoming serious, he said, "But I suppose now you'll want a real home, someplace from which to direct your shipping empire and raise a flock of children."

Larissa smiled, putting her arms around Nathan's neck and pulling his face close to hers. "Some empire! The aging *Queen of Cathay* and the *Lorelei*!"

After pausing to think, she said quietly, "I don't know, Nathan. I suppose we will need a permanent base, though I can't say I'm anxious to make it Boston. But let's leave a few problems for the future. For now, I'm content on the *Lorelei,* and Sean loves it, too. After all, our life together began on a ship. Perhaps that's where we belong."

Chuckling, he lay back on the bunk and pulled her down beside him, pressing his body against hers. "At least," he murmured as he nuzzled her ear, "we'll have a hard time losing one another on a ship. And I, for one, don't want any more separations."

"Neither do I," she whispered. "Not for the rest of our lives."

ABOUT THE AUTHOR

LYNN LOWERY was born and raised in Cleveland, Ohio. As a student at Northwestern University she combined a major in Russian with a major in journalism. She learned to read, write and speak Russian fluently and developed a special love for Russian history, so that nineteenth-century Russia was a logical choice in setting for her first two romantic historical novels, *Sweet Rush of Passion* and *Loveswept*. With her husband, James Hahn, she has published several articles and books on sociological subjects and community affairs and has written several juvenile books. Lynn Lowery lives in Evanston, Illinois.

Lynn Lowery

A novelist whose name is fast rising in the historical romance firmament, she is a student of Russian history and culture. Lynn Lowery continues to win a devoted readership because of her talent for creating distinctive, passionate heroines whose adventures in pursuit of love take them to exotic lands. Ms. Lowery's three novels are also noted for their historical accuracy.

SWEET RUSH OF PASSION

Golden-haired innocent, Katherina Andreivna marries a man thirty years older than she. All men are bewitched by her beauty, tantalized by her purity. However, Katherina is truly in love with handsome, dark-eyed Aleksandr. And she must roam the world—from the glittering courts of the Czar to the savage outposts of the Empire—to finally find him.

LOVESWEPT

Tasha, innocent of the secret of her birth, curses her wealthy father for sending her to the barbarous Alaska coast. During the sea crossing, fate hurls her into the arms of a young Yankee sailor. Because of a sudden parting the sailor must pursue her to San Francisco and, ultimately, to the glittering drawing rooms of Washington before he finds her.

LARISSA

The dazzling darling of Boston society, her fine-bred innocence is stripped by a scandalous man. Her life becomes a series of tempestuous adventures from being kidnapped by Turks to being ravaged by the Sultan. It is only when Larissa finally reaches the American west that she is reunited with the only man she loves.

Read these Lynn Lowery novels published by Bantam Books, available now wherever paperbacks are sold.